FARTHEST HOUSE

Margaret Lukas

writelife®
publishing

Published by WriteLife
(an imprint of Boutique of Quality Books Publishing Company)
www.writelife.com

Cover Photo: "Textured Old Paper Background with White Datura Flower" © Tamara Kulikova

Printed in the United States of America

978-1-60808-080-9 (paperback)
978-1-60808-093-9 (ebook)

First Edition

Acknowlegments

I wish to thank Pat Craig, Jan Novack, and Gail Weiland for graciously reading the manuscript not once, but twice, and offering their sage wisdom. Thanks to David Martin, Stu Burns and Marcia Calhoun Forecki for their helpful critiques. Thanks also to Jeff Kurrus, whose unwavering belief in me has kept me writing, and to Sam Rutten for letting me peer into his world of bees. My teachers, Ann Pancake, Kent Myers, Jonis Agee, Anna Monardo and Richard Duggin, thank you for your instruction and friendship. A special thanks to Stan Rubin and Judith Kitchen for welcoming me into the Rainier Writers Workshop. Cindy Grady and Erin Reel at WriteLife, thank you for your support and acumen. I couldn't have done it without you.

And to my family, my husband Jim, and my children: Jen, Emily, Julie, and Dan, thank you. You've been an infallible source of encouragement and inspiration.

1

Should I begin this recounting with my early childhood in the 1860s along the Rhine River in eastern France? Begin there with life in the villa across the water from Germany's Black Forest and its wellspring of fantastic tales? There at the foothills of the Vosges Mountains and its rock cliffs—the perfect height for young women no longer able to bear the weight of their lives?

Let me begin many years later, after my arrival in America and finally Nebraska. Let me begin with Jeannie and Farthest House. On the 3rd of May, 1960, I stood unseen in the sad bedroom, watching the small group huddled around her: the doctor, her husband Julian, and his mother. As Jeannie struggled in childbirth, we all prayed the doctor could somehow stop the excessive flow of blood. Had I been alive, I might have been of use, for I'd been something of an herbalist, picking up my skirts as a girl and trampling through the French countryside. Later, as a grown woman, I walked through trees and along the banks of the Elkhorn River searching for the medicinal plants I needed. But I'd been dead nineteen years. What could I do?

Jeannie's husband, Julian, knelt beside the bed, holding her hand, whispering encouragements and placing cool cloths on her forehead. Watching grief and fear harden the muscles in his jaw—a man who at thirty-eight had already seen so much—tore at me.

The middle-aged family physician, Dr. Mahoney, placed shiny metal forceps on a clean white cloth, but he kept his scalpel tucked deep in his aging leather bag. He would not use it. He thought Jeannie a bleeder.

Need I say a person's thoughts are never a secret? The living pretend not to know another's thinking, but this is partly a human attempt at propriety, and partly a means of self-defense. The truth is, all things are energy with shape and color. Seen from the spirit world, all thoughts are as bright as washed jewels.

And so, I knew Dr. Mahoney was considering how every year medicine made bounding strides and how in 1960 the advances were nothing short of miraculous. However, he knew no doctor or procedure that could stop this volume of blood, and he had no intention of cutting into a hemophiliac—she must be—to try and perform a C-section. He wouldn't try that during a home-delivery, not without assistants ready with clamps and pints of blood. He saw no point either in waking a volunteer to crank up the village's old ambulance. A driver would need a few minutes to pull on his pants, find his boots, get to the fire station, and bring the ambulance up the hill. There'd be the time it would take to load Jeannie onto a stretcher, the strain and jostling she'd suffer being hoisted down the stairs on a gurney, and the thirty-mile trip to a hospital in Omaha. She'd be dead before the ambulance lights swung into the emergency lot. The infant with her. For the infant's sake, it was best to keep Jeannie as still as possible. If the newborn's head miraculously descended within reach of the forceps, he'd harvest the child. Then, if the mother still had a pulse, he'd pack her and call for the ambulance.

Julian's mother, Luessy, paced but never stepped more than a few feet away before turning back, often needing to touch her son's shoulder, only to pace again. Her hands went in and out of her sweater pockets. Her long gray braid lay quiet over one shoulder, and she watched the laundry basket in the corner with its growing heap of bloody, rubber-backed pads. She was a mystery writer, and she knew the human body held as many as a dozen pints of blood. How much more could Jeannie lose before she bled out?

As that last dark hour wore on, Jeannie, who through the evening endured stages of pain and sobbing, now only moaned. Softly, semi-consciously. Dr. Mahoney had given her sedation, and she'd lost so much blood that she also lost her desire to try and speak. She used her waning strength to will her heart to keep pumping until her baby entered the world. She knew she'd not walk Luessy's rose garden again or live to raise her infant, but she'd fight for breath until she saw her child alive. She'd know whether she'd given life to a boy or a girl. She'd look into the infant's eyes so that she could recognize her child when they met again.

I imagined Death pacing at the foot of her bed, rubbing his arid hands together, grinning at the blood—rose after rose, a garden blooming from between the young and too pale legs.

Julian whispered what we all knew were lies. "You're doing great. The baby is almost here. Everything is fine." He kept hold—as well as he could—of any display of the panic and sorrow he felt, letting the ocean fill his body, flood the air from his lungs, and slosh deluge through his heart. He'd offer up his 6' 2" frame, but he'd not add to Jeannie's pain and fear by revealing his own.

Finally, when we'd all given up hope, the bloody infant was pulled free. At the sight of the baby girl, and realizing the life they'd not share, Jeannie's slowing heart cried out with dark grief, and her mind formed a single word: *Murder.* Though her fading awareness couldn't process an explanation, a deep ticking told her that her death was from more than childbirth. She tried to move her lips, to speak the word "murder," but Julian was staring at his daughter held in the air by her tiny feet, deep red half-circles—bite marks from the forceps, ringing her temples. And my mark, the protrusion on her right shoulder blade like the bud of a wing.

"It's over," he said to Jeannie. He kissed her lips, her cheeks, her eyes— already appearing haunted—and he imagined she tried to tell him something. "It's all right," his voice more frantic as he prayed that the birth meant the bleeding would stop now. "Just rest." Again, he dressed her face in kisses, desperate to keep her conscious. He wanted to say of the infant, "She's beautiful," but the shoulder, the still-blue silence, *shouldn't she be crying*, and his fear for Jeannie kept the words locked in his mouth.

Despite a flurry of effort and commotion on the doctor's part, Jeannie's eyes stared.

Several minutes passed before Luessy could blow her nose, yet again, and put the infant she'd cleaned and swaddled into the arms of Mable, her housekeeper and friend. Afraid the baby would not live, she avoided Julian's arms, the weeping arms of her son. She picked up the small, bloody scissors from the cold pan holding the afterbirth, cut through the thick rope of tissue, and tucked a small piece of the infant's string into her sweater pocket. This she took out into the night, swaying and chanting across the wide yard to where the bodies of my husband, Thomas, and I lay buried. Rocks as our headstones. Under the stars, she wept again for Jeannie, for her son, and for the motherless infant. She buried the string there, at the foot of our graves, praying the act would keep the child alive and bind her to the land. Land which Luessy no longer saw as her own.

I feared the act tethered the child to graves.

Since slipping out of my own old body, I'd been waiting to find peace. At first believing the casket lid shushing closed over my wrinkled and powdered corpse meant my indecent affairs were also being buried—the ragged ends of my stained life finally knotted and vanquished beneath the overhead thud, the skittish and crumbling roll of shoveled dank earth. Jeannie's slow and painful dying, however, proved there would be no rest for me. The family's saga that began when I was eight years old, and the *Affliction* that struck years later, still groped like one of my uncle's ring-decked hands up my childhood skirts, reaching now to the fourth generation. What was I to do? Here was a child bearing my mark on her shoulder, her string was now attached to my grave, and I carried guilt for Jeannie's death. I vowed to stay with the infant. To comfort and help her however I could, for as long as she needed me.

Doubts plagued my decision, weeds in my mind, but if I could unwittingly slay from thousands of miles and across an ocean, couldn't I companion from just beyond the veil of death?

2

✦

Three days after Jeannie's death, with her body put to rest only that morning in the village cemetery, the whole of Farthest House lay under a pall. By evening, Julian's sister, my dear Tory, already middle aged but still living there, had poured herself a glass of sherry to still her nerves and gone up to her room for the night. In the kitchen, Mable stood at the sink in a navy caftan and washed the last of the day's dishes. She turned to glance with concern at the black gardener sitting at the table. She'd made him fresh coffee and set out a plate of homemade cookies, but he stared straight ahead, ignoring both. His name was Jonah, and the outside corners of his eyes, which fell when he was still a young man, now gave him the appearance of a small and forlorn basset hound. The radio was on low, and a commentator talked about the signing that day of the Civil Rights Act and how Negroes celebrated in the streets. At sixty-one, with all he'd seen in his life, Jonah scarcely cared whether or not a new law had been signed. Earlier laws hadn't helped, and he couldn't rid his mind of thinking about the number of lynchings there'd been in just his lifetime. *Lynchings.* Human beings at their most inhuman and the sight of busted up black bodies swinging. On top of that, not three days since there'd been another death in the house. Some homes went a hundred years and crumbled in on themselves and never felt death.

I couldn't watch his misery. Sorrow and guilt sent me from the room and into the library where Julian stood at a window holding his daughter, her body snug against his. After the mortician came and removed Jeannie's body, Julian reached for the infant and took her to his room—as though only the two of them could understand what they'd lost. Since then, he'd not let the housekeeper, his sister, or even his mother tend to the infant. He gave the newborn each feeding, watching the clock regimentally for two-hour intervals, and changing each diaper, though he asked constantly, "Like this?" and "This way?" but not giving her over to other hands. Even during the funeral and at the graveside, he hung on to the infant.

Luessy stepped through the library door, her reading spectacles in one hand. Her wide skirt reached to mid-calf, and her shoes were "sensible." She came quietly down the short aisle, scarcely glancing at the rows of books on either side. Avoiding the wide desk where she liked to spend her evenings reading, she studied her tall son. His time in France during the Second World War and his training at the Police Academy were years behind him, but he'd remained lean and strong. Until now. Now he looked fragile. She approached him slowly, "Your baby needs a name."

Out the window, a young willow tree blew in an approaching spring storm, branches swaying back and forth in the evening light and fronds floating in the air. Julian's gaze lifted from the young trembling tree and settled on his daughter. "Willow."

"Willow," Luessy repeated, pleased with the sound.

He turned back to the window and the first drops of rain. "I shouldn't have brought Jeannie here," he said. "I should have made sure she was in a hospital. That quack of a doctor should be thrown in jail."

"Nonsense. Jeannie wanted to be here. Dr. Mahoney has delivered hundreds of babies. Nearly all of them in their homes. How could any of us have known?"

The skin along Julian's clenched jaw blanched. "She trusted him. I shouldn't have let her talk me into it."

"You were born in this house. So was your sister. We just didn't know."

"Doctors are paid to know."

Luessy saw the eyes of a hurt boy. "They aren't gods."

Willow stirred in his arms but didn't wake. He'd not argue with his mother. It wouldn't change anything. Dr. Mahoney failed Jeannie, but so had he. In that, he also failed Willow. His mind tripped over the name, Willow. His daughter. He would not fail her again. "You think I've got it?" he asked. "You think I understand what she needs? How to do it all?"

Luessy's eyes dampened, and she looked to the small, sleeping face and the tuft of dark hair on the crown of her head. Julian, with his determined purpose and strong hands, had swaddled the infant so tight in her yellow receiving blanket it was a wonder she could breathe. And the way Julian held her, not rocking or cooing, but tight and tucked, he might have been holding a football. Luessy hesitated. She wanted to say, *Heavens no, you're not thinking of returning to Omaha so soon.* Instead, she heard herself say, "Willow will teach you what she needs."

"I can't come back here."

Swinging her hands behind her back was Luessy's only way of keeping herself from grabbing her granddaughter. She thought of insisting that he leave the child there to be raised by the household of females, but this was Julian's child, and he needed the infant. "I know how much you loved Jeannie, but someday this house will be Willow's. I want this to be a second home for her while she's growing up."

Julian shifted his weight, ready to leave, but he stopped when Luessy dropped a hand on his forearm. "Take some time," she said. And then, to keep him close a minute longer, "I know death can take years to heal. When you're ready, bring Willow back here. I'll be waiting."

He lifted the baby to his shoulder, touching her soft cheek with his rougher one. He couldn't explain his wanting to cut all ties to the house and everyone who lived there, but he did. "I need space. Don't call, don't hound me."

"*Hound* you?" Luessy needed to sit, but she didn't want to leave his side for a chair.

His brows pinched, apology grabbed his face. "I just mean you can't fix this. You can't mother me through and make it all right." She looked tired—the last three days had aged her, too. She'd also lost Jeannie, and death had entered her house. "I know it sounds cold," he said, "but let us go."

He left her standing there. He couldn't explain what he couldn't understand. Loss for certain, shock, maybe even pity for himself and Willow, but that wasn't all. Jeannie had needed him to understand something, to give her dying moment some assurance. He'd failed to understand, failed to give her what she needed. Now Willow needed away from where everything went bad, and she needed kept away until the world righted itself. If ever the world would be right again.

3

---❦---

When they left, no one imagined six years would pass so quickly. Willow lived in Omaha with hardly any knowledge of family outside of *Papa*. And me, Amelie-Anais, the ghost of her great aunt. I was the one Papa called *imaginary* each time she spoke of me, until at last, she quit mentioning me, though she often sensed me standing over her bed at night, soothing away tummy aches and restlessness. She moved me into ever lower regions of consciousness, but I never left her.

On a May morning in 1966, she woke from a night of especially vivid dreams. Her right shoulder blade felt bruised from having spent another night on the hardwood floor, but she lay watching the sunlight stream in through her bedroom windows. Tiny dots of red, blue, green, yellow. Already she had an acute sense of color.

A faint sound grew and overtook her fascination with the bright motes. With a start, she realized the vibrations rivering through the floorboards came from boot heels striking the polished wood in the short hallway. Papa. She scrambled to her feet, and using both arms—even the weaker one she didn't like—she grabbed up her blanket, pillow, and last of all Doll, shoveling them onto her bed. Falling onto the heap, she shut her eyes as tightly as she could and fought to keep them closed. Papa frowned when he caught her sleeping on the floor, and *his* frowns went into *her* mouth and down to *her* stomach and stayed there a long time.

When the sound said he'd entered the room, she peeked with one eye to be sure he saw her in bed. Now she could be awake, and she yawned and stretched and smiled at him. Her smile faded when he gave her only a distracted glance, only half his attention. He went instead to the wicker basket holding her clothes, moving the easy way she wanted to move, but not coming to her bed to ask her about bed bugs or to lean over and kiss her cheek with his whiskery face, maybe even to swing her into the air. He dropped a knee to the floor before the basket and began picking through her clothing. Watching him, Willow remembered what she'd seen the evening before, and her stomach began feeling saggy and heavy. Was he still so sad? She scooted off the heap of her blanket, kissed Doll, and hurried to stand beside him, aching to have him tell her everything was all right. "The bedbugs didn't bite me."

"That's good."

He hadn't turned to her, and her cheeks pinked in determination. She stood still, taking in his every movement. The basket he rummaged through sat beside an empty and never-used clothes dresser with yellow-duckling handles. That piece of furniture, like the white curtains, the yellow rocker, and the wallpaper—hundreds of baby ducks, all with one foot in the air—was the work of Jeannie. A woman she'd never seen. A stranger Papa said was her mother. He didn't use the dresser, Willow knew, because like the photographs of Jeannie hanging in his room, it made him close his eyes and take deep breaths.

He lifted her favorite pair of pants, the ones the color of a ripe apple. At least they were that red the summer before when they hung over her shoe-tops. They only touched her anklebones now, and matched the red-but-not-red color of her lips.

One of his discarded T-shirts served as her nightgown, and she lifted the cotton over her head and twisted out. Standing beside him in her Friday panties on a Saturday, she ached for him to turn, face her, and smile in a way that told her she was pretty, maybe even as pretty as her best friend in kindergarten, Mary Wolfe.

He looked over the front of one shirt and then another.

Waiting to be noticed was too hard, and Willow grabbed her stomach, pinching her skin to try and make an outside hurt bigger than her inside hurt. The outside hurt she could stop when she wanted.

If I could have pulled Julian aside and scolded him, just as I'd done when he was a boy, I'd have done so. He never let his eyes really see her shoulder when he helped her dress or when she sat naked in the bathtub. Did he suppose she didn't sense his aversion? She knew he loved her, though. She knew because she'd ridden his shoulders and listened to his thoughts since before she could walk. At first, her arms had been so short she needed to stretch to wrap them around his forehead, his sweat filling her palms on hot days while he held her with one big hand low on her back, and with the other hand he folded laundry, washed dishes, and picked groceries from store shelves. She'd often napped sitting on his shoulders, one cheek and one ear on top of his head, his thoughts mixing with hers. Even awake, watching him walk across the room, or smoke a cigarette, the words in his head mostly said he loved her. Sometimes, they said things like *she'll suffer for her shoulder.* Leaving her own thoughts and sliding into his, she first heard directly from him what he never wanted her to hear at all: She needed to be "fixed."

Standing beside him now, she wouldn't let herself think about sad things; she'd think about things that matched. Her favorite game was "Memory," where small playing cards, each with a different, brightly-colored object, were turned over two at a time until matches were found. Those cards she got to keep. Bits of winning and order. Things fitting together and making sense. Even if her mother was dead.

She swayed, leaning her weight onto one foot and then the other. Her and Papa's bodies matched and didn't match. They had the same dark brown hair, though he had a few white hairs by his ears, and they had the same green-blue-brown eyes. Mostly though, their bodies didn't match. She didn't have the thing she once peeked into the shower and saw hanging off him from out of a mitten-sized patch of fur. (Mary Wolfe was right—boys did have ding-dongs.) But the main reason her body didn't match his was because his back went straight across. Both his shoulder blades stayed inside him and as flat as the floor she slept on. Her right scapula—a word she knew from her trips to the doctors—pushed out with a knot of bone the size of her fist and not even sleeping on the hard floor made it go away. The bone huddled beneath her clothes and made her right arm slightly shorter than her left. Her right hand was stupid, too, because it was still five when she was six. Girls could have yellow hair and straight backs and be pretty like Mary Wolfe, and girls could have brown hair and crooked backs and stupid hands and be ugly.

Watching Willow, I ached for her. I thought myself ugly throughout my childhood, even believing my scapula, gnarled in the same way, made me deserving of my uncle: The Beast.

Julian continued picking through her things, and because he didn't say it this time, she did. "I'm growing like a weed."

"Uh, huh."

"We can go to a store." Her left hand pulled the fingers on her right. "You can buy me a dress."

"You wear a dress to school every day."

She put both hands on her hips, letting all the ducks on her walls watch. "Papa. My school uniform is not a dress!"

Now he did look at her, an almost smile she didn't like. She wasn't making a joke. She wanted a dress. If he bought her one, she'd wear it every day. Mary had a hundred dresses. Willow let her hands drop. Mary had a mother—that was the reason she had dresses. Jeannie, the mother Willow didn't have, looked at her new baby and the thing on her new baby's back, and died.

Five afternoons a week, as one of Willow's many sitters napped or polished her nails, Willow sat rapt, her attention on a television show, *I Dream of Jeannie*. Then she practiced crossing her arms over her chest and giving a quick nod. When she got her powers—she believed absolutely it was a matter of nodding and winking just right—she'd make two things: first, she'd make herself pretty so Papa didn't think she needed to be fixed, and then, she'd make a dress. But she wouldn't make her mother come alive. She didn't want *that* Jeannie; *that* Jeannie had left her.

She moved behind Julian and stretched over his back, wrapping her arms around his neck, as though he'd put a knee to the floor just to give her a piggyback ride. "How come your bones don't poke?"

He rose slowly, so that she slid off without falling. He handed her the soft pants and shirt he'd chosen. Trailing a thumb down her cheek, he said, "Get yourself dressed now." He shoved his hands into the pockets of his jeans and moved to the window where he could stare out and think.

The room faded around Willow as she watched him, found his thoughts, and slipped in behind a curtain of his mind. *Damn doctors,* his mind said, *can't fix Willow. Couldn't save Jeannie.*

He had never raised his hand or even his voice to Willow, but hearing again how he thought she needed to be *fixed* made her eyes burn like skinned knees. She sank to the floor to put on her pants. If he only wanted a little girl who could sing and dance, she'd practice until she won a hundred prizes. He wanted her to be a pretty girl though, and she was trying, but no matter how hard she prayed, her fingers going around and around the rosary the kindergarten nun passed out, touching each bead and saying "Hail Mary," then moving on to the next bead, "Hail Mary," or how many nights she slept on the hard floor trying to push the bone away, she couldn't make herself pretty.

Don't cry, her mind said. Tears blurred her vision, and she stuck both feet into the same pant leg, rolled to her knees, and tried to stand. The tangle pitched her forward, her weaker right arm folding and even the left arm lacking the strength to catch her. Her chin struck the floor. Hot pain rammed up through her jaw, and one cheek scraped over a thorn of the basket's broken wicker. She grabbed the hurt and felt wetness and warmth. "Papa! Blood!"

Julian wheeled around at the sound of her fall, his hands jerking from his pockets, his eyes anxious as he took quick steps to her. He stopped, his will forcing hesitation into his bones. "It's all right," he said. "You're hardly bleeding. Go wash your face."

She heard what he said, and what he managed not to say: *Today is the day. She's gotta learn I can't always be there.*

She never lost a drop of blood without Papa making a fuss over her, and his rejection now, when bleeding proved she really was hurt, stung worse than her injuries. Running from the room and him, she wailed again, though not even her howling made him follow. In the bathroom, she grabbed the damp towel from the bar on the wall and pushed the cool wad against her chin. Still, Papa didn't come. He wasn't acting the way she wanted, and she'd cry until he felt sorry, came and held her. Or turned her upside down, ran her feet across the ceiling, and made her forget what she'd heard his mind say.

She climbed onto the footstool she used to brush her teeth, spied her reflection in the mirror, and sobbed along with it, slow tears running down her cheeks, meeting the smeared blood and turning a watery red. She noticed how her two cuts, her red eyes, and tears changed her face, making it a not-match to her usual face. Every new thing could be a sign telling her that the round bone grabbing ahold of her scapula had gone away.

For extra powers, she dropped the towel, folded her arms over her chest, and gave a quick nod. Satisfied, she let her gaze creep down her reflection, over her chin, her neck, and her chest with its two button-sized and cinnamon-colored circles. Her front looked the same, but she promised herself that her back could still be changed. Turning inch by inch on the stool, afraid of looking too fast, she pivoted to see her shoulder.

Her heart sank. The stupid bone that made her different and Papa sad, still clung to her.

4

The bleeding stopped, but Willow needed longer to accept Papa wasn't coming and she hadn't been fixed. Finally, she stepped off the stool, shuffled back to her room, and dressed. When she returned to the main room with its sofa, television, and the desk where Papa wrote out checks and licked envelopes and stamps, he was waiting for her by the front door. He hadn't made himself coffee or her a slice of melty peanut butter toast. The *I Dream of Jeannie* book bag she carried to school dangled from a strap in his hand. It looked puffy. Not book puffy, the school year had just ended. *Clothes.*

Now she knew why everything about the morning had been different. They were going someplace she wouldn't like. To see another doctor? Was that why he packed clothes for her and wanted her dressed nice on a Saturday and thought she needed to learn to get along without him? She wanted to hear his thoughts again, but the thoughts in her own head shouted *doctor, doctor,* and *hospital, hospital.*

She ran for Doll.

Julian made the toy for Willow when she was two, balling together a couple of pairs of his socks and tying them into the center of one of her old baby blankets. The socks created a head, and with Willow beside him at the kitchen table, he'd drawn on eyes and red lips. The rest of the blanket hung soft and empty, and though Doll didn't have shoulders, Willow could see arms and legs. She knew how to work a finger under the string around Doll's neck so that they didn't become separated at night. She also knew how Doll's fading eyes cried real tears whenever Papa wanted them to see a new doctor.

With his longer strides, Julian followed, walking to her run, letting her reach her toy. He was thankful she remembered and would have the familiar object with her. He swung her and her doll into the air. "Come on, Little Bird. We'll get through this."

In his arms, she could almost quit worrying, except that *he* was worrying. "I need my sweater," she cried.

He grabbed it, and because she loved to swing, he carried her slung under his arm like a bedroll, across the porch and down the steps. At the curb, he put her down and opened the passenger-side door of his black Ford. The odor of stale cigarette smoke rushed her nose, but she didn't mind the stink; it meant him: a match. Still, she couldn't relax. She remembered doctors and nurses in white clothes and smelling of soap and medicine pulling her out of his arms and carrying her down long hallways to cold rooms where machines, ceiling-high, whirled and hissed. Because she was afraid and kicked and screamed, they wrapped her in tight blankets and held her down. With her arms and legs bound, she screamed louder, her heart pounding in her chest. Both times, the doctors shook their heads at Julian. No brace would correct the shoulder, and shaving off the burl was impossible without weakening the bone too severely.

Climbing onto the seat of the car, Willow looked back at him. "You don't have to take me to any more doctors. I'm starting to grow pretty."

Lines etched between his brows, and he looked over the top of his car to the empty street. He sighed, "Willow."

Her name sounded far away or spoken from inside a bottle holding too many other things. When he got into the car, she leaned her right shoulder forward, pressing both hands flat on the dashboard. "See, Papa, my arms are the same long. They match now. You don't have to take me to any more doctors."

"Quacks," he said. "Every one of them."

She believed she'd convinced him. She sank back against the seat, smiling. "They can't make me pretty, can they?"

He reached, cupping her chin, touching his thumb to her cuts, and for the first time looking hard at them. Thankfully, she didn't need a stitch or two. He pulled a pack of cigarettes from his shirt pocket. "My mother, your grandmother, wants to see you." He tapped the bottom of the pack against the heel of his hand and pulled a cigarette free. "I promised her. She's right, too. Every time I see you with that little friend of yours, I know you deserve more family than just your old man. If something were to happen to me . . . my line of work . . . ," he didn't finish.

The thought of a stranger, even a grandmother, made Willow put on her sweater, just in case. She hadn't known she had a grandmother. There was a voice on the phone, and sometimes Papa instructed her to say, "Hello." And from time to time, there'd been an old woman standing in the living room, a woman who even tried to hug her. But Papa never made the woman coffee, never asked her to sit awhile. "How come she isn't dead?"

The sudden set of Julian's mouth made her regret asking. His scapula was flat; his mother didn't have to die.

5

The drive back to Farthest House, to the place where my body lay buried, as did the body of my husband, and where Tory and Luessy still lived, filled me with heavy emotion. I struggled to keep my attention on the farms we passed with their flat acres of newly planted corn and hilly pastures with herds of cows and spindly-legged calves. Mile after mile, Julian's cigarette smoke lifted and slipped out through the top inch of the car window he'd cracked. As the long white exhales trailed away, my memories drifted in.

I was seventeen when my savior arrived in the form of a tall, American photographer traveling through France. He, Thomas, helped me escape, stealing me out of the villa, across the Atlantic, and finally to Nebraska. He built us a small place with logs that he cut and the rocks he found strewn over miles. Both materials needed to be hoisted onto a wagon and drawn up the hill with a four-horse team. The big draft horses with their stomping and blowing air were powerful animals, but Thomas pushed them together with his shoulders, harnessed and commanded them. I thought him a god. I called our home *Peu de Nid*: Little Nest.

I loved him for who he was and the sacrifices he made for me, and I tried to be happy. I owed him that. Putting away the past, however, wasn't as easy as just getting my body free. He never pressed me with questions about my childhood, or my night terrors, or how young I'd been the first time, or how often it happened. Did he pray that one day I would come to him, trusting him enough to speak my story? He asked no questions either, when only a year-and-a-half into our marriage, I asked him to help me return to France and kidnap, no *rescue*, my infant niece, Luessy.

He risked his life, certainly imprisonment, doing so. He understood this better than I; I was blinded by my need to have Luessy with me.

I never bore a child of my own. Thomas and I raised Luessy within those safe and solid walls of Little Nest. Luessy an infant, toddler, little girl, young woman, and still she kept her pure emerald eyes, the same emerald eyes of her mother, my sister, Sabine.

As Thomas's wife and Luessy's mother, my past was for years a shadow that squatted and cowered at night beside the ashy and cold hearth. With Thomas asleep at my side and Luessy sleeping across the room, I watched the dark and trembling silhouette and kept the blankets high under my chin lest it try to crawl into the bed and consume me. In the morning, I stood and put on a woman's dress, tended my cooking and washing, wifed and mothered, and when I had the time, I painted flowers from our yard. As best I could, I kept the hearth swept of the shadow being's tatters and loose hairs.

Thomas died years later, and Luessy grew to become a mystery writer, something I never fathomed for her, though her whole life must have seemed mysterious. In her late twenties, when she'd sold a couple of books, the local banker let her sign a note to add to her monies. She wasn't leaving me, though. On the same hill as Little Nest, she built Farthest House with three stories, more porches than folks to stand on them, five bedrooms, a library, and even a glass turret reaching out greedily for sunshine and starlight. Later, she hired Jonah, her gardener, and the wide Nebraska hilltop became even more of an Eden: cobble stone paths, flowerbeds, blooming shrubs, ornate trees, and roses. Everywhere, there were roses. How Luessy and I loved them. Damask mostly. The wood Thomas planted before he died matured: burr oaks, red maples, and walnut trees. Over the decades, his ten-acres of forest became a place of enchantment with cottonwoods seeding themselves amongst the other varieties and a host of wild and flowering plants taking root. And for those who knew the recipes, many of those native species made deadly poisons.

Julian, motioning for Willow, brought my attention back. She slid across the seat and pressed herself against him. Her legs stuck out over the edge of the seat, her scuffed Keds rubbed against his denim jeans. "Are we almost there?" she asked.

He swung an arm around her. Then, slowly, "Little Bird, you're the prettiest girl in the world."

She pulled her right hand, which she didn't think was a *right* hand, but a *wrong* hand, up into her sleeve. Sometimes Papa lied. "Where does she live?"

"We just drove through Greenburr. Her house is up ahead."

"Is it in Ebraska?"

"Yes, we're still in Nebraska. With an 'n.'"

"I know," she gave him a stern look. "I like saying Ebraska."

He glanced down at her, slowing the car and turning up the long drive of Farthest House. "Sure you do."

The tires hummed on the brick. Huge oaks, grown even larger in our six years away, still lined the sides of the drive, the branches lacing overhead like giant threaded fingers.

Willow watched the limbs and the magical spray of sunlight poking down through them. "I've never been here," she said.

"You were born here." Julian ground the tip of another cigarette into the ashtray, gripped the steering wheel with both hands, and tried to put the memory of that night out of his mind. "You'll be all right. I'll be back for you tomorrow."

"You have to stay, too. I don't want to stay alone."

He couldn't answer.

She pulled Doll to her chin, and her eyes filled. "I don't want to stay."

Again, he didn't answer, only stopped the car at the top of the drive, stepped out, and waited for her to slide under the steering wheel and exit using his door. The sight of the four wide stairs leading up to a massive porch, and his plan to leave her, made her scoot back across the seat away from him.

Farthest House seemed looming even to Julian, and he ached to please Willow by getting back in the car and driving them straight home to Omaha, but they'd come this far. His mother waited, and he'd promised her. He did want to see her, and he was uneasy about the cold distance he'd kept all these years. Phone conversations, an occasional short visit from Tory or her, it hadn't been enough. He'd only avoided facing the place where Jeannie died; she was still dead. But her bleeding out, the blood running no different than it did from a thug dying in the street, made no sense. If he just understood, but what? What did he need to see that he wasn't seeing?

"It'll be all right," he said, the words as much for himself as Willow. She needed women, some feminine influence. He'd drop her off, and when he returned tomorrow, he'd step inside the house and spend an hour or two.

She saw his patient face, his tired face, his sad face, and even his wanting-away face all at once. "How come you don't want to stay?"

He took her bag from the back and bent down to look in at her. "Suit yourself, but I'm going up there." He turned as if to leave.

Despite her fear of being abandoned at the strange house, the safest place in the world was at his side, and though she knew she was doing exactly what he wanted, she didn't want to be left alone. Using her heels to help pull herself, she worked back across the seat, hurrying to where she didn't want to go. "I'm not staying, and anyway, how come you don't want to stay?"

Following him, she'd taken only a few steps before she stopped and stared at the house. She counted up the three rows of windows, a house as tall as her school, Our Lady of Supplication, and on that third floor was a small porch tree-top high. At the other end of the house, a wide glass turret like the turrets of picture-book castles rose from the ground to the roof. The sun broke partially through clouds, and the glass reflected a brilliant splash of light, sky, and shadow. In the moving reflection, Willow saw a silver and blue dragon climbing the turret.

6

Willow clutched Doll in her left hand, keeping her right tucked up and out of sight. Following Julian up the front steps, she moved as slowly as she dared. White wicker tables sat in shady corners on the porch and held pots of bushy red geraniums with green asparagus ferns spilling over the sides. Six wooden rockers, each painted a different bright color, sat lined in a row. They looked empty but quivered like breath, just enough to make her unsure. She hurried and caught Papa's hand. She still didn't want him to leave, but the house, even with the not-for-sure-empty rocking chairs and the glass dragon, felt good.

Julian reached for the bell and hesitated. Was he really a guest? Before he decided to ring, or walk in, the front door with its thick leaded-glass panel opened. A brown and yellow dog, its long hair sweeping from side to side, sprung out at them. Willow let out a cry and hugged Julian's waist.

Twisting around Papa and away from the animal sniffing at her face, she first saw the woman's long, gray skirt and the pinkish-orange sweater with orange buttons down the front. The last button was open because the woman's stomach was a little bit fat. The woman, who was surely her grandmother, held a cane topped with a carved cat's head. The feline's yellow stone eyes peered out from between the woman's curving fingers.

Willow pushed at the dog, keeping her hand clear of its mouth, and watched the woman who stood in Papa's arms. She fit under his chin. "It's all right," she heard the woman say, her voice against Papa's chest. "It's time you came home."

I let myself dwell a moment on the words: *It's all right* and *home.* Would that ever be true again? If only I could have taken her into my arms, too. Luessy, my niece, my daughter.

Neither Luessy, nor Julian, paid attention to how the dog tried to salve Willow's sore cheek with its tongue. She pushed at the animal again. "Go away."

"Friar," Luessy commanded. The dog stepped to her side and sat back on its haunches. She patted its coppery head, "You've found us a little girl."

The dog yapped as if speaking, and Willow believed the animal was lying, claiming it *had* found her. She kept tight against Julian's leg. "Papa brought me in his car."

Luessy pointed. "You came in that car?"

Pulling Willow in front of him, Julian planted his hands on her shoulders. "You remember your grandmother."

"I see my dreams are true," Luessy said, her eyes filling with tears.

"No, Ma," Julian stopped her. "Willow's got to live in this world." His finger stabbed the air, pointing down at the porch floor. "She's got to live in this world right here." They'd had the same argument before, but when he spoke again, his voice was softer. "Here. Not in a world based on dreams and superstitions."

She remained as calm as the braid over her shoulder. "Your ancestors aren't gone just because you've quit believing in them. You think I don't know who she is?"

"The dead *are* gone."

Luessy shrugged at Julian and bent to Willow. "You're hurt."

"It's just a couple of scratches," he said.

Willow's mind flashed back to the fall, her chin striking the floor, the pain and the familiar smell of wax polish and then to the previous night when she also smelled floor wax. Papa had tucked her into bed, and after a few minutes, when she was sure he wasn't coming back to kiss her again, she crawled onto the floor to sleep. There, she stared at the shadowy ceiling, her eyes finally closing and her mind drifting. Papa was there in her twilight sleep, walking back and forth at the foot of his bed, his face sad. He stopped, finally, his long legs folding like a grasshopper's as he sank onto the small tapestry-covered stool in front of Jeannie's vanity. His straight back bent forward, and he lifted Jeannie's hairbrush, rubbing a thumb over the bristles, flattening them and letting them spring back one by one. He cried. A sound so quiet Willow needed to look hard at his trembling shoulders to be sure.

Standing on the porch now, she knew he shouldn't leave her, and he shouldn't always be thinking about Jeannie. "My blood was in the sink," she said to Luessy, "and all over the towel."

Julian chuckled. "Come on, it wasn't that bad."

"It was," she insisted. He'd leave her now with the strange old woman whose dreams and visions he didn't like. While she stayed, he'd go back to Omaha to be with the pictures of *dead* Jeannie on his bedroom walls. Willow hated them. They smiled at Papa from behind cold glass but never at her. The pictures, like the other things Jeannie left behind—as if she'd only gone to the store and would be right back—her hand mirror, lipstick, nail polish, perfumes, hairbrush, all stole Papa away.

"It looks like you'll heal just fine," Luessy said of the cuts. "Will you call me Mémé?"

My Luessy, or *Mémé*, French for grandmother, was an old woman now and still in her functional clothes—something I never could break her of. Her wrinkled skin reminded Willow of the Catechism she covered with a brown grocery sack in September and carried and crushed and stuffed into her bag until school ended just days before. She also saw sparkle in her mémé's eyes, as though another kid played hide-and-seek from behind the wrinkles.

"Come," Luessy said to Julian, "say 'hello,' to your sister. Have a cup of tea with us."

With his hands still on Willow's shoulders, he stiffened. Couldn't they just chat for a minute on the porch? "You and Tory getting along these days?"

"I have my work, and," she suppressed a wry smile, "Tory has hers."

Julian chuckled again, "I'm sure her dolls make a lot of little girls happy."

Luessy's expression changed. "Any news I can give Jonah?"

"No," Julian said, needing another cigarette. "I wish I had something."

"Well, come along."

"Not today." What to say? "They're expecting me at the station."

Willow's heart kicked. She tucked Doll between her knees and not caring about her smaller hand, reached up with both, filling her fists with Julian's thick fingers. She stared hard at the *Jeannie* bag he'd set on the porch floor, willing *that* Jeannie to make him change his mind. "You're going to stay with me aren't you, Papa?"

Luessy studied her son. Her liver-spotted hand clutched and unclutched the cat's head on top of her cane. "Jeannie's not in there. It's just the house where your mother and sister live."

"I'm sorry," he said, and was sorry for things he couldn't name. "We'll talk tomorrow, when I pick her up."

"I'm sure you're the best the precinct has, but a man needs more than his work. Even when he wins awards."

"Aren't you the one always writing?" he asked. "Wrestling with plots and motives? Remember how you used to drill Tory and me on the criminal mind and red herrings? How many mysteries now? Two dozen?"

Luessy's emerald eyes sparkled. "I need to keep busy," she said, "but what *you* need is a lady."

One hand slipped from Willow's grasp, and he dropped it on her head like a heavy, too-large cap. "Here is my lady." He hesitated, "Willow doesn't know you. She's likely to get homesick and —"

Raising a curved finger, Luessy stopped him. "She needs to learn who she is. No one owns a child. She belongs to the family, to all the ancestors responsible for her being here."

Though she didn't fully understand the words, Willow understood enough to frown. She and Papa were a whole family. No one else could be in it.

His hand slid off her head, down over her shoulder, and halfway to her elbow. He pulled her up against him, the hug lifting her onto her toes. He reached, hugged his mother, and started down the steps.

"Papa!" Her scream struck his back. She saw the flinch of his shoulders beneath his shirt, but then he hurried even faster. She screamed again, but he went around the front of the car and opened the door. She started after him, but Luessy bent over her, and the cat-head cane landed thick and sure as a post on the white porch floor, smack between her Keds. The movement excited Friar, and he jumped up and came around to help block Willow's way, licking her face as if Luessy had given the command.

By the time Willow squirmed away, Papa's car was rolling into the shady tunnel of trees, light and shadow sliding over the top and trunk, leaving her at the place that made him run away.

Luessy tapped her cane to the edge of the porch. She watched the car leave the drive, turn back onto Old Squaw Road, and vanish around the curve. "He's still in pain," she said. "Losing your mother weighs on him." Her eyes remained on the empty drive. "Jeannie turned bad so quickly, and there was nothing he could do to save her. He believed he could protect a city, but he failed to save his wife. It's blaming himself that won't let him heal." She forced herself to turn back and smile. "My moons dried up so long ago, it's hard to believe that man came from my body. I remember being stretched like a pear though, my skin too tight instead of too loose."

Willow knew no one had moons, dried up or not. She quit pushing at Friar, and the dog stood at her side, wagging his tail back and forth. "I don't want to stay here," she said.

"It's time you were back. I didn't go through all the pain of squeezing out two wet seals not to have one of them give me a grandchild. You and I need time while I'm still here." She rapped the tip of her cane on the porch floor. "In this world." She started down the stairs Julian just descended. "Come and see how our flowers are doing."

Doll smelled of Papa's cigarettes, and Willow stood unmoving, inhaling the scent. Mémé didn't match anything, but Friar was nice. His tail never stopped wagging, and his breath smelled stinky. She'd tell Mary Wolfe because Mary didn't have a dog. Maybe, Mary didn't even have a grandmother with a cat cane and twinkling eyes and a long braid hanging over her shoulder. Willow frowned, not wanting to think of good things. She hadn't agreed to stay.

Luessy reached the bottom stair. "You and I are old family. In time, you'll understand the circle doesn't break."

Goose bumps peppered Willow's arms. Mémé's orange sweater stretched over her back. A misshapen back, a bumpy back, not flat like on pretty people. "You should get fixed."

A large smile broke across Luessy's face, widening her lips and showing her old teeth. "I've become a crone, haven't I?"

Willow had meant to be a little bit mean, but Mémé's smile was so big she didn't need to be fixed. In Willow's mind, Mémé knew a secret about being broken that made it all right. Watching her, Willow felt as if she almost knew the secret, too. She let the fingertips of her right hand peek out from her sweater

7

They moved at Luessy's relishing pace around the corner and alongside the manor. With each step gained, I felt myself growing heavier, but Luessy was happy and used her cane to point: "Boxwood hedges, George Tabor Azaleas, peonies, Damask roses."

To Willow, who wasn't listening to the plant names, Mémé smelled something like the powder and perfumes still on Jeannie's dresser. This made Mémé almost a match to all the things Willow wanted when she closed her eyes in the dark, or snuck into Papa's room and licked the glass over Jeannie's pictures and tried to taste her.

"After all these years," Luessy said, "you'll need new paints."

Before Willow could ask if Mémé really was going to buy her paints, Mémé stopped and looked upward. The corners of her mouth turned down. Willow frowned, too.

Standing on a second-story porch was a skinny woman with thin folded arms. Her nose and eyes resembled Papa's, but Papa smiled at people, and his black hair wasn't pulled back as tight as a swim cap.

Luessy tugged Willow's hand. "Come on, don't mind her."

They'd gone only a few feet when Willow glanced back, hoping that this time she'd see the woman smiling. The porch was empty. The woman had vanished as if she'd never been.

"Your aunt," Luessy said. "She doesn't go by Victoria now. She's chopped off her name like a goddess her hair. She's *Tory*. Just the butt end of a beautiful name."

"My name is a tree."

"Yes, I remember. I'll show you the tree. I'm glad your father settled on

Willow and left off the 'weeping.' I think he's keeping that part for himself." The thought of Julian's unhappiness tightened her chest. "It takes time, still, by now."

"That lady doesn't like me."

"She doesn't know who you are. She's angry with me, though she stays right here. Same as the child's handprints she pressed into the walk decades ago."

Luessy bent, pulled a small weed in their path, and rubbed the dirt from her fingers on her skirt. "I don't know what went wrong," she continued. "I think both my children are dragging around bones. Tory is waiting to inherit this place, but those old handprints aren't a hold on a piece of land. Not like birth string."

"What's that?"

"Don't mind me. I was remembering the night you were born, that's all. Stars roaring so bright I could barely tolerate the noise. Birth and death mixed up. Nothing solid, and those stars."

Willow knew she'd eventually have to go inside the house, and when she did, the skinny woman would be there. For comfort, she reached out and touched Friar whenever his back and forth trotting brought him close enough. She also let her eyes take sidelong glances at Mémé's back and the bump larger than her own. "How come you look like that?"

"Life grows a woman down. One day, she's as bowed as a spent flower. Not to worry though, that's when she's strongest. She loves mightily, and she creates. She's alive here," Luessy's finger touched her forehead and then tapped her wool sweater over her heart, "and here. When a body curls, a woman knows it's time to start making plans, giving away her things."

"Why?"

"She needs the space to journey *inside*. The clutter's too cumbersome."

Willow pressed her lips together. Her mouth wanted to tell Mémé she talked funny, but the issue of Mémé's back was more important. "How come a doctor can't fix you?"

"There's no hocus pocus for old age; I don't need to be fixed." Her eyes narrowed. "Your father isn't still hunting doctors for you?"

"They can't fix me."

They reached knee-high lavender growing wide and round alongside the flagstone path. The swish of Luessy's skirt against the small, dusty-green stems and leaves sent perfume into the air. "Our bodies are memory," Luessy said. "Unfinished work. Your back is what's right with you. And mine? Well, by the time you've reached my age, you'll have seen such a world of sorrow and nonsense you'll know you're something just for staying. A dowager's hump means I've been blessed with a long life. I'm proud of that." She paused, "Besides, one person looks silly as the next. I don't care how beautiful they suppose they are."

"Do I have a dowager's hump?"

"No. Yours is so special that it came with you. You didn't need to earn it."

They finished rounding the house. Three acres of manicured grounds, flowering trees in pink, white, and lavender, and a host of ground color, widened Willow's eyes. "Our house has yellow dandy, um, lions," she said.

The cat cane swung again, moving left to right in the air. "Magnolias, lilacs, tulips, jonquils, peonies, bleeding hearts." The cane stopped. "That tree there is your tree."

She led Willow to the far side of the yard, rather than into the garden. They looked down a long and steep hillside covered in clover, wild phlox, Dutchman's breeches, and Bloodroot. Bees hummed over the acres. The plunge of wild and unfarmable land ended at a field with green shoots of corn just breaking ground. Beyond that ran the same band of trees I remembered so well. The shiny belt of the Elkhorn River running through them. Still farther was the squat settlement of Greenburr: one street of businesses, skirted by a compact grid of square blocks holding both small homes and one-hundred-year old stately mansions.

"It's beggarly to never know land," Luessy said. "I've lived on this hill all my life. I know its shape, sound, and what the trees want. I know the path the wind takes coming up here and how that changes with the seasons." As if conjured, a sudden breeze blew over Luessy's face, and she breathed deep. "A person must take root and commit to staying before the spirit of the land speaks to him."

Willow listened less to Luessy's actual words than to their tone and numbers. Mémé talked funny and constantly, not a match to Papa.

Turning from the slope, Luessy nodded in the direction of an old and crumbling foundation with plugs of thick-growing grass studding the cracks, the remains of Peu de Nid. The chiseled rocks, the size of kitchen kettles, were still stained black by the sweeps of flame that ravaged it so many years before. Though the home had been rugged and cold in the winter and Thomas dead many years, I still refused to leave it and move across the yard to live with Luessy. Until the fire.

"Do you remember that small house?" Luessy asked. When Willow shrugged, 'no,' Luessy continued, "My uncle built the place for my aunt, Amelie-Anais. He'd traveled to Europe and met her in France." There was still no reaction from Willow. "She eventually learned English, but for a long time her speech was halting. When she went down the hill to shop, a few folks there—only second-generation immigrants themselves—snickered over her accent and sparse vocabulary. They liked to ask each time where she lived. She must have thought them fools for never remembering, but she was a lady. She'd point up here over and over and tell them again, 'Farthest house.' The town began referring to her place by that name. They called the road coming up here 'Old Squaw Road' because of the Indian women who came to Amelie for help."

"Real Indians were here?"

"At times. Much of my uncle's work was with the Omaha Tribe. They trusted him, and the women came to trust my aunt."

Willow had no interest in the ruined foundation, but she stared at the waist-high stack of grave rocks where I unknowingly drifted. I hadn't meant to settle on the gravestones, and I never expected I'd taken on such weight that she could see me. She pointed. "Who's that?"

"Do you mean the crosses? My aunt and uncle are buried there." It wasn't what Willow had asked, but the child's comment was unnerving. Luessy scolded herself. What was she doing? Trying to force Willow to remember things she shouldn't be remembering? "It's a good thing your father isn't here," she said. "He'd have plenty to say about my carrying on." She took Willow's hand again and steered her in the opposite direction. "See those white boxes? Jonah's tending his bees. He's anxious to meet you."

Turning from the stones was hard for Willow, but Luessy insisted. "Don't get too close to the hives, not until we're sure the bees know you." Her voice lifted, "Jonah! Willow is here."

Seeing Jonah eased some of my pain, if not my guilt. He'd survived the years and still lived at Farthest House, though I knew living was not thriving.

He stepped from the shadows between the four columns of stacked white boxes: four hives, each three crates high. Willow saw a small man with skin the same black/brown of Friar's eyes. He held a dented and rusty smoker and wore bib overalls with two faded shirts beneath. *Old too,* Willow thought, a *match to Mémé.* At his temples, gray wooly hair sprang from beneath a fraying straw hat, the hair sparkling in the sunlight. As they started for him, he set down the smoker and started for them. Willow marveled at the droop of his eyes; the outside corners had slid down, closing his eyes by half. The skin beneath his eyes, pads thick as thumbs, sagged. Her stomach danced as it did whenever she found new picture books in the library: flying carpets, Babar going to the circus, cows sneezing, and Jack climbing a bean stalk straight into a giant's house. Mémé's place, too, was full of magic.

"Here's Willow," Luessy said.

Willow heard the pride riding the tops of her grandmother's words, and she wanted to speak for herself. "My name comes from a tree."

Jonah removed his hat and wiped his forehead with the cuff of his shirt. "My name is Bug, and that's because of a bug."

She stared. His face was geography.

"Wasn't no bigger than you," he said. "Oh, was it a hot day at my colored school." He nodded slowly, as if the memory rolled toward him from a distance and needed waiting on. "A brown roach crawled outta my sleeve. It was a bad morning already, my clothes stinking something awful and nobody wanting near me. Seemed to me that I walked alone in the world. Then, here come that bug right smack out onto the plank table. The only thing willing to get close to me. I stared at them two little feelers on his head just a twitchin', him trying to figure out where to hide. That bug had crawled up and down my arm without my even knowin'. I owed it something for not minding me and my black skin, and I hurt so bad with loneliness, I wanted him back in my clothes."

Luessy listened quietly, giving Jonah's story its time.

He leaned closer, and Willow closer to him. "I was considering on that," he continued, "when a little girl about your size, sitting way down at the end, a pretty thing I'd set my eyes on, started crying and pointing at my bug. You'd a thought the feller a ten-foot rattler. Teacher locked me the whole afternoon in the outhouse. Said I smelled like I belonged there." Jonah waited again on the story, glancing from Luessy back to Willow. "Once that door closed, ah, the stink and heat in there, I'd like to have fainted straight into the privy. Spiders and beetles black as me come out after a bit, covering the floor and wanting on my bare feet. Dancing was no good lest I wanted them under instead of over. I was too mean to scream. I had to get my mind around them bugs, tell myself they liked me, and there was no difference between us." He nodded toward the hives, "I guess that's stayed with me."

He put his hat back on. "That was my last day of school. When teacher let me out, I ran all the way to the shack where I'd been holing up by myself. I never went back. Still, I'd gotten the name Bug, and it followed me to the streets. Caused me many a black eye and bloody nose before I figured if I was goin' lose all the fights, I was too runty a fellow to mind name calling."

When he finished, Willow told a story about herself. "Jeannie died."

Luessy's eyes widened, but Jonah's continued to droop. "Yup. That's a fact," he said.

The two had said a lot to each other. They were friends now, Willow believed, even if she couldn't say exactly how. "Do the bees sting you?"

"It's me steals their honey, and a sting's good medicine for what ails you."

"If I was a bee," she whispered, her eyes lowering to the neat patches on the knees of his pants, "I wouldn't ever sting you."

"Yup. I wouldn't ever sting you either."

Luessy and Jonah began talking roses, and Willow snuck a peek back to where I sat. "A lady is there."

The two adults glanced in the direction of her pointing. Seeing she indicated the graves, Jonah took a small, but quick step back. "Best be finishing my work." The last thing he wanted, and with good reason, was a child able to see the buried dead.

Willow headed for me and Luessy followed. I looked at myself, surprised to see I wore the pale blue dress I'd been married in. Rows of beads decorated the waist and cuffs, caught light, and sparkled. To my further surprise, a drawing lay in my lap. The picture was of Sabine. My poor Sabine. She hadn't been cursed with my back, and were it not for my shoulder and our age difference, we might have looked like twins. Perhaps I only wished it true, needing us to have that sisters' bond. When I fled to America with Thomas, she'd still been full of a child's playfulness, romping with the dogs and sheep, sticking her nose into everything from the baking in the kitchen to the milking and grape pressing, her hair always flying free of its ribbons and pins. Then, the letter came from France and Mme. Francoise, the ancient apothecary who lived on a stool in the corner of The Beast's kitchen. The letter explained Sabine was a new mother with a daughter she named Luessy. The letter went on telling how Sabine cut her hair off and cleaved two fingers to the first knuckle.

In the drawing, a picture I painted long ago and lost when Little Nest burned, Sabine's beautiful hair was short and ragged-edged. I'd imagined her cutting it in a wild frenzy of self-hatred, sorrow, and panic. I painted her hands twisting in her lap, two fingertips on the right hand severed. Bright red blood and thick darker clots ran from the wounds. Now, that blood was alive, rolling off the paper, bleeding onto and soiling my blue dress.

Willow reached me. Her stomach told her not to look in my lap, but she did. She let out a small cry, cringing and pulling Doll to her face, only peeking over the top of the toy's bald head.

Luessy put a hand on her shoulder and wanted to say, "Nothing is there," but she knew better. "Let's go inside now. I have someone else I want you to meet."

The dress, the picture, the blood? Seeing my Luessy so much older, Tory with the taste of ashes in her mouth, Jonah in his decrepitude, returning to Farthest House and Thomas's grave, I'd been sucked back in. It wasn't that I needed Willow to help me find Tory, Luessy, and Jonah, but because of her I could no longer escape doing so.

They left the yard, Willow reluctantly, while I remained mired, the slick ether of time sucking me back to my childhood. I felt myself back in my child's body, struggling, fighting for life. I was wedged into the tightness of the long cave tunnel. My breathing was ragged with the effort of staying alive, my toes pushing, my fingertips blistered from clawing stone. I counted: " . . . twelve, thirteen, fourteen . . . " my age. The counting helped keep panic at bay and measured my progress. At the count of thirty, I'd find the cave and be able to fill my lungs with air. And for as long as *I chose* to remain—I'd be safe.

The numbers also distracted me, however briefly, from my self-loathing. I bore the weight of a hundred mortal sins when a single one meant eternal damnation.

Backing out of the tight passage was impossible. I had no choice but to keep struggling, keep inching ahead on my raw knees. Alone in the rock, my whimpering burbled out along the uneven walls, rolling out ahead of me into the pitch darkness and sounding like a trapped animal. I prayed no rock had dropped into the passage since the last time, since even something small would turn the shaft into my grave. I prayed, too, that I hadn't gained an ounce of weight in the days since my last visit and the cave itself hadn't imploded or filled with water in my absence. I prayed hardest that the spirits, who first called me, still haunted the stone.

Crawling, the body-tight rock scraping and bruising, the sharp juts of stone cutting my shoulders, I welcomed the yarn-thin rivulets of blood trailing down my arms and the tears dripping from my chin. Le Bête, The Beast, might have preached, "Washing you in the blood of the Lamb." But I believed I could never be cleansed on either side of death.

Inside the stone, only my labored breathing accompanied me, not his voice booming down the ornate villa hallways, replete with religious paintings in gilded frames, my name spilling over his fat, wet lips. "Amelie-Anais!"

And my mother pushing, "Go. Go. Your bishop uncle has interest in your salvation." Seeing what happened in the bishop's wing, using the eyes of her heart, would have caused her untold grief and possibly that especially bitter sin against the church, doubt. He was the village priest, prêtre, though he called himself an Auxiliary Bishop, and told us all he'd soon be appointed Titular Bishop and then ordained a full bishop. It was far easier for my mother to stay blinded by the bright fury of her household duties, managing the melee of servants who saw to his meals and laundry, the totting of her accounts and meager allowance, and the tending to her religious duties: morning Mass, rosaries, visits to grottos, and her ornate book of prayers.

8

A year passed with Willow and I spending weekends at Farthest House. Julian came on Sunday evenings to get her for the week and gradually overcame his aversion to stepping inside. Often, he sat at the table over a plate of Mable's cookies, conversing with his sister and mother. An outsider might have watched them and believed everything was good.

That spring, Willow stood on the school playground of Our Lady of Supplication, Sister Dominic Agnes at her side. She watched her classmates form a circle, one child skipping around the outside of the others, deciding at whose heels to drop a scarf. For the fourth day, the nun hadn't let her join in, and for the fourth day, the nun was angry.

Sister Dominic Agnes's immaculate white habit hissed, and the beads of her long rosary, hanging from her waist to nearly the ground, trembled, "Because I said, 'No.'"

Willow's good hand clenched a fistful of her blue-plaid skirt; her right hand hid in her sweater sleeve, invisible, but trembling.

When a boy dropped the scarf at the heels of Mary Wolfe, both he and Mary started running, but it was only Mary that Willow watched. Mary had the holiest girl's name you could have and skin as pink as the painted statues in church. She had blue eyes, too, also like the statues and long hair as yellow as an angel's. Every day, her hair was brushed back into a smooth and shiny ponytail and tied with a freshly ironed ribbon. Mary had a mother.

Willow blinked back tears. Through kindergarten and most of first grade, Mary had been her best friend. They skipped together at recess and sat side by side at lunch—Willow's left ankle wrapped around Mary's right, their legs swinging as though between them they had only three.

Then in early December, Sister Dominic Agnes rustled and puffed into the classroom to announce that Mary had been badly hurt. In order for Mary to live, they needed to pray hard. If they said enough rosaries, and if they were *good* rosaries, if the children prayed sincerely, no one's mind wandering off the Sorrowful Mysteries, and no eyes getting sleepy, the Blessed Mother would count up all the numbers and tell Jesus, who would think about it, and *maybe* He'd trade the prayers and let Mary Wolfe get well.

With that burden on their shoulders, Willow's class lifted the tops of their desks and pulled out strings of beads and offered up "Hail Marys" like dropping pennies in a jar for Jesus. Three rosaries every school day: the first thing in the morning, after they'd eaten their peanut butter sandwiches at lunch, and before leaving in the afternoon—struggling to pay off whatever ransom Jesus wanted. Each time they said a rosary, Sister Dominic Agnes cut and pasted another link to her black construction paper chain. Jesus needed to know they were very sad. Willow imagined Jesus visiting the dark and empty classroom with his mother at night (because He let only very special people see Him), walking in His sandals alongside the chain, counting the links, three new black circles each night. The number was always three, always matching.

Now, five months later, Mary had returned. On Monday of that week, with the chain draping across the top of the blackboard and down the sides and up to snake over the tops of all the classroom windows, Mary walked into the room.

Jesus had let her get well. All that day, the other grades, K through twelve, filed into the first-grade room with their nuns or lay teachers and admired the funereal rope, their heads swinging back and forth as they looked from one end to the other and then at the beaming Sister Dominic Agnes and then at Mary sitting shyly in a chair placed at the front of the room. Even Father Steinhouse, the parish priest, came into the classroom and nodded approvingly at Sister Dominic Agnes and laid a hand on Mary's head. Tuesday, a few parishioners visited. Wednesday and Thursday, no one came. No footsteps in the hallway resulted in believers entering, though each time someone passed the door, Sister Dominic Agnes stopped her instructions and waited. Now, on Friday, she'd hung a sign beneath the chain: *Sister Dominic Agnes's Miracle.*

All of which Willow knew, meant Mary was a saint. Jesus let her get really hurt, and then the rosaries changed His mind, and He fixed her. Something He'd not done for Willow.

On the playground, Sister Dominic Agnes's habit rustled again, and she buried her right hand into her left sleeve and her left hand into her right sleeve. "I've looked through my book of Catholic Saints," she said. "There's no saint named *Willow*. I think I must remove you from the May procession."

Willow's breath caught. She and her class had been practicing and planning for the procession, and she told both Mémé and Papa how the girls would march up the center aisle of the church in two lines, and then "fold open like wings," and one line would go down each of the side aisles and into their pews. She'd practiced walking back and forth in front of Papa, taking slow, careful steps while keeping her eyes straight ahead. The procession was also special because Mary's parents bought each girl a small, white basket to be filled with flower petals.

"I've taught school at Our Lady of Supplication for thirty-seven years," Sister Dominic Agnes said. "The children have always had at least one Catholic name to put on their scapulars." She looked down her nose at Willow. "Missionaries got around these problems by assigning Christian names, but our problem is more serious."

Willow's finger found a small hole in the seam of her skirt. She pushed at it. How could she walk down the aisle, her blue-felt scapular the size of a valentine hanging around her neck, but with a different name on it? "How come Willow isn't a saint's name?"

"It isn't. There's nothing holy about it."

Willow pushed harder, heard one thread pop and then a second, her whole fingertip breaking through the seam. Standing still was too hard, and she rocked. "Papa named me for a tree." It didn't seem enough. "Mémé writes stories, so you can't change my name."

"Don't tell me what I can and cannot do." She waited, letting her scolding hang in the air. "We all know your grandmother writes mysteries. That's likely part of your problem. I'm told they are sacrilegious, full of pagan ideas."

Willow kept rocking. "When I grow up, I'm going to read all her books."

The nun's hands came out of her sleeves and swung behind her back making a slapping sound. "You ought to read from the wealth of good *Catholic* literature."

Willow's stomach squeezed. The week had been the worst ever. Mary turned away whenever Willow came close, and during every recess, Willow was made to stand beside Sister Dominic Agnes. At lunch, Mary sat at a different cafeteria table and made it the best table. For five lunches, Willow had crossed her ankles and swung her own feet and tried to pretend one foot was Mary's.

"I don't see you and your father in church on Sundays." The rosary, hanging from the thick belt around Sister Dominic Agnes's waist, trembled. "Are you practicing Catholics?"

Willow hadn't known being a Catholic took practice. She couldn't remember practicing, but she wasn't going to admit to anything that would make things worse. Her Sunday mornings were usually spent in Mémé's attic drawing pictures while Mémé typed. She studied the nun with a boy's name and a girl's name, the long white gown hanging round as a snowman, and the white wimple squeezing her teacher's pale face. Even the nun's lips looked gone, so pale they might have been erased. The only color on her face was the darkness in her eyes. "Do you practice?" she asked.

The nun's hand shot out, grabbed and pinched Willow's ear so fast all Willow saw before she felt the sting was the jump of the two lowest mysteries on the long rosary. "You should be punished," Sister Dominic Agnes scolded, "for asking such a thing." She pinched harder, and Willow cried out. The first grade class forgot their game and turned to stare.

Sister Dominic Agnes didn't mind upsetting the class. All children needed to be reminded to respect authority, but poor little Mary looked shocked. It wouldn't do to have her father back at the school, throwing about more accusations. She eased her thumbnail out of the flesh of Willow's ear but kept hold. "I've had half a mind to punish you for a long time."

Slumped and rubbing her ear with her cuffed hand, Willow felt dazed. Sister Dominic Agnes had wanted to punish her for a long time, and *Willow* was not a holy name.

"Stand up straight, and pull your hand out of your sleeve. You can't hide God's markings, and you can tell your father to start bringing you to Mass on Sundays. Maybe that will help you learn your place. Is he able to do that? Or does he spend his Sundays sleeping off his Saturdays? We don't want him stumbling into church. I know about Frenchmen and their wine."

Willow didn't know about Frenchmen, but they sounded bad. She wished for Doll or Papa and wondered why her teacher would think Papa stumbled. His back was straight. "Papa never falls down."

"Don't correct me."

All through recess, stones had been dropping into Willow's stomach, and their weight threatened to make her throw up. She wouldn't, wouldn't, do that in front of all her classmates. She had to make Sister Dominic Agnes like her. "Sometimes . . . Papa does fall down." The first words were slow, but the next ones came in a rush. "He crashes down on his head, and the table falls over."

The nun nodded knowingly, her lips relaxing, and for a moment things seemed better. But Willow had told a lie about Papa, and she knew he would never tell a lie about her. Worse yet, what if he found out what she'd said?

"What does your father say about the pictures you draw?"

Stung by the lie she told, Willow felt mute. Using her index finger, she pushed, widening the hole in her skirt.

The after-recess bell rang and the other first graders began forming a line behind Sister Dominic Agnes. Willow let them push her back, as one at a time, they stepped in front of her. Finally, with Mary Wolfe at the head, the long tails of her pink hair bow swinging and her hand in Sister Dominic Agnes's, they started in. Willow took baby steps. What if Papa looked at her and saw the lie she told about him? Or what if he didn't see the lie, but her mouth told him anyway?

At her desk, her throat made little popping, sucking sounds she couldn't stop. She could think of only one thing to keep herself from crying—drawing pictures. Since Mary's return on Monday, Willow had drawn several pictures, and each made her feel better. She reached for her thick pencil and a piece of ruled school paper. Drawing made the world around her quiet, and she didn't need to think about Sister Dominic Agnes or Papa.

Minutes passed as she concentrated first on drawing the monster's head, giving it one great big eye, one little tiny eye, a witch's nose, and jagged teeth. When she finally looked up, she sat alone in an empty row. Sister Dominic Agnes had brought her chair from behind her desk, put it in the story-time place, and the rest of the first graders sat on the floor clustered around her ankles. Not even Mary saved Willow a place. Had Sister Dominic Agnes called Willow up front with the others, or did she want her to stay and keep drawing?

Willow knew the nun loved her drawings, so much so that all week she'd let Willow draw and draw whenever she wanted and then collected the drawings for herself.

The creature needed a body. Willow considered some of her favorite things to draw: birds, bugs, and zoo animals. Maybe she would draw clothes like Sister Dominic Agnes's, which were almost like Doll's. She went back to work and didn't look up until the nun closed the last story book and started down the aisle, the folds of her long habit sweeping the sides of desks. Willow smiled, the finished drawing was one of her best, and looking at it made the lie she told about Papa feel far away. If the *I Dream of Jeannie,* Jeannie, were to come into the room and cross her arms and nod and make the monster alive, everyone would scream and run away.

"Is this supposed to be me?"

Willow looked again at the drawing and the monster's habit, complete even to the rosary. The room began creeping slowly around her.

"This time, you've gone too far."

It wasn't hard for me to see the nun's heartbreak. Here, she believed, was more of the mockery of everything she thought sacred. This time it wasn't coming from the young nuns rejecting their habits for street clothes, convent life for apartments where they entertained, served unblessed wine, and lived without curfews, supervised morning prayers, and mandatory silences. Their very life-styles thumbed their noses at her life of service and tried to discredit every sacrifice she'd made for the order. As if all her renunciations, past and future, were without value, the disciplines sent down from Rome worthless, needless dark-age trappings practiced by the foolish, the thousands and thousands of women's lives given over to convents, all for nothing! Now, there was a *modern* pope who would discard even Latin Mass, discard so many foundations of ritual, history, and the established institution. If all that could be so easily discarded, then couldn't she also be?

She lifted her gaze to the black paper chain. Wasn't it proof enough of her spirituality, of how the church must hold fast? She would not take denunciation from a seven-year old who'd already caused her untold trouble with Mr. Wolfe and Father Steinhouse. She would not take it from this misshapen half-orphan whose father never brought her to church on Sundays. She narrowed her eyes on Willow. "I should have guessed. This picture proves your attitude toward me and Mother Church."

Willow trembled as the classroom turned to winter. Even Sister's rushing and flapping back up to the front of the room sounded like ice flaking and dropping from bare trees. First graders, some already in their seats, some still in the aisles, froze as the nun pulled open her top desk drawer and brought out her flat disciplinary paddle. She headed back for Willow.

The wide, short-handled instrument rose in the air, and Sister Dominic Agnes grabbed hold of Willow's right wrist, pulling back the sweater cuff in one motion and pinning the hand to the desk. The paddle whistled down, smacking, biting again, and then a third time.

Willow screamed with each blow. She'd never been struck before, not so much as a swat on her backside, and she didn't understand what was happening. As she screamed, she tried to twist and pull away, but the nun's anger and strength funneled down through the heel of her large white hand, crushing Willow's to the desk. The next series of strikes turned the skin on Willow's hand red and purple.

Then came the words that would for years shut Willow in: "You are disfigured to match your soul!"

9

Those words lifted the paper chain from the tops of the windows and threatened to send it slithering to the floor.

Drums beat in Willow's head, her hand burned, and still Sister Dominic Agnes pulled, jerking her out of her seat and dragging her up the aisle past girls who cried and Mary who only stared. Derrick Crat, the oldest boy in the class, stood beside his desk, his mouth contorted in mock sobs, his hands fisted, feigning the motion of rubbing his eyes. "Whaa, whaa." When he had the attention of those nearest, he pulled his right hand up into the sleeve of his sweater and waved the empty cuff.

"This is nothing compared to what you deserve," Sister Dominic Agnes said, both hands on Willow's shoulders, turning her into the tight corner. "Stand here until I say."

Willow's head dropped into the vee of the abutted walls, and she cupped her hands to the sides of her face like blinders, or closing doors. Wall dust crawled up her nose, and the taste of wet salt rolled over her lips. Even if the class couldn't see her face, she knew they saw her back: her worst thing. She fought against slumping or crumbling onto the floor. As minutes drug through one hour and then another, the eyes of her class stomping around and around the bulge on her shoulder, she imagined the bone growing until it became a whole head lifting out of her back to make ugly faces and say, "I hate you. I hate you." Especially to Derrick. Sister Dominic Agnes had never made him stand in the corner, and he'd never been hit. Neither had Mary. Willow licked snot from her lips. Derrick and Mary hadn't told lies about their dads.

By the time the dismissal bell rang and doors all along the corridor outside the room opened and the hall filled with the sounds of happy kids, Willow's eyes were dry. Doll would cry when she heard what happened, but Willow wouldn't cry any more. She let the classroom empty, wanting everyone gone before she turned to show her face.

"Is your father home?" the nun asked.

Willow's legs ached. She hadn't been given permission to turn around.

"Willow!"

She jumped. She wasn't sure if Papa was home. Sometimes he was, and sometimes a sitter was there. She shrugged into the wall.

"Look at me when I'm talking to you. I'm taking you home, and we'll just see."

Willow never wanted Papa to hear the lie she told about him. She turned and ran to the back of the room, grabbed her *Jeannie* bag—the last backpack still hanging on the row of low hooks—and for a long second she held her bag up, picture facing out, Jeannie's powers staring at Sister Dominic Agnes. If that bag, pushed defiantly in the air between them was held a moment longer than Willow intended, it was by my hand. She ran.

"Stop!"

Her life at school was over; she was never coming back. They'd called Jonah a bug and he never went back. She'd been called "disfigured to match her soul," and she wasn't ever coming back either.

"Willow Starmore, get back here!"

She kept running, down the hall, out the door, and into the schoolyard full of students waiting for rides or milling about in clusters of friends. Careful not to touch anyone, she wove her way through, and when she cleared the largest knots, she started running down the first of the two blocks home. By the end of it, her lungs ached, and her knees trembled, but she could see Julian getting out of his car in front of their house. "Papa!"

He didn't hear, and she ran harder, screaming his name until he stopped on the walk and looked up in her direction, his face filling with questions. She ran, out of breath now, Julian starting for her, not running, but coming with his long strides, the distance between them closing. She hit the wall of his body and wrapped her arms around his waist.

"Hey, hey." He rubbed her back, and when she caught a semblance of breath, he held her back a step and lifted her skirt over one knee and then the other looking for a scrape. "What is it?"

How could she explain without confessing her lie? She looked back to see Sister Dominic Agnes and a younger nun hurrying toward them. A ragged sob bleated from her throat.

"It looks like I'm about to find out," Julian said. "It can't be this bad. Let's go inside. Whatever's happened, it's not for the whole neighborhood."

He carried her, her arms around his neck and her legs around his waist. The screen banged closed behind them, but the wooden door Willow wanted shut and locked, Julian left open. Crossing the first room into the kitchen, he tossed her backpack onto the table and set her down. "You want to tell me something before they get here?"

She shook her head.

"All right." He looked around his own kitchen. "How about a glass of milk?"

She could just manage to keep breathing; she didn't want to try and drink milk. She ached to ask him about being "disfigured to match her soul." Did that mean she couldn't ever go to Heaven? Was *disfigured* the reason Mary Wolfe and Sister Dominic Agnes didn't like her? She wouldn't ask. She wouldn't say the words because she never wanted Papa to know about them.

Each time she looked through the screen door, her fear increased. Only the wire mesh stood between her and Papa learning what she said about him. Shadows climbed onto the porch and then toes of black shoes beneath glimpses of white-hosed ankles. Willow dropped her head onto her arms, and her heart banged as Papa took his time despite the knocking and opened the refrigerator, poured milk into a glass, and set it in front of her. He shook a cigarette from the pack in his pocket, still not hurrying when Sister Dominic Agnes knocked a second time, but lighting the cigarette and pressing it into a small groove on the side of the kitchen ashtray. How many times had Willow heard him and his partner, Red, chuckling about the length of some interrogations, how they counted the number of cigarettes that burned away—the slow crawl of the smoke unnerving to their suspects. A good confession didn't cost them more than a couple of cigarettes.

He took a step toward the door, but Willow let out such a sob, he stopped and turned back. "Hey now," he winked at her. "We'll get this figured out."

She kept her head down, wanting to beg him to slam the big door and take her to the back yard where they'd play catch with a football, his newest plan for strengthening her right arm. This was their house, only theirs, and she had a new rule: "No nuns allowed."

She heard the squeak of the screen and Papa say, "Good afternoon."

"I'm Sister Dominic Agnes. This is Sister Beatrice."

Willow snuck a glance. Her teacher was inside, looking around the room at Papa's shiny floors, his desk with the top rolled down, and the clean kitchen counter tops. Only when her eyes landed on a stack of folded towels, did she seem to relax. Willow wanted to jump up and put them away, but she was too scared to move.

"We've come to speak to you about Willow," the nun said.

Papa looked over at her. "Drink your milk."

Sister Dominic Agnes held out the sheets of Big Chief paper she'd rolled into a scroll. "Look at these. Something must be done."

Surprised, Willow looked up to see Papa thumbing through the drawings. Had her teacher come to talk about the pictures? Not the lie?

Julian's brow lifted quizzically. "Gnomes, maybe trolls, what's the problem?"

An angry finger rapped the top picture, "It's disrespectful," Sister Dominic Agnes said, "mocking, even demonic."

"Demonic?" He needed a moment. "She's got a wild imagination, but they aren't evil. She spends a lot of time in her grandmother's garden, imagines fairies, trolls, and she reads make-believe." He looked through a few again. "They're pretty good. She's trying to copy Arthur Rackham, Walter Crane, Dore, that kind of thing."

The nervousness in Willow's stomach eased. Maybe, Papa could make things all right.

"Her grandmother has quite a collection of the old books," Julian continued, "I grew up with them. Some of those pictures are graphic but harmless."

"What you are holding," Sister Dominic Agnes said, "is not what a normal Catholic child draws. I am responsible," she expelled her breath and needed to draw another, "and no small responsibility it is, for the welfare of my first graders, at home and at school."

Willow crossed her arms over her stomach and held the hurt. Sister Beatrice was looking down at her shoes, and Papa considered her before looking back to Sister Dominic Agnes. "You're responsible for your first graders? Even when they are at home?"

"And for their pure minds," the nun continued. "These kinds of things," she motioned again to the drawings in Julian's hand, "are sinful."

"Sinful?" His brows narrowed, and for a long moment, he said nothing. Then, "You're experienced in this sort of thing." He was nodding along with her. "You know enough to have brought all the pictures? I'm seeing *all* the evidence?"

"Of course. I wanted you to see everything. If she doesn't stop this, I'll take her to see Father Steinhouse. He'll likely want to meet with you, and he may well decide she's not suited for Our Lady of Supplication. As it is, I'm taking her out of the May procession."

Willow slid off her chair and ran to stand beside Julian. "Mémé bought me a dress, and you're coming to the procession too, aren't you Papa? You're coming to church."

"Adults are talking," Sister Dominic Agnes said.

Willow's eyes met Sister Beatrice's eyes, which looked kind and sorry. Sister Beatrice couldn't help though, and Willow turned for her room and Doll. Julian caught her arm, pulling her up short. As she tugged, stretching for her room, though he didn't seem to notice her struggle, he raised the pictures. "You're taking her out of the procession because of these?"

"She draws when she shouldn't. She did all those this week. I cannot tolerate such misbehavior. We take time for coloring the last hour on Fridays, and it's not the devil we color at Our Lady of Supplication."

The pictures hung at Papa's side, the corners fluttering as he tapped them against his leg, his thoughts loud in Willow's head. *She can't be getting in trouble over her drawings again, can't be drawing when the rest are getting ahead. Jeannie attended that school; she wanted her kids to go there. I don't want Willow in rough public schools . . . not where they'll pick on her.*

She stopped fighting his grip. Why had his mind said *getting in trouble again*? She'd never been in trouble for drawing.

He let her go and re-rolled the pictures into a tight scroll. "I'll see this stops."

"Very well," Sister Dominic Agnes sighed with satisfaction. "However, as punishment, I'm still removing her from the procession."

A squeak from Sister Beatrice. "Perhaps, if she—"

"I must maintain discipline," Sister Dominic Agnes cut in, "or risk having none at all." She motioned to the pictures in Julian's hand, "I'll take those back with me."

To both nuns, he gave a slow, gracious smile. "Why don't I keep them? We'd hate to see them land in a file somewhere. Especially if someone might think they're inappropriate."

Willow saw red wash up from Sister Dominic Agnes's neck and onto her cheeks. "They are school property. They were drawn at school and, therefore, belong in her school records. Father Steinhouse may wish to see them."

"Well, then, I'm sincerely indebted to you for bringing them *all* to me. That was a real act of kindness." He stepped around the women and held open the screen door with an outstretched arm. "I'll talk to Willow. She won't give you any more trouble."

Sister Beatrice leaned down, and her kind eyes met Willow's again. "Angels are coming tonight."

The elder nun gasped, "Sister! Wait outside." She glared at the pictures and then again at Julian. "I *insist* you return those to me."

He feigned a smile, "I'll keep them."

The nun reached, and Willow's mouth opened when she saw Papa swing the pictures behind his back. Sister Dominic Agnes would have to touch his arm to reach again. Wasn't Papa committing a mortal sin?

He stood still, waiting until Sister Dominic Agnes stepped out onto the porch beside Sister Beatrice. He stood still until they descended the steps and reached the sidewalk. He crossed the room, picked up his cigarette, inhaled smoke, and blew it toward the ceiling.

"Only half a cigarette, Papa. You did good."

"Why are you drawing while others are being taught? If all you do is draw, how do you expect to learn how to take care of yourself?"

There it was, more of the rejection and loneliness she'd felt all week. This time not from Mary or Sister Dominic Agnes but from Papa. He was even telling her she needed to know how to take care of herself because he wouldn't always be with her. She hurried down the hall to her room. With Doll in her arms, she curled into a ball on the bed, making herself as small as she could. Doll was crying, too.

She didn't hear his footsteps enter her room, but she heard his thoughts as he stood over her. *So small. Still only bird bones. How's she going to make it if I don't keep pushing her? Some punishment, but nothing Jeannie would think too harsh.*

Willow screamed and rolled over on top of Doll, hugging her. A tug and Doll was gone. Willow's arms were empty, as though she hugged herself. But that was hugging nothing.

10

---·❧·---

Willow cried many nights for Doll. I knew she cried in part for what she supposed losing Doll represented, that she deserved to be alone. She pulled off her pillowcase, stuffed a shirt in the bottom, and hugged it.

Julian was sorry. For her birthday, he bought her a plastic doll with yellow hair. It came in a colorful box with a cellophane front. Willow thought the object an intruder, too hard to lie on, smelling like bad oatmeal, and nothing like Doll. It reminded her of Mary Wolfe and things she wanted to forget: having her hand struck with a paddle, Derrick making the class laugh, missing the May Procession, and Sister Dominic Agnes's proclamation.

At first, Willow stuffed it under her bed, but at night, sleeping on the floor, the hard blue eyes stared at her. She pushed the doll to the back of her closet floor and threw a towel over it. Julian asked only once, wondering if she'd packed her new doll for the weekend with Mémé. She shook her head. He looked at her for a long moment. "That's all right," he said. When she rushed to him, throwing her arms around his waist, he held her.

January of her ninth year, a far deeper loss loomed unseen on the horizon. At Farthest House, dark clouds were gathering, proving my worst fears true. I could only watch and wait.

It was a Friday afternoon. Snow had been falling for an hour. Julian considered not taking Willow out on the roads, but he was scheduled for work later in the evening. With his weekends free, he picked up extra hours, and given the weather predictions, the precinct was going to need every hand. His mother also expected Willow, and Willow loved going and came home happy. While he wished he could be her whole world, he understood she needed her Farthest House family, too. And if some day he took a bullet to the chest?

Sitting beside him in the car, Willow tried to look innocent as she kept one hand pressed to the front of her coat, hoping the week's worth of drawings hidden beneath weren't getting wrinkled. Not since that bad day had she let anyone other than Mémé see her pictures.

The windshield wipers whipped back and forth, and she watched Papa light a cigarette, turning his head with each exhale to send the smoke through his half inch of rolled-down window. She suspected he knew she still drew pictures, though never at school. He sometimes passed by her room when she was drawing, and she closed her tablet and put both hands on top. Sometimes, when he came home from work before she and the babysitter expected, he'd catch her drawing in front of the television, and she'd jump and quickly stuff her pad of paper under the sofa. Though she felt he wanted her to share with him, he never asked. In return, she studied hard and gave him the "A's" he wanted on her report cards.

As they left the city limits and hit the highway, the snowflakes grew heavier and thicker and the wind buffeted the side of the car. Usually, she enjoyed the drive, but as the minutes passed, her restlessness increased. "We're driving so slow."

"Everyone is. We've likely got three inches already."

Something was wrong. The *wrong* thing seemed more than the storm, the noisy wipers, or the slow going. She wanted to tell Papa about the unquiet thing, but she didn't know what it was, and telling him stuff he didn't know, and didn't think she should know, worried him. He wanted her to be like other children: not getting in trouble at school, not drawing odd pictures, and never saying things that made people's eyebrows go up. Or down.

Julian fiddled with the radio, trying to find a station without static and with an updated weather report. "Twelve inches," he repeated the announcer. "We won't be dug out until spring."

She heard someone call her name. She sat up straighter, looking to Julian, but he only clutched the steering wheel, which meant he hadn't heard. If she told him, his brows would go up, then down.

"A couple of Ginn stations were robbed last weekend," he said. "Two more robberies this week."

She rarely went into his thoughts now. To hear them, she had to leave her own and go into his, which were boring and usually about things like Ginn stations. She was in fourth grade with Sister Beatrice, and she had a friend. They called themselves "The Two-Girls Club," and they had a rule: To be a member you had to hate Derrick Crat and Mary Wolfe.

"Thirty inches last month," Julian said. "A new record. You suppose this month'll be worse?"

He didn't usually talk so much, which meant he did feel the thing without a name. She tried to distract herself. She'd think about pretty things like the blue coat over her pictures with its rabbit-fur collar, dyed-to-match blue mittens, and the dresses Mémé bought her, dresses as pretty as Mary Wolfe's.

Julian kept his hands on the steering wheel until they'd started up the drive of Farthest House. He reached across the seat and brushed back a lock of Willow's hair from the side of her face. "Tell Ma, I'll see her on Sunday. If I waste time on coffee, I won't make it back." The car wheels began to spin, and the car veered sideways. He stepped on the brake and looked at the house still ten yards up and Willow's short rubber boots leaving her legs bare to her knees. The car slid backwards a few inches and caught. "If I carry you, I'm going to lose the car."

"I can walk."

"No, I got it." He put the car in reverse and turning around threw one arm across the seat top. "I'll park at the bottom and carry you up."

"Papa. I can do it." She grabbed her bag and opened the door. The dread in her stomach rolled, but she'd soon be with Mémé and could talk over her feelings. The cold wind lunged at her bare legs, stinging the flesh. For weeks, winter had felt like a cat clawing at her calves and knees, and now it tried to pull open her coat and get her pictures. Hurrying, slipping, she heard Papa's car idling behind her. She thought to wave him off, but she knew he wouldn't leave until she reached the porch. She trudged up, holding her bag with one hand, the other still pressed against her coat.

The third-floor attic door was closed, and the light behind it off. Across the house, the turret was also dark. The upset in her stomach increased. At the porch, she turned and waved to Julian and watched the car's wobbly slide down.

"He ought to stay." Jonah stepped from the shadows near the door and crossed to the top of the stairs. He wore a light jacket and his ears and hands were bare.

She started up. "What are you doing here?"

"Sweeping."

He held a broom, but the majority of the snow fell on the porch roof. Of the snow that had blown in, she saw no signs of sweeping. He'd been waiting for her, something he didn't usually do. Foreboding washed over her again. When she reached the top stair, he made an almost imperceptible motion, angling his elbow an inch in her direction. If she didn't take it, they could pretend she hadn't seen the gesture. Black men, Tory told her, couldn't touch little white girls. There'd been the hot afternoon when Mable made a pitcher of lemonade for Jonah, and Willow asked to be the one to take it to him. She kicked at his door, her hands full, and his delight on opening it was everything she hoped for. He bent and took the pitcher, wet with condensation, and thanked her, but he didn't ask her in to share a glass.

Back in the kitchen of Farthest House, Tory's pinched face leaned in close. "Don't you *ever* go in his cabin."

Can't he even touch little white girls, Willow wondered, that have a stupid hand and shoulder?

On the cold porch, she juggled her things, freed a hand and clutched Jonah's arm. He pulled his arm in tight. "Miss Willow, you're here now."

His eyes looked as if snow melted in them. She knew all people had the same color of blood, and she wanted to tell him people all had the same color of tears, too. But saying so might be stupid, and then there was the reason for his coming. It wasn't to sweep.

He walked her across the porch and turned the handle on the front door, pushing it just enough to clear the lock. "Hurry now. I was afraid the storm might keep your daddy from bringing you." He left her there, and when he'd gone down the stairs and stepped into the snow, he looked back, surprised she still watched him. Snow fell on his white hair and disappeared. It clung to his shoulders. "Hurry, your grandma been calling for you."

Now that she'd arrived and knew Mémé called for her, Willow didn't want to hurry. "If I lie down in the snow, I could be a snow angel and disappear."

"Yup." He gave her a moment, the broom clutched in his hands. "Now, Willow, you got to go on in there."

She leaned her weight against the door and stepped into the round foyer of polished walnut floors and walls, always like stepping inside a big tree. The foyer was a clock, and she could lift an arm and tick off all the rooms. On her left, seven o'clock to ten o'clock was the dining room. Tick, tick to eleven o'clock to the kitchen. All the lights were on there, and she could smell baking. Tick, tick to one o'clock up the wide staircase, then tick, tick to two o'clock to the library, and tick, tick again to the best room, the den full of Mémé's things: the blue, tufted and buttoned chairs and sofa where Mémé read aloud to her—stories and poems—Mémé's old phonograph and records, her silver candlesticks sitting on small tables alongside books and plants and framed pictures. Willow's favorite place in the room was the wall holding a few of the watercolor flowers I painted and many of the rescued photos Thomas had taken of Native Americans, especially one of an Indian woman who, in her grief, severed two of her own fingers to the first knuckle.

Standing in the foyer, Willow thought to twirl twice, something she always did, but not this time. Mémé hadn't met her at the door and wasn't coming down the stairs, her cat-head cane tapping and Friar bounding ahead of her. The empty staircase looked too big. Even the crystal chandelier over her head, hanging from the second story on its long, long chain, normally a magical spray of light and color, hung solemn and dark.

She toed one rubber boot and then the other. With her wet boots off, she headed up the stairs. A mitten landed on one stair, the second mitten on another, and her coat at the top. She knew Mable "preferred" the coat be hung in the closet by the front door, "fitting for the poor rabbit skinned just for a child's coat collar." But Mable never really got angry.

The upstairs didn't make a clock. Two large bedrooms ran straight along the right side of the hall, then a large walk-in closet for linens and storage of every sort, followed by Tory's room at the far end. The left side of the hall had only two bedrooms, Mémé's, and then a long railing Willow loved to look over, spying on people in the foyer below. There she could also get a closer look at the chandelier and the colors when light struck the prisms. The last bedroom on the left was directly across from Tory's. Willow slept on Mémé's end of the long hall, their rooms directly across. Tossing her *Jeannie* bag at the door of her room, she kept hold of her pictures and hurried to Mémé's door.

Her grandmother lay in bed across the dim room, the blankets drawn to her chin, her cheeks and lips chalk colored. Her eyes looked ringed in purple, but they were open. "I was worried," her words a whisper.

"How come you're in bed?"

Friar lay stretched out alongside Luessy. He rolled his eyes in Willow's direction when she approached, but he didn't lift his head or wag his tail. "Why is Friar sad?" When her grandmother didn't answer, Willow looked away and around the room for reassurance. On the bedside table, though they added little illumination to the room made gray by the December late-afternoon light and the storm, a dozen tapers and pillars burned in various sizes and shapes on silver candlesticks. Each shiny stick reflected a hundred tiny flames, so that they seemed to burn, too. Willow's older drawings still hung on the oak-paneled wall, and the small door to the attic, which even Mémé had to duck to enter, was just ajar, the way Mémé liked, as if someone might come down, or she, dreaming, might want to float up. The crocheted bedspread named "Mother Moses" lay over the back of the rose-colored bedside chair. Except for Friar not jumping up to lick Willow's face and Mémé being in bed, everything *looked* the same. She felt the difference then, and her eyes ran over the room again. Others were there. Mémé had company neither of them could see. Willow could almost count them, five, no six. She didn't question how they'd come from their world to hers. They simply had.

I felt Thomas's presence and Sabine's. I ached to be at the reunion of Sabine and Luessy, but I couldn't be. Though we all inhabited the same space, they were as distanced from me as they were from Willow. I'd entered a labyrinth and shut down my focus to the pinpoint of Willow's life. They were there for Luessy, to walk her across. I prayed Sabine felt my desire to undo my mistakes and that Thomas watched me and smiled at my journey.

Luessy's lips moved so slowly into a smile that they seemed to drift back from her teeth. "I knew it was time for you."

The heavy clouds, the snow, and the winter hour meant there were no shadows moving on the walls or on the floor. Willow marveled; Mémé never wore a watch or checked a clock. Shadows and their motion told her the time, and she could read their minute hands.

Wanting to keep her drawings a secret until later, because secrets were a full thing she liked to hold in her belly, Willow carried them to Luessy's desk.

She stopped at seeing the top cleared of everything but a few loose pages of poems: Mémé's favorites, which the two of them had read so many times they'd fallen free of their book binding. "Where are your stories?"

"I've written them," Luessy breathed. "Someone else must find the rest."

Willow couldn't take her eyes from the desktop. Mémé did the majority of her writing upstairs in the large attic room, the room Tory called the "Never-used ballroom, where no one has ever danced." But every flat and stable surface in Farthest House normally had books and notebooks and scattered typed pages with pencil marks like mazes, sentences circled and arrows going here and there. And no matter how thick the clutter, Mable knew not to touch it.

Feeling unsettled again, Willow shoved the pages of poetry to the far edge of the desk, giving herself room to spread out her pictures. She turned back, "I don't want your stories to be done."

"Come." Luessy waited for her thin granddaughter, with her long dark hair and serious eyes, to reach the bed. How to say what she must? "Tory thinks I'm dying. I'm not. This isn't death."

Willow believed her; Mémé never lied. If what was happening wasn't death, then Mémé wasn't going away, wasn't going to leave the way Jeannie had. Mémé would get up in the morning, and they'd go to the attic. While Willow painted, Mémé would write. Mémé had always been old. She leaned over her cane the first day Willow came to Farthest House. Just the week before, they put on coats and hats and gloves and walked through the garden looking at the clumps of roses Jonah cut back and bundled in burlap. While they walked, the cat-head cane swung and pointed just like always. This time to the sky, "Ducks, geese. Willow, look how they fly."

Luessy turned her head toward the door, the movement putting strain on her face. "Is my son here?"

"You mean, Papa?" She didn't like the mournful-sounding *my son*. "It's snowing too hard."

With her eyes on her granddaughter, Luessy opened an arthritic hand, and Willow put her right hand into the bowl of cold skin. Mémé's hands were moons: moon-shaped, moon-thin, even moon-colored. Willow had seen them glow.

"But you came," Luessy said. "You weren't afraid to come."

"Papa wasn't afraid. He has a stakeout." Sliding her hand free of Mémé's, Willow hurried back out the door, across the hall, and pulled a four-inch strip of velvet ribbon from her bag. "I brought you blue," she yelled over her shoulder. By the time she reached Mémé's bed again, she'd explained, "Not dark blue, it's light blue."

"Oh, sky blue," Luessy said. She closed her eyes as if the color sated her. "Blue."

For four years they'd shared their dreams, their secrets, even their spoons and pockets. Willow crawled across the mattress, not considering herself near enough until she reached Mémé's shoulder. Poking her thin legs under the heavy blankets, she squeezed in beside Mémé, her toes pushing under Friar. She felt the warmth from both bodies, but as she wiggled deeper, she felt Mémé's bones. They poked through flesh no thicker than her flannel gown.

Luessy's fingers opened to clutch the blue, but not before the velvet sheen caught shine from the candlelight. Willow smiled at how Mémé clutched two things: color and light. She watched her grandmother's bent hand slide up her body, not lifting but dragging with the ribbon to rest over her heart.

Willow's first piece of velvet ribbon had come on a birthday gift from Luessy, a wide, flat tin of watercolors with Disney characters painted on the lid. Luessy cut that ribbon in half, tied a length around her wrist and tied a length around Willow's. They wore the matching bracelets to frays before snipping them into long threads and placing them around the railing on the small attic porch. Throughout that day they watched as sparrows and robins came and took the color for their nests. After that, Willow asked Julian, and he drove her to a fabric store and let her pick out several lengths of ribbon in bright colors. These, she cut into four-inch pieces and brought one each time she visited.

"You should have heard her earlier," Luessy said, her voice sounding hoarse, "insisting I change my mind."

Though Willow didn't know what they argued over, she knew Mémé's disagreement had been with Tory. She liked when the two argued because that meant she was still Mémé's favorite. "Tory is mean."

"It's my body going, not my mind," Luessy said. She closed her eyes, rested, and took a breath. "I know what I'm doing."

Willow rested too, close to Mémé's warmth and with the pleasant feel of Friar's weight on her feet.

"I see you," Luessy said. "You're beautiful."

Willow stiffened. She was in the fourth grade now, no one seemed to remember that, and too big for pretending. She no longer believed in Santa Claus, the Easter Bunny, or the Tooth Fairy. "You aren't even looking at me."

"The eyes are the poorest. See the world with your heart." She rested. "If you love anything, there's a beauty in you."

A small knock sounded at the door, and without waiting for an answer, Mable entered. Nearly thirty years younger than Luessy, her short silver hair lay flat as a doily on her head. She still wore only long caftans, just as she had in my day, this one a deep red, with a gold and fringed shawl around her shoulders. She smiled at Willow, not mentioning the trail of winter wear cluttering the stairs, and leaned down to Luessy. "How is your stomach? Would you try and eat something? Just a bit of broth and toast?"

Luessy struggled with her fatigue, wanting only sleep and Willow beside her. "Bring some for Willow." She looked into Mable's eyes and the pain there, "Don't be afraid."

Mable laid a hand over Luessy's, the fringe on her shawl swinging down and brushing the bed. "Can I call Dr. Mahoney again?"

At the word *doctor*, Willow felt her heart jump.

Luessy tried to smile, but lacked the energy. "No." She rested. "He came this morning. Give me Mother Moses."

Mable's eyes filled with tears, and she blinked before forcing herself to turn away to the upholstered chair. Mother Moses was draped over the back. Holding the crocheted spread against her body, she slapped her thigh several times trying to coax Friar onto the floor. "Here boy." Then she scolded, "You're a stubborn fellow. Get off that bed."

Willow watched Friar. She knew he didn't want to leave Mémé and that he was trained to stay off Mother Moses. The sight of the crocheting meant time on the floor. She crawled out from beneath the blankets, grabbed his collar, and coaxed him down. "Stay," she said, but felt sorry for him. She and Friar were Mémé's *right-now world*. Mother Moses meant something else. She kissed Friar's cold nose and helped Mable unfold and unfold Mother Moses across the bed.

"Time to go outside," Mable said stepping to the doorway. Friar followed her.

Luessy's hand lay limp on the cream-colored traceries: birds, flowers, and butterflies. Only one tired finger slid half an inch to the left, and then back. "Not cotton string . . . ."

Willow had heard the pronouncement so many times she finished the words, " . . . but the bone and muscle of a strong spirit."

11

Luessy concentrated on Willow, fighting for a few more hours with her granddaughter. "Tell the story of Mother Moses."

"Do I have to tell the whole story?"

"If you don't know your stories," Luessy managed, her breath halting and heavy, "you don't know who you are or who you can be." She needed another breath, but the drawn-in air seemed hardly able to do more than fill her mouth. "Your stories tell you," a breath, "where you are, and how far you've come." Another breath. "They're your blood."

Despite Luessy's insistence, Willow almost dared to start in the middle, but Mémé could never be that tired. "You were at your after-school job in a store, and a bad woman came in."

"1902. Not *bad*," another necessary rest and breath, "afraid."

"But being afraid made her mean. She was going west in a wagon with her husband. She had four kids. All the kids were hungry, and she wanted to trade the blanket for food. That's the only thing she had, but your boss said, 'No.' He said the string wasn't worth any of his beans or flour, but you loved the blanket so much, you said 'yes.' You traded your pay and bought her some food."

Luessy's heavy eyelids fluttered closed. "Why did we disagree?"

"You kept asking her the name of the woman who made it, and she kept saying, 'A slave.'"

With so much energy in the room, I felt cleaved into segments: There was the heartbreak of Tory and her actions—but that puts me ahead of the story— the excitement of those gathered over Luessy's imminent return, Luessy's grief at leaving Willow, and my concern for Willow. Who would be her confidant now?

Luessy stirred, "Go on."

Willow stared at the brass light fixture over the bed, her eyes going around the scrolls, as she tried to remember everything. "The woman didn't think a slave's name mattered. She thought people like you, who cared about a slave's name, caused the war and made her daddy lose everything he ever worked for." She puffed out her cheeks, letting the air ease out with a sigh. "Mostly, people rode the train to California, but this family was in an old wagon, because the husband wanted to save all his money to buy land. He was letting the children starve because he could get more of those. One kid," Willow remembered, "already died."

Sixty years hadn't erased the memory of looking into the eyes of those starving children, and Luessy's sudden emotion fed her a spate of energy. "The wife played the chattel, because the man had a dream." She breathed and rested. "Her dream was for her children to live, but she handed that over." Luessy labored for breath but would not stop. "Black women, red women too, were chained and herded with whips and guns. White women follow their captors."

"They are," Willow parroted from the countless times she'd heard the story, "the slaves even Northerners aren't too proud to own."

"The name?"

Willow stroked the knobby but soft string, her fingers following the outline of a butterfly, certain she felt it stirring. "You named it Mother Moses." Mother Moses wasn't just a bedcover, Willow knew. Mother Moses breathed as much as did the angels in the room. She even mended herself when necessary.

Turning to look at Mémé, Willow was amazed to see her grandmother had fallen asleep in the space between two sentences, her eyes skating under lids as thin as the cloudy tissue paper she used to wrap her good sweaters. With Mémé asleep, Willow didn't need to tell the rest of the story, and she snuggled closer, closing her own eyes, putting her head on Mémé's shoulder and catching the scent of her neck. Not perfume, but something sweet and yeasty as Mable's rising bread dough.

I'd heard the story of Mother Moses more times than Willow. It was a tale Luessy conjured up just as she did with her mysteries. She based it on the facts found in history and what she knew of the human heart. According to Luessy, the slave was old when she crocheted the blanket because mastery requires years of patience and practice. The woman had also spent her life as a house slave. Field laborers, especially the women, rarely lived beyond the age of forty and had no access even to something as simple and cheap as string. Field slaves had bloody, calloused, and ruined hands, and they dropped at night from exhaustion. As a house slave, the artist may have been burdened with a physical defect, possibly from an injury, a bone that hadn't been set by a doctor, possibly the result of a beating, something that likely kept her in constant pain and made the grueling work of picking cotton or plowing and planting fields impossible.

Or worse. As a young woman the slave might have caught her owner's eye, or the eye of her owner's son, and whoever it was, he wanted her kept close for his convenience. Sweet smelling, not with tobacco juice or red clay ground deep in her heels, rooted in the creases of her skin, sun-cooked into her hair. The artist would have crocheted at night, after she completed her other work, when the house slept, and even *he* had gone back to his wife's bed. She'd have worked by candlelight, squinting close to the flame, learning how to shape and tie during endless hours of trial and error.

Having that one art must also have helped her carry the weight of her life. For years, butterflies, birds, and flowers must have sculpted themselves in her mind as she scrubbed floors, trimmed wicks, and lay under him. Only then, was Mother Moses born, coming to life in the woman's aged hands.

The slave had not done the work for her own pallet or to keep a loved one warm. As a slave, she couldn't own property—even something fashioned with her own hands. She hoped the spread would be beautiful enough to be taken up by whites, off the plantation, and out of the South. There was a world she ached to see, which is why she bled her spirit into the string, a magic only crones possess. The butterflies and birds and things that grew were her wings.

There was more to the whole affair that Luessy hadn't shared with Willow. Only weeks before Luessy bought the spread, I told her the truth about her mother's death, not childbirth as I let her believe growing up, but Sabine taking her own life in order to get her infant to America. "She escaped in you," I promised Luessy, "and her escape is greater with every book you write."

When Luessy examined the crocheting that first afternoon, she looked at the wide-eyed children waiting in the wagon, she thought with reverence

of how the artist's work had ended up in her hands, and she thought of her
mother's need to escape.

In those first years with Mother Moses, Luessy often asked me why her
mother didn't send word, why she hadn't asked for help. Luessy well knew
Thomas and I would have sailed instantly for France, if only we'd known she
was in such grave trouble. The hard truth is, Thomas was innocent, but I was
not. Failure to acknowledge another's pain is not the same as not knowing
about it. Denial is not innocence. As for Sabine, did she assume I disowned
her and wouldn't heed her pleas? Or did she feel such darkness that she lost
all visions of a future self and all hope of escape? Afraid to tell her story, sure
she was the only one and deserving of her fate, she believed I'd be a better
mother for her child.

Luessy slept, but Willow scooted off the bed to the small bookcase where
she pulled out one of her favorite books, the paintings of Frida Kahlo. Mémé
loved them, too, and in Kahlo's work, Willow found both the bright colors and
the mystery she loved. Kahlo's intense and often macabre pictures felt a match
to the picture Willow saw in my lap years earlier—Sabine and the blood from
her fingers alive and moving. Kahlo's work would also make Sister Dominic
Agnes frown and get a red face. But the best thing about the pictures was that
despite how doctors tried, Kahlo couldn't be fixed. Willow couldn't name all
Kahlo's needing-to-be-fixed places; there were too many. Kahlo wasn't hiding
her unfixed places, and she made pictures of bones and skin cut open and
blood. One painting showed her in a brace because her back was broken.
She wasn't crying, even though her body had nails in it. She looked straight
ahead. Had Kahlo, Willow wondered, escaped like Mother Moses, changing
into pictures and color?

Mable opened the door again, Friar bounding past her before she could
nudge the light switch with her elbow. She carried a large silver tray with two
small plates, one with a sandwich and cookies, and the other with a slice of
toast. The tray also held two cups of tea, and Willow smiled. Hers would be
sweetened with honey and cream. Hers was the cup with the purple pansies. At
the beginning of her visits to Farthest House, when she'd been only six, Mémé
let her select a china cup from the collection in the kitchen hutch. They were

Spode, thin as breath on cold mornings, and she chose purple. Luessy chose roses. Being served tea in her special cup, as she was every weekend, made Willow feel loved and fitted at Farthest House.

Blowing out all but one candle, Mable nudged the smoking pillars back and set the tray on the nightstand. Although Luessy stirred at the noise and the bed trembling as Willow crawled back in beside her, she gave only a small shake of her head at the toast and tea.

"I'm going to stay the night," Mable said. "You may need me."

Luessy eyes were closed, "I have Willow."

"Let me stay."

Around the bed the air stirred. "Go," Luessy whispered. "Have Jonah drive you."

Did Mable feel ordered by some fate larger than herself? She'd talked the situation over with Tory, and what was there left to do? Call Dr. Mahoney, who'd come every day that week? He told them to relax, give Luessy—who refused to leave Farthest House—a few more days before they physically removed her to a hospital. Now, with the heavy snow falling, even if the man could be persuaded to come for a second time that day, he very likely would not make it up the hill, and someone would have to rescue him.

"You sleep right there," Mable said to Willow. "If she needs help, get Tory."

Willow wasn't sure why she might need Tory. "Mémé's just sick." She wasn't dying. Tomorrow, even though her stories were done, they'd step through the little door in the wall, like Alice through a too-small door, and they'd climb the white steps and spend the day in the attic.

Mable fussed, stalling, handing Willow her food, and finally whispering close to Luessy. "I'll talk to Tory. She may want me to stay."

When Mable could be heard going down the stairs, Friar stepped to the nightstand and with a tongue deft and quick as fingers, picked off each section of Luessy's toast, swallowing before Willow could think to try and stop him. He looked at the food Willow held and then stared a minute at Luessy and whined, but he resisted the urge to jump onto the spread. He circled in place and plopped back to the floor beside the bed.

After some time, Luessy's voice floated, "I'm up here. Out here."

Willow finished her food, even sticking two fingers into her cup and scooping up the last dregs of cookie she soaked until the bottom edge melted into her tea. "Do you want to see my pictures?"

"Show me," and as Willow rushed to the desk, "draw every day."

"I do."

"Laziness and fear," Luessy struggled to be heard, "especially fear, they wait to steal talent."

"I'm not scared." She was scared though. People didn't like her pictures. With the paper rustling, she snuggled back against Luessy. "I drew two."

They were of old and barefoot women, their clothes ragged at the sleeves and hems, and their faces etched with lines. They didn't match the pictures Willow saw in her mind, but she liked them, especially how she'd crossed and re-crossed their face wrinkles so that the lines made tiny stars and how she shaded in dark backgrounds, smudging the shadows with an eraser and a finger she sucked to keep wet.

"You paint stories."

Remembering the warm Sunday afternoon when Mémé took her to the Josyln Art Museum in Omaha, Willow smiled. She'd been surprised that people could have their pictures hung in such a big place and other people paid money to see them. "Will my pictures hang in a museum?"

"Life is what you do. Tomorrow obeys only you."

In her excitement, Willow kicked free of the covers and scrambled off the bed. "I'll hang them up." Glancing back at Mémé, she hesitated. The sight of her grandmother, looking stiff and frail in her white gown, a stranger too skinny, her hair a long tail of unbraided cloud matted to her pillow, was frightening. Fighting an inclination to run back, she decided the best thing was to hang the work because the pictures made Mémé happy.

The height of the drawings already on the wall matched the height of Willow's reach, and she worked on her whole display, changing the positions of several pieces, getting fresh pieces of tape, lining the drawings up this way, and then that, according to her favorites.

I watched Luessy, trying to keep focused on her arrival *there*, rather than on what her leaving would mean here. I thought of how it would affect Tory. The hour Jeannie died, Tory was in her room, pacing, wringing her hands with nervousness. My beautiful Tory, once a child of wild hair and sparkling emerald eyes, grown too soon, and unable to watch Death yet again, to bear witnessing that too-close ghost's rattle. Was she pacing now? Or were her hands steady on her tumbler of sherry, death easier with the numbers?

When Willow's two new drawings were added and everything was arranged to her liking, she marveled. On the wall she didn't need to be fixed. On the wall, she danced and wasn't disfigured to match her soul.

Admiring her one-girl show, she thought of pretty Mary Wolfe, her old friend who wouldn't be her friend anymore. What would Mary say if she saw the drawings and watercolors? Sometimes, at recess, or after school when no one watched, Mary came too close and put her mouth by Willow's ear. "Do you still draw pictures?"

"No," Willow always lied.

She turned and faced the bed again. Mémé hadn't changed her position, but she trembled, looking like a child who'd fallen or was pushed from a tree. Realizing she left Mémé entirely exposed, and Mémé hadn't been able to cover herself, Willow ran the few steps, reaching the end of the bed, making the whole bed bounce as she crawled up the mattress. She pulled the blankets over them, tucking them under Mémé's chin and then her own, willing Mother Moses to help make Mémé warm again. She snuggled still closer and felt cold striking her legs. A wet cold, and for a moment she didn't understand. Then she realized Mémé had wet the bed, and the moisture had chilled in the open air. She threw her arm across her grandmother's chest, hugging her, "I'm sorry, I'm sorry."

Luessy lacked the strength to answer.

Only babies wet the bed, Willow knew, and doing it when you weren't a baby was the worst thing. No one could know, and this *worst thing* was her fault. She'd spent too long hanging up her pictures and being proud. "I'm really sorry," she tried again. "I'm really, really, really sorry." She rubbed Mémé's arm, trying not to cry, and then raised herself onto one elbow and patted Mémé's cheek. "Mémé, I'm sorry. I love you."

She didn't know what to do. Mémé couldn't get up and change her bedding and nightgown. Mable was gone, and Tory was too mean to ask. Going to Tory would be the same as *telling* on Mémé. There was Papa, but he was working, and even if she could reach him on the phone, he was too far away to help and couldn't come in the snow. He'd tell her to put Tory on the line. Jonah was strong and he would help. She was sure that even with the dark and snow she could find his house at the back of the garden, but she couldn't sneak him upstairs without Tory knowing. If Tory caught him, she'd be furious, and anyway, Jonah couldn't see Mémé naked because he was a man.

She could see her grandmother without clothes, but she couldn't lift Mémé. If she were as strong as other fourth graders—with two good arms—maybe she could, but she wasn't.

The smell of old urine, as though Mémé were rotting inside, and the decay had come out between her legs and seeped up from under the blankets, made Willow gag. She hoped Mémé hadn't heard. She gagged again. "It's okay," she whispered, "it doesn't stink very bad."

A breath of sound, "Willow . . . "

Pulling herself up on one elbow again, Willow pressed her ear to her grandmother's mouth and strained to hear more. Was Mémé trying to say she still loved her and wasn't angry? No other sound came, and Willow sank back down, nudging against her grandmother, harder this time, trying to shove her out of the wettest area, pushing her own legs deeper into the cold. She scrubbed at tears. She deserved to be there. "You still love me. Don't you!"

Tory appeared, already halfway across the room, her nightly glass of sherry in hand. Seeing her, Willow jumped. In her mind, Tory could move through the house, coming and going without sound and staying invisible until she appeared just inches away. Did she love to scare Willow, or like Sister Dominic Agnes, did she want to catch her being bad?

At least Tory didn't have her sewing basket with her. Papa liked how his sister made dolls for poor children, but Willow hated seeing the dismembered arms and legs stuck full of pins and looking as though they'd been torn off soft bodies. And heads, too, with sharp pins run through their empty faces, marking the placement of absent eyes, noses, and lips. To Willow, the pins were just the sort of thing doctors would do to her given the chance.

Studying the emaciated figure of her mother, the red in Tory's glass began to shiver. Her mother looked grave. She caught hold of her emotion, turning to Willow. "Why are you crying?" And at Willow's shrug, "Go on, it's time for bed."

Willow wanted to go to her own bed, but she wouldn't leave Mémé or let Tory discover the wet. She gripped Mother Moses. "I'm supposed to sleep here. Mable said so."

"Did she eat anything?"

On the floor, Friar hadn't moved since his meal, and Willow told her eyes not to look at him.

Tory hesitated a moment longer before leaning over the table, blowing out the last candle, and starting for the door. "Sleep there if you want, I don't suppose it matters."

In the quiet, motion at the dark turret windows caught Willow's attention. Nickel-sized white flakes swooped inward, the snow kissing the glass and melting. Then movement from Mémé's desk where the top sheet of paper Willow had pushed to the corner earlier drifted to the floor.

Making sure the blankets didn't lift this time, Willow wiggled out and ran for the page. Her damp dress, especially a wet place along the hem, stuck to her leg. Her mind said, *Yuck, yuck.* She crawled back into bed with her treasure. Fighting an urge to throw up, she wedged her legs into the wet.

The tiny black words swam and made her rub her eyes again. She knew many of them by heart. Week after week, Luessy had read the lines to her. Familiar words here and there helped her remember whole lines.

> "The soul,
> Forever and forever . . .
> longer than the soil is brown and solid
> longer than water ebbs and flows . . ."

She read as slowly as she could, spending the words as carefully as nickels and dimes, wanting them never to run out.

> "I will make the true poem of riches,
> to earn for the body and the mind whatever
> ad . . . here . . . is, adheres,
> and goes forward and is not dropt by death."

Mémé was listening. Willow felt sure of it, and she turned the page over, reading words Mémé had underlined.

> "Of your real body . . .
> item for item it will ee . . . lude
> the hands of the cor . . . pus, corpse-cleaners
> and pass to fitting spheres . . . ."

A tear rolled from Mémé's eye, moving down the side of her face and into her thin hair. Willow had never seen her grandmother cry, and the sight made her moan. She let go of the page she'd been holding and using a finger, pushed the next tear back towards Mémé's eye. The skin under Willow's finger stretched and smoothed, as though she pushed through frosting.

She tried again to read. She wanted to read louder than the pounding in her chest, louder than how sorry she was, louder than Mémé's tears, and louder than the awful, quitting sounds coming from Mémé's mouth.

Friar stood and whined, as he paced back and forth at Luessy's bedside. He trotted to the foot of the bed, and despite Mother Moses, jumped up. On his belly, his tail dragging behind him, he used his forelegs and pulled himself over the crocheting to Luessy. He dropped his head on the rise of her stomach and lay still, staring off into the room.

The weight of her grandmother's body leaned against her, but Willow knew Mémé had left her.

12

❧

The bed trembled. Willow shook so hard her legs kicked in tiny jerks. She'd never lain beside a dead person. She didn't know what she should do. She knew you weren't supposed to disturb the dead. Would sliding away, if she didn't hardly move the blankets one inch, be disturbing the dead?

Lying beside Mémé, without a clock in the room and no moon or stars sliding across the windows to prove the passage of time, she felt like she was in a strange world where time didn't exist at all, where being rescued might never happen. She shut her eyes tight but was afraid to scream. She wanted Tory to hear from down the long hallway and through her closed door, but even the thought of screaming added to Willow's fear. What if she screamed, scaring herself more, and still Tory didn't come?

She cried for Papa to come and for Mémé to stop being dead, and for her own shaking, so hard her knees bounced together, to stop.

I sat beside her, tried to sooth her, until finally her body gave into exhaustion, and she sank into a fitful sleep. She dreamed she ran through a forest of thick black trees, and no matter how loud she screamed, no one came to help. She dreamed she stood on the steps of Our Lady of Supplication, a black chain binding her to Sister Dominic Agnes, and Mémé, her cat-head cane tapping, walked by and away, never turning to see Willow.

She woke having to go to the bathroom, and her head pounded and buzzed as though filled with a hive of Jonah's bees, angry bees. She couldn't see Mémé's face without turning, which she wouldn't do, but Friar was still with her, and so she wasn't alone.

She rolled away. Mémé's body shifted. Standing at the far side of the bed, panting with fear at how Mémé had moved, Willow thought even of crawling back in. Mémé couldn't be dead, couldn't be. But her skin had changed to the wrong color, as had her lips, and her eyes looked too deep, poked in. Only her hand on the spread looked right, though the ribbon had dropped onto her chest. Willow hurried around, picked up the piece of sky, and because Mémé couldn't hold it, Willow wove it through her grandmother's cold fingers.

Mémé had sky again, and Willow rushed across the carpet and over the last few feet of wood flooring and into the hall. Friar watched, his head not lifting from Luessy. "Come," Willow whispered. He didn't stir. "Come Friar, you have to come." The urine on Willow's dress had dried and smelled worse now. "Come," she begged. "Please come with me."

The blessed dog rose, stepped off the bed, and with his tail hanging went to Willow and let her press her face into the ruff of his neck and hold onto him.

In the bathroom at the near end of the hall, away from Tory's bath at the far end, Friar kept close to Willow. She sat on the toilet wondering how it was possible that everything looked the same. White towels were still folded and stacked on their white shelves. The bathtub still sat with its claw feet pointed straight ahead, as though it might get up and run. The black and white floor tiles still ran in straight lines. Standing naked and washing her legs, her clothes rolled into a ball that she would hide under her bed, she could see that even her back was the same. She told herself Mémé was there, too, watching her wash, reminding her to hang up her washcloth, and waiting while she put on clean pajamas. "She is, isn't she Friar."

She was certain Mémé didn't want her to sleep in her room across the hall. Mémé wanted her to sleep in the attic, in the white cottage bed where the two of them often took afternoon naps. With Friar at her heels, she followed Mémé up the main attic staircase, hearing the sound of the stairs sighing just ahead of her, each one bearing and releasing an invisible weight.

She woke hours later to the sound of her name being called. The attic with its white floor, walls, and ceiling held the faintest light, not morning light, or moonlight, but an ethereal light.

Luessy stood at the foot of the bed looking radiant. I wasn't as surprised to see her as she was to see me. She'd been so sure that Willow and I were the same person.

Willow stared at Mémé's appearance. Her grandmother looked thirty years younger than Willow had ever seen her. She stood whole and solid, not floating on a wire like pretend angels in a school play, not with clouds swirling around her feet like holy cards of Jesus. She also stood taller than she had before, and her back was straight.

For every inch of Mémé's new health, Willow felt more disfigured and alone. This Mémé wasn't old and didn't need a cane or pictures on her wall. This Mémé didn't need to be read to, and she didn't need Willow. She had plans and meant to leave and be happy away from Willow.

The younger, not-Mémé nodded toward the foot of the bed. Willow's gaze followed the direction. Mother Moses lay folded in a thick pad, and on top lay a fresh-picked Damask rose.

Mother Moses had been down on Mémé's bed a floor below, and Willow knew exactly where in the summer garden the Damasks bloomed. But a winter storm blew outside, and the roses had been pruned and wrapped in burlap. She looked back up. Mémé was gone.

As the heater churned in the basement and north winds buffeted, the wood, brick, and glass of Farthest House creaked and sighed.

In the morning, the sound of Papa hurrying up the stairs and into the attic startled Willow awake. Sun reflected off the snow outside, bouncing light up the three stories and over the creamy walls. Papa stepped into the attic, his face relaxing on seeing she was all right. He crossed the room and squatted beside her bed. "Willow, I have something to tell you."

She slapped her hands over her ears. Her body wouldn't be still. She sat up, rose to her knees and slumped, sitting back between her heels. "Where's Friar?"

"He's all right." Julian's eyes searched hers. "You know? Your grandmother has died."

Her hands slid from her cheeks and came down together, steepled as if she meant to pray. Then her fingers spread and clasped together, and her hands formed a tight ball. Mémé wasn't dead. Dead meant you never moved. Dead meant you were buried and turned into ashes. That's why there was Ash Wednesday. But she'd seen Mémé young and moving, and that was different from dead. Mémé had pulled out of her old skin like a locust, leaving Willow behind. "She's not dead."

Julian had no soothing words for death. Losing Jeannie still hollowed out a pit in his stomach. He sat down on the bed beside Willow and stroked her sleep-tousled hair. "She loved you very much."

Willow flopped back, away from his touch. She remembered Mother Moses and the rose. If they weren't there, she couldn't be sure Mémé had visited in the night. Mémé might only have been a dream, and if only a dream, then Papa was right and Mémé was dead. Never-coming-back dead. Jeannie dead. If the things were there, then Mémé was alive, maybe not in the regular way, but alive, which meant she could visit again if she wanted.

Her heart leapt, and she rolled up onto her knees again and flopped forward and stretched out, grabbing the flower and back, almost crawling into Julian's lap. She told the story as quickly as she could—except for how Mémé's back was straight.

When she finished, Julian couldn't speak. How many times had he asked for some small sign from Jeannie? Anything.

"They mean she's not dead," Willow said.

He pulled her close, pressing her cheek against his chest and setting his hard chin on top of her head. "She is dead, Willow. I don't know how to explain this." He indicated the crocheting and the rose. He didn't want to destroy whatever fantasy Willow needed to tell herself, and so he wouldn't insist the things were carried up by either Tory or Mable. "Your grandmother loved you, and she still loves you, but she's gone." He realized for the millionth time that the same applied to Jeannie. She was gone, and if she sent signs, tossing coins into his path or white feathers, the tokens wouldn't change the fact that he was never going to hear her laugh again, never going to hold her again, never going to carry her to their bed.

On Tuesday, the morning of Luessy's funeral, Willow woke with a start. She and Papa had spent the night at Farthest House, and she could hear Tory yelling from the floor below. She hurried into the hall in her pajamas and across to peer again into Mémé's room. The mattress was gone, the bed stripped to the box springs, the door to the attic shut tight, and the wall of her pictures bare. No one had asked if she wanted her drawings, and though she supposed Mable knew if they'd been thrown into the trash, she didn't want to ask. For two reasons, she hoped they had been. If Papa saw them, he'd be sad to see how many secrets she kept from him. And it was because of the pictures that Mémé died.

Again, the sound of Tory yelling from the kitchen echoed through the tree of the foyer and up the stairs. Knowing Papa was in the house gave Willow courage, but she pressed her back to the wall at the top of the stairs and slid as much as walked down. Tiptoeing across the foyer, she stopped behind the kitchen door and peered in through the split between the jamb and the door. Lumpy dishtowels covered cakes and pies on the counters. She stretched to try and see more.

Papa sat in a chair, not facing the table, but his long legs stretched out parallel to it, one elbow on the oak for support. Willow could see, as well as I, that he hadn't been up long. Still barefoot, he wore blue jeans and a flannel shirt left open, the way he dressed in the mornings at home, coming into the kitchen to start coffee and Willow's toast, not bothering with shirt buttons before stepping into the shower.

While his clothes reminded Willow of their regular life, nothing on his face or in his posture did. He sat slumped, as though Tory's yelling whacked him down. His eyes were shut, and his mouth formed a hard line. When he came to the attic for her and told her Mémé was dead, he was sad, but this sadness was different.

"Stop and think," Tory said, her voice ripe with irony, "how much it would hurt Mom's reputation and the good name she cared so much about. Jonah, too. How much are you willing to put him through? Jail time? Even Willow, what would it do to her?" She paused and with more emphasis, "I'm your sister. You owe me, Julian. Cop." She stopped, letting the words sizzle in the air. Then, "You lied to me."

Julian's elbow shifted on the table, his palm rose, and he dropped his forehead into it, hooding his eyes as if to shut Tory out.

Careful not to lose her balance and make the door bang, Willow shifted her weight to see more. Tory wore a narrow black dress that reached to mid-calf. On her feet were long black pumps. Her hair was knotted tight at the nape of her neck, her lipstick red.

It's not fair, Willow thought. *Papa was tricked.* He came into the kitchen just to have coffee with Tory, but she'd gotten up earlier, dressed, and waited for him. Willow wanted to crash into the room and tell Tory to *shut up!* She wondered why Papa wasn't defending himself.

A shadow on the ceiling above his head caught her eye. Thin and gray at first, she tried to ignore the gloom. As she watched color draining from her father's face, the stain darkened, morphing through several shades until it reached black ink. The shape began to tremble. She closed her eyes, willed it gone and looked again. The sight pushed her to her knees. Out of the blackness, wings were forming, heavy and thick with plumage. Her heart pounded as she felt the drag and weight of the wings struggling to loosen themselves, as if unearthing from a grave.

Then it happened. Papa's head lifted from his hand, dropped back, and his face lay exposed to the ceiling. The black—a table-sized raven now—peeled off the ceiling, talons and keen eyes swooping down. The specter shadowed Papa's face, seemed to bleed into it, and vanished.

Julian's head came forward slowly, and he opened his eyes. Willow wanted to believe she only dreamed the darkness. If what she saw could be a dream, she'd trade away the rose and Mother Moses and say Mémé's visit had also only been a dream. He stood and walked out of the kitchen, passing her without seeing her hiding there. She watched him cross the foyer and step barefoot onto the icy porch. His feet were on the exact spot where he said of her to Mémé, "She's got to live in this world. This one right here."

A large reception followed Luessy's funeral. It pleased me to see so many drive up Old Squaw Road, aging faces that had been young when I lived. Writers from all points in the state came and news crews from Omaha and Lincoln. They filled the lower rooms of Farthest House, milling about with small plates of food and ready conversation. Only the library was kept locked, the skeleton key deep in Tory's sewing basket.

As Julian wandered from one room to the next, Willow followed. He moved between people, nodding, but always stepping away too quickly for conversation. Having seen the raven, and not understanding, she feared he might die, too. Everyone did. On his third pass through the dining room, avoiding the people making their way around the long table with its platters of food, he stopped before the tall windows, shoved his hands into the pockets of his black suit pants, and stared out, looking into faraway places Willow couldn't go.

It was Red, Julian's partner, dressed in a suit rather than his uniform, who caught sight of Willow standing with a stricken face watching her father. He leaned down, "Hey, Little Bird, how you doing?"

He smelled of cigarettes and aftershave and handed her a plate. "Have you eaten today? I'm starved. What looks good to you?"

Jonah fell into line behind them, and Willow was distracted enough to nearly smile. The three men didn't match at all. Red had white skin and red hair. Papa's skin was darker, and he was taller and skinnier. Jonah had white hair, black skin, and he was short. But they did match, too, because they were her three favorite men, and they loved her.

Red hadn't yet filled his plate when Julian stepped up to him. "Let's get some air." They left through the kitchen and stepped out the back door. Willow hadn't been invited. Neither had Jonah.

The twelve dining room chairs were pulled back and set along the walls. She took one and patted the next in line for Jonah. "You can sit by me." She never saw him in anything but overalls, and he looked funny in his new navy blue suit. His hands looked awkward holding a small plate rather than a rake. She watched him eat, hunting for an introduction into her missing pictures, Mémé's wetting the bed, Tory's screaming at Papa, and the raven. "You shouldn't be in this house. Bad things happen here."

He'd lost so much peripheral vision that he needed to turn his head and look at her straight on. So often she spooked him. He didn't need to be reminded that bad things happened at Farthest House, and now Luessy was gone. His appetite left, and he ignored the plate in his hands.

"I saw Mémé in the attic," Willow said. "She brought me the blanket and a rose. It was a rose from the garden."

Tory stepped in front of them. "Where's your father? Go and get him." And to Jonah, "I need you in the library, too."

Five cane-backed chairs sat in a row in front of Luessy's enormous desk. By the time Willow returned with Papa, Tory, Mable, and Jonah were seated.

Tory nodded to the man sitting behind the library desk, and he opened a briefcase with two loud snaps and removed a folder.

"As the attorney representing the estate of Luessy Starmore . . . ."

I watched the actor. Had he ever before been hired for such a stunt? He played his role as convincingly as Raymond Burr. "I, Luessy Starmore, being of sound mind . . . . "

Willow peered down the row: Tory, Mable and Jonah looked intent, waiting, but Papa was silent and angry. She heard that Mable and Jonah were to receive bonuses for their years of loyalty. Money, too, for Papa. She heard her name and how on her nineteenth birthday she'd begin receiving a stipend for college, $500 a month. It sounded like more money than she could spend, but having to wait ten long years was the same as getting nothing.

The man continued reading: Tory would remain custodian of Farthest House until her death, at which time the house would be given to Greenburr, provided said township did not disturb the graves of Mémé's ancestors for a period of one hundred years.

Finished, the man closed the folder and looked around for questions. When they were done, he shook Julian's hand and then Tory's and left the room. Mable stood, "I better tend to our guests." Jonah and Tory followed her out. Julian continued staring straight ahead. Willow sat with him. "Papa?"

"Get your things."

13

Willow struggled to carry the double weights of Mémé's leaving and the raven's coming. She no longer visited Farthest House. Around the end of the first month, she stood in the doorway of Julian's bedroom in Omaha and stared in. He'd gone out, a "quick trip," he said, leaving her alone—something he'd not done before the raven. She knew he'd return with bread, bologna, dry packaged cookies, and wine he'd hide quickly in a high cupboard, as though she didn't see it.

His room felt not just empty, but hollowed out. He hadn't made his bed since the raven, and so she hadn't made hers. Papa didn't care. He hadn't worked since then either, despite Red's coaxing. Instead, he spent his days pacing and staring out empty windows. Often, he spent the entire afternoon sitting at the kitchen table sipping wine.

She picked up his pillow, hugged it to her chest, and sat on the bed. She'd seen Mémé at the foot of the attic bed, proof that Mémé could come if she wanted. Proof Mémé's staying away now, not coming even one time, was a choice. On the walls, Jeannie looked out from framed pictures. One, two, three, four, five smiling Jeannies behind glass. Jeannie had never visited either—not one time.

Throwing the pillow onto the floor, Willow pushed off the bed and ran to the kitchen. She needed a hard, smashing thing. She grabbed a sauce pan from the sink and ran back, using all the strength in her thin arms to swing the pan again and again into the glass over Jeannie's pictures, shards of sharp silver raining onto the floor and over her shoes. The glass on the last picture shattered but didn't fall out of the frame. She needed to stab at it with the pan's handle. More stabbing then, destroying the paper picture, too. Jeannie's dumb eyes and dumb lips. Five ruined Jeannies broken on the floor.

That night, she lay awake in the dark, staying in her bed until finally Papa turned off the kitchen light, and she heard him walk into his room. Silence. She waited. He'd come yelling down the hall. She hoped he told her she couldn't watch television or read books ever again. She hoped he marched her back down the hall and gave her her first spanking and shook her and made her say *why*. She'd tell him she did it because she hated Jeannie, and she hated Mémé.

Minutes passed, and then came the sound of slow footsteps. He stood in her doorway, looking like a shadow but for the faint yellow light from his room falling across one side of his face. He didn't speak at first. He shifted his weight, and a floorboard under him moaned. He whispered, "You all right?"

She bit her bottom lip.

He waited. Finally, the floor moaned again as he turned to leave, and he whispered even more softly, "Good night, Little Bird."

When the sweeping and tinkling of broken glass ended and the house was quiet, she pulled out her old *I Dream of Jeannie* bag. She carried a solid pink backpack to school now, but she kept the Jeannie bag, using it to help practice her blinking and nodding. With her school scissors, she poked and shredded that Jeannie's face, too.

Through January, February and March, she missed a day or two of school each week. Those days she sat with Julian. He scolded her for missing school, but not too seriously, and she scolded him for not going to work. Neither mentioned his drinking. She watched the letters coming from school, first from Sister Beatrice, her favorite teacher ever, then from the Office of the Principal. She read sentences about her "lack of initiative" and her "high absenteeism." The new letters began warning that without a "marked improvement," she would need to repeat the fourth grade. For a few days, Julian made sure she went, but then her screaming and crying to stay home made him abandon his resolve. In his mind, the situation was temporary, he'd get himself together, he'd find a way to go back to work, and Willow would want to go to school again.

For Willow, too much school was impossible. She needed to stay close to

Papa and keep him from dying the way Jeannie and Mémé had. When he lay snoring, sprawled on the sofa or his bed, she needed to cover him in warm blankets and keep watch.

Red came to the house most days, asking Willow how she was doing and trying to coax Julian into returning to work or seeking help for his depression. "If you won't talk to me man, talk to someone." With each visit Red's anger grew, and by April he came through the door with his face as fiery as his hair and shaking his head at the newspapers piling up. "You've got to get your shit together." By May his attitude was cold. "All right, you bastard, drink yourself to death. But what about Willow? You thought that far?" He shoved Julian, his hands flat on his ex-partner's chest, pushing and forcing him out the back door while Willow screamed for him to stop.

Red's eyes never left Julian's. "I want to break your fucking neck." On the scrub of what had been grass, he moved around Julian, his fists up, but Julian kept his hands slack at his side. Reason enough for Red to hit him. No real man quit like this, not an ounce of fight in him. Especially not a man with a child.

Red pulled back his fist and slammed it into Julian's face.

Willow screamed. Papa lay on the ground with blood rolling from his nose and upper lip.

"Get up," Red yelled. "Come on, you bastard. Fight. Show some dignity."

As Red dropped to a knee beside Julian and pulled his fist back a second time, Willow screamed and threw herself over his back, slugging his arms. "Go away. We don't want you here."

Red stopped, one hand reaching back, pulling her off and around to his chest and holding her tight until she quit struggling. "I'm not going to hurt him." He looked away from Julian and all that was unreadable in Julian's eyes and into Willow's. "You ever need anything, anything, you call me. All right?" Willow nodded. "I'll be there," he said. "You got my number?" More silent nodding. He whispered close to her ear. "Write it down, a couple of places. Not just once. Keep it close."

Red walked away, and Willow helped Papa stand. His weight against her proved he needed her, and she'd saved his life. She wasn't a little girl any longer and couldn't ever be again. She had to be strong, not die like Jeannie and Mémé.

Papa needed her. She'd fix their food, wash their clothes, help him to bed at night, and then be the one to lock the doors and turn out the lights. "It's all right," she said. "You're hardly bleeding. Let's go wash your face."

In the fall, she was back in the fourth grade. The classroom was the same, and she had Sister Beatrice again, but her classmates were different. They taunted her at recess and snickered when they could, only dumb kids were held back. After school, Derrick Crat and others from the fifth grade called: "Hey, fourth grader!" Mary Wolfe watched.

"The Two-Girls Club," ended. "You have to be in the same grade to be in the club," her friend told her.

Sister Beatrice watched. On a cold, October day, she asked Willow to stay after and help clean erasers. When they were alone, she put her arms around her. "If you do very well over the next few months," she stopped. She couldn't promise too much, couldn't set Willow up for another disappointment. She rolled Willow's right sweater sleeve up over her hand, patted the hand, and placed it back at Willow's side. "If you study hard, I mean scoring 100% in every subject, and you don't miss any school, not one day," her eyes were kind, "*maybe* after Christmas I can have you promoted into the fifth grade."

Willow nodded. She wanted to be in the fifth grade, but she couldn't promise she'd have better attendance. What if Papa needed her at home? What if Red was there at that very minute trying to knock off Papa's head?

Sister Beatrice bent and kissed Willow's forehead. "You can go now." And just as she told her fourth graders each afternoon before they left for the day—sending them off again to who knew what worlds, "Remember, angels are coming tonight."

When Willow entered the house, she saw Papa still sitting at the kitchen table, just as she'd left him that morning, only now with wine and cigarettes. She thought of him as a "pretend" detective. Every day, he read the *Omaha World Herald* and the *Lincoln Journal Star* for reports of crimes and sentencings. When he finished, he refolded the papers and placed them on top of the yellowing stacks growing along the back wall of the main room.

He lifted the sheet he'd been reading and flicked his wrists. The paper folded inward, and he spoke around the cigarette between his lips. "You're late, I was getting worried."

You shouldn't be sitting here, she wanted to say. The old Papa would be at work. Even if she was in fourth grade again, she knew that. Why didn't he? She thought to tell him what Sister Beatrice said, but what if there were too many days she couldn't leave him and it didn't happen?

An envelope lay on the table, and he pushed it in her direction with a nicotine-stained finger, but he kept the finger there, pinning the envelope to the table. She saw it was from the Nebraska Department of Health and Human Services, but when she reached for it, his hand flattened and covered it.

"So, here's the deal," he said. "There are laws. It's a law kids have to go to school." His eyes bore into hers. "A law." He paused. "You understand what I'm saying?"

She did. Laws that weren't obeyed meant someone was going to jail. One or the other of them could be taken away. She fought back tears, and he put a thumb under her chin, lifting it.

"It's all right. You'll go now. Every day."

She nodded. She knew of a thing called foster care. They could take her away from Papa.

"Now," Julian said, "go and get changed before you get your uniform dirty."

She headed for her room, not reminding him that she was the one who turned on the washer, and when they had it, poured in soap. At the end of the hall, she stopped. Her bedroom door was closed, something she hadn't done since Mémé's death when she quit drawing and had nothing more to hide. Why would Papa close her door? From inside, her bed squeaked. She stared at the knob. She heard walking. Backing away, she retraced her steps, and at the end of the hall, she turned and ran into the kitchen. "Somebody's in my room."

Though his face looked gray, light twinkled in his glassy eyes. "How come you aren't changed?"

She willed herself to see only the wine-happy in his eyes. She tried to find a match there to her old memories of him, but those were deep now and nearly lost. "Somebody's in my room." Already that seemed unlikely.

He swallowed wine and then flicked the ash from his cigarette. "You aren't scared are you? Go on now. Holler if you need me."

Her stomach kicked. She glanced in the direction of her room and then back to Papa. His lips had lifted to a half grin, telling her he knew something, and he believed she'd like it. The kicking increased. She hated when he tried to make her happy, the strain on his face only moving around. Like his joke about how she was likely to start mooing—given that dinner the last two weeks had been milk and grilled cheese sandwiches. His teasing was supposed to make up for things, make her happy. But when he saw she wasn't laughing, his face fell, and she knew she'd hurt him again.

He leaned forward, meeting her gaze at eye level. "You don't suppose that big hairy thing I saw running around here got into your room?"

Willow knew only one big hairy thing. Her mind cried *No, no, it's a trick.* She didn't want to remember Friar, and she knew not to believe in good things: Papa promising they'd go for ice cream and never taking her, promising trips to the library, promising new socks and panties. Broken promises made her feel slapped inside. She shook her head, she shouldn't believe because Friar was Jonah's dog now. She'd been in the kitchen after Mémé's will was read, her arms wrapped around Friar's neck while Papa carried their bags to the car and stood outside the front door and yelled at her to "Come on."

Mable stopped stirring whatever was in her bowl. "Don't you worry about Friar," she said, "he loves Jonah, and I have a feeling he'll do Jonah some good."

Then Papa called again, louder this time, and Willow stood at the kitchen window and watched Friar and Mable cross the yard and Jonah's door open and Friar's tail begin to wag for the first time in three days.

Now, these months later, she searched Papa's face, wanting real assurances. With his sallow skin and cheeks sinking in like palms, he'd turned into an old man. She rocked on her toes and grabbed his forearm. "I wish, I wish," she said, wishing that she never wished.

He put a hand over hers. "Go on, take a look."

She couldn't move. Never knowing would be better than disappointment.

He squeezed her hand. "I know," he said. "You go on now and have a look."

She ran down the hall, hurrying so fast hope couldn't catch her. Her hand shook as she turned the knob and swung open the door. Friar lunged at her, both forepaws hitting her chest as they went over together, spilling into the hall in a tangle of Willow's thin arms and legs and Friar's heavy fur and wet tongue.

Only after they rolled on the floor did Willow notice the large black easel from Mémé's attic and the other things: blank canvases, brushes, and tubes of paint. Mother Moses lay on the bed.

She ran back, Friar at her heels, and into Papa's arms.

He held her. "I figured some things belonged to you."

He had wine and cigarettes and newspapers. She had permission to paint and Mother Moses and Friar. She'd study herself into the fifth grade, and while she did—going to school every day—Friar would take care of Papa.

Only much later, did she notice the box of books in the corner. On her knees, she unpacked them, showing each to Friar: a book on cave art, one on mythology, a book of French painters, *Grimm's Complete Fairy Tales*, a few of my watercolor journals, and the book she'd loved of Frida Kahlo's work. She opened the book to a painting of monkeys draped around Kahlo's neck and turned pages to see masks that cried real tears, two Fridas hooked together by a long vein, a painting with bones in Frida's head. The book also had a photograph of Frida in bed, her back in traction, and a brace of white sheeting keeping even her head immobile. The picture proved Frida had a real mustache and eyebrows like two black wooly caterpillars butting heads. Neither Frida's back nor her face were fixed. Not one bit fixed. Her eyes, looking straight at the camera, said it too: *Not one bit fixed.* Willow had already known people with stupid backs could paint, and now she wondered if people with stupid backs had to paint no matter what.

The book was license. She had permission to paint, like Frida, telling whatever stories came to her, no matter all the Sister Dominic Ageneses in the world.

She considered how only Mémé knew her favorite books. Mémé must have been at Farthest House to tell Papa which ones to take.

That night, with Mother Moses over them, she and Friar slept in her bed.

14

Growing up, I hadn't been entirely without support. I had Mme. Francoise, who saw not just with the eyes in her head but also with the eyes in her heart. She didn't turn from the pain she saw in me, not like the rest of the maids and cooks who averted their eyes when I was near. But what could they have done? To question out loud what they suspected would have meant immediate dismissal. They were women lucky to have employment. Coming forth wouldn't have changed The Beast's routines or his beliefs. They'd have simply been replaced with others more willing to look away in exchange for bread to place in their children's hands.

Mme. Francoise was tiny and bent and seldom spoke. I don't know how many years she sat on her little stool in the stone kitchen before she approached me. I had walked by her a hundred times, and seen nothing, maybe a shadow, or a fixture as meaningless to my child's mind as a stick broom. Then she came. I was outside, hiding between bushes. Crying, with my bloomers torn off, I rubbed and scratched between my legs. Such itching and burning I'd never known.

She took me inside, sat me in a bucket of warm water, cloudy with herbs. I recognized some of the things she boiled before adding them: lavender, chamomile, walnut, anise, and Damask rose. There in the kitchen, no clothing beneath, and the skirt of my dress blossoming over the pail sides, as though I simply sat on a little stool, I soaked. I don't remember how often she needed to save me in this way, but I remember the instant relief of sinking into her remedy, antibiotic and restorative and being content to sit there long after the water was cold. At the time, I didn't know enough to associate the infections with The Beast, though she must have.

I'm convinced that she was allowed to stay at the villa in part because she went nearly unnoticed. She was half phantom, hunched alone in her corner, an old wool scarf tied around her head, a gnome or ancient fairy. Under certain slants of light, I could catch a tincture of the fiery red hair she once had. When she wasn't walking the hills harvesting wild things, she worked soundlessly at her table with her herbs and flowers, chopping, pressing, and grinding for her creams and powders. Sitting in her concoctions, I watched the staff approach her with their colds, flu, and female troubles. They would stroll to her stool, waiting until she looked up. She studied them, at times there was whispering, and after a few minutes, she shook powders or crushed leaves onto tiny squares of paper, and with her chloroform-stained fingers and nails, she folded the paper and gave instructions. "Boil a cloth along with this. Wrap it tight around the wound," or "Make a warm tea, strained well. Drink it three days. No more."

I loved the scents rising from her table and her peaceful silence. While the others chatted and cackled amongst themselves, her quiet was louder. There was the afternoon, too, after my having been with The Beast, the sky black and slicing with lightning, when I feared running across the fields and climbing into my cave. Mme. Francoise saw my sorrow, and her eyes told me she knew about the morning I had. Her concern doctored me, the acknowledgment of my sorrow, and I sat down next to her eager to be taught. Later that afternoon, when The Beast was ready for his tea, when it sat on his tray ready to be delivered, she opened my palm, put a pinch of something in it, and with her eyes motioned to the tea cup. Then, she screeched at a rat that dropped out of the air, and as the maids screamed and grabbed brooms, I hurried and opened my hand over the waiting cup. The powder vanished, like a white leaf sucked down a drain. For three days, the house was in an uproar, The Beast fuming with unstoppable diarrhea.

My desire to learn everything she knew increased. I picked flowers for her, learned the weeds around there and their properties. At least for a short time. Was it my mother who pulled me from the kitchen and the company of women "beneath" me? With so many secrets needing kept, was she afraid of Mme. Francoise and her crone sight?

I'd already spent enough time in the kitchen to learn something of dyes. I began making tints and painting the local weeds and flowers. My mother and The Beast found the pastime acceptable. Wanting me complacent, they were happy to supply me with books of botanical prints done by other artists. While I painted, they knew where I was, who I wasn't talking to, and I didn't return from the mountain after hours away with torn undergarments. Painting, I became a young Mme. Francoise, quiet, unseen, learning everything I could.

Living with Thomas in Peu de Nid, I continued painting. He gifted me with a magnifying glass, a wonderful aid, and studying the tiny fibers and gradations of colors, I learned more about herbs and apothecary, even as I searched for my reflection, painting what I could of my soul. I worked studiously, as Luessy did after me in the medium of words, and Willow did in the years after having my easel brought to her. She, too, was a young Mme. Francoise, alone in her room, working, learning, searching for a handhold on her wobbling world. Julian was happy to see her there—surviving despite him.

How often, as her paintbrush lifted color from her palette to a canvas, did she feel my presence in the room and my attachment to the easel? Thomas built it, hid the gift until he finished and presented it to me on our first anniversary. Did he not realize it was too heavy and required my calling him every time I wanted it moved? Or did he want to be called from his curry brush or his photographic plates to move the piece of furniture when I needed help?

Often, over the next few years, as Willow turned the pages of my old journals, her fingers brailing the fading colors and shapes of orchids, roses, and datura, she must have believed the works held some largess simply for having survived the decades and for having a connection to Farthest House.

Through the remainder of grade school and her first year of high school, structure sustained her: school, homework, housework, reading, and when she could, coaxing Papa to throw the football in the backyard because he needed the exercise. And painting. At school, her friendships were casual and with girls as unpopular as herself. They sat together at lunch, but she avoided getting too chummy. She had no desire for a *best* friend who might want to visit, have sleep-overs, and who'd see Papa sitting at the table with yellowing newspapers and green wine bottles. She owed Papa all his secrets and kept confidences only with Friar.

Age and puberty finally changed that. Not her love of painting, but its ability to be enough.

The last day of her freshman year, she walked out of Our Lady of Supplication High School hearing the cars pulling from the parking lot and vibrating with music by the Beatles. Some headed for the nearest golden arches, others to the mall to buy summer shorts, halter-tops, and swimsuits. She had no money for the first, or the second, and no desire to try on revealing clothes.

"Chicken," the girl at her side said.

Willow, a head taller, tried to shrink her height, slumping ever so slightly. "I'm not chicken, I just don't want to go shopping."

"Chicken."

With everyone off and excited about the summer, the thought of going home to her static life filled Willow with dread. She headed for the library, her only free resource. She didn't put her new books in her satchel. She held them against her chest like a shield, proclaiming to any kids who saw her that she didn't mind being alone, and she preferred books over friends. *Brainyack* stung less than *loser* or *loner*. She carried the books that way up the porch steps and across, not a shield against Papa, but against the gloom holding them both captive.

As she opened the front door, Friar bounded to her with his tail wagging. She bent, dropped her books and wrapped her arms around his neck. "How's my best friend?" She tilted her face up so his tongue scoured her chin and not her lips.

Julian sat at the table unshaven and holding a cigarette that was hardly more than a stained brown filter between his thumb and index finger. Spread out before him was his customary newspaper and two wine bottles, sitting like sentries. He snuffed the cigarette out in his ashtray already heaped with matchsticks and cigarette butts. "All done?"

Foreboding tracked a thin line of heat up Willow's spine. The ashtray looked like the site where a tiny house had burned down. She hated things she could almost see and had to push away before she did. She put her books on the table. "Yup. Freshman year is over."

He refolded the newspaper. The still-growing paper towers hugged the back wall of the main room in shoulder-high drifts and added staleness to the already foul air. He called them his *records* and Willow made herself believe him. Mémé had kept stacks of books and papers piled everywhere, and they'd all been important to her. If Papa read and kept up on recent crimes and who'd been sentenced, then when the time came, he could go right back to his job as if he'd never left. On that day, Red would have a hundred pending cases only Papa could solve.

Julian lifted one green wine bottle, tipped it, and set it down. Empty. He squinted at the other. Empty.

He no longer hid his drained bottles. Willow found them not just on the table, but crawling from beneath the sofa, sitting beside the toilet, teetering atop the television, and even on the back step where they cupped bits of shine in slants of light: street, sun and moon.

She opened the refrigerator—no milk, no soda, no orange juice. She closed the door and saw Papa using a stained finger and pushing her top library book back an inch, then the second and the third, reading the spines and forming a tiny stairs as he did.

"*Mad Apple?*" His voice more startled than questioning. He picked the Luessy Starmore Mystery from the stack and flung it in the direction of the overflowing trashcan. "You got your report card?"

She went for the book splayed open on the dusty floor. "Why'd you do that?"

His gaze drifted over the wine bottles on the table, but what he saw was a past she was too young to understand. He hoped she never had to, and certainly not at . . . fifteen. God Dammit, he missed her birthday, remembering only the anniversary of Jeannie's death. "You got a report card?"

She brushed crumbs and long strands of Friar's hair from the novel pages. Papa could get the card himself if he cared so much. "It's in my backpack."

He took his time, unzipping her bag, reading the grades again and again, and finally, nearly to himself, "We're showing 'em, aren't we?"

Willow's heart gripped. She shrugged. She didn't study because she believed they were *showing* anyone or even to make him proud. She liked pleasing him, though the responsibility of having to do so always threatened to sit her down. She studied because she'd never be pushed behind again, because paying rapt attention to instructors kept her mind from roaming around the room, wondering what others did the night before or seeing someone whispering about her. Even waving an empty sweater cuff. She studied because receiving high marks made her back matter less.

Julian and I could see that as she grew, (she'd be tall like him) the gnarl on her back didn't keep up. Year by year the bone was smaller in proportion to her increasing height. Her mind kept hold of an old picture though, and she thought of herself as *disfigured*, like her soul.

"Those grades call for a celebration," Julian said, "and hey, happy birthday."

His raw need made her ache and search for some distraction. "How come you never read Mémé's books?"

"I've read them."

"Really? Did you hate *Mad Apple* so much you think it belongs in the trash?"

His smile faded. "That's enough."

She stood beside him at the table. "You always do that," she said. "You quit talking."

"I said, 'That's enough.'"

"You can't just clam up like I'm not here."

He slapped open his newspaper.

By seven o'clock, the sun still two hours from setting, Julian had left the house, returned with more wine, and celebrated so much he lay draped across his bed, snoring. Standing at the door of his room, Willow stared at the figure on the bed. *Not Papa. Not the man she still remembered him being.*

She thought about calling Tory. Maybe there was something Tory could do or undo. Maybe Tory would come, bringing her sewing basket and doll parts and sit at the kitchen table. Maybe the two could talk and fix things. But Papa didn't want his sister there any more than he wanted *Mad Apple* in the house.

She tried but wasn't strong enough to roll Julian to his side and free some blanket to cover him. She hated leaving him exposed, not because he'd chill, but because she left Mémé that way. He looked unprotected and vulnerable. She'd take the blanket from her bed.

In her room, she swung back Mother Moses and grabbed up the blanket beneath. Before starting back, she stopped at her easel to study the picture she was working on, a painting she'd named *White Mask*. It stared at her, pleasing and unsettling, prickling her skin and reminding her that Papa lay unprotected in a world full of ravens. She dropped the blanket she'd been hugging, took up Mother Moses and hurried back to him.

Spreading the crocheting over his body—long thin bones, hard-cut shoulders and hands—she fought back tears. "Sure, Papa," she whispered, "we're *showing* them."

I tried to make my presence felt. She looked frail staring down at a man who, like Jeannie and Mémé, seemed to have orphaned her. His walls murmured around her, and she turned, taking them in. They were bare but for areas of chipped paint and cracks, one running from the leaky window to the floor, and one small picture of Jeannie, frameless and hanging by a thumbtack, its corners curling. This was the last likeness of her mother, punched and ruined by the handle of a sauce pan, but still recognizable. She turned back. Papa, mute on his bed beneath the pale lattice of Mother Moses, looked a broken and ghostly match to it.

She approached the photograph. "I killed you," she whispered. An infant wasn't really guilty, she knew that, and yet without the delivery Jeannie would be alive. Smashing the photographs had just been more of it, bringing the murder up to date.

She shut his bedroom door and returned to the kitchen where she tipped the empty wine bottles on the table into her mouth. She brought others from the trash, let the drops of cheap alcohol drip on her tongue, and she licked the bottle rims, her hunger still ravishing.

The kitchen cupboard held two cans of tomato soup and a can of green beans. She had no appetite, and it made no difference if she ate at all, except that she had a whole evening to fill while Papa slept and other high schoolers were out enjoying their first night of summer vacation. She opened a can of the soup, scooped it into a pan, and grimaced at the sight. Too red without milk. She added the beans. While she waited for the meal to heat, she lined the wine bottles across the table, something she started doing on the coldest winter nights when she studied alone and Papa slept—a row of the tall and thin-necked containers jutting across the table or in front of the sofa like witch's teeth. She could talk to the shapes, even with their dejected color, and she liked the way the empty bottles caught the steady room light. They made a conduit to Papa. He'd reached with his thick fingers and palms and put his hand around them. Hands that long ago reached and wrapped strands of her loose hair behind her ear and took up her hand in crowded places—afraid of losing her.

Only when she saw her own face in the bottles, a row of tiny and sickly Willows, did she push them over.

She sat down with the bottles and her five books. The check-out limit was fifteen, but if she checked out a smaller number, she could return to the library more often. One of the books demonstrated painting techniques, two were pictorial history books of Native Americans, and the last two were Luessy's mysteries. Willow opened the first of the history books, squinting at the bottom corners of the pictures for two letters: T.S., Thomas Starmore. My Thomas. Even in the absence of her great uncle's initials, she looked for matches to photographs she remembered hanging on the den walls at Farthest House. Over time, a photographer's initials were often lost, she knew, ignored in the multiple reproductions. Pictures became copies made from copies, reduced or enlarged with little concern for the notations. In the end, their source was credited only to the historical society that owned them, not the original photographer. If she found even one picture, either familiar or with the initials, she felt she could follow the print back through time, the way other families followed photos in scrapbooks, and she'd have legs carrying her to Farthest House.

This was not so different from what I knew of Mary Wolfe, who at that moment was running up Willow's street, her long hair and most of her face hidden beneath a silk hood. Mary still visited the first-grade classroom where Sister Dominic Agnes spent as many hours as possible, even evenings and weekends, sometimes sleeping on the hard floor. When Mary appeared at the classroom door, Sister Dominic Agnes lifted her eyes from her prayers and drew the young girl in. Together, they knelt on the two kneelers the nun had requisitioned and placed before the black chain still draping from the windows. The construction-paper, now with tiny rips, sagged with age, dust, scotch tape, and the weight of the hundreds of staples used to keep it together.

A knock sounded on Willow's door, and she sighed at the disruption but didn't leave the table. She pretended she wasn't home. The second knock was more insistent, and she knew she wasn't fooling anyone. Papa's car sat at the curb, and the house lights were on. Still, she hesitated, hoping whomever, selling whatever, or predicting some whenever end-of-time apocalypse would simply give up and go away. On the third knock, more a hammering, she thought of Papa sleeping and didn't want him back in the kitchen with his need to "show 'em." She hurried to the door.

Mary Wolfe stood with the screen already open. "Let me in before someone sees me."

Not wanting her to see the interior, Willow tried to step outside, but Mary pushed her way in. "You can't tell anyone I came. Not even your dad."

The house, with its floors growing porous and rough and its sagging-seat sofa and row of wine bottles alert as disciples, dropped from Willow's concerns. Mary had pushed back the hood of her silk jacket, and her long golden hair looked just-brushed. No matter how Willow wished it weren't true, Mary was beautiful. Whether walking down a school hallway or sitting at lunch with a crowd around her, she was beautiful. Her blouses were always ironed and snow white, buttoned to the top with a tiny knot of white grosgrain ribbon at her throat. And while everyone else's skirts looked snatched off the floor and stepped back into each morning, Mary's had crisp, starched pleats. Even the denim jeans she wore now had pressed vertical creases straight as plumb lines. Beneath her silk jacket, she wore a blue satin blouse the same light blue color as her eyes. The cowl neck of her blouse reached nearly to her chin, and her painted nails, pink, not harsh red, stroked the lush fabric as if pointing to her own flawless face.

On the sofa, Friar lifted his head and pulled back his ears. He stepped off and came to Willow with his tail hanging low. She heard the unrest in his throat, more harrumph than growl, and she reached down and placed her hand on his head.

Mary eyed the large dog, then dismissed him, and returned her attention to Willow. "Promise you won't tell. Promise! No one can know I came here."

"I promise." If Mary didn't want anyone to know, Willow would never breathe a word of it. She felt ashamed in her beat-up shorts and old T-shirt, and she watched Mary's gaze pan the room. Sister Dominic Agnes once stood in that very spot and looked at a clean and kept-up house. Now, everything was just as the nun had hoped to find it then.

The more Mary scrutinized the room, missing nothing but Willow, the more ashamed and out of place Willow felt. On the stove, the soup boiled and spat, and she went to turn off the burner, glad for an excuse to move and leave Mary, even if only for a moment.

Mary followed her, "Show me your paintings."

Willow's breath caught, and she slowly slid the pan off the heat. Her paintings? She hadn't shown anyone her art since Mémé's death. Being asked threatened old and unhealed wounds. "I don't have any."

Mary started down the hall. "I can see them through your bedroom windows."

Fresh embarrassment rolled over Willow; she'd been caught lying. She followed Mary, keeping Friar at her side.

"I want to see the one you're doing right now," Mary said, as they passed Julian's door.

Willow's pace slowed. If Mary couldn't be seen by anyone, not even Papa, and his car was slumped at the curb, then she knew he was down for the night and that not even knocking and conversation would wake him. Had she seen him stagger to his room? How many nights had she watched before she felt confident enough of his routine to knock?

Most days, Willow didn't notice the state of her room, but walking in with Mary made the room's condition striking. The wallpaper, with its once bright and high-stepping ducks, was faded and peeling at the corners. Her floor was dull and rough, and the old lace curtains on the windows hung uneven and gray. The blanket she pulled off and then only tossed back onto the bed revealed sheets worn so thin the stripes of the mattress showed through. She wished Mother Moses were there, the corners of the old crocheting pooling onto the floor, and the butterflies and birds alive.

Mary shut the door and turned around. "Pull the shades."

Friar had relaxed somewhat, but as the door shut, his ears turned keen again. Willow reached down a second time and put a steadying hand on his head. Did he know Mary? Had Mary been sneaking around outside the house and he picked up her scent, or had he seen her at a window? Maybe some evening, when he'd gone out to lift his leg and relieve himself on the sole tree in the backyard, she threw sticks at him.

Pulling the shades as slow as she dared, Willow scanned the street for Mary's friends, the jerk Derrick Crat or girls hiding in the shadows to see how far Mary would take the dare.

Earlier paintings leaned against the walls, but Mary had no interest in the ones visible from the windows. She stood at the easel. "It's creepy." She stroked her throat again. "Why do you paint such weird stuff?"

On the canvas, grays, greens, umbers, and sables dominated. A girl, half hidden in the shadows of overarching trees, crouched in undergrowth along a forest's edge. She wore a mask: a wide square of bone-colored birch bark with two dark eyeholes.

Willow smiled to herself and sat down on her bed. She never imagined Mary would one day be standing in her room, having all but broken in, to see a painting. "It's not weird or creepy, she's just hiding," Willow said. "She's scared to come out of the woods and into this world. It's called *White Mask*."

Mary glowered, "Stupid."

"When she does come out, the mask will fall off. She's been hiding her whole life because she knows if she takes a face everything will change." Willow loved the story so far. She was doing exactly as Mémé had done in writing Mother Moses' story. "If she takes a face, she can't ever go back into hiding. That's the scary part."

"Repeat. Stupid."

"I'll bet Eve just wanted to have a face when she ate the apple, and then Adam, too. But he was scared to go first." Keeping a straight face was hard, not because of Mary's shocked look, but because the story poured forth as easily as if it were being read from a book. As easily as if *White Mask* herself were telling the story through Willow.

"Can I have it when it's done?"

"No." Willow would keep it and look at it and find more story. She wouldn't pass her work out into a world that reached back and cursed her each time she did. "No," she said again. "I have to keep it."

Mary folded her arms across her chest and unfolded them. "Well anyway, everyone already has a face. I was scared to come here, but I did. My parents would kill me if they found out."

"Why?" She wished she hadn't asked. Given the differences in their appearance, they obviously originated on different planets. Of course Mary's parents wouldn't want her there. Still, Willow had always thought Mary didn't like her because of her shoulder, or because she was a book nerd, or for a hundred other reasons. "Who cares what they think?"

A slow smirk touched Mary's lips. "At least they aren't alcoholics." She nodded, "Yeah, everyone at school knows."

Willow felt blown back years, and when Mary started to leave, she jumped up, catching her by the arm. She hadn't wanted Mary in her house, but now with re-opened wounds and new embarrassments, she didn't want to be alone. "I promised not to tell anyone you came."

"Show me your back."

Willow's face blanched, and she imagined it turning as fixed as the white birch mask. "No," she whispered.

"Do it!"

The world saw too much of her back through her clothes, but Mary stared at her, declaring with cold eyes that Willow's only chance at friendship was through obedience. Willow glanced sidelong at the painting. Mary and her friends probably dressed in front of each other all the time, though this wasn't about comparing cup sizes or the amount of lace on their bras. This was about rank, Mary wanting to see Willow at her most vulnerable.

"Chicken!"

Slowly, inch by inch—giving Mary plenty of time to change her mind—Willow turned around and began lifting her shirt.

15

At Willow's age, I often stood looking out over lavender fields, wave after wave of purplish-blue color. I envied the women and young girls doing the harvesting. They worked hunched over the rows with short sickle-shaped knives, their faces immersed in all that perfume and color, the bags slung across their shoulders swelling with the cuttings. The Beast's chambers were also rich with color: his bedding, tapestries, paintings, even his vestments—elaborate robes, and like all ceremonial robes, designed to mask an ordinary man—reds, greens, blues and lavender. Did his owning all that color, even to his emerald ring, help convince us that God favored him? How else could he have so much?

In my teenage years, I might have been emotionally stronger, but like a bird caged from a hatchling, I had no knowledge of freedom. I'd grown no flight feathers and had no vision of sky. Then one day, word arrived that a photographer from America was some twenty miles away showing his work, photographs of Native Americans. So rare was any sort of cultural event in our region, especially with so many fleeing the border with Prussia, The Beast immediately sent a rider to ask him to come. A week later, Thomas Starmore stepped through the door. Over dinner that evening, when I dared, I peeked at him. I was accustomed to withdrawing and remaining as unseen as possible, and I was happy to let Sabine hold center stage. She was joyful always, and why not?

I raised my eyes from my stewed rabbit just as Thomas looked across the table at me. I realized we were sharing an exact thought: The Beast was far hungrier for someone to impress with his adventures in America than he was to hear about Thomas's work. The thought itself wasn't of any great significance, but the synchronicity of Thomas's mind with mine was. It was flight, if only a moment long. I had experienced something entirely new and made a connection with someone outside of my circumscribed life.

Later, he displayed his photographs across the cleared table. Walking slowly around, I stopped at a picture of a woman who was the photograph's sole subject. No child in the picture labeled her as a mother. No man labeled her as a wife. Not even a basket labeled her as a craftswoman. I stared at the picture, and my feelings can best be described as music in my head. Here was a woman whole unto herself, not beautiful, not wealthy, but complete. I thought of Mme. Francoise. Knowing that such women were also in America brought tears to my eyes, and I longed to go and experience the new world.

That's when I noticed the hand and the woman's soiled lap. Blood.

Sabine came to stand beside me, and she also saw the hand, its two fingers cleaved at the first knuckle. "What happened?" her voice clear and self-confident, calling to Thomas across the room. He came and stood at my shoulder, closer to me than Sabine. Was it because of my tears?

"I only know she cut herself," he said. "I believe she was mourning. It's rumored to be a custom at the loss of a husband or child, but it's got to be rare, because she's the first I've seen."

"She must have been really sad," Sabine said.

Thomas nodded, "I can't imagine inflicting that much pain on yourself."

I looked up at him, my shyness replaced by disbelief. Here was a man who thought a woman's suffering important enough to record.

Years later, when Tory was Sabine's age, I should have been watching out for her. I was her surrogate mother, allowing Luessy, who carried the expense of Farthest House and the feeding and clothing for the four of us, to spend long hours writing. I failed Tory by averting my eyes—however subconsciously I did so. Too afraid of seeing, of revisiting the groundswell of pain I'd experience in my life before Thomas, I also failed Luessy, Julian, Jonah, and myself. I acted no different from my mother, who used her religious "duties" as a thick veil pulled righteously over her eyes.

The day came when an undeniable darkness burst over everything. When that day came for my mother, she crawled into bed and refused food. When it came for me, I fought.

Now, I restated the vow I made at Willow's birth: I would not leave her.

And the vow I made to myself: I would keep my eyes open and feel what I needed to feel.

In the front rooms, she kept the shades drawn. She forbid Mary the newspapers, the wine bottles rising and dancing like clattering bones. And Papa.

Julian didn't object to living in a space of shadow and dusk. His mounting hoards filled him with a subterranean panic, and the less he saw of what he was doing, even as he added new weight, the better. Nothing mattered to him but Willow. She was everything, the reason he had to get himself back. He would, too. Tomorrow. Tomorrow, somehow, he would find his way back. Until then, Willow was taken care of financially. His mother had seen to that. Not him, not her father.

Only to Willow's room did Mary have access, entering and leaving through the side window where Willow kicked out the bottom of the screen so that the wire mesh lifted and lowered like a slow trap door. Mary might have one creamy leg draped over the bedroom windowsill before Willow realized she'd been favored again. Sometimes, too, Willow kept her windows locked and the vinyl shades with their frayed strings pulled down. Hardest were the weeks and even months that passed without Mary visiting. During the long absences, Willow forgave Mary for not coming, and at school, she kept her promise and never acknowledged Mary. She told herself that plenty of girls would envy even the meager time and attention Mary did give her. *Mary Scraps,* she called them, recognizing in herself a hunger too big to refuse even the bits thrown her way.

In December of their junior year, the night of the school's Christmas Prom, which Willow wasn't attending, never having attended any school dance, snow fell and wind gusts struck the house in undulating waves, reminding her of the night Mémé died. She worked at copying a plant from one of my watercolor journals: datura with its long and jagged leaves and showy white flowers.

Just as she prepared to quit for the night and wash up my old brushes, Friar rose and hurried to the window. Willow caught the last of a vanishing motion. The window light extended only an inch beyond the pane, but just enough to reveal a narrow ribbon of color at the window's edge. Lemon yellow, the color of Mary's favorite coat because it matched the same bright color of the sports car she received on her sixteenth birthday. Every time Mary walked about in her yellow, the TR6 was heralded, though it sat in a parking lot out of sight.

Wiping her hands down the thighs of her jeans, Willow glanced at the clock: 12:34. Mary must have insisted Derrick Crat, still her steady, take her home immediately after the dance. She must have hurried out of her dress and into sturdier clothes for the nearly eight-block walk over. Mary never drove there, never parked her identifiable car at the curb. But to walk this late? In a snow storm?

Willow waited for Mary to tap the glass and announce herself. She didn't want to rush for Mary or to be caught looking; both acts would seem needy. Minutes passed. The motion at the window moved, Mary looked in, hid, looked in again. As Willow wondered and then realized what Mary was doing, gloom invaded the small room. Mary stood in the cold, her body pressed against the house, snow falling on her head. She hadn't come for companionship; she'd come to peek in on a freak show. Like staring at the nine-foot man in the *Guinness's Book of World Records*, or the nameless and topless African women in *National Geographic*.

The minutes continued to unspool. Just out in front of Willow, the unfolding of what she would do next waited dark and cold. *All females experience caves,* I thought. *They carry caves within themselves.*

Willow's heart was heavy. She slowly closed my watercolor journal and let her palm rest a moment on the front cover. She tried to gather her will, but she was disfigured to match her soul, Mémé was dead, and Mary wanted to see a freak.

Willow moved over to the light switch, put the room in darkness, and crossed her floor to raise the window. The cold air, indigo and silver with night and snow, sharp and aching, rolled into the room. Willow turned back to her bed on leaden feet, and while Friar watched her, she pulled off her sweatshirt to lie face down, offering her back to Mary.

I saw myself entering The Beast's chamber. Not because my mother had pushed this time or he gripped my arm and drug me, but because I was empty. With what substance could I have refused even his verbal commands?

The whisper of Mary's jeans brushing over the sill and the squeak of nylon sliding under the wire screen were sounds as cold as snow. Friar padded to the door of Willow's room, not leaving, but watching at a distance from Mary. Then Mary's breath, as she stood over the bed, and Willow's gasp at Mary's freezing touch—knife cold. Around and around the blade of Mary's finger traced, while Willow shivered in shame.

16

❧

Five months passed in which Mary didn't visit Willow, though she often visited Sister Dominic Agnes. The three were caught in a web, and when the aging nun and Mary fought against the strings trapping them, the strings on Willow's side of the web tightened. I had only to look across to see Sister Dominic Agnes, ever thinner and paler and more bent at her kneeler, and the black chain hanging heavily above her. When the first graders left in the afternoon, she turned off the lights, lowered herself, and prayed. Weekends too, in the dark, the room had the air of a chapel. Mary slipped into the somber space feeling fitted to the dark and welcome under the funeral chain velvet with dust. They prayed for Mary's vocation, that she could come to accept God's call, and they talked of the days when the paper chain had been new and people paraded in and out to see it, and the two of them had felt most alive.

Winter moved into spring. Though Mary hadn't visited Willow recently, the memory of the last time, the circling, chiseling in of pain, self-doubt, and shame, continued dragging an icy finger over Willow's back. On the night of Spring Prom, she tried again to fill the hours with painting, though finding that deeper space where time passed with no awareness was nearly impossible. Her mind sagged with worry and longing. Mary, and nearly everyone else she knew, had dates and danced in beautiful spaghetti-strapped gowns.

After eleven, she put down her brushes and sat on the bed to study the pale canvas. With one arm around Friar, she asked him what he thought. The picture she struggled to copy was *Pandora,* by the French painter Lefebvre. She'd been working on the painting in her free time for over a week, and one of Pandora's legs still looked seriously off kilter. On another night, she might have scraped off some of the paint and worked another two or three hours, but the thought of Mary possibly showing up, as she had after the Christmas

Prom, crowding the room with her odors of dancing and drinking, filled Willow with dread and shame.

The best tactic was to turn out the light and go to bed. If Mary came, she'd see the dark window and leave. Sweeping her brushes back and forth through turpentine, Willow kept one eye on the painting. The first-woman of the Greek's definitely looked tipsy and ghostly. The oils and acrylics Papa brought from Farthest House were gone. A tiny bit of white remained, smidgeons of a couple of colors, but most tubes were so flat they looked sucked dry. Still others were rolled up as tightly as wire bands around Spam keys. She kept them, needing them the way Julian needed his newspapers. On her saddest days, she picked them up, felt their pinched and squeezed hard surfaces, read their exotic names, and imagined holding full tubes.

"Care only to work," Mémé had said, and Willow wouldn't let the lack of optimal painting supplies keep her from that.

Their small house felt large and empty as she and Friar walked past Papa's doorway and through the kitchen to where she opened the door, and he went out to lift his leg on the big tree in their yard. When he finished, she locked the back door, something Papa never bothered to do. She locked the front door, as well, and turned out the room's light, watching how the newspapers seemed to hold illumination a second longer. Passing Julian's room again, she paused to look in. He lay shirtless in his worn jeans and atop his blankets, his bottom ribs visible, his face in the dark, stony and smudged in shadows, and his hair graying and too long falling back from his sharp-edged face. She'd already begun to think of him as disappearing, and now in the dim light, he looked half erased. Creditors called daily, at least they had before the telephone was shut off, and Papa was anxious about everything.

She pulled herself away and hurried on. She wasn't still a child. She could take care of things. She'd applied for a job at the nearest art store, right on the number 2 bus route, and if they hired her, she could help with groceries. More importantly, she'd be aware of every sale, every damaged tube of paint headed for the trash, and she'd have an employee discount. If only they hired her, she'd never be out of paint again.

In her room, close to Mother Moses, she double-checked the locks on both her windows, and as Friar finished circling on the bed and dropped rump-first with a sigh, she turned off the light and crawled in. Friar snored soon enough, but she tossed, rolling right and left, and finally staring up at the ceiling. She acted horrible the night of the Christmas Prom, rolling over like a dog and exposing herself, so needy she let Mary go on and on with her emotional mauling while snow melted off Mary's shoes and onto the floor.

The shameful memory made Willow take up her pillow and move to the floor, though she couldn't explain why. Friar stepped off the bed, joined her there, and she wrapped her right arm around his neck.

Even half expecting it, the tapping on her window made her jump. She looked at the clock: 12:52. Mary. Why always on nights when the rest of her group surely lied about spending the night at friends' houses and were coupled up four to a bed in motel rooms? Was that it? Was Mary afraid of those situations? The drinking and the sex? More afraid than walking in the dark in the middle of the night? When a car could stop, pull her inside, and no one would see it happen?

The tapping turned to knocking and finally pounding. Willow kept hold of Friar, keeping him quiet and on the floor, while she prayed the banging would stop before it woke Papa. The noise only increased, and as Mary pressed against the window, her dark silhouette grew.

Willow held her breath, not hearing Julian's bare footfalls over the pounding. She noticed him only when he appeared at the door of her room. Too late to rush back into bed. She shut her eyes tight, clenched her teeth and feigned sleep. When Friar pulled free to go to Julian, she had to let him go.

The pounding stopped. The arms of the shadow rose and cupped its shadowed mouth. "Fucking bitch!"

Willow's heart seized. The name-calling would hurt Papa, make him worry. Here was another something hurled at him: her unpopularity. Something he couldn't fix, only carry.

"Fucking bitch!" Mary screamed again, "I've always hated you."

The window cleared, and the soft glow from the nearby streetlight settled again on the glass. A June bug, caught between the window and the screen, whirled and buzzed in distress, and still Julian lingered, listening to the insect, making sure the figure at the window wasn't returning, and watching his teenage daughter curled on the floor. He hadn't seen her there in years. Friar sat on his haunches staring up at him, and he petted the dog's head. He didn't know how to help Willow. "Go on," he whispered. "Stay with her."

As I watched the boy I helped raise, grown now into a beautiful man, drink from a bottle in his room, I thought of my instructions to Tory. "Sip, sip," I said. "Forget this."

The following forenoon, Willow stood at the kitchen sink, holes under the arms of her old T-shirt and in the knees of her sweatpants. Using her fingernail, she scratched at the dried on grit in a soup bowl. Neither she, nor Julian, cared much about food: Campbell's soup still kept them alive. Willow even preferred painting while hungry. She was convinced that on an empty stomach she could work for more hours without tiring and that hunger kept her mind sharp. An emaciated model with large eyes, so like a victim in a concentration camp, was all the rage. Twiggy had even recently recorded her first album.

At the table behind Willow, Julian ground out the stub of his cigarette. "I'm going to pick up a few things."

She rinsed the bowl in her hand. Cigarettes and wine, there was always money for those. She was out of sanitary pads and pinned washcloths to her underwear. She washed them out at night and spread the stained squares under her bed to dry. Papa hadn't mentioned the midnight incident, hadn't asked how school was going or if she had any friends, hadn't said, "We're showing 'em." He smoked more than usual that morning, snapped his newspapers with unnecessary force, and avoided looking at her. She was thankful; she couldn't have explained Mary to him. She didn't understand Mary herself.

By the time the taillights of his rusted Ford rounded the corner at the end of the block, Mary crossed the porch and slipped through the unlocked door. "Why didn't you let me in last night?"

Willow turned. Beautiful Mary. Less than twelve hours earlier, Willow wanted nothing to do with her, but in the hours since, she'd heard Mary scream "bitch" over and over and felt Papa's gloom. Mary with her bright hair, eyes, and clothes, represented the good stuff: money, beauty, and popularity. How could Willow turn her back on that, cutting off her only possible lifeline to the world where teenagers lived in the safety of numbers, never alone like herself? What she and Mary shared was crazy and stupidly painful, and yet, here Mary was again, the second time in hours, wanting something. Friendship? She'd called Willow a "fucking bitch," but did she even remember? Had she been drunk? Was she visiting now, in daylight, to apologize?

"Why didn't I let you in?" Willow repeated the question, as if she'd been trying to remember the reason. "I wasn't home. A couple of us without dates had a sleep over."

"Liar." She started for Willow's room, the long ties of her white espadrilles winding up her ankles, her pink shorts and sleeveless pink silk blouse with its mandarin collar making Willow vow that once out of high school and away, she'd copy Mary's style: every blouse and sweater. She might even learn to stroke her neck like Mary, as though absent-mindedly petting some fine, porcelain thing.

The bedroom was thick with heat and humidity, and the heaviness added to its over-crowding. The large easel, the table holding art supplies, her bed, the boxes of books, and the dresser all looked pathetic to Willow. Adding to the muddle was the wallpaper with its close and untidy mass of static and discoloring ducks.

Standing in front of the easel, Mary's gaze went from the Pandora painting to *White Mask* leaning against the wall and back to Pandora. "You're just like everyone else."

The picture looked no better to Willow than it had the night before, and she considered how she'd have to start at the hip and paint the entire leg over again, maybe start as high as the waist.

"Sex is the only thing people think about," Mary said.

"That's not sex. Haven't you ever looked in an art book?"

"She's naked under that see-through . . . , whatever."

Mary's eyes were especially pale and cold, winter blue and titanium white. Willow wanted to blame the pallid color on the sunlight coming through the windows.

"My parents," Mary said, "would kill me if I painted something like that."

Mary was jealous, and Willow hoped the pride she felt wasn't spreading over her face. Her art was her single comeuppance. It was little in comparison to Mary's beauty, to the silk blouses, her friends, and the dances. But it was something. "Why'd you come over last night? Not enough compliments on your prom dress?"

"I still want that painting." She pointed to *White Mask*. "You've had it long enough."

"That's not why you came. At least, it's not the whole reason."

Mary turned, lifting both hands and slamming the heels into Willow's chest, sending her stumbling backwards, just missing Friar, nearly catching herself with an arm on the bed but not, feeling like Mo and Curly and Larry in a slapstick routine, then landing on her behind with a plop and an elbow smacking the floor. Surprised by the duration of her fall and how ungracefully she'd gone down, she started to laugh. "You are cra-Azy!"

Friar rose, his eyes sharp as he gave one quick bark in Mary's direction.

"That dog hates me," she said. "Get rid of him."

Willow's palms dampened, "What?"

Mary's arms swung, motioning around the room. "At least I have a life. I don't spend it in this hovel, painting naked women."

Willow might still have laughed. She'd survived the dumbest fall ever, and Mary couldn't paint at all. She wanted to tell Mary to calm down, but Mary's words also held a truth Willow couldn't deny. Only a single year of high school remained, which meant she was about to lose something she'd not yet tasted. For three years she'd been telling herself, "Next year," but like the ducks, she never gained an inch of ground. Now, with her junior year ending, *next year* was her last chance.

Rising from the floor she had a daring thought. "Maybe, we could," she took a deep breath, "go out some night. A double date. You and Derrick, and me with one of his friends."

Mary faced the painting, but Willow's request made her pivot slowly again, her brows pinching. "You're kidding, right?"

A door Willow dared to open slammed shut. "For someone who can't be seen with me, you sure visit a lot."

A draft passed through Mary's eyes, and they seemed to empty even of the sickly blue. Willow drew back. Wolf eyes. She expected fangs and fur to appear. Afraid of enraging the eyes any more than she already had, she kept her voice low. "You don't come to see me. You don't even like being here. So why does perfect Mary visit *me*?"

Just as Willow thought Mary meant to use both hands to hit her again,

Mary's expression changed, her face softening, nearly crumbling into tears. "I'm sorry. I don't hate you." She paused, "Tell me about this painting."

The flame of anger Willow had seen only the second before and the effort Mary took now to rein it in was frightening. Did Papa need to know that Mary had been the one at the window, and that she changed personalities as quickly as a pair of shoes?

Not wanting to see the colorless eyes again, playing along, acting as though nothing happened and talking about the painting, seemed safest. Papa would be back soon and Mary would go, hopefully for another five months.

"Pandora's story?" *Who didn't know that?* She'd make up a very quick version, but first, she ran her thumb and forefinger across her lips as though zipping Mary's. "Pandora is the first version of the Eve myth."

"You're still on that?"

"You asked."

"Okay, okay."

"Pandora and Eve both wanted knowledge, a life bigger than what they had, something they weren't supposed to want."

Mary pointed to *White Mask.* "Like her?"

Willow hadn't thought to include *White Mask,* and it surprised her that Mary did. "Yeah. Eve and Pandora were both supposedly living in Paradise; they were both called the first woman, and they were both accused of letting evil into the world. Though that evil had obviously already been created by someone. Had to be God, right?"

Mary watched her.

"If Eve and Pandora had really been in Paradise, they'd have been perfectly happy, with faces and knowledge. So whose paradise was it?" No reaction from Mary, and Willow considered what she'd just said. She was starting to sound like Mémé. "Anyway, Eve and Pandora are the same story. The End."

"She's a whore."

Cold brushed across Willow's shoulders, and she glanced out the room's street-facing window and onto the empty street. What was taking Papa so long? She wanted to say, *It's just a crappy painting, Mary, no one's in competition with you,* but she didn't dare. Mary frightened her. Even joking felt dangerous.

But Mary wasn't always like this, not *this* mean, and Willow thought of the day she'd felt so much anger and upset that she destroyed Jeannie's pictures, the pot handle like a knife in her hands. Mary was hurting; they matched. They both had weeping places, deep and unseen. But what could the source of Mary's pain be? "Is your mom sick or something?"

Mary's fingers drew quotation marks in the air. "She 'worries' about me. 'Worries.'" Her hands came down, and she looked hard at Willow. "Does your dad know you painted that?"

Willow shrugged. "He hasn't seen it, but I know he doesn't care what I paint."

"Does he know you show me your back?"

From my place, I shuddered watching the two teenagers, remembering Julian and Tory at that age. Was there no end to the sources of pain?

Out Willow's bedroom window Julian's car rumbled back to the curb. Mary groaned. "What's he doing back already?"

They watched him come around the car and start up the walk, each hand holding a brown paper sack twisted around what had to be the neck of a bottle.

"Alcoholic," Mary said.

"You woke him up last night."

"Quick, show me your back."

"No."

"Turn around," Mary hissed, and then louder when Willow didn't move. "I said, 'turn around.'"

"Leave," Willow managed. "Don't ever come back."

Using the same quick and angry motion she used earlier, Mary slammed the heels of her hands, but this time into the canvas. The canvas slid up and off. She looked at the wet paint on her hands and lifted them to her face, streaking the ghostly paint down her cheeks, across her forehead and drawing a wide circle around her mouth. "You'll be sorry when I tell everyone about you. Your senior year is going to be hell."

Willow could only gape at Mary's face, but Friar stood, his ears back. He gave a sharp rap.

"That stupid dog," Mary said, "will be dead before the summer is over. Just wait."

17

✣

The first day of Willow's senior year, a math instructor scratched geometry problems on the blackboard, while Derrick Crat, sitting several desks ahead of Willow, kept turning to look at her. She ignored him, too, and looked at the bank of windows. An oak tree swayed in the breeze and rained fall leaves. She'd spent the previous week sitting on the back stoop at home, watching leaves just like these drop onto the mound of Friar's grave.

She'd painted late and let Friar out the back door, slamming it quickly against the cloud of moths orbiting the outside light. Through the door's smallish window, she watched him trot out of the circle of light, and then exhausted, she sat down at the kitchen table to wait. When she woke, two hours had passed. She opened the door, but Friar wasn't there. She called. He didn't come. She stepped out and listened. Nothing but the screech and flutters of night insects and farther away a car on Dodge Street. Friar wasn't digging at a molehill or his feet padding over the weedy yard toward her. She moved off the steps, and then slower from the light into the darkness, letting her eyes adjust to the night. Only then did she hear the barely audible panting. At the fence, Friar lay on his side. She dropped to her knees, stroked his head, his neck, her fingers going deep into his neck fur. "What is it, boy? What's wrong?"

In the classroom, Derrick Crat paid no more attention to the instructor than Willow did. Each time he turned, she felt the prick of invasion. Was he waiting for her to turn scarlet with embarrassment? Did he think he could still make her pull her hand up into her sleeve?

She'd left Friar in his distress and run back inside to shake Julian awake. "Come on! It's Friar!" Julian's fumbling for his worn jeans on the floor, trying to get them on while still under the blanket, wasting precious seconds, angered her. Did he think the sight of his skinny legs, or something hinting of walnuts beneath his holey briefs, in a dark room, mattered now?

"Calm down," he growled, "I'm coming."

Outside she continued rushing him, staying hard at his elbow though her heart raced yards ahead. Friar hadn't moved, but now his one exposed eye stared lifelessly at the night sky. Julian knelt, rolled the dog to his back, and pressed a palm over Friar's heart, an ear to his mouth. He rocked from his knees back onto his heels. "He's gone."

"He can't be. He was alive."

"I'm sorry."

"I know he's still alive. We have to take him to a vet."

"Willow, it's too late."

"You just don't want to take him in. Please!"

"There's nothing to be done. He's dead."

Through tears she glared at Julian. Maybe Friar was dead, but Papa hadn't done anything to help. "Go back to bed."

"I'm not leaving you out here. Come in, we'll deal with this in the morning."

"This? You mean Friar being dead? This?" She was on her knees, stroking Friar's long body.

Julian tried several times more to coax Willow into the house, but she wouldn't listen to him. He moved to sit on the back stoop. As the stars drifted overhead, Willow, still in tears, stretched out alongside Friar.

Derrick was still glancing back, causing those nearest him to glance back as well. Even the instructor noticed: "Mr. Crat, can I have your attention, please."

She woke beside Friar's body, thin streams of mauve and purple colored the eastern sky in weeping strokes. Ants walked in her hair, mosquitoes marked her arms in bumpy red seams, and Friar lay stiff. A few yards away, fully dressed, Julian worked with a shovel. She sat up and shuddered, her lungs quivering as if she'd continued sobbing in her sleep. She forced herself up from the dewy weeds. "Mary killed him."

Julian stopped and leaned on his shovel, "Mary who?"

"Mary Wolfe. She said he'd be dead before school starts. School starts next week."

He dug. "When did she threaten that?"

"Remember the night in May? She was the one pounding on the window."

"May? Three months ago? That's a long time. You can't start pointing fingers without any proof." He shoved the tip of the shovel into the dirt and used his foot and weight to force the blade deep. His hair, too long, swept against his cheeks.

Willow brushed a black ant off her arm. "Who says that? That they're going to kill your dog? Now, he's dead. We have to take him to a vet and have an autopsy."

"What exactly did she say?"

"I don't know exactly. Quit digging. That's what she meant."

Julian lifted another shovelful of dirt and dumped it on the ring growing around the grave rim. "I know how much you loved him. I did too, but he was old."

"Can we just take him to a vet?"

"You're going to have to face the facts."

"Can we?"

He leaned on the shovel again. "We've had him seven years. Mom had him five or six before that. He was an old dog."

Her body was taut with anger. Hadn't Friar held them together, been the good spirit in the house, kept them from shattering like dropped bottles? Hadn't he loved her, never seeing her as too tall, or too weird, or needing to be fixed? "Mary killed him!"

The cresting sun struck the oak tree, throwing shadow over them and the house. "Don't go looking for trouble," Julian said. "You don't have any proof. This is over here."

She swiped at tears. Friar never counted wine bottles, never wondered why Papa's days were spent sitting at the kitchen table. "I can't believe you. Mary killed him, and you won't even take him in."

"I said, 'No.'"

Her lungs grabbed air. "Red would. He'd do something!"

Julian looked up. No anger in his eyes, only hurt. Exactly what Willow wanted. She wasn't finished. "You don't want to spend the money. You've always got it for cigarettes and wine. If you're that broke, get a job." She turned and ran for the house and her room.

By the time she could force herself back outside, opening and closing the door as quietly as possible, Friar was curled in his grave. Julian sat back on the stoop waiting for her.

"Please," she tried again. Anger and loss were cold hands around her throat.

Julian's fatigue, his shame at not being able to grant Willow her wish, and his own grief over the loss of Friar, all angered him. "You don't have any proof. Why would Mary care about your dog?" His voice was near shouting. "Why would she go through plotting and then killing him? Stop being stupid. He lived a long life, and he died."

"He should have lived longer."

Julian closed his eyes, and when he opened them, his expression had softened. "I know. It's never long enough."

His mind had clearly gone back years to Jeannie's death, and Willow wondered how he expected her to forget Friar and move on in one night when he couldn't after so long.

He walked to where Friar's body waited. "You want to do anything more here?"

"You can't just shovel dirt on him."

"That's what I'm asking."

She started back for the house, thinking to grab a towel for a shroud, maybe even Mother Moses. Why not bury the blanket and its fictionalized story of hope? She wanted no more to do with fantasy and pretending, and Friar had been with the crocheting all his life.

The newspapers running along the front-room wall caught her attention. She took up a thick wad from the most recent stack, papers still white rather than urine-yellow, and hopefully, the ones Papa cared most about. At the back door, she stopped, turned back, and filled her arms with all she could carry. Just let him object.

Julian frowned, embarrassed by the statement and angry over the volume he was losing, but he wouldn't tell her to get something from her own life. He wiped sweat from his forehead onto his sleeve. "We're goin' need a bigger hole."

Lame. She wouldn't smile. She dropped to her knees and tried reaching in to wrap papers around Friar, but she lacked the strength in her right arm to brace herself while she tried to lift his rump with the left. She switched arms, no better, and for a fleeting second she realized how little the difference was between the two. Without measuring, could people even tell? But Friar was dead, and then, Papa was kneeling beside her, taking the newspapers, quilt-thick handfuls, reaching in and wrapping them around the edges of Friar's body, lifting Friar's stiff legs, taking extra care to wrap his head, tucking out of sight the long belly hairs, working carefully, filling even the corners of the grave, as if packing frail china for a long journey.

Derrick had turned, again. Willow felt jerked from her memories and then wondered if Derrick knew anything about Friar's death? She doubted it. He was too much the center-stage showoff to bother going out after dark to help Mary poison a dog. And Mary wouldn't have told him what she'd done. He'd never understand why she cared enough to bother. When Derrick smiled again, Willow made a gawking face back, as if to ask, *what?*

That evening, knocking at the door brought her from her bedroom. Television lights flickered over Julian who snored on the sofa, the gloaming across his face making his chin sharp and jutting, his neck ropy. She was still angry at him, but as each additional day passed, she was more certain that Mary killed Friar. She didn't need a vet to say so.

The knocking continued. She hurried for the door. This wasn't Mary; she wouldn't dare. Besides, Mary preferred slinking in windows to walking through doors.

The instant Willow opened the door she wanted to slam it shut again. Shock and panic washed hot and quick over her face.

Derrick Crat smiled, and his eyes looked straight into hers. "How you doing? I thought I'd stop by and see if you wanted to take a ride."

Her knees trembled. He had dark eyes, not brown, not slate exactly. Dark. She swallowed. "In your car?"

"I'm sure I'm the last guy you ever expected to see, but you'll give me a chance. Won't you?"

She didn't miss the fact that he waited for near darkness, but he at least parked at her curb. He shoved his hands into his pockets, something Papa once did. Innocent. Boyish. She thought of sweater cuffs.

"We won't stay out late," he said. "I've got curfew."

She considered how there might be legitimate reasons for his coming late:

the football team often practiced late, then he had to shower, go home, have dinner, maybe he even did some homework. His proposal still scared her, and she had no intention of going, but wasn't something as surreal as Derrick standing on her doorstep exactly what she'd been waiting for? She didn't want to tell him to leave, and she couldn't ask him in with their sorry lives on full display, and Papa like a dead man on the sofa.

"Just a few minutes?" There was the same loose, sloppy smile from class.

Suppose the world was finally opening a door for her, and she didn't walk in because she was scared? When *was* she going to be more than a stupid static duckling with one foot in the air? When *was* she going to jump into her face, as *White Mask* needed to do? The first leap was the worst. That one you wanted over ASAP. She looked down at the hole in her cut offs and the long ragged threads from the unhemmed bottoms.

"It's just a car ride. We won't go in any place people will see you."

No they wouldn't. Derrick Crat wasn't taking Willow Starmore any place public because Mary might find out and go berserk. Seeing them together, though, was exactly the punishment Mary deserved for killing Friar. Behind Willow, Julian continued his snoring. He still refused to even discuss Friar's death, and he would never admit he was wrong about Mary. "Sure," she heard herself say.

The click of his car engine and then the hum made her marvel. She was in an entirely new space. The leather bucket seats were warm, and his sunglasses swung from the rear-view mirror. Casey Kasem introduced a song on the radio. With the windows down, they drove slowly, the dash lights layering a soft wash over Derrick's face. He fumbled at conversation, and she felt herself relaxing. The song ended, and Kasem's melodic voice announced it was the first anniversary of Elvis's death. "Seventy-five thousand flocked to Graceland the first night," he said. "The roads were a traffic jam for miles, forcing the Presley family to close the gates."

Derrick laughed, "Who the hell cares about that old, dead fart?"

"My dog died." She watched him, but there was no change in his expression. "Friar," she said.

He flashed a sideways grin. "Friar? What happened to Spot? But then who names a kid, Elvis?"

"He was my grandmother's dog. She was going for *brother*."

She watched Derrick, sensing there was something he wanted to say, but he struggled to get it out. He cleared his throat and more than once adjusted the rear view mirror. "Mary doesn't need to know about this," he said. "She's got a temper you wouldn't believe."

Willow wanted to tell him she knew all about Mary's temper, and then just as quickly, she didn't want to think about Mary or for him to think about Mary. "Don't you love this song?"

"Yeah," relief in his voice. "And you and I are talking."

"We are." That fact bewildered her, too.

"If you want to punch me or something," he said, "go ahead. I deserve it."

She laughed with surprise and turned at an angle to face him more squarely, her right scapula safely pressed against the door. "Don't push your luck." This was what it meant to be a teenager, out after dark, talking with a boy in a car, a radio playing. She'd grab up the night with both hands.

An hour later, he pulled back to the curb in front of her house, keeping the engine idling. Convinced he'd never be back, because she hadn't been good enough at whatever it was he wanted her to be good at, she didn't want to get out. She could do better. "Where are you going for college?" The question sounded stupid to her, left field stupid, and she wanted it back.

He didn't laugh. "As far from Omaha as I can get." He raised a finger, touched the air here and there, going clockwise around the extreme edges of an imaginary U.S. map. "Bangor Maine, Miami, Brownville, San Francisco, Seattle. Europe, if I could."

"Why?" She understood wanting to get away, but Derrick? He had everything going for him.

He made a point of looking at his watch. "Curfew. I won't be going anywhere if I don't get through high school." He leaned over the gearshift, fresh waves of his aftershave reaching Willow like a balm of promises. "Can I kiss you?"

She held her breath, even as she told herself to breathe. He kissed her, only a peck, and pulled back to study her expression. "I'm not very good at that," she said.

He laughed. "You'll learn." He kissed her again, this time with one hand around the back of her neck, gently holding her, pulling her closer to him. They separated, and he grinned, "You're cute. I could fall in love with you."

She didn't answer.

"Curfew."

Julian hadn't moved, dishes still sat in the sink, and clutter lay everywhere. She thought of Cinderella returned to her scullery. Would she ever dance with the Prince again? Had he meant what he said, that he thought her cute and could fall in love with her?

Lying awake in her bed, with Friar's absence a gaping hole in the room, she replayed the evening: the car ride, Derrick's kiss, and his voice. She heard him repeat endless times how he thought she was cute and how he could fall in love with her.

The next night, they parked in a field a half-mile from the end of the airport runway. The roar of jet engines, the flashing lights, and what seemed like huge silver whales rising and lifting over them, felt magical. The great-bellied beings thundered with power and mysterious comings and goings to places she only saw in books or on television and while sitting slumped on a bleak and ratty sofa. This was being alive. She failed Friar, and she continued to fail Papa by not finding a way to bring him back from his shadowed wanderings. But sitting next to Derrick, power surging over and through her, all that was a world away.

"Let's get in the back seat," he said.

Crawling between the seats to the back, she landed first and then he, all legs and arms between them. Derrick kissing, unsnapping his jeans first, then hers, tugging hers down over her hips.

His speed shocked her. Was getting in the back seat a code word for *yes*? "I don't think we should," she said, but she didn't pull his hands from her clothes and didn't push him back. "Wait, just wait a sec."

"You want to be my girlfriend, don't you?"

Of course she did, just as she wanted him to desire her, but she needed a minute.

"You got a rubber?" he asked.

A rubber? So, they were really going to do it? She wasn't saying, "No," but she also wasn't saying, "Yes." Her jeans were off, then her panties, and her heart banged with so much noise she feared he would hear and laugh at her. "Derrick—"

"You don't have a rubber? You're good then?" He mumbled the question into her neck, kissing and breathing, hugging and rocking against her. His bare thighs on hers.

A plane roared so low overhead the car's windows rattled.

Yes, she was good in the sense that she wanted him to love her. She didn't really want to have sex, but she *did* want to feel desired. And despite the planes, the world outside the car seemed far away, along with her worries about tomorrow and Papa. There was only Derrick pressing his lips on hers, the weight of his body on hers. Her mind flitted over the idea that she might get pregnant, but she let it go. Tomorrow was a million miles away. It would never come, and not having a rubber wasn't slowing Derrick down. If he wasn't concerned, she wouldn't be the one to ruin everything. Besides, everyone knew you couldn't get pregnant the first time.

As I left them alone, I considered how I never conceived, never gave Thomas children of our own. After a year of marriage, I gathered the courage to see a doctor. He examined me, and then we sat opposite each other, his wide desk between us.

"I'm sorry," he said, "You'll never have a child." His face was tight with questions. Or knowing. Had he seen other cases? "You're full of scars. Pelvic adhesions and bands of scar tissue." My eyes were filling with tears, and he slowed down. "Bad infections in children, before the cervix is fully mature . . . ."

His office filled with the scents of lavender, Damask, and Mme. Francoise's baths. I knew then why I was barren. I rose and left the office before he finished explaining. On the list of things *Le Bête* took from me, I could add my children.

In the dark that night, I whispered to Thomas, "There won't be any children." I turned to the wall. The bed moved as he rolled after me and pulled me into his big arms. "Then I get to keep you all to myself."

We never spoke of children again. A few months later, I received word of Luessy.

18

Immediately after that encounter, certainly I can't call it lovemaking, they left the thundering overhead planes bounding to places unknown. Within minutes Derrick had her home again, his car idling in front of her house. "Wish I didn't have to go," he said, "but I've got curfew."

Her jeans felt tight, and the seams twisted and uncomfortable, wrong on her body. Her underwear was soiled. The Beatles sang on the radio, but she heard only the idling engine and Derrick's readiness to leave.

"You okay?" he asked, and before she could answer, he looked purposefully again at his watch.

She shifted in the seat, pulled her long hair over one shoulder and twisted it around and around. They just had sex. She wanted to talk about it, to find her place in its meaning. He'd fumbled and hurried through as though a classroom bell might ring at any moment signaling their time was up. Now, she wanted the rest, the non-rushing part where he made her feel loved, not gutted.

When he opened his door to step out and come around, she opened her own door and stepped out before he reached her. She'd act on her own, not have him standing there with her door open, all but saying, "go."

He planted a kiss on her lips and grinned. "I'll see you tomorrow night." He started back around the car, "I'm sure I can get away."

She wanted to stop him and say that it had been her first time, but she was afraid he'd shrug, "You're kidding, right?"

His car moved down the street and turned at the corner and vanished. Only then did she look at the listing porch and the house without Friar. Derrick's car had been stuffy hot, and lying under him, her head wedged against the door while his was in the cleaner air, she smelled the seat and a saturation of odors rising from impossible crevices: dust, sweat, splashes of beer, stale French fries.

Derrick hadn't taken his jeans all the way off, had only slid them down over his hips. If a policeman, or night watchman, had come to the window and tapped on the glass, Derrick could have covered himself in an instant. Their different states of undress seemed a metaphor for the evening, a feeling that she'd been the only one who'd really taken risks.

The lights in the front room and kitchen and even the television were still on. Snoring rumbled and caught and rumbled again from Papa's room. She locked the front door, turned off the lights and television, and in the dark walked through the kitchen to stare out into the backyard. The mound beneath the tree chilled her. She and Friar were both buried.

She wiped at her tears, left the window, and walked to the doorway of Papa's room. The same streetlight, giving his room dim illumination each night, outlined his form on the bed. She once ended nightmares and did away with monsters by running down the hall into his room. On those nights, he lifted the blanket, she snuggled into the warmth and security, he kissed her cheek, and he snored again—the best lullaby in the world.

She tiptoed into his room. "Papa, are you awake?"

He hadn't removed his shoes, and the sole of each one had a quarter-sized hole. The two openings stared at her like a pair of animal eyes. She imagined how he'd staggered, *Yes, Sister Dominic Agnes, he staggered down the hall and fell onto his bed.* "Papa?"

He didn't move.

A little louder. "Papa?"

He still didn't move, and she took the last step to the side of his bed. He smelled of stale wine, cigarettes, and old clothes. His whiskers were a salt and pepper stubble. She didn't want to confess what she'd done with Derrick, she'd never tell him that, but she wanted to hear his voice, to have proof she wasn't alone. "Papa? You want to talk?" She put her hand on his shoulder. "I'm sorry for what I said. I don't blame you for Friar."

He groaned, but his eyes remained closed.

She stood a long moment, sucking and biting her bottom lip. "I need you to wake up." She shook him, and his shoulder felt thin and lifeless. Still he didn't move. Her anger rose. She whispered, "You're leaving me. Just like

Jeannie and Mémé did. Just like Friar." She slapped his shoulder. "Papa! Wake up! You stupid drunk!"

Over the next few days, especially in the mornings before leaving for school and before Julian started drinking, she stayed close to him. As he made coffee, she stood at his shoulder, and as he smoked his first morning cigarette, she kept her chair close to his. She thought if she stayed near enough he'd notice she was different, and he'd know how to fix it. For certain, he'd see the fear in her eyes, and he'd know what she knew: If she didn't keep having sex with Derrick, he'd dump her. She couldn't go back to her life with mired ducks, and she couldn't let Mary win and have Derrick back.

Julian did notice her, but he believed she only missed Friar, and the way he'd disappointed her by not taking the dog to a vet, weighed on him. Though he thought his non-action was justified, she respected him less, and knowing that, hurt. He was proud of her. She'd become a beautiful woman: tall and sleek. Many days, wandering through the empty house, he looked in at her canvases or sketch book, and what he saw could make him weep with pride and shame. His emotions closed his throat against saying he loved her and made him pour more wine into his glass.

When Willow and Derrick next crawled into the back seat, she knew she should ask him to wear a condom, but she couldn't find the courage. *Rubber* was such a gross word and subject. She just didn't know him that well, and their relationship felt too fragile for such clinical talk. She could talk about math, science, art, but not say the word *rubber*. She was also tired of worrying about the future. Derrick was all she had, the only thing that mattered, and they'd already done it once, all of which was a kind of box fitted over her. When he started unbuckling his belt, she wiggled her pants over her hips. This time, too, Derrick fumbled with her breasts only through her bra, not reaching behind to open hooks and eyes, and she wondered if he avoided getting his hands near her shoulder. Embarrassed, she quit wearing a bra. They'd come from the Goodwill two years earlier, were old, gray, and still fit only because the elastic was stretched out. She didn't want him seeing them anyway. Without a bra, button by button, as nonchalantly as possible, she could open her own blouse, and Derrick would fondle her breasts, and she'd fight back tears of shame over her beggarly act. Who was *that* needy? How was it different from offering Mary her back?

After the first few times, with the fall days growing colder and shorter, her hopelessness grew. She'd lost so much already, why protest now? Lying beneath him in the backseat of his car, the radio low, she never resisted him, and she never joined him. While he pumped and grunted, she let her mind ride around and around the circle of whatever song played in the background. The lyrics taking her all the distance of a carousel horse.

19

"Willow?" The old school nurse leaned close to the door of the bathroom stall. "Is that you in there? You've been sick every morning this week."

Kneeling on the floor, Willow puked again, more of the same green crap. She spit four, five times, trying to suck traces of bile from her teeth and tongue and rid the bitter taste from her mouth.

"I must ask," the nurse's voice lowered to a whisper, though they were alone in the bathroom, "could you be pregnant?"

Hearts and initials scratched into the paint, covered the metal panels of the stall, and Willow sank back against the words, "True Love." The nurse didn't know, but Willow had been sick through the last two weeks of October, through Halloween and All Saints Day.

She could see only the nurse's white hose and shoes. The heels were worn down, but the leather, with layers of chalky polish, was titanium white. She could have reached and untied the laces. She dropped her head onto her drawn-up knees. "I can't believe this is happening to me."

The nurse sighed. "Honey, you can refuse to believe whatever you want, but it's not the mind that gets pregnant."

Willow rode the bus to the free clinic alone. Receiving a confirmation, she knew she had to tell Derrick. He didn't avoid her at school—not exactly. Walking into geometry class, he always said, "Hi," but with alphabetical seating assignments, Crat sat up front, Starmore in the back. They shared no other classes and sat tables apart at lunch. He was always beside Mary Wolfe, though he wasn't shy about smiling at Willow when passed in the halls. Something Mary noticed.

Willow spent that weekend at the library, telling Julian she had a massive research project. There she walked the aisles or cried in the bathroom. She made a phone call.

Derrick came for her again on Monday. She waited until after he'd lain on her. A few blocks from her house, she asked him to pull over. She didn't want Papa accidentally coming to the window and seeing them fighting.

Her stricken face made Derrick comply. "What's up?" he asked. When she hesitated, trying to find the words to begin, he glanced at his watch, "It's getting late."

"I'm pregnant."

He stammered. Was she sure? What free clinic? The questions went on until he slammed the steering wheel with the heels of his hands. "Fuck, no!"

Moths fluttered around the streetlight. The black dart of a bat flashed and vanished.

"Nothing?" Derrick shouted at her. "You weren't using a goddamned thing?"

"You weren't either."

"I asked about a rubber." His hands gripped the steering wheel. "I thought you were on the pill. Everyone takes the fucking pill. Or uses one of those . . . UD . . . I . . . things. What the fuck's wrong with you?"

She glanced at him. His face was the color of the ghostly moths. She looked away.

"You weren't using anything? How fucking stupid are you?"

There was nothing more to say. He knew now, and they weren't going to have a little chat about baby names. He wasn't going to smile and say, "Wow, I'm going to be a father," and she *was* fucking stupid. She stepped out of the car and away, meeting his cold stare, and then turning and starting down the walk. She'd gone only a few feet when his car tires squealed off. The noise pleased her, that cry ripping through the unfeeling night and taking him away.

He'd thought she was using something, taking care of herself. The ugly truth rocked her, felt like a soggy rag in the pit of her stomach. Why hadn't she been taking care of herself? How could she ace school and be so stupid when it came to sex? How could she spout all her liberated ideas about Eve and Pandora and not champion herself? Had she secretly wanted to ruin her life? To follow Papa's lead? Would that bring them closer in some sick way?

Her stomach rolled, the rag was coming up, gagging her. She rushed off the sidewalk and onto a browning, leaf-strewn lawn and ran for the deeper darkness between two houses. She puked and finished and half rolled, half collapsed away from the mess. Lying on her side, she hugged herself. She had no reason to go home. No one waited up for her. By this time, Papa had passed out with no awareness that she was even gone.

The low moon was an orange globe. Voices trailed from the house to her left, people leading regular lives. Sometime later, a cat sniffed at her, then streaked away when she reached out to pet it. Since having her pregnancy confirmed, she'd been promising herself everything was Derrick's fault. Blaming him fashioned a tiny room where she curled and kept herself out of the worst wind. Those walls were blowing in.

She'd stood in a phone booth, its glass so dirty she could hardly see out, and tried to make her voice sound casual. "Tory, hello. It's Willow." Would she need to say, *your niece?*

"What a surprise," Tory said. "How are you? How is Julian? I worry so about both of you."

For a brief moment, Willow wondered why Tory worried about them, but why wouldn't she? "We're fine," she started, but the lie opened the door on her emotions. She was weeping, the sobs coming from her stomach, deep as had all her puking. "I'm pregnant."

She imagined the two words traveling through the wire, flying over the city, over the fields and pastures, down into Farthest House, Tory standing in the kitchen, and the words hitting her. In the silence, she imagined Tory's words coming back, crossing the miles. "That's all right," Tory said. "It's already done then?" Her comments clipped, a bit floundering as she tried to factor in this new situation and decide how best to handle it. "So there's no use fretting about what's done. I know it seems impossible now, but these things happen. Girls get through them."

Willow was nodding, sniffling. She'd not meant to break apart.

"Are you going to keep the child?"

"Yes. And I want to give my baby a family. More than anything."

"Do you need to come here?"

That option had never crossed Willow's mind. Tory wasn't Mémé, but still she represented Willow's best years, when Papa was healthy and she'd spent her weeks with him and her weekends at Farthest House. "Could I?"

"Of course."

"Papa would kill me."

"Has he been giving you the cards and letters I've sent over the years?"

"Uh . . . " she caught herself, only just managing not to cry out, *No*.

Then Tory was talking again. "You know I have room for you. You can stay during your pregnancy. After, we'll figure out what's best."

Willow's minutes were running out, and she had no more change to feed the meter. She also found it hard to say more. At that point, she hadn't told Derrick or Papa, and she didn't want to imply Papa was certain to throw her out. Nor did she want to hint she might actually accept Tory's offer. "I have to go," she said, "but how's Jonah?"

"Older, more foolish than ever," Tory answered. "Promise to think about my offer."

In the grass between two houses of strangers, Willow stood and looked up and down the street for Derrick. Was he coming back for her? She walked toward home. The night was chilly, but still she didn't hurry. However dishonest Papa had been in hiding Tory's attempts to keep in contact, and however mad he'd be when he heard she was pregnant, she wouldn't leave him and run to Tory. The fact that she *could*, however, that Farthest House was an option, eased a bit of her fears. She wouldn't be returning to Mémé, but she'd be returning to the house she loved with its big rooms and big gardens where Jonah trimmed roses.

She'd just hold on. Mémé had said, "Care only to work," and now especially, she needed to sink down into her art, feel her way into it. Let art carry her through again. Life was easy there, not fighting any battles, where she could wink and nod and have her powers manifest on the canvas. When she did that, somehow, even if only briefly, some of what she found there followed her out like paint on her shoes.

She wiped her nose on the sleeve of her jacket. Things would be all right. Derrick was just pissed, and who could blame him? She'd known she was pregnant before the nurse called her out. She'd had days of crying and pacing. Derrick just needed more time.

The following Friday, as Willow walked home from school, Derrick's car pulled up alongside her. In the daylight, a hundred eyes were able to see them. At McDonald's, he ordered cheeseburgers, fries, and Cokes. They sat in a booth, the food untouched on the tray between them.

"I told my folks," he said.

She waited. At least he wasn't screaming, and he didn't intend to start, or he wouldn't have brought her to a public place.

"Mom went through the roof. Six hours later, she was still screaming how I was killing her. 'You love Mary Wolfe!'" he mimicked her higher voice. "Dad called me a 'jack-off,' said I'd always thought with my little head."

Willow stared at the straw jutting from the center of her flimsy lid.

"Mom bawled all night. First thing in the morning, before early Mass, she went to see Father Steinhouse. She came home telling me I was from a 'good Catholic family.' She wants us to marry."

"Marry?" Willow reached for the drink. Her mind scrambled over the word. *Marry?* Should she scream for joy, or should she run? "What'd your dad say?"

"He's so pissed, he won't speak to me again. I figure I'll get a good decade of silence out of this." He picked up a straw, tapped it end over end on the table. "He takes his rants out on Mom, and she spreads the joy onto me. He doesn't want Omaha, his cronies I should say, talking about how his son ran out on some pregnant girl. He says I've fucked up and need to face the consequences. Actually, I think he's glad. He thinks this is the lesson I need." He bit the paper tip off the straw, spit it to the side. "Like he's such a good family man, coming home at dawn smelling of gin and ass. Mom's already dragged me to Father Steinhouse."

Willow flopped back against the seat. The conversation was moving too fast, had gotten way ahead of her. "Father Steinhouse! I don't want him to know."

"Well, he does. How the hell else are we going to get married?"

Her throat felt jammed shut. She swallowed. "Who says we're getting married?"

"That's what people do. Catholics at least." He looked down at the tray of untouched food. "What else can I do?"

Willow's mind spun around lyrics of a Paul Simon song: *You just slip out the back, Jack.* "You don't have to do it."

"I do if I want to ever see my parents again, if I want them to pay for college, if I want to stay in the church. I'm not giving up my inheritance."

She knew he was an only child, and his father co-owned a large construction company. He wouldn't want to throw that all away, but still, he didn't *have* to marry her. Plenty of guys would walk away, no, run away from everything, even money. His being willing to marry her had to mean he thought they'd be all right together. Her heart was drumming, pounding the way it did in nightmares. "When?"

"Steinhouse says as soon as possible. He has an opening the Saturday after Thanksgiving."

"This Thanksgiving?"

"No, next." He glared at his untouched food. "He's probably crowding us in for Mom's sake. Those two are tight. She can't stand the thought of us possibly screwing one more time without being married." One side of his mouth lifted at the irony and dropped back. "Steinhouse says it's a busy season: The Fall Festival next weekend, then Thanksgiving, Advent, and Christmas. We have to take a shit-load of classes between now and then."

Willow was staring at him. "That's just over two weeks. Doesn't he have to post banns or something?"

"I told you, he and Mom are tight. She doesn't want this broadcast to the whole parish."

"Why?"

"Why do you think?"

"I mean why are you marrying me?"

He lifted a French fry, started it toward his mouth, but when he saw the way she fought back tears, he dropped it onto the tray. He took a deep breath. "It's not like I hate you or anything. I just didn't plan on this." He picked up the fry again, waved it in the air at her. "You got a better idea? Babies need their dads. We're Catholics."

He hadn't mentioned love, but she wasn't sure she loved him either. She'd pray that would come as it did in stories. She wanted her baby to have two parents, something she never had, and brothers and sisters. If Derrick was willing to try, she would too. She'd have six kids, and she'd never be lonely again.

"We're history at school," Derrick said. "Expelled. I think we've got a week. I'm surprised we've got a day. The week is probably Mom's doing."

"Expelled?" The news was as shocking as hearing she was pregnant.

"You'll be getting the news."

Was this really happening? "Papa will be thrilled."

20

Willow let the next week pass, going to school as usual, waiting for the best opportunity to tell Julian. When Monday came again, she told him she was sick and couldn't make it to school. On Tuesday, four days before the wedding, she stood in the kitchen doorway. There was no easy way. "I'm getting married on Saturday."

Julian looked up with surprise. What sort of joke was this? She faced him, blinking back tears, her left hand clutching the right in a choking grasp. His heart felt the touch of a hot poker. "What'd you say?"

"F.S. and . . . I mean Father Steinhouse and Derrick's mom . . . "

He wasn't hearing the names, only the seriousness in her voice. "A grasshopper's ass you are!" He studied her, still disbelieving. "You aren't marrying anybody. What are you talking about?"

"Father Steinhouse," it wasn't just him, "the church says we *have* to."

He didn't move from his place at the table, as if holding still could hold off what he was hearing. His face reddened. Ultramarine veins rose on his neck. "Have to?" His face was full of disbelief. "What are you telling me, Willow?"

She thought the words might not come out. "I'm pregnant, Papa."

"Ahh. No." He closed his eyes. Opened them. "Jesus Christ! How could you!"

She needed to lock the backs of her shaking knees, concentrate on them to keep from buckling onto the floor. She wanted to tell him she was sorry and scared, but the weight of her emotions and his crestfallen expression made her say, "I love Derrick. He loves me, too."

Julian's hands rose above the table and then dropped slack at his sides. He heard Jeannie starting to cry from the area of the sofa. He had to fight the urge to look over his shoulder for her. A tiny quake started in his knees. "Don't tell me this." He pushed back his chair, struggled to rise under the weight of the blow she'd delivered, opened the back door despite the cold, and stood facing the larger space and the bare oak tree. Wind smelling of winter blew in through the sagging screen. Jeannie was still weeping, his gut twisting.

She turned for her room.

"I promised your mother." The tremor had risen into his throat muscles. "I promised her I'd take care of you."

Willow spun back around. "What did you promise me? When do I become half as important?" Her shaking voice and his were a match. She hated that. "And just for the record, I didn't promise her a thing. She didn't stay to hear what I wanted."

He charged back to the table. "You're talking crazy. She didn't choose to die." He swung his arm, knocking a wine bottle to the floor. The green glass rolled and spun, blood red wine squirted out in tongues.

"Papa!"

"No!" He shouted the word without looking at her, his hand in the air as if to keep her from getting close. "I'll have nothing to do with you getting married. Nothing. Get out of here."

"To where? Tory said I could live there." As she turned for her room, she saw the color leave his face.

21

Going into Father Steinhouse's office with Derrick never got easier for me or for Willow. We both needed to gather our will to step inside those walls. I fortified myself by repeating over and over my resolve to stay at Willow's side, to both companion and learn. Still, going into the private chamber of a priest caused dread. Father Steinhouse never touched a child inappropriately. He thought priests guilty of the crime should be tarred, feathered, and imprisoned. Yet, he abused little girls every day in his belief that they were lesser than. Let me repeat that one's beliefs are always evident, are always communicated. His too, were suffused in his person: the way he stood, sat, spoke, and looked at her. It was in his clothes, the fat of his hands, the slack of his tired chin.

Willow sat on a chair before the priest's desk, her plaid school skirt pushed down over her knees, Derrick in a chair at her side. The walls held as many as twenty crucifixion pictures, all in sorrowful colors: charcoals, burnt umbers, deep-night navies, and shades of blood-red scarlets. She considered the paintings, fitting them into three categories: reprints of the old masters but on cheap paper and with cheap frames; oils by fair-enough artists, most better than her own work and likely purchased at starving artists' sales, and there were several that looked like paint-by-number kits done by children or palsied parishioners.

"Willow," Farther Steinhouse drew her attention back to his instruction, "you haven't listened to a word I've said in the last thirty minutes." His elbows were wide on his shiny desktop, and his short, round fingers steepled beneath his chins. "Did you hear that you must make a confession before Saturday? I won't perform the ceremony, otherwise."

She wanted to like him, even thank him; he was the shepherd taking them to the altar. He'd been the loudest voice in favor of their marriage, and she believed marrying Derrick was her only chance of having the future and family she wanted. She accepted her guilt, knew she'd been so *sick* for love that even Derrick's need for sex had been an acceptable substitute. What she objected to was Father Steinhouse's insistence that she feel shame and repentant before *him*. As if the evil thing about her pregnancy was that she usurped church authority. She had sex, used her body as though it were hers, before a priest gave his permission.

Derrick nudged her, wanting the session over as much as she. "I've already made my confession." *Agree already,* his eyes said.

She told her head to nod, yes. What was the big deal? Throughout her years at Our Lady of Supplication, the nuns routinely ushered all the students, class by class, to confession in September—as if to launder them of their sinful summers—and again at the onset of Advent and Lent, and before saints' days and Holy Days. She'd confessed a hundred times, always trembling at the gravity of her big sin, the one that never went away, the one she whispered every time she entered his black-draped, coffin-sized confessional: "I told a lie about Papa." However, being commanded to confess now felt different. Was it forgiveness he wanted for her or to see her on her knees?

The priest's eyes were narrow. "It's mandatory before the sacrament of marriage."

"Yes, Father," Willow managed. In the charged air, she shifted in her chair, straightened her skirt again, and looked sidelong at Derrick for support. Nothing. He had already confessed and was absolved. He was now blameless. She wondered too, just how much blame Father Steinhouse thought was Derrick's. Fifty percent or a number far lower?

The tired priest turned to Derrick. "You're enrolled in public school? The coaches here will miss you, but you understand we have rules."

"I start next Monday. I've already met with the basketball coach."

Father Steinhouse smiled at Derrick, and his expression fell again on Willow. "We expect our standards to be upheld at Our Lady of Supplication," he paused for five, maybe six seconds, "especially by our financially-challenged students."

I wanted to knock the man's hands out from beneath his chin, to have his head slam down onto the desktop, and do a John-the-Baptist roll.

Willow felt herself beginning to sway. She widened her hands off her lap and onto the sides of her seat and held on. She should have known all along, but had somehow managed to keep the secret from her heart. She was a charity case. Other families, like Derrick's, and of course, Mary Wolfe's, paid a higher tuition to cover her costs. Shame burned her cheeks, and her knees began vibrating, trembling the hem of her skirt. The counseling session felt twisted up with things going clear back to Sister Dominic Agnes and being "disfigured," the black paper chain that still snaked around the first-grade classroom, Mary destroying the Pandora painting out of some rage Willow didn't understand. The incidents seemed like puzzle pieces she couldn't quite fit together, and yet she knew they were somehow connected. If only she turned them at just the right angle, this into that, or if she had a few more pieces.

She stood. "I have to go. I promised Papa I'd be home early."

Father Steinhouse rose and leaned forward on his desk. "If you won't make your confession, I can't perform the ceremony."

Willow had her arms in her coat sleeves. "I've made my confession. I didn't want to say so because I was too embarrassed, but I went to someone else." It wasn't a lie. She'd told Papa. He was a priest to her, and her condition hurt him as much as anyone. "I wish I could tell you where I went, but I know you guys take oaths and can't discuss confessions. If I make another confession," she shrugged, "wouldn't that be like calling the absolution he gave me a lie?"

As she walked toward the door, I cheered her. At the same time, I wanted to linger, hoping the priest would realize how even his unspoken beliefs about females, the church doctrine he greedily accepted as his own, bled through and bruised Willow. I ached to discuss with him the church's insistence that females confess their angers, doubts, and fears (mostly church inflicted) to males. How different might the world be if through the centuries males were required to confess their deeds to women: their wars, genocides, and the perpetrated lies about females in their "good" books. Suppose they had to confess their rapes and acts of incest to women, and women meted out the punishments? On what strange planet did sinners only confess to their equally-guilty cronies?

My war was not with all males. There was always Thomas to remember, beautiful and gentle, and every inch male. A man who could pull me close and without hesitancy whisper, "I'm sorry." A man who could carry stones up a ladder for a chimney, heft a massive wooden yoke over the shoulders of a pair of oxen, kill a rattle snake with a rock in his hand, and weep over the genocide of the American Indian. A man who thought a woman's cleaved fingers important enough to document and an infant girl half way around the world worth risking his life to rescue.

Willow hesitated at the door. She felt how wrong the session had gone, again. She did want to marry Derrick, and though she couldn't stay a moment longer, she didn't want to leave things so negative. "Angels are coming, tonight," she said.

Father Steinhouse stared at her.

They left the rectory and drove back to Willow's house. Trees with leafless branches clawed against a gray, cold sky. Derrick pulled to the curb, his bloodless hands gripping the steering wheel. Willow pressed herself against the opposite door, feeling claustrophobic and depressed.

He broke the silence. "Did you tell your dad I'm moving in?"

She hated the thought. What would Derrick think of Papa's silences, the newspapers, the wine bottles, and how her house unraveled day by day like a rag in the wind? His house looked beautiful, at least from the outside, but Mary lived next door. "I will," she said.

"You were just great in Steinhouse's office. Really great, Willow."

"Because I didn't ass-kiss? I'll ask Papa if we can stay here."

"*Tell* him we are. I'm doing you a favor. You couldn't stand listening to my mother all day, and my old man . . . forget it. I'll be gone a lot with ball practice and working weekends, you might as well be home."

She buttoned her coat for the walk to the house. He didn't intend to spend any more time with her than he had to. Marriage wasn't going to cramp his style. "On my nineteenth birthday," she said, "I start getting five hundred dollars a month from my grandmother's estate."

"Five hundred? Every month?"

"Mémé left it for college. I think." She was seized by the thought that Mémé, with her visionary dreams, may have seen this coming. She whispered as if to Mémé's ghost, "I'll start school again as soon as the baby is born."

They hadn't said "hello" or "good-bye" in days—the niceties felt too taxing on top of their stress. She stepped out of the car and walked up the sidewalk toward the house Derrick had not yet entered.

Papa sat in the dark at one end of the sofa. The television was on, but soundless, and Willow doubted if he saw the moving images. She tried to tiptoe past him.

"How was your meeting?"

She still felt sick from the pall Father Steinhouse had thrown over her. She swallowed, hugging herself through the bulk of her coat. "Could we live here? Just until my birthday?"

He stood, taking the few steps to her. He'd cut his graying hair, making him look years younger. His face was still thin and gaunt and riddled with stress, but his eyes were clear, not glassy with alcohol. In them, she saw sorrow and something else. Was it guilt? Not anger?

She turned to the newspapers stacked along the wall. Why was he blaming himself for what she'd done? She couldn't carry that weight, too. Couldn't he see? "Where's your wine?" She hated herself, but how dare he be sober now? What about all the years he hadn't been? She wanted to scream, to bust up the room. "Why aren't you drinking now?"

He lifted his hands and spread his fingers in a gesture meant to calm her. "We'll be all right," he said. His voice even, as if he'd not heard her anger. "You and I. The baby. But marrying that boy?"

She took quick steps back. "His name is Derrick. You can't stop us." Did he know that by hurting him she tracked a razor over her own wrists? "I'm expelled from school too, just so you know."

His eyes darkened. "You're quitting school? No. Wait, come here."

She couldn't step into the arms he opened, couldn't let him hold her. She'd shatter. "Remember, you want nothing to do with my wedding, which is fine with me." She turned and hurried down the hall for her room.

Her paintbrushes and pencils lay still, and the Pandora canvas she scrapped clean weeks earlier looked as sickly and nauseated as she felt. She paced back and forth before the ducks on her wall and *White Mask*. Sobbed. Why was she hurting Papa and unable to stop herself? She loved him. *How many aspirin would it take to go to sleep and never wake up?* How easy, easy, easy.

But not for Papa. He didn't deserve that.

The hours trudged on as she paced and flopped across Mother Moses. Was Papa right? Could he help her raise a child? Ha! He hadn't raised his own child. Her baby's life would be different.

In his room, Julian also paced, then opened the top drawer of Jeannie's dressing table and pushed in her things: tubes of lipstick withered to kidney beans, her hairbrush and hand mirror, and the perfume bottles, the contents evaporated to dry and smoky rings. He closed the drawer and saw the tracks on top where his fingers had dragged through the dust. He pulled the thumbtack from her last picture and stared at the image briefly before he opened the top drawer again and placed it inside, facedown.

22

We watch, we wait, and we pray that our loved ones find their way. There are no other roads to take. Who prayed for Sabine when at Willow's age, in an era when there was little tolerance for women, and none for those who found themselves pregnant out of wedlock?

On Thanksgiving, Willow woke to the predawn light and the sound of the front door opening and closing. She wiped sleep from her eyes, rolled over, and on her elbows stretched to look out the window. Papa, in his shoes with holes, his breath steamy, was running down the frosty sidewalk. Loping really, as though his knees and hips pained him, and yet, he pushed himself.

Later, when families up and down the block were sitting down to turkey and stuffing, he ran again. The other hours of the day he spent in his room, avoiding the kitchen table where he normally drank. Instead, it was Willow who sat there, hoping he would come out and talk to her. She looked through newspapers from two years earlier when they discussed the earthquake in China, Nadia Comaneci's perfect 10, and Howard Hughes's death. Julian did not come out, and the only sounds assuring her he was still alive came from his constant pacing that agitated the walls and floors.

On the way to bed that night, she paused at this room and dropped her head against his closed door. Sometime after midnight, she was awakened again, this time to the sound of hushed male voices: Julian's and one only half remembered. The front door opened and closed. Again. Each time, cold air rolled down the hall and into her room. She left her bed, sat on the floor in front of her window with its pushed out screen, and watched. The two dark figures moved in and out of the streetlight's glow—Papa and Red filling Red's truck with newspapers.

She watched for several minutes, wanting to run out into the night and help, but Papa had chosen the cover of darkness. He hadn't wanted any witnesses other than Red, not even her. As the work continued, her emotions changed. Now, she wanted to run out into the night and make them stop. This was all her fault, and she didn't want to lose the secret she and Papa shared. The hoards had been just between them, a tether that was being cut.

She wondered about the emotional price Julian paid in walking to Red's house and, after seven years, asking for help. How did a proud man admit to hoarding and say he needed a friend to come in the middle of the night?

Through most of Friday, Julian again kept in motion, walking the streets until his feet were numb with cold and every couple of hours showering until the hot water ran out and cold drummed his naked body. The mirror still weeping after he left the room.

Watching it all, I thought of Thomas's pictures of sweat lodges and how Julian grew up with photographs of Native Americans on the den walls at Farthest House. And how he'd spent his childhood living on Old Squaw Road.

Late Friday afternoon, with dusk descending, Willow finished washing out the refrigerator and scrubbing the floor in preparation for Derrick's move in. He was out with his friends, a stag party this time.

She ran hot water through her dishrag and wiped off the table, marveling that it was clear, no wine bottles sitting on top, no wet glasses with burgundy-brown rings in the bottom. It was day three of Papa's abstinence, not that he was likely to stay sober. He had good intentions, she knew, but he was stunned by her pregnancy and upcoming marriage. Soon enough, he'd start drinking again. Still, she couldn't remember if she'd ever seen him *try* to quit before. Maybe a man, sober until forty-eight, didn't become an alcoholic in seven years. Drinking hadn't been the demon that forced him out of work; drinking was the demon that masked his quitting.

He surprised her when he stepped into the kitchen. His wet hair was combed, the comb's teeth marks still visible, and his clothes were clean. "I remember," he said, his eyes misting, "how you always liked dresses."

Willow's throat tightened. "I had some cute ones."

"But not for a lot of years." He cleared his throat. "Your mother's wedding dress went clear to the floor. I think there were white beads."

"Papa, I know where this is going, and I don't need a dress." She planned on her white sweater from the Goodwill and the black skirt required for all school programs. The service would be only minutes long, just the skeletal requirements for legality. The only thing that mattered was *after* the service, that she and Derrick built a life together. "It's not going to be that kind of wedding. Really, it's okay."

He opened his hand, revealing four ten-dollar bills. "There's a bridal shop just up Dodge Street. I know it's late, but I'll walk you up there."

The bit of money made her wish she could disappear. Forty dollars wouldn't buy the kind of dress he was thinking of, floor length and beads. He had no idea about prices, but the hope in his eyes was huge. He wanted her to have a nice dress. He was her father, and he had one simple wish for her, that she have a nice dress for her wedding.

Her hands lifted, her fingers intertwining and resting on the top of her head. She knew how to deal with his being drunk, how to blame him when she needed a scapegoat, and at times even how to make herself believe she hated him. She also knew how to shut off feeling until she could sit alone in the evenings without tears, or lie still under Derrick, but she didn't know how to survive this. Julian, too, was close to tears, and she felt separate from the hand that came down and accepted the money. She wrapped her arms around his neck.

"I remember how you were always asking," he said. "You've always been beautiful, but tomorrow I want you to feel it, too."

When he let go, she folded the money in half, then again, giving her hands something to do. *Forty dollars would buy so much paint.* The thought made her weak, she couldn't. If only she'd gotten the job.

"Come on, I'll walk you up there."

She couldn't have him see what dresses cost, nor have sales clerks eye him with pitying looks. She wanted to give the money back, but his hope was too high. "You've walked enough today." Was there no gas in the car for them to drive? "Let me go alone, you're going to kill yourself with all this exercise."

"I know it's not much."

She reached and kissed his cheek. It smelled of bar soap. Since Friar's death she'd said so many cruel things to him and done so many cruel things to him.

Acts she could never take back. And yet, for her, he'd swallowed his pride and called Red. "I'll bet I can find something," she said.

"While you're gone, I'll move my things into your room. You and Derrick will need the bigger bed."

She hadn't let herself think about a bed. "You can't sleep in my room."

"You think I'm afraid of a few ducklings? Get going."

"You won't even fit on that bed."

"I'll fit better than the two of you. Now go."

She obeyed, needing to get away before she lost hold of her emotions again. At the door, she reached for her coat and opened it. Mary stood there, one hand in the air as if she were just about to knock. A dress bag lay over one arm.

"What," Willow asked, "are you doing here?" *And why now?* The timing felt like stalking.

"Hello, Mr. Starmore," Mary said as she stepped inside. "How are you? I wanted to talk to Willow. Is this a good time?"

The sight of a strange teenager, acting as if they were old friends, surprised him. He looked to Willow with a raised brow.

"Papa, this is Mary Wolfe." Her own brow lifted. "Mary Wolfe."

His eyes narrowed. He didn't know Mary had been at Willow's window in May or that she'd been Derrick's long-standing girlfriend. He didn't even remember she was the one Willow accused of killing Friar, but he remembered other, older confrontations with her father.

"Can we talk in your room?" She had turned to Willow, her voice calm. "Maybe we can make a trade?"

The surprise and anger Willow first felt was changing into something more slippery. Mary had a dress to trade, now, right in the middle of a conversation about dresses? *You killed Friar.* But Willow didn't say it. Didn't for her father's sake and the expectant way he eyed the dress bag. Bringing up Friar yet again, reminding Papa of all the cruel things she'd said, would only hurt him again. Besides, there was also a tiny, or not so tiny, pleasure in the whole situation. The last time Mary was over, she acted aghast at the thought of even double-dating with Willow, and now Willow was marrying Derrick.

Mary opened her coat to reveal a creamy turtleneck blouse, and she smiled again at Julian. "When I heard the big news about tomorrow, I hoped this was my chance. I want a painting she has, and she won't give it to me." Joking, her voice a girlish chuckle. "I'm hoping this time she'll trade."

"*White Mask*?" Willow asked. "You really want it that bad?"

"You know I do. Come on." She started down the hall, knowing she left Willow no choice but to follow. In Willow's room, she closed the door and stretched the dress bag out across the bed. "You got pregnant just to hurt me."

"Trust me, you aren't that important."

Mary unzipped the bag and exposed a floor-length sheath of pale lavender brocade. The neckline had an inch-high mandarin collar, and the sleeves were tiny and capped. The dress was beautiful, slender, and elegant. "Well?" Mary asked. "You know you have nothing to wear, and I have a closet full of dresses. You can always paint another picture."

"Did you kill Friar?"

"Who?"

Papa was in his room. Willow could hear drawers opening and clothes being pulled from his closet. Would he use her dresser with the duckling handles? She felt pushed and pulled with warring emotions. "I need to know, did you kill my dog?"

"Why would I kill your dog? Is that why you got pregnant?"

Mary was never the same two visits in a row, but Papa was right, there was no evidence to prove she killed Friar, nor was there a way to bring him back. What mattered now was Papa wanting her to have a nice dress. And *White Mask*? The picture was small in comparison. "Do you want that so much just because I wouldn't give it to you?"

"What Mary wants, Mary gets. Remember that. Where's that other one, that naked one? Did you give it to Derrick? I told him about you. I wouldn't do it with him, but when he heard about your pictures, he knew you would."

"You're lying. That would be admitting to him that you snuck in and out of my house."

Mary smiled, and carrying the painting, left. With her safely out the front door, Willow returned to her room and pulled the dress from the garment bag. An index card fluttered to the floor. She picked it up. *Your baby will die, too.*

23

In the morning, Willow stood looking out the window of Papa's bedroom, her and Derrick's bedroom now. Only a few colorless leaves, more beige than copper, still trembled on the trees, and the air shuffled between drizzle and snowflakes, the temperature well below zero.

She moved around the room. With neither a basement nor a garage for storage, she and Papa had carried the dressing table to the curb where he taped a sign to the front: FREE. He stood at the front window then, looking out on the wet weather, hoping someone came soon. She returned to her new room, thinking all the while about the card in the dress bag. "Your baby will die, too."

Mother Moses lay across the bed, and Willow folded up the talisman and put it on the closet shelf. Derrick knew nothing of Mother Moses, and he'd never understand her significance.

He's going to be my husband. The thought sat her down. Now, making love to him would be fun. He'd whisper sweet things in her ear like Omar Sharif in *Dr. Zhivago.* Afterwards, she wouldn't feel like she was drowning, she'd feel loved.

With her hair washed and dried, she slipped into the dress and back into the bathroom for a look at herself. Standing on the side of the bathtub, one hand on the ceiling for balance, she tried to turn wedge-wise, her best shoulder forward. The brocade hugged her body and her still-thin waist. Derrick too, would grin at how pretty she looked, and he'd feel better about the day.

At 1:45, fifteen minutes late, Derrick's car pulled to the curb. She hurried half-mad with excitement around the edge of the main room where Julian sat in front of the television, staying out of his direct line of sight and trying to restrain the goofy smile sweeping across her face. She didn't want him to see her, not yet. She wanted him to see her and Derrick together, a couple. She opened the front door grinning.

For a long minute, Derrick looked up and down at the dress. His eyes raked the high neckline and tiny-capped sleeves and then they narrowed. "What the fuck?"

A cold blade of betrayal slid into Willow's heart, fitting itself there as though her life would always hold open a place for pain. Before Derrick could say, "Mary's prom dress!" she knew.

His face softened as he watched hers crumble. "She gave that to you?"

Willow managed to stay standing, telling herself that Derrick understood Mary's plotting. Still, she felt sick with shame, her hands folding over her stomach.

He carried a suitcase and stepped around her and into the room. Julian, not ten feet away, remained sitting on the sofa, his back to them. Derrick headed across the room.

The more pain Willow felt, the more she determined Papa wouldn't feel any. No matter the number of people who didn't understand her—or the tricks they played—they weren't her family. She rushed after Derrick.

At the sofa, Derrick, extended his hand. "Sir."

Julian's eyes were on Willow, smiling. "Look at you."

Still embarrassed by the dress, she was glad he ignored Derrick. But Derrick hadn't been the one who tricked her. She walked dumb as snot into Mary's trap. If Papa and Derrick were to get along living under the same roof, they needed to begin now. She sat down beside her father. He'd showered and shaved, and his wet hair was combed, but he wore his oldest pair of jeans. She took up his hand. They hadn't talked about his coming to her wedding. They only screamed at each other about how he wouldn't. Had she been secretly afraid he'd be drunk, and did he believe she was ashamed of him? "Papa, will you please come?"

Derrick made a point of checking the time on his watch. "I'd be happy if you came, but Father Steinhouse will be pissed, sorry sir, I mean angry, if we aren't there in about five minutes."

Willow's teeth clenched. "I will throw your damn watch in the toilet, first chance I get." She fixed her eyes on his before turning back. "Papa, we'll wait for you. Please, I really want you there."

Julian raised a hand, quieting Derrick who seemed to pace inside the space of his trousers. "You kids go on. I'll change."

Resignation dropped cloud-like over Willow. She could feel herself sinking into it, her mind passing into that middling space of obedience. That narrow shelf where the weak curled up and pretended to rest, where women were their own wicked stepmothers, passing themselves poisoned apples so that their sleep was deep, easy, and without incident.

She grabbed her old coat and followed Derrick to the door and out. She was surprised to see Mrs. Crat sitting stone-faced in the front seat of Derrick's car. No Mr. Crat. The man obviously wasn't attending, or the couple would have ridden together. She could tell Papa that Derrick's dad hadn't been there either. Maybe the absence explained how Derrick could so easily leave Papa out.

Mrs. Crat's face contracted, the eyes, mouth, even the woman's ears seemed to pull in with a pucker. *The dress,* Willow realized. Her coat quit at her waist, and the long lavender brocade swept to the ground. Mrs. Crat had likely admired every facet of it on prom night, lined Derrick and Mary up before the fireplace, and taken an entire roll of pictures.

Derrick opened the back car door for Willow, as though no other seating arrangement existed. She crawled in. "Hello, Mrs. Crat."

Silence. At least nothing loud enough for Willow to be certain she heard. As Derrick drove, she watched the back of his mother's head. Pitch-dyed hair rode above a half inch of hoar frost at her scalp. If the wedding hadn't merited a trip to the hairdresser, or even a cheap box of Clairol to *wash that gray right out of her hair,* how could she look askance at a used dress? Thank God they weren't going to live at Derrick's.

Her thoughts went back to Julian. He hadn't had a drink, at least not that she'd seen, since Wednesday when he'd swung his arm, sending wine spraying across the floor. That night, he confessed to Jeannie, the apology Willow heard creep through the floorboards to her room and up into her bones. Thanksgiving and yesterday he walked and stood in the shower, but he didn't take a drink.

She turned and looked back toward the house. The black and rusted Ford sat at the curb, likely out of gas. To come to her wedding, he'd need to walk. He wouldn't make it in time, even if he tried. She shouldn't have left him, not even with both him and Derrick telling her to do so. She should have forced him into the car with them, dressed in old jeans or not. Now, he was alone, while they were off getting married without him. Under a cloud that heavy, what father wouldn't take a drink?

There was no point trying to insist they turn back. Derrick wouldn't, and Papa would only refuse her again. The best thing was to hurry through the "I do's," pray he'd hang on that long, and get back to him. Maybe, once the formalities were over, everyone would relax.

Derrick turned into the parking lot. Only then did Mrs. Crat break her silence. "I knew your grandmother." She spoke still looking straight ahead. "I heard her speak once at a luncheon."

The comment sounded moralizing, accusing, as if to remind Willow of character she lacked. The comment also sounded absurd. Willow could picture Mémé behind a podium, her long braid and bright sweater, a room full of women listening to her read for twenty minutes from her latest novel. Then the women returning to their salads and Chablis. From one such event, Mrs. Crat supposed she knew Luessy Starmore. If a person hadn't spent days with Mémé in her attic, seen the way Mémé's whole body softened at the sight of her Damask roses in bloom, heard her read Tennyson or Whitman, they didn't know her. Willow leaned forward between the bucket seats. "Which of her novels did she read from?"

At the same instant, Derrick, nervous and distracted, pulled too fast into a parking space and hit the brake. Willow slid forward, catching herself on the console between the two front bucket seats. She saw the white gloves Derrick's mother wore and how the gloved hands clinched and cowered in her lap like a single wounded dove. At Willow's sudden nearness, the dove startled and broke apart, each wing flying up, one of the woman's hands bracing against the dash and the other rising against Willow.

After the dress and her fear of having hurt Julian terribly by not asking him earlier to her wedding, Willow wanted to crawl completely through the seats to the front and into Mrs. Crat's spreading lap. That would shock the stupid toad.

Mrs. Crat opened her door, stepped out, and hurried for the church.

Derrick walked beside Willow at a slower pace. At the bottom of the church steps, he stopped. "Jesus," he mumbled, "it's happening."

Looking across the street to the empty playground was easier for Willow than looking at him. There, the slide, swings, and monkey bars cut stark lines against the gray sky.

"So far, it's been okay," Derrick said. He continued with a thin-sounding voice, "You'll be getting money soon, Central High is a cool enough school, and ... " He stopped.

Her money and the fact that his new school was okay made a list of two. He'd tried to think of a third and failed. He hadn't mentioned her or the baby. Across from the playground sat the school and the dark windows she knew belonged to the first grade classroom. She imagined Sister Dominic Agnes there, standing just back in the shadows watching.

They climbed the wide steps of the hundred-year-old church to where his mother waited. Mrs. Crat pulled a white chapel veil from her purse and placed it on her head, the two long lacy ends hanging over her ears. She glanced at Willow's bare head, opened her purse again, one gloved hand digging, and brought up a folded Kleenex. "You better wear this."

As Derrick opened one of the heavily carved double doors, warm cavernous air, faint with the scent of parishioners and incense from a morning funeral wafted over them. Willow stepped through and past the proffered tissue, "No thank you."

I followed them down the aisle. Our Lady of Supplication was no Cave of the Bulls, had no ochered handprints on rock walls, but here too was the stuff of rites, the human need to mark life's passages with ceremony. Top to bottom, the church had its own variety of totems: friezes and moldings around the domed ceiling, gilded crosses, and a melee of richly painted statues, both winged and unwinged, with staring eyes. The two-dozen stained glass windows sent rainbows through the charged air and floated medallions of color over the slate floor. A tall bank of votive candles burned, blinking in red glasses: petitions for healings, financial gains, absolutions, quarters and dollar bills dropped into the gold collection box for hoped-for deals struck with the Divine.

Willow noticed the ten-foot statue of the Blessed Mary was moved from the elevated chancel and placed at the far end of the communion rail on the main floor. She wasn't sure when Father Steinhouse had the Holy Mother's image all but removed. Was he backing it out a bit at a time so that no one realized the actual moment it vanished?

Mrs. Crat, her face still strained and her gloves still stark, gave Derrick and then Willow a tormented look and dropped into the first pew alongside Derrick's two cousins who would serve as best man and maid-of-honor. She pressed to her mouth the tissue Willow refused and lowered her head. Her shoulders began to tremble.

"Derrick," Willow whispered, "she's crying."

He frowned and then shrugged. "She bawls at card stands and baby food displays."

Despite his offhanded comment, Willow knew his mother's distress upset him. It was there in the way he kept glancing at her and his shoulder muscles tensed.

As if on cue, Father Steinhouse stepped through a nearly invisible door from the sacristy, walked across the altar, and down. He said nothing to Willow or Derrick, but went to the first pew and sat down beside Mrs. Crat. He put his arm around her shoulder, and she sank against him, the ends of her white chapel veil falling onto his chest. Her words were muffled.

Willow had never seen F. S. touch anyone other than to shake the occasional hand after Mass. This familiarity went far beyond the cursory, "Hello," though their relationship didn't feel sexual. Willow was fairly certain that sleepy Father Steinhouse didn't have the stamina for that, but certainly their relationship went farther back than just the upset of Derrick's marriage.

Mrs. Crat cried briefly and then sat up straight, shifting away from the priest, as if suddenly aware they were being watched. He stood and motioned for the cousins to follow and then to Derrick, "You have the rings?"

While Derrick brought out their two gold bands, Willow watched Mrs. Crat sitting alone. What had she said to Father Steinhouse? When Mrs. Crat looked up, Willow held her gaze. *Just wait,* Mrs. Crat's eyes seemed to say, *you'll learn real heartbreak, too.*

"Let's begin," Father Steinhouse said.

The wedding party followed on his heels and climbed the three wide marble steps to the altar. Willow turned away from Mrs. Crat. Willow had been experiencing a slight dizziness since entering the church, and rather than abating, it grew. The air around her felt charged, buzzing, the yawning space filling with the sound of bees.

"Miss Starmore," Father Steinhouse sighed, "can we begin?"

Derrick stepped back to her, his voice nearly a whisper, "Come on. Let's get this over with."

She ignored him. The buzzing sense of *otherness* had goose bumps splashing over her shoulders. Something, she couldn't decide what, wanted her attention. She looked around at the statues on plinths with their imploring hands and saintly eyes lifted heavenward. She'd seen it all through a hundred school Masses. Still, something was terribly wrong. Or terribly right. She sat down on the step, using dizziness as an excuse. "I just need half a sec, or I'll faint."

She saw it then, lying on the far end of the communion rail and in front of the statue of the Holy Mother, a place she'd looked not more than five minutes earlier. A Damask rose.

Derrick squatted at her elbow. "Come on, you're pissing everyone off. Your old man isn't coming."

"I know, but look," she pointed. "It's a Damask." Her face widened in a smile. "It has to be from Mémé."

"That flower? You want that flower? I'll get it."

"No. I will."

"Come on, Willow, don't start this."

"Your mom's here," she said, "F.S. has to be nice in front of her." She didn't want to cause a scene, but Mémé was also there. That realization changed her mood suddenly from elation to shame. Mémé was seeing her pregnant at eighteen, wearing a dress she'd been tricked into, Papa's absence, and all of that after Mémé had dreamed so much for her.

She stood. She didn't doubt Mémé's ability to join them, but trusting Mémé wanted to join them required a bigger leap of faith. Why would Mémé come now, after so many years in which Willow ached for some sign from her? Why hadn't Mémé appeared in the back seat of Derrick's car and kept their clothes from coming off? Why hadn't she come the night Friar needed protection from Mary?

"She's coming," Derrick was saying, "she found a flower."

Going as slowly as she dared, Willow went back down the chancel step and down the length of the long communion rail. She picked up the flower, and as she did so, it twisted in her hand, a single quick wrench that sent a thick bristle, sharp as a thorn, into her finger. A garnet of blood beaded from the wound. Mémé had indeed come to her wedding.

A shaft of light broke into the back of the church, and before Willow could look up to see who had opened the door, she knew Papa had arrived.

The sunlight backlit his silhouette. His height and the light combined to fill the doorway. He stepped inside, slightly out of breath, his eyes adjusting to the dim and scanning the altar area where the body of the wedding party stood. His lips were pressed together, hardly more than a line until he saw her, by herself. His lips turned up at the corners, and he started down the aisle, not hurrying now, but purposeful, his old shoes with a hole in each sole, polished. To Derrick's casual khakis and navy blue blazer, Julian wore his dark suit, something Willow had not seen him wear since Mémé's funeral and the raven's visit. In the suit, his shoulders rounder and thinner than when she'd ridden them, he looked a generation past and representative of something lost in her own generation. He meant to carry on. He was an old-time man who from this day forward intended to act with honor.

He moved as balanced as the dancer Mémé had seen in him, and Willow thought of Sister Dominic Agnes across the street in the convent or classroom. The nun once asked Willow if he avoided going to church because he couldn't walk straight down the aisle. Someday, in some eternal mind-reel, Willow hoped the nun would have to watch this moment over and over.

She glanced down at the rose and the garnet of blood on her fingertip. Mémé had sent both, but the bigger gift had been holding up the service for Papa.

While the group on the altar stood hushed, and even Mrs. Crat turned to look, Julian passed through the varied colors of light streaming through the stained-glass windows. His suit changed hues as he was touched by scarlet, maroon, and gold. He didn't come far though before he stopped and held out his hand. Willow walked to him carrying her rose and put her arm through his. He walked her down the aisle.

Papa had returned, she was positive, even if he'd be unsure himself for months or years. He'd bested the raven, and that was bigger than her wedding.

24

The sun not yet up, Derrick gathered his things in the dark and crept from the bedroom. Willow pretended to sleep, though she'd spent the last few hours awake. He showered and dressed in the bathroom and tiptoed through the main room with his books and shoes in hand. When she heard the soft click of the front door close behind him and then the louder, freer sound of his car accelerating down the street—the sound of someone believing they'd escaped—she rolled from her side onto her back.

Her head pounded. The first thirty-six hours of Holy Matrimony had been anything but holy. Saturday night, their first night as an officially wed couple, he stepped into the bedroom, looked around at the walls in need of paint, the shabbily dressed windows, the old bed, and in his throat cursed, "Holy shit."

With his disbelief and disappointment still hot on her skin, he crawled into bed. Before their marriage, he'd used sweet-talk. She thought of it as white-lies, a form of posturing and pandering. It was beggarly and dishonest, but it was still a form of asking. The last two nights as her husband, he acted as if her body were a purchased object, certainly an entitlement. When he finished, he rolled off, turned his back to her, and retreated into a space as small and hard as a walnut chamber. His attitude hurt as much as the empty sweater cuff he raised years earlier to make the class laugh at her.

She continued staring at the ceiling, her gaze following a plaster crack, the fracture creeping from one end to the other and looking like a child's black magic-marker line. She once set up rows of empty wine bottles to see her reflection there, to fool herself into believing she existed despite Papa's drinking, or existed in his drinking, and now if it were possible, she'd set up more rows of fun-house mirrors that let Derrick see only her best side. She'd spend her life standing wedge-wise, her feet planted heel to insole, like photographs of women trying to hide their wide hips. She'd be whatever he wanted her to be, and then he'd fall in love with her. He'd have to; she'd be his creation.

The thought of that future scared her, but all futures were scary. At least her baby would have two parents.

The smell of coffee brewing and the sound of Papa closing a cupboard door finally made her push back the blankets and swing her feet over the side of the bed. She reached back and slugged Derrick's pillow. "Take that, Crat!" She went to the closet and brought Mother Moses down from the shelf and wrapped herself in it.

Julian leaned against the kitchen counter dressed in the suit he'd worn to her wedding, steam lifting from his coffee cup. At the table, a cigarette burned in the ashtray. He smiled. "How's the new bride?"

"Restless. Where you going?"

He hesitated, "To see a man about a job."

"A job?" She wanted to hug him, but his severe nonchalance told her he didn't want fanfare. He wasn't proud of his situation. "You're getting back on the force?"

He set his coffee down and turned the mug back and forth before stepping to the table, taking a drag on his cigarette, and returning it to the ashtray rim. "Not exactly."

"Why not go back to your old job? They didn't fire you. You're trained; your record is clean."

"I'm done with that."

"Why?"

"I'm applying for a security cop job."

"You mean a mall cop? You're kidding."

He didn't look at her. "Yes. Different events too, it depends where they need me. Teenagers acting up in food courts, shoplifting, that's as deep into crime as I want to go."

"You loved your work."

"A man changes." He nodded a good-bye and walked from the room. The front door opened and closed.

Happy for him, though frustrated, she sat at the table considering. What secret was he always so determined to keep from her? She'd never know because he never gave clues.

On the table, his cigarette still burned in the ashtray. He'd left another cigarette burning the day before, but that one hadn't given her much thought, except to be thankful the stacks of fire-thirsty newspapers had been carted off. Studying this cigarette, she lifted her hair off her shoulders, twisting it until the length coiled up tight against her head. The burning cigarette didn't mean anything, she promised herself. Papa deserved to be taken off her list of worries. Was it any wonder he was distracted: his slaying his netherworld raven, Derrick invading their house, her pregnancy and marriage, and now, after so long, his going to apply for a job.

She watched the cigarette smoke rising, the thin patterns drifting into the air, the smoldering and morphing, the streaming ashen color and the lazy curves climbing, tugging on her tired brain. Her hair fell from her hands and uncoiled to fan across her back. The hypnotic spirals of smoke twisted up into one lazy bloom after another and made tiny, smoky roads and pathways that led into other flowering shapes. Some of the forms might have risen off Mother Moses, winged birds, fronds in a breeze. She thought of Farthest House and the gardens and Mémé with her long skirts and cat-head cane. She considered how the flowers, one on top of the next, were at first tight blooms before they spread and disappeared. The longer she sat and watched the ever-changing drifting images, the more she saw female faces in the smoke. Or parts of faces: a chin, an eye, the curl of a lip, only to reach a height and fade. But easy, easy the letting go, giving up their space for the next.

She looked down at Mother Moses, feeling admiration for the slave woman who in surviving the unimaginable helped birth the next generation of daughters and the one after that. A woman who hadn't had the right to say who touched her, either to rape her or whip her, because her body was property and owned by someone else. Yet, she endured, carried by her art.

Willow smiled, wanting to stand and twirl around the kitchen. She, of course, would do the same. There was so much inside her waiting to be discovered. What was Derrick's mood, good or bad, in light of this volume? She was a painter. With *her* work to do.

The eyes of the crocheting stretched wide over her shoulders, and she felt that if she only dared, she could slip like Alice through one of the thousands of gathered up spaces. How like the gaps between those stitches the world was proving to be, the knots having less substance than the space between them.

She looked again at the smoke, watched it unspool before her, and knew she needed to tell the stories of the women on whose backs she'd come. They weren't recorded in history, which made her work that much more important, but like all women, they were part of the chain, each link of equal importance. Her line of female ancestors: Mother Moses, Mémé, Sabine, and I, the strange woman from the rocks were as vital and as mythical as any from the Greeks.

She rose grinning and looked around the kitchen as if she saw us all there. She would tell our stories, just as Mémé told the story of Mother Moses. Her medium wouldn't be words, but paint, and in telling them, she'd be telling the stories of countless women. Women who were ignored in history texts, but who could shout from gallery walls.

Julian's cigarette was nearly burned away, but she snuffed out the remaining butt as if to put an explanation point on the inspiration she'd received. The paintings, several of each woman and depicting the different phases of their lives, was a long commission that could take a few years. The length of the project felt fitted and welcome. Derrick could go on with school; she'd return soon enough. Meanwhile, she'd be just as busy learning and painting.

She wondered how without tintypes, sepia prints, and even grainy photographs, she could execute the images. She didn't even have a picture of her own mother. She'd destroyed them. Frida Kahlo had gotten around the problem by painting her face into her ancestor's faces, and that idea felt as fitted to Willow as the entire project.

She needed paints, and with Mother Moses still wrapped around her, she headed back to her room. When she tried to give Julian back the forty dollars, he closed her fingers around it. "You need other things." She supposed he meant maternity clothes, but she didn't need them yet, and she didn't need anything else as badly as art supplies.

On the dresser, Mémé's rose stood in a tall glass of water. Willow lifted the flower and watched clear droplets slide off the end of the stem. The outer petals of the rose were drying and spreading, just as she'd seen in the smoke, but the heart of the rose still held rich color and even the pure and sweet Damask scent. On the wet stem, what began as no more than a series of tiny barbs at the top grew stouter and sharper, until at the bottom they were thick thorns. She pressed the longest and sharpest into her upper arm, piercing the skin, twisting the thorn, until it tore flesh and drew a bead of blood, just as Mémé had done to her in the church. She repeated the process, remembering and promising each woman who had visited her in the kitchen.

25

✦

In July, Derrick stood beside Willow, using the neck of a beer bottle to point at the picture on her easel. "What kind of weird shit is that?"

Engrossed in her work and with the July heat so thick she had to lean into it the way she leaned into strong winds, she hadn't heard him coming up the apartment stairs or opening the door. She'd lost track even of the hours she sat tipped forward, her fingers clutching a brush. Now, torn from that quiet, interior space, she felt the ache in the small of her back. Already two days past her due date, she thought herself a porpoise. She leaned back and kneaded her pain. The clock over the stove read almost 6:30. "You worked late," she said.

Derrick took another drink, longer this time. He shifted his weight. "Who's that? You?"

Standing, hoisting her stomach, she looked from his beer bottle hanging at groin level, to the picture. He'd spent the day working on a cement crew for his father's construction company and now, still in his dirty jeans, steel-toed boots, and with sweat and dust coating his arms and hair, he looked as uncomfortable as she felt. "It's not suppose to be me," she said, "though her face is modeled after mine. It's my great-grandmother, Mémé's mother. Her name was Sabine."

"Paint clothes, that's gross."

"Gross because she's pregnant?"

"How many hours did you waste today, doing that?"

She crossed her arms, one hand on the pattern of thorn scars. "What should I have done? Practiced my high dive?"

They'd argued before about her paintings, and when they stopped, she was never sure what exactly the arguments had been over. Papa had never objected to the long hours she spent in front of her easel, and she couldn't imagine why Derrick would either. She suspected he was vaguely jealous—even if he had no desire to paint. It wasn't envy of her art, but of her having it. As the summer progressed, he was becoming more depressed about the fall. No college recruited him to play football, and he was enrolled at the local Jesuit University, which didn't even have a football team. Nor did he have a campus life to look forward to. He'd be there, with her and a child, studying with an undeclared major. He didn't blame her for his not being recruited, and he admitted that high school heroes were often third-string bench warmers when it came to the college level. Still, she feared he saw her as a symbol of his lost dream—leaving Omaha and playing for a Division I team.

His scowling and half-concealed anger over her painting ate away at her vision. She briefly thought of turning the picture around, but didn't. The point of the painting *was* Sabine's pregnancy, and to get the strongest sense of that, the figure needed to be naked with the unborn child just visible in the womb. The long piece of rich brocade draped over her lap, represented modesty, innocence, and even privilege. Though Willow knew wealth didn't separate one woman from another when it came to childbearing.

Derrick wiped the cold beer across his dusty forehead, "Just asking."

She took the beer from his hand, wiped the cold across her own forehead, handed it back, and headed for the wall holding their kitchen appliances. She had another painting started and leaned up to the wall behind the easel. *Prairie's Coming* was a simpler painting: just an unborn child curled in a sea of blue, which symbolized both amniotic fluid and the idea that babies are born from, and into, a global space.

"You want a hamburger?" she asked. "Actually, that'll have to be a hamberdog. We only have hot dog buns."

She watched beads of sweat track down the sides of his face and how he pulled her straight-back chair away from the easel and sat down. He'd need most of his beer before he stepped into the shower. Without taking his eyes from the picture, or answering her, he worked at untying his laces, jerking wide the mouth of his shoe, and accidentally banging his hand against a front leg of the easel. "This thing gets on my nerves. It's too damn big. Can't you get something smaller?"

She turned on the kitchen faucet to splash water over her own sweaty face and wash paint from her hands. The easel felt alive to her. Some days, when she thought she might do something other than paint, it called her. This was one of the reasons she wasn't interested in a new one, the cheap kind with three skinny legs and less heft than a toy balsa wood plane. "Are you hungry or not? It's too hot to turn on the stove, if you're not going to eat."

Tugging one shoe at a time, he let them drop on the floor and peeled off his sweaty socks. Taking the last swallows of his beer, he headed for the bathroom. "It's a fucking furnace up here." The door slammed.

Willow frowned and slid the frying pan from the back of the stove to the front burner—the one of the four burners that actually worked. Sitting at the easel, she'd leaned forward, her breasts resting on the dome of her stomach, where patches of hot skin had met patches of hot skin, and sweat pooled. Now that she stood, the moisture trickled down her sides. She pushed her fingers into the blood-red meat she'd taken from the refrigerator and pulled off a fistful.

Grease splattered and sweat continued to roll down her sides. She felt she'd been sweating since they moved into the place in May. The day they first looked at the two rooms, the space was empty. It seemed larger and was definitely twenty degrees cooler. She'd smiled at the hardwood floors, the same color stain as the floors at home and just as worn. She'd gone to the window and looked out at the sky, grinning at the idea of living on the third floor, so like the attic at Farthest House. Their soon-to-be landlord pointed out there was no central air, but he assured them they were high enough to get a good breeze. Standing at the window that day and looking out at the neighborhood grocery store where she'd ridden up and down the aisles on Papa's shoulders, Willow picked out his rooftop just two blocks over. "It's perfect."

Derrick also liked the place. The rent was the cheapest they'd found, and he meant to work as many summer hours as he could. Neither of them imagined summer heat and humidity where milk curdled in the refrigerator and sleep was nearly impossible. Their furniture came from the Goodwill: a kitchen table and two straight-back chairs, a bruised red velvet sofa with a matching and equally lumpy velvet chair, a coffee table, and a black and white television. The lava lamp Derrick brought from home. They could sit at the kitchen table and rest their elbows on the back of the sofa.

Space in the bedroom was just as tight. With their bed and a crib squeezed in, they couldn't walk between the two pieces and had to enter and leave the bed by crawling in and out at the foot.

Derrick came from the bedroom dressed in clean shorts and holding his shirt in his hands. He took another beer from the refrigerator, while she halved the hamburgers with her spatula and placed the halves lengthwise in hot dog buns. "You going out?"

"Maybe."

"Which means you are."

He looked at her, "You want to come?"

"Sure. I'll put on something slinky and we'll do the town."

"You think tonight's the night?"

His question made the baby in her womb stir. She reached for the ketchup bottle. "I've thought it was *the night* for the last two weeks. Maybe the baby knows it's cooler inside, and she's not coming out until fall. Look." She put down the ketchup and lifted her shirt to show the slow motion of an unborn heel or knee move across the top of her stomach.

Derrick's brows came together, and he spoke through a mouthful of food. "Who'd ever believe a stomach could stretch that much?"

She pulled down her shirt. "I'm part Latex. It was in the marriage contract."

He finished eating and headed for the door, the shirt he'd hung over the back of his chair in his hand again. "I'm just going to have a few beers."

"Where?"

He held the door open, ready to step out. "In air conditioning. This guy's house. You don't know him."

"Derrick?"

He turned back and waited while she stared at him. He'd become even better looking over the summer, tanner, and stronger. His life felt almost alien to hers, and she didn't know how to ask for what she needed. If she asked him not to go, that would be an excuse to leave because she was a clinging nag who suffocated him. If she said go, that would be an excuse to leave because she didn't care about him. Either way he was leaving, and either way it was her fault.

"Nothing," she said.

She stood at one of the street-facing windows. Like all the windows in the apartment, this one was raised, but there wasn't enough breeze to stir the dust on the sill. She lifted damp strands of hair that had fallen out of her ponytail, twisted them up and off her sweaty neck and tucked them back into her rubber band. She'd never lived in a house with the distractions of small chatter, never needed someone in the room with her, but now she was huge and uncomfortable, and that changed things.

Derrick appeared on the walk below her and headed for his car, his shirt swinging over his shoulders, his arms punching into the sleeves, jubilant and athletic in his motions.

A flash of bright color at the end of the block, no more than a half-second streak of lemon yellow caught her eye: Mary's car. Or had the color been mango, maybe gold? She turned back into the room. She was probably letting her imagination get the best of her; the low sun added a golden wash to everything. Mary had been calling though, even if Derrick denied it. Did he suppose her too pregnant to notice how he jumped for the phone, saying nothing beyond, "Hello," but listening, then after a minute placing the phone back on the cradle? "Wrong number."

Willow didn't know where Mary had been in the months since the wedding, but she was back now, *when I look most like Flipper,* she thought. Still, she trusted Derrick wasn't having sex with Mary. They hadn't been doing it in high school when everyone else was, and when he came home after an evening out, he always insisted on it no matter how long Willow had been asleep or how exhausted she was. At least, he had until a few months ago, but who could blame him now.

She wouldn't spend the evening thinking about Derrick, or Mary, and she went to her easel. The unfinished painting of Sabine showed her in profile and looking into a mirror. With the majority of her face seen only in reflection, there was a slight psychic disconnect. Sabine's body was on the chair, and her sad face in the mirror opposite her.

To find the place where she spent the afternoon, the breathing place, Willow had only to begin. Inspiration found her when she began dabbing her brush in color, feeling the slight weight of it in her hand, stroking crimson onto the canvas.

As she worked in the quiet, and I studied the picture of my sister, I couldn't stop the memories from flooding through me. The Beast's room, too, had rich brocades, along with silks and satins on the walls and bed, ancient hanging tapestries, and a ceiling painted to look like a garden. I could hear his voice in my ear, "God says you must stop crying."

Lying on his bed, quaking, I imagined my body full of birds: rock doves, skylarks, redstarts, and nightjars. When he pushed into me, the birds burst out of my mouth, my ears, my eyes, flying away until only my empty skin remained, silenced, because what was left to make noise?

Trapped inside by stained-glass windows, the birds flew to the ceiling where trees were never touched by wind, clouds never sent rain, and lifeless flowers had no scent. Reaching that ungarden, the birds flapped and beat against the dry plaster. Feathers dropped. Then, whole birds fell all around, soft thuds beside me on the bed, on the crimson carpets, dying, dying.

When he was done, The Beast walked to the basin across the room, poured water from a pitcher frosted in gold, and washed himself. "Kneel, Amelie-Anais. Confess your sin to me. Ask God to forgive you."

All this I left for Sabine.

26

Early afternoon of the next day, with the heat and humidity churning the air and tracking sweat down her body, Willow's contractions began. Derrick hadn't come home the night before—a first, though he often came home late—and his steel-toed shoes still sat wide-mouthed in front of her easel. Protective shoes were mandatory on the job site, which meant he was not at work. There was no use calling there, and if she did, and Derrick had called in sick, she'd be ratting on him.

She paced and cleaned, pouring out the curdled milk in the refrigerator, wiping down the shelves and making the bed. She needed to keep busy, and she kept reminding herself that Derrick's absence might not be for the worst reason she could imagine, Mary. A whole host of things might have happened.

Not wanting to time her contractions and frighten herself, she timed her trips to the window, not letting herself go more than once in any ten-minute period. Each time, looking down on the empty street and seeing that Derrick wasn't there, she felt something pitch inside her. Then pressure built behind her eyes, her hands started shaking, and her mind played old tapes. She needed to be fixed; she was disfigured.

She swept the floor with a worn broom, dust bunnies coming from the corners, sand and white dust from Derrick's shoes. Her doctor had told her not to rush to the hospital, overreacting when labor was sure to take several hours. She still had plenty of time for Derrick to screech his car to a stop in front of the apartment building, sprint like a madman up the three flights of stairs, and gather her in his arms.

The sweepings slid from her dustpan into the trash. She could call Papa or walk over to his house, but then he'd know before Derrick, and he'd be full of shameful questions about Derrick's whereabouts.

Late into the previous night, she'd worked on the painting of Sabine, but she took that work off the easel, the still-damp oils sticky, and leaned *Prairie's Coming* on the ledge. She chose the name Prairie for her daughter because the name was not listed in *The Book of Catholic Saints*. This meant it would never be written with a black marker on a square of blue felt and worn for a scapular. *Prairie* meant place: land and a physical spot on the Earth where one belonged. *Prairie* was a prayer that the infant's life be grounded, as Mémé had wished for Willow when she buried Willow's cord at Farthest House.

Derrick scoffed at the name, confident the child would be a boy. "Derrick II."

Squeezing small dabs of blue and then white onto her palette, she took up her brush, determined to stay at the task until inspiration caught her up, transporting her beyond even the deep skin of art to where time had no meaning and waiting a minute or an hour would be the same thing.

By ten o'clock, the streetlights below her apartment windows were globes of yellow and lightning bugs blinked like scattered, nocturnal eyes, opening and closing. Long gripping contractions burrowed across her lower back, wrapped around to carve equally deep trails across the front of her stomach. Their strength scared her. She had no choice now but to call Papa, and she held the phone ashamed of what she knew would be his first question.

"Where's Derrick? How long you been hurting?"

She twisted the telephone cord around two fingers. "He called a while ago. I was fine then."

"Where is he?"

"Can you come? I think it's time."

Julian was there. Hurrying up the three flights of stairs before Willow put the phone back and thought to step into her rubber flip-flops and pull the bag she'd packed from under the bed. In his car, she watched his hands gripping the steering wheel, as every half block he asked her again how she was doing and then answered himself before she could. "Having a baby is a lot safer these days. Hospitals are the best way to go. Yeah, being in the hospital, you'll be all right." He slowed the car minimally at a red light and went through. "In a hospital, they'll have everything you need, good doctors."

"I'm scared," she heard herself admit. "Damn doctors couldn't save Jeannie and couldn't fix me." *Where was Derrick?*

He glanced at her and took the next corner so fast she rocked against the door.

"What if she has my shoulder? What if both her shoulders . . . "

"All right, now, that's enough of that."

"We don't know what—"

"Don't Willow."

"I'm not six. You can't scold me for talking."

He walked at her side through the wide emergency doors, so close she could slump against him if need be, and into the lobby where one of her shaking hands brushed one of his shaking hands, and the two sets of fingers slid one into the other and held on.

The night receptionist called a nurse, and Willow answered questions and received a wrist band and was helped into a wheelchair. She and Julian didn't speak to each other.

"I'll take her to maternity," the nurse told Julian. "You fill out the paperwork here, and I'll come back for you."

At the end of the hall, the nurse turned a corner, and Willow, from her wheelchair, glanced back at her father. She did not take her eyes off his aging face until she could no longer see it.

The morning sky still held pink, azure, and opal, when first Julian entered the room and then Derrick on his father-in-law's heels. Julian stood on one side of the bed, asking her how she was doing, while he absentmindedly pestered the coins in his pocket, bouncing change in his hand, only to drop it in the linty bottoms of his pockets and pick it up again. His eyes kept flashing anger at Derrick, who stood on the other side of the bed.

Derrick's right jaw was scraped and red. He had the beginnings of a black eye and two black stitches in his brow where a nurse first used a tiny razor and shaved a thin, white clearing. He smelled of Mercurochrome and put his face too close to Willow's, showing her every injury.

Julian had remained at the hospital during Prairie's birth and came into the room after to grab Willow's hand and hold his granddaughter, tears filling his eyes. He hadn't left until Prairie was taken to the nursery and Willow dozed. When she next opened her eyes, the chair he'd occupied was empty. Now she knew he'd gone and found Derrick, and there'd been a reason to hit him. She wanted to throw back the sheets, get on her knees, and blacken Derrick's other eye.

At the same time, she was exhausted, and her body felt full of a dreamy lightness. The birth was over, and her body reclaimed. Most importantly, Prairie was beautiful. Her soft, pink back, smaller even than Willow's hand, was smooth and symmetrical. With so much to be thankful for, couldn't she forgive Derrick, pretend his absence hardly mattered? She wanted to tell Papa to *stop, don't ruin the morning, act like a woman and deny you're in pain,* but she couldn't shut out his anger. His thoughts, full of rage, threw a red arc over her to Derrick.

"Prairie is beautiful," she said, a peace offering to the room.

Derrick's head bobbed too much in agreement, proving he hadn't yet walked down to the nursery. He sputtered for words, an easy joviality. "We thought it was going to be a boy, didn't we?"

"Yes, she is," Julian said, but his emotions roiled with a far different concern. These slammed into Willow, and she tried to shut them out, but couldn't. *You bastard*, his mind was wild. *You don't deserve to be a father. She could have died having your baby!*

Willow's fingertips were white on the sides of the mattress she clutched. She felt herself dropping through the floor of the room and on through floor after floor of the hospital, dropping like some hapless Alice into another world. She saw it then. Papa walked through the door of the Wolfe house. Mrs. Wolfe gasped at the sight of a stranger and then recognized him. Grief and acceptance pulled her face and sent her back to the kitchen where she'd been sitting at the table, a cocktail in her hands, her eyes staring straight ahead. Her actions telling Papa both that Mr. Wolfe was not home and that his instincts were correct.

"You all right?" Julian asked Willow, his gaze washing back and over her face. "She's a beautiful baby."

Willow's breath was ice, and the frigid air moving in and out of her lungs painful. She couldn't immediately unpack everything she'd seen in Papa's mind. There was too much shocking information. She'd have to break it into pieces, just as she did any too-heavy weight. She wanted them both gone: Derrick for being with Mary, and Papa for making her see it.

"You better rest," Julian said, his eyes narrowing with concern. When she failed even to nod, he took up her hand. "I'm sending in a nurse. Prairie is beautiful, and you're fine. That's all that matters."

She wanted to reach for him, to have him hold her, and take her back to when they watched football games on television, threw a ball in the backyard, and he made all boogeymen go away.

Eyeing Derrick, he nodded at the door, and the two started out, single file again, Papa in the rear.

Kill him! Willow's mind shouted. *I wish he was dead!*

Julian hesitated, glanced back with questioning eyes, winked, and the two left.

She couldn't close her eyes against what she'd seen through his. How he took the stairs in Mary's house, threw open the only closed door on the second floor, hit the light switch, saw Mary and Derrick on the bed scrambling apart, both naked, Derrick jumping to his feet to stand beside the bed, his low and frantic, "Fuck, fuck," Mary wailing and reaching out for some covering she didn't find because both the blanket and sheet were on the floor, Mary's hands on her chest, slapping as though a fire still raged there, trying to cover up every inch at once, not cupping her breasts to hide them, the dark areolas of her nipples burned and scarred away, only the exposure of her scars mattering, not her blond pubis, not being caught in bed with Derrick, only trying to hide the white froth of scars that puckered her skin from armpit to armpit and from her throat halfway to her navel.

Lying in her hospital bed, Willow struggled not to make any noise that would alarm the nurses. She turned on her side, and even catching the scent of the bleached and disinfected sheets, she wiped her eyes and nose with the hem of the pillowcase. Mary's burns had likely happened in first grade when the class cut and glued the black paper chain and prayed endless rosaries. The scars explained why Mary needed to run her fingers around the ridge of Willow's bone—all the time keeping her own larger disfigurement hidden. The scars explained her turtlenecks and mandarin collars, her anger over the Pandora painting with its bare chest visible through gossamer, her visits after Christmas dances and proms when other couples were crowding eight to a motel room, shedding tuxes and dresses and four to a bed, passing out rubbers and shots of whiskey.

"Willow?"

Rolled in a ball, she wiped her face again on the pillowcase, a wet, slick hem now, and looked out at the nurse holding Prairie. "It's not quite feeding time, but your dad asked me to bring her in for you."

Willow held out her arms.

In the evening, Papa and Derrick stepped back into the room. The purple around Derrick's eye had deepened, the bruising reaching down onto his cheek, the bridge of his nose was newly swollen and knotty, and Papa's right hand was wrapped in an ace bandage. They'd fought again, and the hatred that raged between them earlier in the day was still cold and bitter, but also changed.

She hated that they'd reached even this frigid resolution, and the rest of what happened the previous evening flooded over her: Mary screaming at Papa, "Don't look at me you fucking pig!" Derrick's eyes droopy and slow, looking at Mary, wincing at the sight of her chest in the light, turning back to Julian, and only then looking down at his own nakedness, covering himself with his hands, Mary's hysteria increasing, her rolling over, her white buttocks in full view, "Get the fuck out of here!" Papa stepping up to Derrick, his fist rising, Derrick's head snapping back with the hit, and Mary wailing, "I'll kill you for this, you fucking pig." Papa's eyes lifting to *White Mask* hanging on the wall above the bed.

27

Stepping back into the apartment, this time with Prairie in her arms, things at first looked the same to Willow: cramped space with a sagging sofa, a lava lamp with its constant regurgitation, and oppressive heat muscling in from the outdoors, the hallway, and up through the two lower floors.

Julian and Derrick followed her in, neither suspecting she knew what had happened. She wondered just how long Papa planned to tail Derrick, keep him out of trouble, and carry the secret of Derrick's betraying them both. Secrets, however, were Papa's forte.

Both men angered her, and she went into the bedroom with Prairie. At least she had her baby home, and no nurse would be walking in to take the infant back to the nursery. Curled on the bed, she studied Prairie's tiny dark lashes against her translucent skin, her soft auburn hair already half an inch long, her bit of upturned nose, and her lips the color of innocence. She tucked one hand beneath Prairie's perfectly flat back, closed her eyes, and tried to rest.

The apartment looked the same as she passed through, hadn't it? Her eyes opened. The easel shelf was empty. The painting with the blue wash and infant, *Prairie's Coming*, was gone.

She threw open the bedroom door. Julian stood at one of the windows. Derrick sat on the sofa staring straight ahead, and the feeling in the room was moratorium rather than celebratory. "Derrick, where's my picture?"

He jumped, his face both dull and surprised, and he looked first at Julian, then around the room. Was he, Willow wondered, looking for other proofs that Mary had been there: a shoe, maybe a bra he hadn't tucked away?

"What picture?" Julian asked.

She wanted to scream at him, too. She wouldn't have known anything if he hadn't gone looking for Derrick. He ought to go home and mind his own business. She couldn't tell him that—how insane. Who didn't know facing the truth was better than living a lie? But this truth threatened to buckle her knees. "Never mind," she managed, turning back for the bedroom and Prairie. Now that Mary had touched it, she didn't want the painting back.

A week passed in a blur of nursing and sleeping. Merciful sleep that invaded Willow's bones and blood and head, keeping some part of her mind in lockdown, insisting on it. A week in which she did no painting and didn't move from the bed but to use the bathroom or go to the refrigerator, forcing herself to nibble on food so that her body would continue producing milk for Prairie.

She sat in her bed now, leaning against the headboard, pillows behind her back, Prairie in her arms and nursing, a tugging sensation that flooded Willow's blue-veined breast. She felt shaky and kept glancing at the doorway. Rain had fallen most of the night, but she'd left the bedroom window open, unable to bear shutting out the sound and the cooler, clean air that helped to rid the room of the faint smell of dirty diapers and grief. The old and porous wooden sill was swollen with water, and on her last trip to the bathroom, she opened the closet, grabbed up an armload of Derrick's clothes, hangers and all, and dumped them in front of the window to keep the rain from flooding the room and dripping down on the tenants below. Derrick, already gone for two hours, was hardly pouring cement in the rain.

She stroked Prairie's cheek and cupped her hand protectively over the infant's head. She glanced again at the doorway, still empty. In the middle of the night, with Derrick snoring on the sofa, she fed Prairie and was returning from the bathroom when she stepped into the bedroom and saw the dark form lying on her bed—an arm through the bars of the crib, a shadowy hand on her infant's back. She gasped and took a step back, her heart racing. The apparition disappeared. She thought to run, and for one brief second to wake Derrick for help. Instead, she gathered her courage and crawled very slowly up from the foot of the bed, putting her hand through the crib slats as she'd done so often that week—a hand needing to rest on Prairie and feel Prairie's breathing—her own body taking up the space where she'd seen the darkness.

The rain increased as Prairie finished and burped on Willow's shoulder.

She'd sleep now for a couple of hours, but Willow couldn't, not another day of lying there, her mind chewing on the fat of how she'd been betrayed. She needed to be up, if not painting, then at least moving, even if only to kick over chairs and punch pillows.

In the main room, her eyes avoided the sofa where Derrick spent the last week of nights. She had no appetite, but again, there was the responsibility to eat for Prairie. Hopefully, the milk Papa brought the night before was still cool and smelled like milk instead of the cow. Taking a glass from the cupboard, she poured, but her hand began to shake when she sensed otherness. First visible only out of the corner of one eye, she saw it beside the sofa: a bleak haze. Milk splashed onto her feet. The apparition looked down at the pillow where the imprint of Derrick's head remained.

"He's not staying," Willow's voice was a whisper, but the Poe-like phantom had already vanished. For some time, Willow sat at the table, stared out at the rain, and thought of a movie she had once seen—the ghosts of dead soldiers walking up and down the battlefield where they'd died, unable to leave the horror, stuck in the memory of the worst thing that ever happened to them. But she wasn't dead. She wasn't.

Later in the shower, she let the water drum over her skin, flatten her hair to dark oil down her back, and create a tunnel of sound that mixed with the noise of the storm's increasing rancor. Every few minutes, she listened for Prairie and then turned the overhead rush back on.

How like Julian she seemed to me, letting the water wash her and then batter her.

When finally her fingers and toes had puckered, she turned off the water for the final time. She stood stock-still, knowing the shadow waited for her behind the curtain. She could feel its nearness, loathsome and needing her. She pushed back the plastic, heavy with hard water stains, the curtain rings scratching along the aluminum rod. The shadow sat on the closed toilet lid, its legs drawn up.

Water ran off Willow's breasts, over her spongy belly, and from her kneecaps. She stared, less afraid this time. Derrick would never touch her again, but she hadn't told him to leave because doing so would free him to go to Mary, where he'd be happy. As long as he slept on the sofa, with Papa visiting every evening to be sure he was home—under the guise of wanting to hold Prairie—Derrick was miserable. *Miserable.* She hadn't even told him she knew he'd been with Mary because bringing up that bit of news would also force a showdown guaranteed to end in his leaving and going to her. So he remained, not because there was any hope for them, but because she fed more on her anger than she did on milk, vegetables, and protein. All the while, she passed her loathing of him into her breast milk, making it worse than anything in the refrigerator, feeding Prairie swill.

The shadow, dark and sluggish, passed through the steamy air and disappeared.

Willow clutched a towel to herself. She knew the figure was a projection of her mind, very real emotion in psychic form. She was at a crossroads. She could fight to reclaim a life, or she could let the shadowbeing with its slow vibration move permanently into the apartment, into her life, and into her heart until she forgot how to live without envy and hatred. The darkness had already spent over a week passing on torpid sleep, keeping Willow's thoughts miserly and too dull for honesty. How long was she willing to live off anger— justified as it was? How long would she let bitterness so consume her that it followed her like a specter?

Over the next two days, the shadow spent more time sitting on chairs, staring out windows, and refusing to let Willow near the easel. With each sighting, Willow felt torn. She still wanted her grief, had earned her grief. She'd been wronged, and other than Papa's watching him, Derrick wasn't suffering. Maybe he'd even confessed to Father Steinhouse, and for ten Our Fathers bartered an absolution.

Watching her, I wondered, was I her guardian, as I fancied myself, or was I there to learn from her? I was likely too young to save Sabine, but had I released my shadow being, my resentments toward my mother and The Beast, would I have found the sight necessary to prevent what happened those many years later?

The next day, Willow brought Prairie out of the bedroom. She bathed her, admiring the tiny body, the loose skin on her knees, the down of her hair, and especially the grace of her perfect, ivory shoulders. When Prairie slept, Willow painted.

Late that afternoon, she sat on the sofa holding Prairie. She waited for Derrick, even letting him go to the refrigerator for a beer. Earlier, she thought to wait for July to end, not wanting Derrick's leaving to be in the same month as Prairie's birth, the way her own birthday fell on the day Jeannie died, the worst day in Papa's life. Every day Derrick stayed though, the shadowbeing also stayed, and she healed less than she would without him.

"Pack your things and go," she said. He *had* come to her for the sex Mary wasn't giving him. He figured he'd settle for the bicycle with the bent wheel and work his way up. "If you hurry, you'll be out of here before Papa arrives."

Derrick stood fixed beside the refrigerator. The motor clicked on.

"I don't care if you go to Mary's bed," Willow said. She glanced at him over her shoulder. "Yeah, I know about your little screw fest. Just go. I need you gone so I can quit haunting myself." All day she'd considered how she'd only be divorcing her fantasies of what they could be together. She had no actual memories of them that she'd re-live with longing. "Prairie doesn't deserve to live with how much I hate you."

He took a long drink of his beer. "What about your old man?"

Not, *what about us*? Or *what about Prairie*? "Well, Derrick, if some night he steps up to your bed, nestles his gun barrel in your ear, and pulls the trigger, you've been warned."

"Nice Willow. That's real nice talk."

"You know what ex-cops are like." She knew what Derrick wanted: an angry scene he could hold up over his blame and use for the reason they split. He needed something he could tell his dad that would keep the old man in his corner and his inheritance safe.

His belongings fit in a 48-count Pampers box and two soggy pillowcases. He stopped at the door, looking over the apartment. "I think I've got everything."

Willow snuggled Prairie closer and whispered, not wanting Prairie to hear the hiss of her anger. "You're not sticking me with that lava lamp."

He set the box and pillowcases in the hall, came back and picked up the lamp. "I thought you liked the colors."

"That's not color." Her gaze leveled on him. "It's upchuck. I'll keep myself supplied with color."

He hesitated a second time at the door. "Remember, this is all your idea."

"Get the hell—"

"I'm going. It's just," another long pause followed, his throat full of hesitation, "we thought for sure it would be a boy."

Willow's breath felt sucked from her lungs. Shock kept her mute, able only to say, "Destroy the picture Mary stole. I don't want her, or you, looking at anything having to do with Prairie." He started to shake his head, saying Mary didn't have it, but she stopped him. "Do it Derrick."

He closed the door, and she heard him struggling with his load down the stairs. They'd shared nothing: no books, no hobbies, no souvenirs, not even something as simple as a bauble won together at the state fair. He hadn't held up a single item and wondered which one of them it most belonged to. His trashy lamp didn't count. Prairie was the one precious thing they shared, and he'd not once held her. He hadn't even opened her tiny hand and let her wrap her fingers around one of his. She kissed Prairie's forehead, Derrick's words ripping through her: *We thought for sure it would be a boy.*

She shed no tears when he left, and if I'd been physical enough to weep, my tears would have been for joy, not because Derrick was gone, but because Willow dared to face a dragon, and in the process she learned much about herself. Would it be enough?

28

Willow named the shadow Perpetual, sure Sister Dominic Agnes would approve of the name. She wasn't certain of the exact day or week when Perpetual moved entirely out, though she knew if she cared to sit and spend an evening remembering all the wrongs done to her, Perpetual would walk eagerly back through the door and snuggle close and bring out long colored fabrics from her basket of memories.

In October, she took the GED, and in January she started college, thanks to the woman who took drop-ins and to whom Prairie went eagerly.

The March afternoon Mrs. Crat called to say she had something she needed to bring right over, Willow had just put Prairie down for a nap and pulled out a geology book, hoping to grab an hour of study before picking up the apartment and starting dinner. As he did a couple of nights a week, Julian was stopping by for dinner. She'd be serving him the only thing she had in the cupboard: canned tuna with noodles. Again.

With Mrs. Crat sitting on the red sofa, Willow was annoyed, even angry. She had things to do, and since Mrs. Crat hadn't once visited before, why was *now* so important? According to Papa, she'd come to the hospital after Prairie's birth. He and Derrick were in the parking lot ready to leave when Derrick saw her car, hurried over, and a moment later, she drove off. Willow supposed Derrick's bruised face might have had something to do with it.

Sitting with her gloved hands clamped over the top of her purse, Mrs. Crat pushed back her wool headscarf, but she refused Willow's offer to take her coat. Perched on the edge of the sofa, a simple push of her thick legs would have her standing and out the door.

The clock on the stove read only 2:30, early afternoon, but heavy clouds darkened the windows and made the hour seem much later. Another gust of wind snaked between the north window and its casement, sending out a long moan.

"If Derrick fathered your child," Mrs. Crat said, opening her purse, "I don't mind helping." She pulled out a white envelope and extended it. The words CRAT CONSTRUCTION and the address were in large black letters in the upper left-hand corner.

Willow stared at the envelope. She didn't want money. She'd yet to receive any aid from Derrick, and though Papa disagreed with her, she refused to involve the courts. Lawyers and a judge might lead to Derrick getting Prairie for an hour, an afternoon, or god-forbid, a weekend. That time would also be with Mary, who had every reason in the world to hate Prairie. So long as neither Derrick, nor his family, sent even the pittance to buy Prairie a pair of shoes, they couldn't lay claim to her, Willow hoped. Now, Mrs. Crat, her knees locked together, her rutabaga face unmoving, had her hand outstretched.

If I refuse the money, Willow wondered, *will Derrick still get credit? After all, his family tried.* She wondered too, about the hand-delivery rather than simply mailing it? Had Mrs. Crat come in order to relish the sight of her good works and inflate herself to the stature of savior?

Derrick's mother pushed the envelope farther into the space between them. "Oh, heavens," she barked, "take it."

Willow watched her hand lifting and accepting the nearly weightless envelope—a check, not bulkier bills—which meant there would be a cancelled check, proof in court. *Thank you* skittered around in her head, but she couldn't force the two slight words off the end of her tongue. She put the envelope beside her on the chair, undecided about what to do with it. "It's March, a couple days shy of April; Prairie was born in July."

Mrs. Crat frowned, her shoulders unmoving inside her dark coat. "Eight months. Your child is hardly grown."

Willow wanted to chuck the envelope back, but with it lying so close she couldn't help but think of her bills: Rent, utilities, babysitter, food for two, keeping a car running, paints, and tuition. She washed Prairie's clothes in the bathroom sink, hung them on a small wooden drying rack. Month by month since Derrick's leaving, she'd been sinking further into debt, going through Mémé's stipend and charging what she couldn't pay for. The bills arrived in colored envelopes now, and still she lied to Papa: "I'm fine, quit worrying." He most likely wrestled with his own mountain of bills, and asking for help would get him started again on how she should be hauling Derrick's ass to court. Now, here was a check that might be for a thousand or five thousand dollars.

"I didn't expect Derrick to just vanish," she said. *Thank God, he had.* "I thought he'd at least want to come and see Prairie at Christmas."

Mrs. Crat's boots had left a trail of gray and watery prints from the door to the sofa. "But he's living in Texas."

"Texas?"

"You didn't know? It's a small college. They're letting him play football."

"Did Mary go with him?"

"Mary's been sick again." Mrs. Crat's fingers clutched her purse. "She needed medical care and was returned to St. Joe's Psychiatric Hospital."

"No surprise there."

"It's a hospital," her voice was cold, and her eyes glistened. "For people who are sick and suffering."

Willow waited. She was about to get an ear full.

"Derrick was never in any real danger. Your whole affair," she let her emphasis rest there, "has been devastating to Mary, and—"

The word *danger* made Willow's ears perk up, but it was the word *affair* that made her cut in. "The affair of our marriage? Or the affair of—"

"Your marriage, of course," Mrs. Crat stopped her. "Mary's such a beautiful girl. It's awful to watch someone so beautiful suffer."

"Because she's beautiful? Someone a little less beautiful, their suffering wouldn't matter as much?" She didn't need an answer. "Besides, Mary won, if you can call Derrick a win."

"There's so much you don't know. Mary was burned."

"I know that."

"She's struggled over the last few years. You can't blame her. It's hard being a teenage girl when everyone around you is in those god-awful tube tops and bikinis. She's had to hide her body, no sleep-overs, and no city pools."

Willow managed to keep quiet. She pulled one leg up under herself.

"Her mother has spent thousands on clothes, trying to convince Mary she's beautiful, but it hasn't helped. Probably, just as much money has gone into medications. Having two or three doctors, each unaware of the other, with antidepressants, pain pills, and who knows what else. Years of this. I'm fairly certain she's started taking illegal things, too."

"You mean street drugs?"

Mrs. Crat hugged her purse to her stomach. "I'm leaving my husband and moving to Texas. I've rented an apartment very close to Derrick."

The news widened Willow's eyes. "Divorcing? To be with Derrick? I'll bet he's thrilled."

"He's angry, and you know it, but I need to do this. If I don't go, he'll leave the church for good. I hope to bring him back to Omaha, eventually. He should have a share in Crat Construction."

Willow considered the news. "You came to tell Prairie good-bye?"

"I need to explain why I haven't been able to be a grandmother to her." She let go of her purse and slowly lifted her gloved hands. For several seconds, she stared at them. "Derrick and I were at Mary's the day of the accident," she began. "Mary's mother, Sally, and I were in the kitchen. The kids played in Mary's bedroom, drawing pictures." Her eyes sought Willow's. "Innocent things. They were babies, just first graders.

"Mary's father walked in on them and saw something in the pictures. Or said he did. He's an animal. I know that's why Sally never had another child. Seeing those drawings, he grabbed Mary by one arm and drug her down the stairs and into the kitchen where Sally and I were making Christmas candy. Laughing, we sipped wine as she chopped pecans, and I stood at the stove stirring syrup for hard candy. My pot had been boiling for several minutes, and finally, the candy thermometer had reached 250 degrees." She began working on a gloved hand, finger by finger, pinching the tip and giving it a slight tug, as if still dealing with pain or the memory of pain. "Just as I was ready to turn the burner off, he barged in. Mary was screaming and scared with his rough treatment. He shook her, making her head snap back and forth as he demanded to know who taught her to draw dirty pictures. He'd been in the kitchen not five minutes earlier and frowned at Sally and me. I suppose we were having too much fun. I know he went looking for something to make a stink over. Sally was trembling, cowering, with panic on her face, and doing nothing." She stopped, letting her breath catch up, still working the glove off. "Of course, she knew him better than I."

Willow pressed her lips together and struggled to keep from showing any aversion to the hand Mrs. Crat revealed.

"I'm sure Sally knew that keeping still was the best way to handle him, but I couldn't. The scene made my blood boil. He kept yelling, wanting to know who taught her to draw like that. Mary didn't understand, other than to know the problem was about drawing. She said your name. You were her friend, and you gave her little pictures from time to time. She used to carry them around. Well, your name *really* set him off. He hated your father for giving him a second DUI. There may have been other brushes with the law, too. There were rumors."

Hearing her name in connection with Mary's burns was both surprising and upsetting to Willow. She watched as Mrs. Crat began working on her second glove. "That's how this all started? My dad arrested him?"

"I wanted to throw my wine at him. Derrick was huddled in the doorway crying, but he was too scared to run home without me. Mary was screaming, and Sally was no help. I told him he was crazy. I even ordered him to put Mary down. Imagine that." She took a breath. "The rage on his face! I'm sure no woman had ever spoken to him like that, and he wasn't going to take it from me. He marched toward me, still holding Mary, swearing I was in *his* house, and she was *his* kid. Then he heaved her at me and said, 'Take the little whore.'

"The distance was only a couple of feet, and she couldn't have weighed more than forty to fifty pounds. I was taken by surprise and couldn't grab her fast enough. She seemed all arms and legs, and I couldn't hold her weight. Her hand slapped the pot handle." Mrs. Crat took in another deep breath, let it ease out of her lungs, and her eyes filled with the memories. "That big pot, that thick syrup, just bubbling away. Mary landed on the floor, and it flipped and landed on her chest."

Willow winced.

"She let out a few awful, terrible, just terrible screams," Mrs. Crat said, "and then," she paused, "I think she went into shock. Her eyes rolled back, and her arms and legs flapped like a child having a seizure. She was dying. Sally was screaming, and Mary's father unleashed a tirade of blame, cursing me and the day I was born and 'look what I'd done.' *He* didn't drop to the floor over his daughter. I did. I grabbed the burning pan, threw it off her, and tried to scoop off what syrup I could. It wasn't like water that cooled fast. It was thick and held the heat. Mary wore a pink T-shirt, no buttons to undo and pulling it over her head would have put the hot mess in her face. At least I knew that."

She lifted her hands to show Willow. Pink and white puckered scar tissue rippled from her fingertips, up over her partially webbing fingers, and to her wrists.

"That pile of thick, boiling syrup," Mrs. Crat continued, as if it were the image she couldn't free herself from. "I kept scooping at it, but that wasn't working. I could only think to put my hands under her shirt and lift the mess up and off her skin." Her scarred palms cupped imaginary fire. "I tried to keep off as much as I could. The men from the rescue squad cut her shirt off up the back. The candy had cooled enough by then so that it was fused to my hands. I went into the hospital still carrying her shirt and layers of her skin, my hands encased." Her hands dropped into her lap. "None of us accepted blame. I didn't, and I provoked him. Seeing his anger, I should have taken Derrick and walked away."

Staring at Mrs. Crat's hands, Willow didn't know what to say.

"Mary told me once," Mrs. Crat continued, "that her parents never talked about that day. She was glad they didn't. She blamed herself, and she didn't want to be reminded of her sin: drawing dirty pictures. Maybe that harmed her most, having to look at her burns year after year, thinking she deserved to be disfigured. She should have been in therapy. She should have heard that she wasn't to blame, but her parents were too afraid. They couldn't bear her telling the story to outsiders. They just kept medicating her moods, buying her more silk to cover up with, the best car of any teenager in Omaha. She never came to see how adults failed her." One scarred hand jerked, "Right after the accident, her father, big, important man, marched up to Our Lady of Supplication and included Sister Dominic Agnes in his blaming. He said if she'd been watching her students, she would have known you were teaching Mary to make smutty drawings. He laid down the law: When Mary returned to school, you were to be kept away from her."

For comfort, Willow glanced at the paintings on her wall. "Mary's dad blamed Sister Dominic Agnes, too? And she believed him? That explains so much." She sank against the soft chair back, considering. A question came to mind, and for a moment she was afraid to ask. "How do you know this? Did Father Steinhouse tell you?"

The eyes of Derrick's mother leveled. "That man has been a great help to me. Why does everyone think that's wrong? He came to the hospital when I needed someone. Every morning since then, he's taken the time after Mass to talk to me. He's the only one willing to listen to me and forgive me. My own husband hasn't." Her thoughts were jagged sparks of shooting energy. She remembered the morning months after the accident, her bandages freshly off, and with her scarred hands she buttered her husband's toast, just as she did mornings before the accident. Proud of what she'd done, she pushed it across the table to him. He'd watched as she struggled with the knife, the scarred hands on his food. He looked at his toast and pushed the plate back.

"You started doing paint-by-number crucifixion pictures."

"Father Steinhouse has them hanging. They were gifts from him. Painting those little numbered spaces and opening those little pots of paint were physical therapy. The work helped keep my mind busy, and the pictures reminded me that my suffering was less than Christ's." She began working her gloves back on. "The state I was in, each finished painting was an accomplishment. I'd gotten through another month, maybe two, and I wanted him to have them."

For so long, Willow had longed for answers, and now that she had so many, she wanted to be alone. She turned to check the time, hoping it would serve as a hint, but the dark windows caught her attention, not the clock. Tiny icy pellets ticked against the glass.

"After the accident," Mrs. Crat went on, "I was hospitalized, too, and went back and forth from my room to Mary's. I went to the cafeteria for candy, ice cream, to the gift shop for stuffed toys, anything to take her mind off the pain and the awful bandaging and rebandaging every few days, the grafting," she shuddered. "I didn't leave her alone with Sally. How could I trust that woman? My hands and the pain, while Sally's hands were pretty as ever. She polished her nails to visit the hospital. I'd earned my place by Mary, and she wanted me there. If her father came, she'd cry until he left. I shouldn't have come between them, but he threw her at me, and she was like a little, broken angel.

"I wanted Derrick and Mary to be together. We owed her that. I told myself he loved her, but I suppose he could have hated her for taking me away from him." She stopped again, her face knitting and fretting, but she needed to say more. "You didn't come between them. It was me, insisting Mary was the one, not letting Derrick feel as though he had a say in the matter. I didn't see who else would marry her. My husband was rejecting me; I didn't want that for her. It wasn't Derrick's life I thought you ruined, it was Mary's."

Willow watched the last of Mrs. Crat's scarring disappear inside her soft, black gloves. The woman wasn't evil, and being honest enough to admit she cared more about Mary than her own son took courage.

The damp boots shuffled on the floor. "I don't wonder that he watched you. We all did. You were mixed up with everything, and we were desperate to blame an outsider. When I learned you were pregnant, I cried for days. I knew I'd failed Mary and that Derrick hooked up with you as a way to hurt me."

Remembering nights in Derrick's car and his urgency in wrestling her out of her jeans, Willow was certain he hadn't been thinking about his mother.

"I'd have celebrated Mary getting pregnant and their marriage."

"So, why did you push him to marry me?"

She shrugged, as if no longer certain. "Our family name. Father Steinhouse believed it was God's will. My dream for Mary seemed ruined by your pregnancy. Even if Derrick didn't marry you, there was still going to be a child. And," for the first time her lips curled, then tipped down as she shook her head, "we were certain it would be a boy and need a strong name. Crats always have boys. My husband is one of six brothers. The brothers all have boys."

A slow, hot burn threatened to make Willow scream, but at the same time she knew Mrs. Crat's Neanderthal thinking meant Prairie was safe. Had Prairie been male, the Crats would be trying to take her.

"Even after you threw Derrick out," Mrs. Crat continued, "I needed to concentrate on Mary. I couldn't have your baby around. I just never knew what Mary might do."

"That's why you've had nothing to do with her? Her being a girl and your fear Mary would harm her? Did you also tell Derrick to stay away, or did he decide that?"

"Trying to share custody from Texas wouldn't be practical."

"Practical," Willow managed, "of course it wouldn't be." And after a moment, "Are you saying Derrick went to Texas to get away from Mary?"

"I don't think Mary really tried to hurt him, certainly not to kill him, like she said. I'm sure she wouldn't actually hurt your child, either. That day, I believe, she flirted with suicide, trying to show Derrick she'd really do it."

"Suicide?" She remembered Mary slapping her chest, going crazy over Papa and Derrick seeing her scars. "And she threatened to hurt Prairie?" The window moaned again. "You came to warn me?" She couldn't stay sitting. She stood and paced back and forth behind her chair. "Yesterday and again this morning, I saw flashes of a yellow car at the end of the street. Does she still drive her convertible?"

"It was her father's car she wrecked. I just don't know, without me being here for her. I must go, though. I'm no use to her."

Willow didn't need to hear more. She stepped back from the chair and motioned to the bedroom door. "You're here and leaving for Texas. Do you at least want to see Prairie?"

"That's really the name you chose?" She stood, pulled her scarf up, and headed for the door leading out. "She's sleeping. Let's not wake her."

"Is that why you came now? Because you supposed she'd be napping?"

The cheeks, just visible behind the wool scarf, turned florid. "I came now because of the storm. I want to get home before the ice hits."

You are the ice, Willow thought. "You may not like me, but you're Prairie's only grandmother."

Mrs. Crat's brows yanked inward again. "Oh, for heaven's sake, haven't you got *any* family?"

Willow didn't watch her walk down the hall. She shut the door as soon as the woman was outside and slid the deadbolt into place with extra force. It would take days to unpack all she'd learned, but a few facts were clear: The months of quiet she'd experienced were because Derrick was in Texas and Mary was in the hospital. Her behavior was so dangerous, or suicidal, it warranted locking her up. Now, she was out and making new threats against Prairie.

Picking up the envelope, she stared at the name again, Crat Construction. She opened it and removed a $50 dollar bill. Her heart sank, and then she laughed. Just as quickly, the window squealed, and her stomach fell again. The apartment felt as if Mrs. Crat had left something evil behind.

Willow opened the door to where Prairie slept and slowly crawled up the bed. She pulled the baby blanket up tighter over Prairie's small shoulders and then wrapped herself in Mother Moses. With birds and butterflies around her, she watched Prairie and tried to calm herself. Prairie was safe, and Papa would be there soon, ice or no ice. Everything was all right. Wasn't it?

29

※

"You've got to stay the night," Willow said to Julian. She nodded toward the sofa Mrs. Crat vacated only a few hours earlier. "I'll sleep there, and you can have the bed."

He sat over his second serving of tuna casserole, eating as though the dish were a rare favorite and holding Prairie on one knee. "There'll be a heap of accidents in that ice. Red'll be out all night," he said. Then, wistfully, "Glad it isn't me."

"Sure you are."

He kissed Prairie again on the top of her curly head and looked at the paintings on the wall. Tonight, they arrested him more than did the weather. He pointed with his fork. "You want to try and explain all this to me?"

He hadn't asked before. He had admired them and often joked about her "museum," but this time Willow sensed he was asking for some deeper connection. He was nervous, or extra lonely, or feeling the gray she'd been feeling since Mrs. Crat's visit. Explaining the paintings though would have to include the story of the morning she watched smoke rising from his cigarette, the rose Mémé sent to her wedding, and the thorns she stabbed into her arm. Those wounds, infected for a week, left puffy scars she still carried. And how to explain paintings she only really understood while in the act of creation? Afterwards, she lacked the language.

Julian put down his fork. "They lived in simpler times."

"Derrick's mom came to see me today."

The hand Julian kept around Prairie's waist tightened. He watched Willow, his eyes some combination of wanting to hear the details and already expecting the worst.

"She came to warn me. Mary is out of the hospital. You knew her father blamed me, at least partially, for her burns. All these years, you've never said a thing."

"The man ain't worth the effort."

Willow carried their plates to the sink. Half an inch of ice coated the ledge where pigeons roosted in the summer. No cars crawled along the street below, which was good because Papa wouldn't slide into anyone, but bad because it proved just how treacherous the streets were. "Please stay the night."

"I can still get myself two blocks."

He didn't hurry home. He built block tower after block tower for Prairie to knock down, her laughter like a cascade that kept him laughing, too. When finally Prairie was asleep, he took up his coat, and despite Willow's insistence, said good-night. She stood at a window, kneading the ache in her stomach and looking down on trees shiny with ice. He stepped from the building and avoided the slick sidewalk, moving to his car by way of the less-slippery grass, wind gusts billowing his coat and forcing him to lean into the cold, one bare hand holding his hat to his head. He'd lived his life on the seams and edges of society: the years he patrolled the night's shadowy streets, the years spent with the ghost of Jeannie, the years as a wine-induced hermit with secrets he told no one. Even now, his figure looked less a father and a grandfather and more a man alone in a storm.

Uneasiness kept her at the glass, leaning into the cold pane, straining to see him creep up the block and the last smear of his taillights vanish. *Already half-way home and fine,* she promised herself.

She still hadn't studied for the next day's class, but it was likely to be canceled, and she felt too restless to concentrate on a book. The image of six-year-old Mary writhing on the floor wouldn't leave her mind.

The pictures on her wall were all crones, even the young faces. They didn't have hooknoses, warts, or toothless smiles. What they possessed was old wisdom, ancient female wisdom, and in that they were beautiful. Taking down a picture of Mémé, she set it on the easel. The cylinders and cubes of the face had already been worked into cheeks and chin and nose. The rough outline of a towering stack of books had already been sketched in as Mémé's perch. An hour of work passed, and still Willow's hand felt heavy, her strokes dull and more weeping daubs of color than fluid additions. She stepped away, looking at the painting from a few feet, then farther back.

"Move on," her college art instructor said of her obsession with the portraits. "Try something new." She'd tried, but bowls of fruit and dull landscapes didn't excite her.

Taking in a deep breath, she tried to shake the tension from her hands. She went back to work. Gradually, her awareness of the apartment faded and even the sound of the sleet striking the windows vanished. Her hands began to move as though to the rhythm of music.

What happened next can best be described as a mental crash or bursting. That quick. One moment her paintbrush was in the air. In the next, she saw Julian, and the horror of the vision knocked the paintbrush from her hand. Papa was consumed in a column of flame.

She jerked toward the nearest window, but stood frozen, telling herself she couldn't have seen what she imagined she saw. In the distance, the sound of sirens, no more than the whine of mosquitoes, touched her ears. *Too far away.* But growing slowly. She took deep breaths, the sound of emergency vehicles creeping on the ice, growing louder, finding their way into her body, rising up from her heels, turning her legs cold, mounting into wails that clawed the inside of her stomach and turned savage in her ears.

She still couldn't approach the window. For the second time that day, she rushed first to Mother Moses, hurrying into the heavy crocheting as if hurrying into Mémé's arms. Only then could she force herself forward, approaching the window as she had so many times since moving into the apartment, locating her childhood rooftop. Smoke and a bright orange glow.

She ran for Prairie, scooped her up, blankets and all, and stopped. Taking a warm and sleeping baby into the storm wasn't just cruel, it was dangerous. She swung Mother Moses across the foot of the bed, added a second thick blanket to the crocheting and then Prairie. She had no other choice.

The bundle was nearly too bulky to carry, but Mother Moses was tied up with Mémé, and Willow needed that good spirit with them. On the street, she jostled her load, trying to jab her keys into her frozen car locks. The ice wouldn't yield, and after several time-wasting attempts, she took off on foot. Cutting across lawns and between houses, the unwieldy bundle of Prairie and blankets made her running slow and clumsy. Her heart pounded through a surreal world: painted silver streets, grass looking like shards of glass, and the dark wash of ash and smoke rolling sickly over dark rooftops.

She didn't feel the ice hitting her hands and face, but the wet cold soaked her sweatshirt and added to her stiff and erratic running. She fell twice, three times, taking the spills on her hip or elbow, believing Mother Moses controlled the trajectory of the falls, protecting Prairie who woke and cried and fought to get her head uncovered. "It's all right," Willow panted. "I'm right here. I'm right here." Her voice ragged with terror and cold and exertion.

The screaming sirens quit as they reached the site. When Willow came between the houses across the street from her childhood home, she saw flashing lights and smoke billowing from the open front door. Behind the windows, flames leaped and fell, and then the quick dark shape of a man in thick protective gear.

"Stop!" A male voice rang out at her shoulder. Strong arms grabbed her. "Stay back."

She wasn't going any closer, not with Prairie, who at times made muffled crying sounds and at other times let out screams that sliced through the blankets.

"I've got her," a familiar voice called out, his arms circling both Willow and her bundle. "Come on," Red coaxed, "we'll wait in my cruiser."

She fought him, begging, as though he didn't know Julian was inside, telling him they had to get Papa out, and just let her see, not hearing herself, not able to control the massive fear engulfing her. Red kept coaxing, steering her over the treacherous ice and away from the sound of breaking glass and groaning timbers.

When a fireman burst through the front door carrying a form over his shoulder, Willow nearly sank to her knees in relief.

I felt no relief. The past and the present engulfed me with their ashes and smoke. I arrived too late to save Little Nest from the fire that destroyed it. I stood back, watching it burn while firemen worked in vain. Through its destruction, I held a weeping Julian to my skirts, a boy terrorized by the power of the fire, too innocent to have ever imagined such hellish and quick destruction. Now, here again, was a house in the family burning down.

30

✣

Willow paced in the surgery waiting room, while Prairie slept in her arms and Red stared straight ahead. All around her, she heard the voices of sickness and death, urine and blood, speaking as they gurgled down drains. Death, cleaned up by staff who never saw the deceased, who only rolled up sheets that would go on other beds, and sent antiseptics washing over floors. Spirits rose up out of bodies and lifted away, while carts with defibrillators crashed into rooms minutes too late.

Later, a doctor used so many terms Willow struggled under their weight. "Second-degree burns over twenty percent of his body, third-degree burns over forty percent, unstable blood pressure, severe smoke inhalation, plasma leakage, airway edema, organ shut down ..." If Julian survived, "There have been unlikely miracles," the doctor said without conviction, recovery would mean years of surgeries, severe disfiguration, skin grafts, and amputations.

Red stood and crossed the room, his outstretched hands bracing shoulder-level against the wall, his head dropped between them. "How long?"

There was a slight hesitation, and then the doctor looked at Willow. "My guess is two, three days. It's impossible to say. We're doing what we can to keep him comfortable."

Willow sat in shock and was still that way when hours later she stood in a baggy gown at the door of Julian's IC unit. A nurse stood beside her. "You won't recognize him. You should prepare yourself."

"Is that possible?" she whispered. "To prepare?"

She stepped inside a small room made even smaller by the large pieces of medical equipment. The smell of burned flesh hit her so hard her stomach lurched. She covered her nose and mouth. She couldn't look at the form on the bed. Only peripherally, a white shape bandaged and sheeted. It wasn't Papa yet, not until she said so.

Monitors, beeping screens, and tubes ran to and from the bed. The whole of it was terrible machinery. Her gaze inched upward, and she saw the shape of Papa's feet and calves under a swath of white bandages—only white cloth, she could handle that. Higher, a sheet was draped modestly across his groin. His hands were wrapped to his elbows, and the skin of his upper arms and the shoulder nearest her were crimson with large weeping splotches of open flesh. His chest was bandaged. A face?

She slumped into the chair, willing herself to keep hold of her screams. Tubes up a black nose, another tube, garden-hose width, disappearing into what had to be a mouth, but couldn't be Papa's mouth, wasn't any man's mouth. Swelling, blistering, red and purple putty rather than flesh, indentations in dough rather than eyes. Maybe not a man at all, a kill, bear-mauled.

She wanted to run out of the room and take her screams up and down the halls. This wasn't Papa, couldn't be, but she'd stood in the sleet as smoke rolled from his roof, gold flame lapped his windows, and a fireman carried out his body.

Over the next few hours the world seemed to come at Willow in fragments, and she struggled to process the commotion. Red stood outside the room, Prairie asleep on his shoulder, his uniform dark on the stomach from holding her with her soaked-through diaper. He told Willow he'd take Prairie to his house and be sure she was kept safe, and, yes, his gun was always at hand. A flux of doctors, nurses, chaplains, techs, social workers, administrators with thick pads of paper and questions about health insurance, and religious affiliations and did she want Julian to receive the last rites? There were scraps of new information about Papa's condition. They'd cut his legs and opened a long seam, from his groin to the arches of his feet, to relieve swelling. A seam on his chest eased the pressure on his heart and lungs.

"Damn pirates," she imagined Papa saying, "couldn't save Jeannie, couldn't fix you, and they can't save me."

Hours later, I sensed Red coming down the hall before he tapped on the room's window. Willow, her eyes puffy from crying, hurried out to him, "Where's Prairie?"

"She's with my wife. She's fine."

"Mary Wolfe did this."

Red's brows narrowed. He held a vase of spring tulips, and a long blue ribbon trailed over his freckled hands. His clothes were clean, and he looked as though he'd gotten a couple of hours of sleep.

"She threatened him," Willow continued, "and yesterday Derrick's mom tried to warn me."

He set the flowers on a table to his right and pulled a small spiral notebook from his chest pocket. "From the initial investigation, and it is just preliminary, it appears the fire started on the sofa with a cigarette. Another was left beside the sink in the bathroom. It burned down and dropped onto towels."

"Those weren't cigarettes he lit." She gasped a deep breath and tried again. "I know how it looks, but my ex-mother-in-law visited yesterday. She warned me about Mary, said Mary was threatening something," she nodded to the room behind her and Papa, "something like this."

"What exactly did she say?"

"I know she was warning me. Mary's threatened Papa before."

"Mary Wolfe." He wrote the name slowly, writing it down for Willow's sake. "When exactly did she threaten Julian and why?"

"You have to believe me."

"How long ago did she threaten him? Were there any witnesses?"

"Derrick, but he was drunk or stoned." The truth shamed her: her husband in bed with someone else while she was having a baby. She tucked her hands under her arms. "The day Prairie was born."

Red closed his notebook. Prairie was already crawling. "Nothing since?"

Having sat so many hours in hard chairs, Willow's legs and back ached, but the fatigue that leaned her against the wall came from not being believed. Again. "It's like trying to convince Papa."

He reopened his notebook, read the name. "Mary Wolfe. And what's her connection to Julian?"

"Mary had, is having," she couldn't push herself from the wall, "I don't know, an affair with my ex. She killed my dog."

He squinted, "Your dog?"

She closed her eyes, dropped her head back. "What's the use? I need to get back. Please go home and stay with Prairie."

"Why don't you find a cot or couch somewhere and get some sleep? The nurses will find you if he changes."

"I'm all right."

"He has a sister. You want me to give her a call?"

For the first time since hearing the whine of sirens in the distance, Willow felt hope. "Tory." The name didn't summon great relief, but it called up others that did, and her mind went over the round, soothing sounds: *Mable, Jonah, Farthest House.* Farthest House, where surely Mémé's ghost still walked the garden and tended Damask roses. "Yes, please call her."

By late afternoon, Tory and Mable stood at the window of Julian's room. Seeing Tory, I felt my energies spiral yet again. Would I soon appear sitting in some strange chair, having taken on such weight that people looked and wondered what world I belonged in? Tory, my grandniece, my daughter, how much I still loved her.

Willow's heart also leapt at seeing the pair. She hurried out to them. She'd not expected Tory until the following morning or afternoon, if Tory decided to come at all. She'd not imagined Mable.

Tory held a potted Easter lily with several yellow-throated blooms. Willow thought her chin and nose had sharpened in the ten years since Mémé's funeral. Her hair held streaks of gray now, but she still wore it the same strict way, wrapped tightly and pinned in a chignon, low on the back of her neck. For all the ways age made her more austere, Willow saw no change in her intense gaze. Still piercing, Willow felt seen-through. There was nothing to explain. What didn't those eyes already know?

Mable wore a smoky-blue shawl over her round shoulders, and like Tory's light-weight trench, it proved a warm front had moved in behind the freezing rain. Mable looked more the peach, flushed and soft in a creamy caftan. Unlike Tory's long, pointed shoes, Mable paddled in wide, sturdy shoes beneath thick ankles. "It's terrible," Mable said before she could draw a handkerchief from a pocket in her shawl and catch the two tears that rolled down her round cheeks.

Both women glanced at the window, but Willow felt protective of Papa. He wouldn't want to be seen. "They don't want you in there. You'd have to suit up."

Tory insisted. Changed into scrubs, she stood dry-eyed, staring mutely at her brother, though the muscles around her mouth looked full of the unspoken. When she was six and Julian four, she often dressed him in her clothes, an act she believed made him more fully hers. She liked him in polka dots, red or blue. She liked him in pink. She told him, "No, you mustn't," when he wanted too many cookies. She found his mittens on winter mornings before she found her own. She tasted his cocoa to be sure it wasn't too hot. She huffed at Luessy, or me, when we carried him to his own bed or replaced her little dresses with small navy sweater vests and clip-on bow ties.

When she emerged from Julian's room, she surprised Willow. "Mable will stay for as long as you need her. Who has your baby now?"

Willow hesitated, Prairie wouldn't be as safe with Mable as she was with Red. "She's with a friend."

Tory nodded, then pinned Willow with a commanding look. "We're family."

Willow wanted to protest: *Red has a gun.* Taking advantage of him wasn't fair, though, and at any rate, he'd already left Prairie with his wife. Prairie wasn't riding around in the safety of his police car, Red's wife most likely did not carry a gun, and who knew how caring or resentful she was of having to babysit Prairie. And poor Prairie probably wanted the bed and toys and surroundings she knew.

"It's all right," Mable said at Willow's hesitation. "I don't mind staying. Taking care of a little one will be a nice change of pace."

"It's not you," Willow said. She looked away and down the long hall, trying to think. Mable *was* almost family; Red wasn't. His boys, redheaded monsters when she was a kid, would be teenagers now. Probably demons that would as soon run over Prairie as step around her.

Willow sighed, "Okay."

The morning of the second day, Willow woke in her chair by Julian's bed to Tory tapping again on the glass. They sat across the hall in a small lounge,

Tory in tailored pants, her legs crossed and the top leg hanging motionless and sleek as a spindle. Calm. So calm, that I felt cold snaking through me.

"Farthest House is such a large place," Tory said. "Seeing you again, and Julian . . . ." her voice trailed off, and for a moment she was quiet. "Well, it's all made me consider."

Distracting odors rose from the scrubs Willow wore. Was it the tang of Papa's seared hair, burned flesh the doctors hadn't cut away, seeping bandages, or decaying lung tissue?

"I'd like for you and Prairie," Tory said, "to come and spend some time with me when . . . well, when this is over."

Nothing short of Julian standing and walking out with her sounded as wonderful to Willow as spending time again at Farthest House. But surely Tory wasn't asking them for more than afternoon tea?

"Spend the summer with me," Tory said. "You love the house, and you'll need the rest."

Shivers raked down Willow's arms. "I love Farthest House, but," she took a breath and found she was crying yet again. Papa, though on the brink of death, was still alive, and she didn't want to talk of a time when he wouldn't be. "Right now, I can't think about the next hour, let alone the next weeks."

"Nonsense," Tory said. "You must think ahead. You have a child. Don't try and get through this alone. It's too much." Her voice softened. "The Damasks will bloom soon. I remember how much your mother loved them."

"Jeannie loved the roses?"

"They were part of why she came to stay those last weeks of her pregnancy."

Willow wondered why she hadn't been told this before. Jeannie not only smelled and cut roses off the same bushes Willow had, she walked the same cobblestone paths, sat in the same blue-tufted chairs, studied the same photographs and botanical prints on the walls, ate off the same plates, and likely had her own floral china cup.

Tory stood to leave, reaching down and squeezing Willow's forearm. "Spend the summer. Give yourself and Prairie at least that much time."

There were a dozen questions Willow wanted to ask. Unlike Papa, Tory might actually give answers. Tory had been in the house, if not in the room, when Jeannie died. She knew whether or not Jeannie had fought death, whether or not Jeannie had asked to hold her newborn.

Through the afternoon, Willow sat beside Julian listening to the barely audible but mechanical sounds of the machines monitoring and keeping him alive. In places, the skin on his shoulder nearest her had rolled back like thick brown potato peels. She feared that even touching him might cause pain. She folded her hands, resting them on the bed, letting only the tips of her knuckles make contact. "Tory came to see you. She told me Jeannie loved your mom's roses. You never told me."

After dark, when the hallways cleared of visitors and the nurses changed shifts and the new ones made their fussing noises over monitors and charts, Willow's heavy eyes closed. All day she'd wanted to open the door to Papa's room, swing her arms wildly, and shoo out Death. If only such a thing were possible. As her tired head bobbed into exhausted sleep, she dreamed Death was still in the room, pacing at the foot of the bed. The dream and Death morphed, as her sleep deepened, and Death became a black and winged raven that vanished through the ceiling, only to swoop over the city in block-wide swaths, searching.

She woke with a start. Death looked for Prairie!

It was only a dream, she promised herself, but an hour later she still paced, warring with her fears. She didn't want to leave Papa, but the dream, lucid and chilling, clung to her. She hurried for the elevator and her car.

Mable sat on the red sofa watching Johnny Carson sign off for the night. Seeing Willow, her eyes widened. Her face paled, and she turned off the set.

"No," Willow said, reading her concern, "it's not over." She hadn't yet *signed* the papers authorizing them to remove his tubes. She'd only *agreed* to do so after the last consultation, when the doctor said, "I'm sorry."

Mable studied her. "You look exhausted. You were right to come home and get some sleep."

Willow dropped her car keys onto the table and let her gaze linger a moment on the crones. She wouldn't confess her nightmare. "I'm not staying; I just need a minute with Prairie."

In the dark bedroom, she crawled up the bed on her knees and bent over the side of the crib. Prairie slept on her back, her head to one side, her tiny lips parted, her arms flung out—innocent, unafraid. Willow listened to the little sweeps of sound purring in and out of her throat. She ran fingers through Prairie's hair and down her cheeks, using long, soft strokes, the motion she used to fill her brushes with oils, taking up warm brown, moonglow, the palest magenta. She wanted Prairie's pink on her hands, to take the blush back with her to Papa's room where she could look down at her fingers and palms and see that Prairie's living had stayed with her.

Mable came to the bedroom doorway, her figure blocking much of the already dim light. "She's fine."

Still leaning over Prairie's crib, still stroking Prairie's cheek, Willow only nodded.

"I made tea earlier. Would you have a cup with me?"

Sitting at the table, she watched as Mable poured warm tea into chipped mugs and then lifted a dishtowel on fresh-baked cookies made with figs and oatmeal.

"You went to the store?" Willow's voice sounded sharp, and she regretted that, but taking Prairie out was dangerous.

"We are getting on fine."

From the wall, the crones watched. Willow picked up her cup, the liquid trembling with the shaking in her hands. Her world felt draped in black: paper chains, shadow beings, vultures, and Death in his robes.

"I know it's bad," Mable said. "It's awful to lose a parent."

"I've got a horrible feeling something else is going to happen. This time to Prairie." Putting her fears into words, added to them, fleshed them out, and gave them power. She tried to force her mind off Prairie. "How do the doctors know he's not in incredible pain? Even with the morphine, how can they be sure?" She set the cup down and picked up a cookie. She felt famished, and yet, she couldn't eat. "The house was set on fire. I know who did it."

Mable's eyes widened. "You've told the police?"

"I tried. She's smart. She probably crawled in through the window of my old bedroom, lit a cigarette, and tossed it onto the sofa."

Mable watched Willow breaking the cookie and then breaking the pieces. "I'm sure that can't be true."

When the cookie lay in a pile of crumbs, Willow spoke. "Maybe my ex has stayed away because he's scared of Papa." She looked toward the bedroom door. "He might try to take her now." She stood, walked the few steps to the nearest window, and looked down on the dark street. "The Crats are rich; it wouldn't be a fair fight."

"You mean he's likely to want full custody?" Mable asked. "After this long? Children are a lot of work." She reached over with a wide hand and pulled Willow's cookie pieces from the table's edge. "If he wants some visitation, wouldn't that be good for Prairie?"

"Not if his girlfriend is a murderer! He's moved, according to his mother, but Papa's death could bring him back. The fire proves she's never going to quit."

Explaining to Mable what deformity could do to a person's mind was impossible.

"I'll take care of Prairie," Mable said. "Go and be with Julian. You can tell all this to the police in the morning."

Willow twisted strands of her hair. She felt torn, not wanting to be away from Prairie and hating the minutes away from Julian. "How will we live without him?"

Mable sniffled, reaching for her second cookie. "How do we survive life? But we do."

Hearing the sadness in Mable's voice made Willow ask, "Were you ever married?" Talking about something other than her fears felt welcome.

"I never married. My prince is still alive, but life didn't have us marry."

"He's with someone else?" Willow was prying, and she sat back down. "I'm sorry, this isn't my business," she reached for another cookie.

Mable's hand slapped Willow's so quick the cookie fell back on the plate. She pointed to the door, the flesh on her underarm swinging. "You're worrying about too much. You can't control it all. When the centipede realized he had a hundred legs to control, he fell down. Far as I know, he's still down. Just go and be with your father."

31

❧

The nighttime corridor leading back to Papa's room was vacant. Doors to patient's rooms were only slightly ajar and the overhead lights dim. She paused at the nurse's station, picked up the pen offered her, and with a trembling hand signed the papers. She walked over waxed floors and through air tasting of aluminum. The sound manufactured was unearthly.

The chair in Julian's room had been pushed back from his bed and his over-head lights were turned off. Only the dim glow of a monitor screen, its sharp-edged pulses cast light on him, not illuminating as much as shrouding. Lying like stone on the white slab of his bed, his wrappings and skin oyster-colored, she thought of pictures she'd seen of ancient sarcophagi.

He would die now. She'd signed papers, and he'd already stepped partially away. Her knowing was keen and terrible. Others were there, too, invisible, but as present as she. They came from their violet world, just as they had at Mémé's death, ready to take up his hands, ready to take him away from her.

She approached his bed, whispered softly into his ear. "Angels are coming tonight." She tried to control her sudden gasping. How did a daughter breathe alongside her father's death? Alongside the terrible awful face that was still Papa?

Through the chain of relentless hours since the fire, she'd worried about how much pain he was suffering, once even praying that he found a quick release from charred skin and muscle. Now, knowing that he would leave her, she wanted to recant that prayer.

She pulled the chair back to him and sank into it, her knees so close they pressed hard against the cold bed frame. The last time she saw Papa whole, he sat at her table eating her cheap flour noodles and holding Prairie. Now this, all for having let Mary in the house that first time, getting into Derrick's car, and spreading her legs for him.

She lifted her right hand, wanting the weaker, wounded limb in his, but she stopped. The wrappings on his arms, and then his hands, looked like papier-mâché clubs, and he might feel pain if she clutched him. She trailed a finger alongside his arm, over the ghostly sheet, and finally lowered her head onto the bed, resting her cheek so close to his shoulder she could feel his warmth. She closed her eyes and tried to conjure a picture of how his face looked before. When she was a toddler, he tossed her in the air, and for airborne seconds, she looked down at him grinning up at her, his arms extended to catch her. She'd try to keep hold of that picture, the healthy, happy father who loved to make her fly.

She ached to start babbling about how much she needed him and how much Prairie needed her grandfather, even if only for a few more days. But how much pain, she asked herself, would she have *him* go through in order to postpone *her* loss?

Someone dressed in white entered the room, but she closed her eyes, not wanting to see a physical man or woman. More sobbing than speaking, she tried to tell Papa again, "Angels are coming tonight." A hand brushed across her back, and a voice asked if she was ready.

She didn't watch the tube being extracted from his throat or the wires being disconnected, and she didn't look up at the person who left with no more than a whisper of soft shoes. Papa would go to Jeannie, now.

He mumbled.

Her heart kicked, and she lifted her head to look at him. Her flicker of hope—that they might have a last bit of communication—died. The distorted face, not his, was quiet, and even without the breathing tube, he couldn't have spoken. "Papa, I'm right here."

I should have killed him.

Clear and sharp with regret, the words hadn't come from his mouth. They leapt and she caught them in the old way. She closed her eyes and covered her face with her hands, trying to still the trembling. How could he, with his mind half freed and wizened with full sight, be thinking of Derrick? She stood, paced, and looked back at his dying form. Did he hate Derrick that much? Or was he so afraid of what Derrick would do? Her heart pounded, what was he seeing?

She forced herself to sit again, and she worked to keep her voice steady. "You don't have to worry about Derrick. You protected us, Papa. We're safe now."

Long minutes melted gray into gray, and she was certain she could feel his body cooling. "Willow," she coaxed. "Say Willow." A part of her was dying, too. In so many ways, a daughter was slain when her father no longer lived to speak her name into the world, no longer held the space of it open, insisted on it. "Say, Willow."

There was only silence and the crowding. She wanted to push at them, shout, tell them to go away, and give her more time. She thought of Mémé's death and how Mémé had dropped blue.

On the small table outside his door were the flowers the hospital hadn't allowed into his IC unit. She stepped out, took the ribbon from each, tied the two together, and went back in. Careful not to bump his hand, she draped one end of the ribbon over and around the bandages on his wrist. The other end she wound through her own fingers so tightly they pulsed. She clung with her other hand to his upper arm. Tears rolled off her cheeks, but to reach for a tissue would mean letting go. She would walk with him as far as she could, holding onto him until the very end.

32

❦

Willow held Prairie in her arms and stared out at the people gathered around Julian's grave, a spattering of fifteen or twenty. She wanted to thank them for giving up their morning and curse those who hadn't, thank them for their prayers and curse what they might be thinking—that Papa had been drunk and smoking.

Prairie reached and touched the tears on Willow's face, tiny round fingers exploring the wetness. "It's all right," Willow whispered in her ear, not imagining how it could ever be so again.

Her gaze lifted above Papa's casket and over the headstones of carved angels, crosses, and wide slabs flat as stone cellar doors. A week before, there had been ice, but the warm front that moved in almost immediately after remained, and the weather was spring-like. She wasn't sure of the exact date, only that the calendar was somewhere in the first week of April. She looked to where the sky rolled, layer upon layer, the blue fading in the distance like unevenly-dyed silk.

In those gathered, she saw half-remembered faces from the years when Papa worked on the force, men who came to the house to watch football and jumped to their feet every time the Huskers scored.

Red stood beside his wife and held his hat in his hands. Willow supposed others were Greenburr locals who'd grown up with Papa or Tory. To her left, Mable sniffed, and the ends of her dark shawl fluttered in the breeze. To her right, Tory stood with no sniffling or display of emotion, her shoulders back and her chin resolute. Willow appreciated both women: Mable's deep feeling and, knowing that Tory and Julian hadn't been close, her aunt's composure and hard honesty, no pantomiming tragedy.

Jonah was half hidden between men and women who stood head and shoulders over him. She'd wanted to spend time with him the night before, but after reaching Farthest House, finalizing the funeral Mass with Tory and the priest, and getting Prairie down for the night in a strange room, the yard to his small cottage lay in darkness. She could have taken a flashlight, but standing at the kitchen window, her face pressed to the glass and her hands cupping her eyes against the inside glare, she'd not seen even the warm glow of a low-watt bulb showing in either of his inky windows. Nor could she bring herself to wake him, just because she ached for his company.

A striking man dressed in a black suit stood next to Jonah, and the two made a study in contrasts: old and young, black and white, short and tall, a concentration of forms. Whether it was because of the interesting composition they made to her artist's eye, or something in their postures and proximity, she believed they came to the funeral together.

She dropped her gaze back to the black casket with its simple silver cross; Papa was dead, and nothing else mattered.

The Greenburr parish priest, having swung his censer over the body in the local church, an aromatic cloud of incense rolling up to accompany the soul, now sprinkled holy water, his final anointing. "Though we are separated from Julian for a time, we all share his destiny and will meet again at the resurrection on the last day."

Hollow words, Willow thought. This was a murder.

Jeannie's grave lay on one side of Julian's, Mémé's on the other, and the closeness of the three plots gave Willow some comfort. Papa wasn't alone. There was no grave for Mémé's husband, Papa's father, and she wondered why Papa never mentioned him. Had Mémé divorced the man?

The priest finished his prayers, and too soon, the undertaker touched Tory's elbow and pointed her to the walk and then touched Willow's, "This way." Well-wishers formed a line to offer final condolences, extending hands Willow shook while holding Prairie close, a blur of faces sliding past, lips moving. She tried to concentrate, and as Tory supplied names, she thanked them for coming and resisted telling each one, "He was murdered." She waited for Jonah so that she could take hold of his old hand and the shaking in her own would stop.

The man she saw standing next to him earlier was alone now. He shook

Tory's hand, smiled at Prairie, and extended his hand to Willow. "I'm sorry for your loss."

"Thank you." Behind him only Red remained, which meant Jonah hadn't stayed to see her.

"How good of you to come," Tory said, her voice flowing. "Willow, I'd like you to meet Dr. Hartford."

He smiled. "It's just Clay."

Handsome, she thought, with his sandy-brown hair and mauve-speckled blue-gray eyes. But the fact that she was making assessments of his looks, dog-faced or dashing, on the day of Papa's funeral threatened to start her crying again.

"Dr. Hartford teaches the English classes at Briarwood. One course is on Mom's novels."

She'd heard of the small college outside of town, but she didn't know anyone who went there. Had someone asked her about its professors, she'd have guessed they were old, matronly women who also taught piano on Saturdays.

Clay smiled at Tory's comment. "I teach three literature classes out of a couple dozen the University offers."

The joking and teasing, when Willow felt half sick with loss and as if her head were full of lead, made her ache for Mémé's old bedroom: the dark and quiet where she spent the previous night.

"Dr. Hartford," Tory said, "is in charge of building the library honoring Mom."

"I help chair a *committee*," he gently corrected. "Every member is important to the project."

"What library?" Willow asked.

He leaned in instinctively, as though he hadn't quite heard, then straightened, his face questioning, telling Willow that her surprise surprised him.

Tory cut in. "Willow, you've been under such stress. Have you forgotten the Luessy Starmore Library?" Then to Clay, "Since my brother's accident, we haven't gotten a chance to talk about the library again."

Again? Willow wondered. Papa hadn't mentioned a library. If he'd known, he'd have told her. "When's it going to be built?"

"You'll have to excuse us," Tory said. She gave a pointed glance to Red and his wife still waiting in line. "You'll be up to the house soon."

"Absolutely," he nodded at Tory and then Willow. "If you're going to be in town for a few days, I'd love to show you the site."

Willow tried to smile and seem interested. She felt made of rain and cloud.

Red offered his condolences to Tory and motioned for Willow to walk with him. As soon as they'd stepped away, she grabbed his forearm. "Have you arrested her?"

"There are no signs of a forced entry."

"What about the back bedroom window? It might have been unlocked."

"The windows were all down. Even if we found a latch open, that's not evidence against Mary Wolfe. The cigarettes—"

"But she lit them and put them where they'd start a fire."

"Walking around without his waking up? She has an alibi." He paused. "She spent the night at the neighbor's. The Crats. Mrs. Crat says she never left. Think about it, that was an ugly night for her to be out driving around looking to set fire to somebody's house."

The fierce headache pounded in Willow's head. "She would have walked, not driven, and it wasn't *somebody's* house. It was Papa's."

"There's one more thing you should know. There were bottles on the kitchen table. It looks like he'd been drinking."

No reception followed the funeral. Prairie and Willow returned to Farthest House, and while Mable took Prairie to the kitchen and Tory went up to her room to change, Willow headed outside for the hilltop air she remembered. Hopefully, Jonah would be out, too.

Standing on the portico, her gaze took in the sweep of the wide lawn and garden. She told herself this is how it will be, nature won't stop. Minutes will pass in the distraction of living, shaking strangers' hands, and taking care of Prairie. The minutes will creep, until after a very long time an hour will have passed and then a second, Papa always receding.

Jonah wasn't uncovering roses or checking his bee hives, which stood nearer to his door than she remembered. The door to the tool shed was closed, and she hated to knock on his. He hadn't remained at the cemetery to talk to her, and she had no way of knowing the depth of his sadness, or fatigue, or his desire to be alone. She'd walk around and hope that he came out, maybe even open his door and invite her in.

The grass held a spring-green cast, thick buds pushed through furry casings on the magnolia trees. Tulips and daffodils poked thick, short fingers out of brown beds.

My attention went to the pile of gray and white sun-splashed rocks where Thomas and I had bones buried. At least this time, my ghostly specter wasn't there. Luessy used to recite a poem I loved, and scraps of those lines returned to me, " . . . death like a shoe without a foot in it, death like a ring stoneless and fingerless . . . "

Willow made her way across the yard to where the formal lawn ended and the uncultivated hillside dropped away to new switch grass, volunteer milo, pigweed, tickseed, and to where Mémé taught her to watch for pheasants and bobolinks. In the valley, the river shimmered through the trees covering its banks, and farther still Greenburr looked small and quaint. A tractor droned in the distance, and Willow wanted to spend the afternoon sitting there, doing nothing more than watching the clouds and the slow tractor cross the field. She'd spent the years since Mémé's death bordered by gray asphalt, rather than living green, light poles rather than trees, and standing on the hill felt as though she stood on the edge of possibility. Her body as interwoven with the trees, grasses, and the farmers in their seasonal work, as a reed in a basket. In the years she'd been away, she tried to untwist herself from the land, but she felt she lived those years with bends and empty kinks, never fitting as well as she had at Farthest House. Now Tory wanted her to stay.

Mable opened the door off the kitchen, her voice rising, "The tea is ready." Willow started back. Jonah wasn't coming out.

Holding Prairie and a small cup of dry Cheerios, she sank into a chair across the table from Tory. The dining room looked unchanged. Mémé's burgundy-colored rugs, the heavy velvet drapes the color of new pears, the polished mahogany dining-room table with its twelve high-backed chairs and cushions of claret and dusk, and one wall, still, with a grouping of half a dozen botanicals I painted.

Willow smiled to see Tory pour tea into the purple pansy cup, "You remembered."

Tory slid the cup and saucer and steaming tea to Willow. She lifted the lid from a silver sugar bowl and slowly sifted sugar into her own tea. "Have you considered my offer?"

"You've already done so much."

Tory stirred slowly. "Having you both here would give me such pleasure."

Taking up the honey, Willow poured a thin, gold stream into her cup. She felt sympathy for her aunt, too. Tory also lost someone in Papa, and even if they hadn't been close, losing him shut a door on any hope of reconciliation.

Prairie picked up pieces of cereal, still clumsy at feeding herself, more eating out of her hand than her hand finding her mouth.

"I believe," Tory continued, "your living here for a bit is what you need, too."

As a child, Willow avoided her aunt, but now, she studied Tory's thin, angular face and how the window light striking the right side added to its equine shape. *Handprints pressed into cement aren't a hold on a piece of land,* Mémé once said, and Willow wondered what Mémé would say now. Hadn't Tory earned Farthest House? Choosing to live simply, staying in her hometown and childhood home? Papa was the one who chose to leave for what he must have thought would be glamorous work fighting crime.

Mémé had also said a person needed to become rooted to a place before the land spoke to him. Surely now, trees whispered to Tory.

Decades ago, I'd given Tory a three-legged sewing basket. Now, she pulled a doll leg from it. With mesmerizing movements and tiny gold, pelican-shaped scissors, she snipped a length of white thread, moistened one end on her tongue, and threaded the strand into a long silver needle. The needle dipped and rose, making two, three, four small stitches before Tory's hand lifted, and she drew the thread through all the stitches at once.

"You must have made hundreds of dolls by now," Willow said.

"I've no idea how many. Do you think Prairie would enjoy one?" Before Willow could answer, Tory continued on, as if she didn't expect an answer or hadn't heard herself ask the question. "I can't offer you a permanent place," she said. "When I die, Greenburr inherits all this. You do remember hearing Mom's will read?"

A vision of Papa's casket suspended over the inky outline of the grave below made Willow shudder. "Let's not talk about dying."

"Well, shall we talk about you?" Tory sipped her tea, and her eyes lowered again to her sewing. "Tell me more about your life."

Willow toyed with Prairie's hair, winding curls behind her daughter's ears and considered what she could handle telling and what she best avoid. "I'd love to stay here. The thought of going back to my apartment, standing at the window, and not seeing Papa's roof creeps me out. Without him there," she took a breath and some time, "we have nothing left in Omaha." *And so many reasons to get as far away as possible.* "I'm afraid, though, that after a couple of days we'll wear out our welcome."

"Nonsense."

"You and I are just getting reacquainted. I'd like us to become close, not enemies. Then, there's my apartment and classes." She slowed considering school, "I've missed a paper and a test." A deeper realization struck her. Even if her instructors let her make up what she missed, dropping Prairie off at a sitter's now was unthinkable. Not with Mary out there. She and Prairie needed allies. With Tory, Mable, Jonah, and the solid security and distance of Farthest House from Omaha, Prairie *would* be safer.

Tory lowered the doll leg onto her lap. "We'll do fine." The petite scissors opened, flashed, and snipped thread. "It takes years to get over a death, and I've lived alone too long. If I'm ever going to have something of a family again, it's time now."

Prairie finished her last Cheerio and squirmed to get down. Willow sat her on the floor and watched her crawl for the kitchen and Mable, as though she already knew and felt comfortable at Farthest House. Mrs. Crat's words rang in her head: *Oh heavens, haven't you any family.* "I paint," she said after a moment. "The oils smell."

Tory looked up from her work. "You still paint, then? My aunt used to paint in the attic. You could work there."

With so little sleep over the last several days, Willow's body felt like a folding-chair collapsing on itself. She struggled to focus. The attic would mean a full-sized studio, her own space to work nights and during Prairie's naps, and where her supplies could be spread out, not piled into a playpen. A dream come true, but the only thing that mattered at the moment was having Prairie in the safest possible place.

"Good," Tory said.

"With his house burned down, Farthest House is the only other place Papa ever lived."

"You don't really believe someone set fire to his house?"

Willow leaned back and looked through the doorway to Prairie on Mable's hip. On the day they buried Papa, Prairie was happy. Farthest House, Mable, Tory, Jonah, they'd all be gifts to Prairie. "There's this crazy person named Mary. She threatened. For Papa to die like he did, because of a fire, and for it to be a coincidence, hardly."

"But wasn't he a heavy smoker? Didn't the fire start with a cigarette?" And then, almost reverently, "There was his drinking, too."

Papa had been lax about burning cigarettes; she couldn't forget the one he left burning in the kitchen, its smoke curling up. "He didn't drink anymore," she said. "I don't understand those bottles."

"Willow, really? He was just a man."

For a few minutes, they sat without speaking. Willow didn't want to hear how Papa had been 'just a man.' She wanted to excuse herself, get an ice pack for her head and sleep, but Tory's long-fingered, masculine-looking hands lifted the cozy off the teapot and poured again. "Who is this Mary?"

There were volumes Willow wouldn't tell. "A blonde, too perfect on the outside, tormented on the inside. She drives a yellow TR6."

Tory's penciled brows rose. She set the doll leg on the table, a needle jutting out. "Yesterday, just before you arrived, I drove down to have my teeth cleaned, and when I came out of the dentist's office, a small yellow car, I might have said gold, was driving very slowly down Main Street, right past me. An unusual, bright color. A roadster type, I don't know models."

Willow's stomach clenched. Had Mary come to check out Greenburr? The location of Farthest House?

"My dentist was surprised to see me, Julian not yet buried," Tory explained, "but I made that appointment months ago, and I've never in my life missed an appointment." She picked up her sewing again, a purposeful set to her lips. "Anyway, a pretty girl sat behind the wheel, and a car that color is not the sort of thing an observant person misses. I didn't recognize her." Tory went on, "I mean she wasn't one of our local girls. I don't know the college students, of course. Briarwood draws them from all over the country."

"Did the car have Omaha plates?"

"I've no idea."

"I'm scared," Willow's voice lowered to a whisper, "for Prairie. I half expect a court order to come any day, forcing me into joint custody with Derrick."

"She'll be a year old this summer. If Derrick hasn't cared yet, why would he now?"

"Because Papa is gone. Because now it's safe. Because Mary has resurfaced, and she'd push him into it just to hurt me. And then, on a day he has her, an accident. Texas is not far enough away." She felt the threat of tears again, and she looked over Tory's shoulder and out to the drive and the canopy of trees beginning to bud. "Please, let's talk about something else."

The doll leg in Tory's hand looked bloodless. "All right, dear."

"It's weird being here, weird that I was born here. Why not a hospital in Omaha?"

"Who can remember so long ago? Was it '59, '60? Just out of the 50's at any rate. Home-births were common. If I remember, Julian was doing a lot of undercover work, spending many nights away, and Jeannie didn't want to be so alone her last trimester. She loved Farthest House and the roses. She even enjoyed Mom. Julian came every chance he got.

"Dr. Mahoney," Tory gave a tiny shake of her head, "what would this town do without him? He preferred home deliveries. Likely still does. With no hospital nearby, he'd waste a lot of time driving back and forth to Omaha, and that distance, especially if you were in heavy labor, with sometimes just awful roads? Who would want to risk having a baby while stuck in a ditch in a snowstorm? His wife always hung out her sheets the day after her babies were born, already bleached and white as snow. She's an admirable woman."

"That's admirable? Who wanted those sheets out? Her, or him?"

Tory was still remembering. "Twenty years ago, doctors didn't have to worry about lawsuits for every little thing. Death was seen as God's will, and women often died in childbirth. Even in hospitals."

The pounding in Willow's head had risen to a crescendo. "I'm sorry. Would you mind if I went upstairs to lie down for just a bit?"

Tory went on. "Having you here will do us all good. You're more stressed than you know, but we won't make any far-reaching plans. Spend the summer, in the fall you can decide if it still suits you."

I wasn't surprised by Willow's relief. She watched her aunt's hands, the thin needle suturing. Each stitch seeming to punctuate the benefits of staying: no rent, food, and childcare expenses. Relief from those, for even a couple of months, would help her pay off some bills. Prairie remained the biggest concern, though, and Willow's mind kept circling around that. Even if Mary had driven to Greenburr to gloat over the impending funeral, she wasn't likely to come every day, cruising by as she'd started doing in Omaha. "You're sure? Maybe over the summer, Red will find proof that Mary killed Papa, and she'll be locked away for good."

"I'll call movers," Tory said. "My expense. And in the fall, if you decide to stay, Briarwood is an excellent university."

Sleep, Willow thought, but after Tory's kindness, movers doing the work, and Tory paying the bills, how could she get up and leave the table? "Dr. Hartford seems nice."

With a practiced motion, Tory rolled the end of her thread between her thumb and index finger, snagging it into a knot. "You'll see plenty of him this summer, he's going to be working here in the library."

"Here?"

"Is there a better place to write Mom's biography? The journals and notes are here. I've never let anyone cart off artifacts, and I won't start now. Those papers are likely worth money. I hope, when his book comes out, the university will want to buy them. I've told him none of Mom's papers are to leave the premises, under any circumstances."

"I'm glad I'm staying." Dr. Hartford would be another, younger set of eyes to warn of Mary.

Tory's stitches slowed and then stopped as she rounded a muslin toe. "He's seven or eight years older than you and already through all his schooling."

"I didn't mean I was looking for a man." The age difference didn't bother her, though. She fingered the handle of her pansy cup. She was sick of boys with shiny faces, errant pimples, and in stupors over what puberty had done to their penises. "I've escaped earning one PHT. I'm not looking to earn another."

"A PHT?"

She sipped her tea, Jonah's honey sweet on her tongue. "A 'Put Husband Through' college." Still, she had no interest in someone like Clay Hartford. Beautiful people like him, like Derrick, were of one world, she another. Though she didn't want to spend the rest of her life alone, raising Prairie the way she'd been raised—with only a single parent—at the moment, she didn't need to add a male to her list of troubles. "Actually," she said, "when the day comes, if it ever comes, I'll be looking for a mud face. Much less trouble. I just want to steal long looks at the guy, material for fantasies when I can't sleep."

Tory's needle bobbed. When she spoke again, Willow was surprised by the turn of her thoughts. "I'm not sure why Mom left you so little. Maybe she thought by the time I died, Farthest House would be an albatross."

33

✦

Willow tossed most of the night and rose in the morning with her head still pounding and her stomach rolling. She thought it odd to still be sick, because she was seldom ever ill. She took two aspirin, dressed Prairie, and they went down to the kitchen. By midmorning, she felt no better, and sitting where Mable rattled pans and cracked eggs by whacking them on the rim of her glass bowl wasn't helping. Fresh air might. More urgently, she'd yet to see Jonah.

With Prairie in her arms, she started across the yard. The bright sunlight and even Prairie's eighteen pounds made her doubt her decision, but Jonah was working to clear a raised flowerbed toward the back of the yard. She hurried.

He didn't see their approach, and when they'd come to within ten yards, Willow stopped to watch. She noticed his slumped posture at the funeral, but only in passing. Grief kept her focused on the casket. Now, she saw his back had become a bow, and his forward lean made his overalls hang from his chest, creating a sling, a place she wished she could crawl into, close to his heart.

"Poor old fool," Mable had said in the kitchen. "That man sees about as much as this egg in my hand."

The emotion in Mable's voice, a cross between frustration and kindness, had made Willow smile. The way Mable kept looking up from her work to glance out the window, her hands going still while her gaze followed Jonah, made Willow feel hope. They were family here.

"Jonah?" Willow said coming up on him, "hello."

He stopped raking and at the edge of the bed turned slowly, using the rake for support and cranking his stiff body around to face her. He'd spent her years away working in the sun and hilltop wind. He looked even more the basset hound, and she imagined one day, his rheumy eyes would not open at all, and he'd simply dream his way into eternity.

He wore three shirts under his work-worn Key overalls, each adding a different color of frayed thread to hang at his wrists. "Willow," he said, one tremulous hand reaching out for her.

She grabbed his knotty hand as Prairie in her arms tipped her head away from Jonah into Willow's neck. "This is my little girl, Prairie. Papa's dead," she heard herself say, the words sounding shamefully like *help me*.

Jonah nodded. "Yup. Your daddy was a good man. Your grandmother was always proud of that one."

"Thanks for coming to the funeral. I don't know how we'll get along without him." A wave of nausea rolled through her stomach, and she hoped she wasn't going to be sick in front of him. "Tory's asked me to live here for a while, and I've accepted her offer."

Jonah's gaze lowered, and he looked down to his shoes or the tines of the rake. He lifted the tool an inch off the ground and punched it back down.

His reaction surprised her. Was his hearing as bad as his sight? Had he misunderstood?

A bee buzzed by her ear and landed on Jonah's hand. Looking like a drop of gold, the insect moved, dipping the upper part of its body into the shadow between two of Jonah's thick black fingers. It walked across the bridge of one finger and dipped again.

"I see you're still keeping as many bees," she said.

"Can't say for certain. Counting 'em is hard. Tory asked you to stay here?"

He had heard correctly. "Does that surprise you? It did me at first."

"Why you want to be here?"

His attitude felt bruising. "I love Farthest House."

"No reason you need to be here."

He only reached her shoulders, but his words felt towering. "I have reasons."

"You best go back home."

On Willow's hip, Prairie was growing heavy. "Tory has more than enough room, and she's family. Right now, Prairie and I need—"

"Ain't you got a job? Ain't no work around here for young folks."

What could she say? He'd been glad to see her, and now he was telling her to pack her bags. She watched the bee on his hand.

"That baby too?" he asked. "She staying?"

She shifted Prairie to her other hip, her eyes narrowing. How could he even ask that?

"Ain't no reason to have a baby here. Just us old fools here."

There was no point in continuing the conversation. He didn't want them there, and because he was half the magic of Farthest House, half her reason for staying felt gone. The other half wasn't: she needed to stay where Prairie was safest. She glanced back at the house and the cobblestone walk she had to travel to get there. If she could just get back inside and lie down, then later, with a cleared head, she'd try and make sense of Jonah's rejection. "Give us a few weeks, at least, and don't worry, we'll try and stay out of your way."

She shifted Prairie again, not realizing a bee had landed in the crook of her arm. With a yelp, she flung the free arm down, and the bee dropped and spun in the grass. She felt doubly betrayed. During the four years she spent weekends at Farthest House, often helping with the hives, she was never stung. Didn't she have a special relationship with the bees? She'd thought the same of her relationship with Jonah, too, but she was wrong.

34

---❦---

Three rows of bookshelves flanked each side of Luessy's library. Moving down the aisle with Willow, I spied books I had read, colored spines, snatches of titles, many in French, ideas picked up and put down. Worlds. They had an equally spellbinding effect on Willow. She not only longed to read each one, for her the worlds of reading and painting were as connected as the two sides of the brain, thick with ropy links and nerve fibers firing impulses. She loved line, color, shading, and negative space. And she loved words.

When she thought of summer's passing, April and May already gone while she tossed in bed with headaches or leaned over the toilet heaving, it depressed her. But she was up now and having a much better day, even managing to shower and come downstairs. Still in her bathrobe, she'd stopped to rest a moment in the wide arboreal foyer, and the door to the library had caught her up and pulled her in.

She walked slowly with no more desire than to be in the space, another space, where Mémé found inspiration. Two mahogany arm chairs in antique leather still flanked a small reading table in front of a wall of French windows. The windows framed a view of the garden where Jonah worked at one of his endless tasks, and the willow tree Papa used as inspiration for her name sat stately and much larger than she remembered. At the front of the library was the desk where Mémé's will was read so many years before. Willow felt she'd never understand what happened that morning: Papa so angry and stunned by the raven. Mémé's death, though he grieved her, hadn't done that. Something else crippled him that winter morning.

The Luessy Starmore Mysteries occupied a prominent place in the first bookcase, middle shelf, and eye level. Like the rest of the library, everything looked in its proper place but spiritless with Mémé and Papa gone.

Willow moved around the desk, sank into the chair, and her hands fanned out over the broad and polished desktop. Mémé had touched and palmed the wood all through her adult life, and Willow felt starved for connection.

I felt a deep ache, too. As Willow's illness drug on, I was losing hope. My worst fears were unfolding.

"Why am I so sick?" she asked of the space. On good days, she managed a few minutes outside, sitting on the portico with Prairie, until a bee, sometimes two or three, came circling. At other times, she found the strength to duck through the low door in the wall of Mémé's bedroom and climb the narrow and crooked attic steps. There she sat and stared at her paintings. Kahlo, she knew, found ways to paint while in pain, the bright primary colors full of blood and heartache, but how?

On her worst days, Willow lay in Mémé's old bed, drifting in and out of fitful sleep, the wall paneling, windows, and the door to the attic winging around her, and the lines of day and night bleeding together or entirely erased.

"Mom read in here every day," Tory said from just outside the door, her voice reaching like one of her long fingers into the library. "But when it came to her writing, she preferred the attic, believing all the books were a distraction."

As Tory appeared, Prairie on one gaunt hip, and behind her Clay Hartford, Willow drew in a quick and frustrated breath. She ran her hands through her damp hair and clutched closed the deep vee of her robe. "Hello," and then, "I'm here. So sorry, Tory, nowhere to hide."

At the sound of her mother's voice, Prairie leaned forward, trying to squirm out of Tory's grasp, her small arms stretching for Willow.

"There's my baby girl," Willow said. She stood too fast, a swoosh of dizziness slamming her head. She dropped back down.

The hems of Tory's black, wide-legged pants fluttered around her thin ankles, and she brought Prairie forward. "I haven't seen anyone sitting behind that desk since Mom died. How strange to see you there. You remember Professor Hartford?"

He reached his hand across the desk. "It's good to see you again. And please, it's just Clay."

His coat was off, and he carried it swung over his shoulder on the hook of a finger. He'd also loosened his tie and rolled his shirtsleeves back from his wrists. *Tall,* Willow thought. *Taller than me, and kill-me-now handsome.* She reached for his hand, trying to keep Prairie balanced on her lap and her robe closed. "I bet I wouldn't find Clay in the *Catholic Book of Saint's Names.*"

"I wouldn't know," he looked amused. "Is that important?" Then after a pause, "Tory tells me you've been sick. I hope this means you're recovering."

Tory stood closer to him than Willow thought necessary. "Dr. Mahoney has left instructions: Willow is to get plenty of bed rest, but she's also to get up and get busy."

The comment made Willow cringe, and she hoped her face wasn't coloring. She disliked the town's old physician and his condescending recommendations. Only for Prairie, who needed a healthy mother, had she allowed him to examine her not once, but twice. Both times he repeated the same diagnosis: "Probably a virus." The second time though, his voice held a thinner, slightly tighter note: "I suspect you've let yourself get depressed. Just the sort of thing viruses like. You need to get over that, now."

She'd stared at him. *Get over Papa's death? Get over caring that Mary murdered him and is still free? Get over worrying about Prairie's safety?*

Still, Dr. Mahoney had drawn blood on her second visit, and when the tests came back, his white brows tangled over his dark eyes, and he scolded: "There's nothing medically wrong with you. When a woman spends her time in bed like you're doing, I tell her she needs to find something useful to occupy her mind."

In the library, Clay stepped back from the desk and to the long line of Luessy's mysteries. "Do the two of you have a favorite?"

Tory's shoulders lifted. "I've never read them. Oh, I've thumbed through some of them, but it wasn't much fun having a mother preoccupied with her work."

Willow swallowed, forcing herself to stay quiet. Mémé always gave her plenty of attention, and Papa never complained about neglect. The criticism seemed as unfair as it was surprising. Even if Tory believed she'd been neglected, she needed to be careful what she said in front of Mémé's biographer.

"I'm interested in her writing habits," Clay said.

"Completely compulsive," Tory said. "The writing always came first."

Clay acknowledged her comment and nodded toward Mémé's titles. "One is missing."

Gazing around, indicating the whole of the library, Tory smiled. "It must be misfiled. You're welcome to try and find it." She turned back to Willow, "Mable is fixing tea, and we're taking it outside. Do you feel up to joining us?"

The bees! How many times had she been stung? The furry little monsters in her face seemed like extensions of Jonah, telling her over and over that she wasn't wanted. "I don't think so, and I'm not dressed. You two go on ahead. Prairie and I will stay inside."

"I wish you would," Clay said. He looked solid and comfortable as he took the few steps back to the desk, light from the nearest window layering a thin sheen over his jaw. "It's a beautiful afternoon, and I'd like to hear your stories of your grandmother."

Was she staring at him?

He looked down at Prairie. "You want your mom to come outside?"

Prairie nodded up and down.

Smart, Willow thought, *use the kid.* Spending more time with him though and being outside with Mémé's roses and Prairie did sound wonderful. She was starved for company other than that of the two sixty-something women who prattled on about the weather or gossiped ceaselessly about folks she didn't know or served up churchy platitudes about how she'd certainly feel better soon. But did she have the strength to climb back up the stairs, get dressed, and make the trek outside? Only to face the bees?

"Having you join us *would* be a treat," Tory said.

They waited for an answer, but Willow continued to hesitate. "I wish the porch were screened in."

"Nonsense," Tory said. "We're going first to see the attic. Dress and join us outside."

They turned to leave, and Prairie squealed and squirmed in Willow's lap. Clay stopped. "You want to come with us?"

He dropped his jacket onto the desk and lifted his palms in invitation. She leaned for him.

The three left the library, and Willow marveled at how Prairie went so easily to Clay, and how Clay hadn't considered himself too busy or too important to reach out and take her. Considering how Prairie had only women in her life now, Clay's kindness was appreciated. The flip-side though made Willow's throat tighten. Prairie was likely to reach for any stranger who smiled at her.

Dressed and feeling gratitude just for having found the strength to do so, Willow stepped onto the covered portico and stopped, breathing in deeply. The air smelled of fading peonies, and new roses. The sky was a clear, liquid blue, maybe cerulean, cobalt light, and titanium. Across the lawn, Jonah worked with pruning shears. Behind him, farther still, stood his hives.

She hadn't spoken to him since their first conversation, and knowing he didn't want her, or Prairie, around still hurt. There had to be some misunderstanding. She'd get well, start helping out in the garden, doing the heaviest jobs, and they'd get things straightened out. He'd come to love Prairie.

She noticed Clay then, sitting alone at the patio table and looking out in the direction of the graves. He'd rolled his blue shirtsleeves up to his elbows, and for a moment, her eyes rested on his bare forearms. She wondered if he remembered he left his coat on the library desk. Hopefully not. If he left the prize behind, she'd wrap herself up and—Reason thumped her on the head. *You're losing it. Might as well bare your breast to an asp as trust a male again.*

He turned, smiled, pushed his chair back and started for her. "I'm glad you decided to join us."

She didn't have a vocabulary for describing scents, not like she had for the nuances of color, and she wondered about his faint suggestion of spice. Not cologne, something warmer and more masculine. How did you describe attar of man? "I'm glad, too."

"The graves over there," he nodded in the direction of the rocks, "they're the aunt and uncle who raised Luessy?"

As much as she enjoyed his standing beside her, she still felt somewhat lighted-headed and moved on to the patio table and a chair. "Did Tory tell you about the graves? Mémé's will says they're to remain undisturbed for a hundred years."

She'd dressed first in a long-sleeved cotton blouse over her cut-offs, a top with no cling over her shoulder, but she thought of how much spring weather she'd already missed lying in bed, and how quickly Prairie was growing and Jonah, Mable and Tory were aging. She wouldn't waste one more afternoon wishing she were prettier and trying to hide herself. She tossed the blouse across the rose chair and reached for a cooler white T-shirt.

Now, Clay stood behind her doing the whole gentlemanly thing, pushing in her chair like he didn't already have carte blanche to the library. How could he not be looking at her shoulder? He hadn't missed her legs. Crossing the portico, she noticed his gaze going down, and up. For years she'd hated them, *gangly and too long,* and now here was a leg-man. Not that it mattered. He was not a potential partner. Tory was right, seven or eight years *was* too much of an age difference, and he had a PhD, and taught at the University. She was barely twenty, already a divorced, single mother who lived off the generosity of an aunt, and according to Dr. Mahoney, a victim of mindless depression.

He came back around the table, the corners of his eyes crinkling ever so slightly against the sharp sunlight. "I love your paintings in the attic."

She struggled to keep from giving the too-big grin of the fool. "Thank you. My last professor thought I wasn't challenging myself by always doing portraits." She wouldn't add, 'of females.' A female painting females—lesser on lesser. "I've been told they don't fit any European model and fall into the category of folk art." She grinned, "You don't want to get me started."

He settled into his chair. "I see them as allegory. They're arresting, rather mythical."

"You see what I'm trying to do. You're good."

One brow lifted. "'Good?' Good for a guy, good for someone who knows nothing about art?"

"Just good."

"Okay, then." They both chuckled at the other. "What would you say to hanging one in the university library? The one of Luessy atop the stack of her novels? We have a lot of wall space to fill."

"You're kidding?"

"I'm not. It's the Luessy Starmore Library, and that's a very arresting and unique painting of her, and it was done by her granddaughter. I think it more than qualifies."

She wanted to reach across the table and hug him. Fighting tears, she looked out across the flowers. "I'd love it," she managed.

"I hope I haven't upset you."

"No. It's just things have been so crazy the last few months. Somehow, having even that simple picture displayed feels like a step forward. I'm grateful."

"Tory says you're mostly self-taught, and you learned a lot by copying figures from mythology?"

Something almost remembered skimmed Willow's awareness, but slipped away ungrasped. "Tory has listened to my ranting for two months now." Was that true? Was she having conversations she didn't remember? "I did do a lot of copying. While other kids were running up and down soccer fields and splashing in swimming pools, I painted."

"You didn't use photographs of the women?"

She framed her face with her fingers, just as she'd isolated areas in art class. She cringed, remembering her hand and recovered. "I stole that idea from Frida Kahlo. The props and clothing come from the scraps of their lives I do know about." A slight breeze funneled under the roof, and she watched it work like an invisible hand smoothing the front of his shirt. "Now your face," she said, "tells me your life has been one big picnic."

"Good guess. A picnic through and through."

She studied him, half expecting the sun would strike him and he'd disappear like any mirage. "Do you write fiction or strictly biography?"

"I'd secretly like to write fiction, but I think I'd better stick to biography, research, and facts."

She hoped she wasn't staring, watching him lean back, his arms relaxed on the arms of his chair. "Maybe you have a couple of pot-smoking colleagues who would make good characters."

"My colleagues wear dark suits and think pot-smokers should be behind bars." He waited, enjoying her amusement. "Actually, they're great people. Tory hopes you'll attend Briarwood in the fall. I wouldn't want you thinking badly of us."

Thinking of fall saddened her. She'd been too ill and uncertain to consider three months ahead. "Tory's been an entire army of help to me, but I have no idea if I'll still be here in the fall."

"We have an excellent studio arts department, and they'd be thrilled to have you."

"There's just so much. All I can manage to think about right now is sitting in this chair." She also wouldn't mention how she could sit and talk to him for an eternity. "Your interest in Mémé is cool, but I have to tell you, she'd think all the library fuss silly."

"Would she? I thought she loved attention?"

"What?"

Taking his time, he looked out over the portico to the roses and Jonah. "This incredibly huge house and the big garden—"

"She wasn't Emily Dickinson," Willow cut in, "but this isn't Monticello either."

"And the name? Farthest House on Old Squaw Road."

"You must already know how the name came about."

"I've heard one version. What do you think? Why build something grand and give it a name that to others is a joke?"

"Because it spits in your eye."

He laughed. "Exactly. But why was that necessary?"

A cumulus cloud moved, blocking the sunlight and deepening the color of the roses. "Maybe she built it for her aunt or for the mother she never knew. I've never thought about it, which probably sounds weird." She shrugged. "Actually, everything about being here is weird. I feel like I'm always dreaming, half loopy."

She looked away and back into the eyes so like shiny river stones. "I can't believe I just admitted that. Being sick rots your brain, makes you start babbling." That admission was at least as bad as the first. Her eyes narrowed. "What I mean is, Mémé's aunt rescued her. Now, here I am, at this house, rescued by my aunt." A chill crawled up her right arm and passed over the scars she'd given herself. Her heart pumped a bit faster. If something happened to her, would Prairie then end up being raised by Tory? Had Farthest House sucked her back to die in its walls and hand Prairie over to another childless aunt? "You're not going to put any of this in your book?"

"I promise. The book is strictly about Luessy. I grew up reading her and Conan Doyle and . . . ."

Willow lost track of the conversation. Jonah stood in the same place as before, but now he had a wheelbarrow. She'd missed seeing his slow slumping away and slow slumping back. She wanted to close her eyes, but she needed to stay awake, concentrate.

" . . . and your grandmother's descriptions of the Midwest," Clay was saying, "spoke to me."

He'd taken off his tie and opened his top shirt button. Low on his throat, there in the bottom of that thumbprint indentation—given by the gods, myth said—she imagined his pulse. "So, you moved to Nebraska instead of Scotland Yard?"

"I couldn't be sure Scotland Yard had as much charisma as Nebraska."

She lifted a hand, held it between them. "Please . . . a Nebraska mystique? Corn and Herbie Husker? What about Bangor, Maine, or Seattle? Points farthest away from here."

"I came from the East, the White Mountains area. Here you have incredibly wide open spaces, a lingering aura of the west, buffalo and sacred sites. Did I mention incredibly wide open spaces, nothing to stop the wind? Or a person who needs to put on track shoes and run."

"You're serious, aren't you?"

"Plus," he said with a chuckle, "Briarwood offered me a job. It's not easy to get that first tenure-track position. I couldn't turn it down."

"How did that come about?"

"I thought I was interviewing you."

"I thought you weren't."

"I'd finished my PhD." He glanced in Jonah's direction, too, then back. "I only had one brother, he was gone, my parents were gone, and I wanted to start fresh somewhere new. When I read about the position, I immediately thought of the Luessy Starmore Mysteries and how she lived in Greenburr. I didn't know she'd died. I thought if Greenburr was a town where she had the freedom to do that much writing, it would be a great place for me to teach and write."

"And?"

"I applied, was granted an interview, flew out in the spring and was hooked: the town, the Victorian homes, old shops, people who looked you in the eye and said 'hello.' I fell in love. Farmers plowed and planted using huge pieces of machinery that rumbled down the roads, Tonkas on steroids."

She wanted him to go on talking. "And?"

"Well, the whole area felt alive. Different from people running around in a city. On the Briarwood campus, flags whipped straight out on their poles, girls turned their faces into the wind, and their hair lifted off their shoulders. Everything moved, no mountains, no high rises, no boundaries of any sort to stop that wind. In every direction, I could see clear into the next state: Iowa, Kansas, Colorado, and South Dakota."

"I've always loved that about Nebraska, being able to keep an eye on the folks in Colorado."

"I could breathe. I came out of my first interview with the search committee and filled my lungs with air and knew I had the job. Even if at that point they had no intention of hiring me, I knew the job was mine. However the chips fell, their first ten choices all changing their minds about moving or suddenly dying of the bubonic plague, the job was mine. Maybe they still aren't sure how I got here."

Willow wondered why he hadn't been able to breathe before he came to Nebraska, but she decided against asking. They didn't know each other that well.

A bee buzzed too close, and she jerked back and saw the insect lift and disappear like a bead on the end of a yanked string. There would be others.

"You're scared of bees?"

"I didn't used to be. What about the library? How'd you get a project that big off the ground?"

"I didn't. The money had already been raised, the plans approved for a larger library. Tory's making too much of my contribution. I did write a persuasive letter suggesting the library be named after her, their local celebrity and a literary one at that.

"And that's why they invited you to serve on the library committee?"

"*Invited* might not be the right word. *Assigned* might be better. Once you're on a committee, and you actually show up to the meetings, you can end up with a truckload of work in your lap. Don't forget, I'm working on her biography, so I've got ulterior motives. Being on the committee, I'm certain of selling at least one copy of my book to the library."

He was fun. She couldn't remember the last time she had such a fun and genuine conversation? He said more in fifteen minutes than Papa had in a year. "I take back what I said, Mémé would love the library."

"I hope so. Wait until you see it. The back of the university butts into open land, acres they own and rent out as pastures and expand into. Some rich and childless widow bequeathed her farm, and the section the library is on holds a slew of massive burr oaks."

The wide patio door opened, and Mable carried Prairie out. She left the door ajar, brought Prairie to Willow, disappeared back into the house, and reappeared carrying a tray with small dessert plates, milk for Prairie in a sippy cup, tiny pitchers of cream and honey, and a plate of cookies. Clay stood and taking a few long strides reached her and took the tray. He eyed the cookies. "You do this every day? Every single day? My mom baked a lot of cookies, but not every single day."

Mable stayed to pass the plates around and see her cookies placed squarely in the middle of the table. "I have to work to keep meat on this one." She leveled her eyes on Willow. "Walnuts, dates, Jonah's wild honey, good, rich butter, now you eat one."

"They smell wonderful," Willow said, though she had no desire to eat one.

Tory appeared with a second tray: a teapot and three cooling cups all with varied patterns. Erect in her chair and presiding, she passed a mug to Clay and the pansy cup to Willow. The flowers still took Willow back in time and made her feel a part of Farthest House. She wasn't yet a burden to Tory.

"Cream?" Tory asked.

Before Willow could agree or refuse, Tory lifted the small creamer and poured. She asked the same question of Clay with the same absent-mindedness and added cream before he could refuse.

Willow felt Clay's amusement, but she dared not look at him for fear of smiling and Tory catching their pleasure and realizing she was the cause. She reached for the honey jar.

"Please, start while your tea is hot," Tory said. "I'll only grab my sewing."

Willow had braided her hair earlier, and now Prairie grabbed for the plait, bringing it over Willow's shoulder. Captivated by the knobby feel, Prairie slid her chubby hands down the long bumpy rope. She grabbed again, higher this time, reading with her tiny palms the many things her mother's hair could be.

The first morning Willow decided to braid her hair, rather than let it hang loose down the sides of her face, she hadn't thought of Luessy's long braid. She walked around Luessy's bedroom with its cooler air and stillness, some slight touch making her wonder if the bedroom door had been shut all the years she was away. Time and isolation might explain how the room seemed to grow its own light and air. She trailed her fingers over her grandmother's big pieces of furniture: the bed, bookcases, desk, and dresser with its aging mirror and what looked like water stains beginning to spatter the silver-backed glass. Mémé touched it all, she thought, and she imagined her grandmother's liver-spotted hands and rounding knuckles. Mémé and the furniture had aged together.

Stopping in front of the mirror, she stood barefoot on the same carpet where Mémé had stood barefoot, likely even Jeannie, and the carpet where she'd stood as a little girl, when the world around her was carnival sized. Her fingers began braiding.

Now that she'd started wearing the single braid, she didn't feel dressed until she'd made the three equal sections, layering the hair over and over, weaving in comfort and history, and calling up ghosts.

35

With Tory not yet returned, Clay swallowed the tea he sipped and set his cup down, his shoulders giving an involuntary shudder. "I do coffee." He reached for a cookie. "This'll help."

Still holding Prairie, Willow laughed, touching her nose to Prairie's in play. "He hates tea." She believed she could see his mind already swinging back to his work, the way her mind so often swung back to her work hours after she'd cleaned her brushes.

"Would you consider Luessy a feminist?" he asked.

Prairie felt heavy in Willow's aching arms. Willow took a quick gulp of her tea, "Ah, cream and honey," and set her cup back before chubby hands could grab for it. "Would her being a feminist bother you?"

"No. The term wasn't even popular in her day, at least not when she began writing. I've never felt her novels carried a political agenda, but being here," his gaze went out over the garden, "the grandeur of this place is quite a statement for a woman of her time. Was it Jung who said our houses are representations of our psyches?"

She squinted as if Clay hadn't heard himself. "What else would our houses represent?"

One side of his mouth lifted in an easy sideways grin. "You'd be challenging in a class room."

Prairie squirmed to get down, and Willow fought to keep hold of her. Returning fatigue crawled up Willow's back, and her stomach began to sway with an all too-familiar roll. She'd been out of bed too long. "Mémé believed in the power of finding and holding tight to a vision. She believed in work." Willow's words sounded loud and too forceful. She tried to fight her symptoms and relax. "Does that make her a *feminist*? What does that word even mean?

Women with visions who work to achieve lives that males believe only they deserve?"

Leaning in, Clay watched her.

Her symptoms were always the same: headaches, nausea, and exhaustion. The tiredness, she supposed, came from the first two, which kept her from sound sleep. If she were to add a fourth, it would be moments of hyper-awareness, almost a dislocation from her body, and this, too, she believed came from her inability to keep food down and sleep soundly.

The door slid open, and Tory stepped out with her sewing. When she sat down at the table, and Clay who stood, sat back down after her, she reached into her basket and drew out the flat round form of a doll's still-empty head. "You were only a child when Mom lived," she said to Willow. "How would you know about her visions?"

"You heard that?" Willow asked. "Do you think Mémé was a feminist?"

Tory's long fingers pinched off wads of batting and stuffed them into the narrow slit she'd left open at the top of the doll's head. "She certainly lived in her own world."

Selfishly? Was that what Tory suggested? But it was 'lived in her own world' that most caught Willow's attention. On her first trip to Farthest House, she stood on the big front porch with Papa, surrounded by geraniums while Friar tried to lick her face, and she heard Papa scold Mémé with nearly the same sentiment: *Willow's got to live in this world right here*. In the years since that bright morning, she'd experienced so many extraordinary things that now she wondered what world was *this world right here*?

The slightest stirring under her feet caught her attention. Had something shivered beneath the flagstones? Not possible. She was just getting crazy tired. She shuffled her feet to rid them of the sensation and wished Prairie, who grew heavier by the minute, would sit still.

The conversation between Clay and Tory drifted away from her. She tried to refocus on them and at the same time hold on tighter to Prairie. From the floor beneath her feet, thin wires of energy, like nerves ticking, sent heat creeping up through her soles. She lifted her cup and sipped, noticing the shaking in her hands. Hopefully, neither Clay nor Tory had. The afternoon heat turned thick and damp over her. Somewhere nearby, bees buzzed, spun, and died. She didn't wonder that she knew, she just knew.

Tory's voice rose and fell. Clay asked questions, and Willow struggled again to jump onto the moving train of their conversation. But their words were big and cumbersome, leaving without her. Prairie squirmed, and tried to stand in Willow's lap. Too much energy, more than Willow had in her tired arms. "Mémé gave me a belief in magic," she blurted. The words were again too loud and likely too far from whatever they were discussing. She couldn't stop herself. "If Mémé said, 'Look, a fairy,' I *saw* a fairy. I want that for Prairie. To give her a world with a Mother Moses around every corner."

Tory's eyes remained on her work, but Clay studied Willow. Gone was the sassiness and confidence she demonstrated only minutes earlier. Distracted, he took another sip of his tea and was forced to swallow. "Mother Moses?"

Settle down, Willow coaxed herself. *Stay one more minute. Don't leave at the stupidest time.* "The story's too long," she tried to sound casual. "Can I tell you another time?" The unrest beneath her feet had become a bulge. The cement grout crumbled and the corner of a stone lifted. Not possible, but sliding a foot, she felt it pass over the knob. She needed to talk, to use the few words she could still manage like a handrail. "Mother Moses is a bed spread. Mémé bought it from a former slave owner. At least the woman's ancestors were." She stopped herself; she was shortening the story.

"Another of Mom's fantasies," Tory said.

"Well, whatever her beliefs," Clay offered, "she's built a beautiful place."

Two of Tory's fingers were buried in her muslin and looked severed. "We all built this place."

Willow wanted to pull Clay aside and repeat every word of Mother Moses' story. She'd also tell him that before Mémé's death, Tory and Mémé had a falling out, and Tory still carried hurt feelings. That conversation, though, would have to wait for another time. At the moment, Prairie kicked with her tiny shoes, sharp and bruising, flagstones moved beneath Willow's feet, and the pounding in her head was warlike.

She broke off a small piece of cookie and put it in Prairie's mouth. In a few hours, she wouldn't be able to hold her head up and wouldn't be able to take care of Prairie, making certain that Prairie stayed safe. Knowing the rest of the day, and probably the next, would mean crippling headaches and dry heaves, she'd stay as long as she possibly could.

She glanced down at the irritation beneath her feet. Thin black vines rose and reached for her ankles.

Tory let her work sink into her lap. "Willow, your face. Are you all right?"

Vines couldn't be sprouting, Willow knew, and the realization that she was hallucinating deepened her fear. Was she losing her mind? Dr. Mahoney would shake his head and tell her to get a grip. "I'm fi-ne." The last word singsong, waltzing.

"This isn't a good time," Clay said. He placed his hands on the chair arms and pushed himself up. "Why don't I come back in the morning?"

The ivy crept, twining tighter and higher around Willow's legs. She had to fight it and keep her panic under control. She wouldn't break down in front of Clay, and especially not in front of Prairie. "Please, don't go," she said. He was stability, and hopefully, a weight to counterbalance the strange sensation at her feet. "I'm all right. Mable fixed all this."

He lowered his body back into the chair, but his hands still gripped the arms. Willow concerned him. "I'd love to hear more about your paintings." And to Tory, "They're something, aren't they."

As Willow watched Tory pinch off more batting and work it into the doll's head, she knew she couldn't really discuss her paintings. She could talk about the paintings' esthetics, color and line, but she couldn't discuss what they meant to her spiritually. That, like a hundred other secrets she needed to keep, including the green/black growing up her calves, was private. She wiped cookie spittle from a corner of Prairie's mouth. Struck by a sudden realization, the shaking in her hands increased. The paintings were not just a way of saving her life; they could save Prairie's as well. She took another sip of tea, praying the liquid would work as a tonic. When she couldn't keep Prairie from standing, she kept hold of her daughter's hands, letting the punch of little shoes strike again and again.

Beyond the portico, the air had become a hot brilliance. Willow turned from the light and felt a sort of slippage in time that might have meant five seconds or five minutes passed. The conversation had moved ahead, and she felt addled and embarrassed. At the same time, evil continued to climb from beneath the flagstones, wanted to pull her down, and wanted her to know.

Now, she did want Clay to leave. He couldn't stop what was happening, and she didn't want him seeing her like this. Another time, they'd get together and toss a football. She'd throw the ball so straight and hard the pigskin would pop and sting his palms, and he'd know she was there.

"No, he's not from here," Tory was saying, as she looked out at Jonah. "He'd been accused of a murder in Omaha, and Mom brought him here to save his life."

Other than his bug story, Willow had never heard anything of Jonah's past and never wondered about a life before Farthest House. The realization was painful.

Clay wrapped his fingers around his nearly full cup, a thumb tapping on the handle. "What happened?"

"He was accused of killing a white woman. How, or why, Mom got involved, I couldn't say. Many people believed him guilty, but she used her name, and well, there he is."

The vines clung, turned Willow's ankles blue, and made her calves ache. She fought to keep her mind off them and on the conversation. "A white woman?" Was killing a white woman more heinous than killing a *black* woman? "Was she *pretty*, too?"

"She was blonde, and I hear quite beautiful," Tory said. "There was talk of a lynching. The Willie Brown incident was still fresh in everyone's minds, and many young men believed they had missed a good time. They wanted their faces on the front page of the newspaper, too." She paused, kneading the doll head in her hands and smoothing out the stuffing. "Jonah is still the only suspect."

"He couldn't have murdered anyone," Willow said. Her voice cracked. She turned to Clay, "Don't put that in your book."

Tory plopped her muslin down. "Willow, really." She glanced sideways around the edge of the table at Willow's legs. "What are you doing?" When Willow didn't answer, she spent another moment watching her before turning away. "She's likely right. Jonah doesn't seem the type to have killed a woman, though it was believed his father was in jail at the time for murder. He had no other family. And he *was* working that day, raking leaves for the woman. His rake was the murder weapon."

Clay pushed his cup back. "When was this?"

"1932."

"The lawless thirties," he nodded. "The era of mobs, cover-ups, and Saturday night lynchings. He's been here ever since?"

Between Tory's pushing and stuffing, she managed to finish her tea. "Nowhere else to go. I imagine that for years he was afraid of showing his face back in Omaha, tempting fate as it were. Getting a traffic ticket, even walking on the wrong street, might have ended in arrest. He owed us, too, for Mom saving his life." She smiled to herself. "When my brother, Willow's father, started police work, he was determined to prove Jonah's innocence. He couldn't do it. He stewed over records for years, questioned people, but he couldn't find any evidence to clear Jonah. That should tell you something."

This was news to Willow, and squinting against the brightness, she looked out to where Jonah worked. The outline of his figure looked hazy in the heat and his straw hat made of gold. He couldn't have murdered anyone, even if he didn't want her and Prairie around. However, if Tory believed he had, maybe that was one of the reasons she and Mémé fought.

Prairie squirmed, this time nearly falling from Willow's aching arms. Thin drops of sweat ran down the sides of Willow's face, and the vines were more insistent. They weren't real, couldn't be, and struggling against imaginary wolves only spread them through your house and filled your closets with growls. She needed to put Prairie down, but she'd waited too long and couldn't trust herself even to set her on the floor without dropping her. And what then? Tory and Clay were deep in their conversation and not paying enough attention to notice if Prairie crawled across the yard and out of sight forever.

Prairie flopped back again and nearly slipped onto the stones.

"Dr. Hartford!" Willow gasped.

He reached a hand across the table, catching Prairie's arm. "Are you okay?" he asked Willow.

"Take Prairie. Don't let her down. Don't let her get to the road."

He stood, reached and plucked the small child into the air. Prairie let out a happy squeal, just as she had in the library, her legs kicking.

There it is again, Willow thought. Their unfair closeness. Prairie belonged to her. No one else. Not Tory, not Mable, not Clay.

She raised her cup to her lips. She'd drink her tea, try and eat a cookie, and she'd remain sitting where Prairie could at least see her. Pain, sharp and hot stung her bottom lip, making her jerk, splash tea down the front of her white T-shirt and drop her cup. The china rolled from her lap and partially down one leg before hitting the flagstones. In a splash of caramel-colored tea, a bee spun, managed to lift, find an unsteady wing, and fly off, but Willow's attention was on her precious cup—a symbol for more than she could say. The cup and its broken handle lay six inches apart. "I can fix it. Tory, don't throw it away. I can fix it."

"Clay, I'll take the baby," Tory was on her feet. "Help Willow." When he scraped his chair back, passed off Prairie, and caught Willow, Tory's voice calmed. "It's not bee stings causing her to be so ill. Dr. Mahoney says she's not allergic to them. She never has any reaction."

In Clay's arms, Willow knew her aunt was right. The stings didn't leave her with swollen eyes, didn't close her throat, and didn't leave her gasping for air. She'd been woozy and seeing things before she was stung. But the assaults, hitting her at her lowest, had the force of fists. "Why," she cried at Tory, "do you let Jonah keep those things?"

36

Much happened over the next month. While Willow stayed inside with her migraines and nausea, Prairie turned one, began walking, and Clay came most mornings to work. He labored through boxes of Luessy's papers, journals, and letters, sometimes pacing the library aisle, sometimes sitting in the attic and working in Luessy's old space. In the afternoons, he tried to show his gratitude by helping Jonah, though he considered hands-on access to the garden, like hands-on access to Luessy's papers, a privilege.

Depending upon how Willow felt, their time together could be a short or long evening. Even on her worst days, when she saw doubles and triples of everything, he went upstairs, looked in on her, and stayed to read from his notes or tell her something interesting he'd discovered. "Your great aunt, Amelie-Anais, grew up in her uncle's villa. He was a priest."

"And she fell in love with a man named Thomas."

Listening to the two of them discuss my life might have been amusing, if only the truth hadn't been so horrifying. Thomas had been at the villa only ten days before The Beast caught us talking in private and ordered him to leave. Did my uncle fear I was confiding in Thomas? As The Beast's bullies rushed forward moments later, to escort Thomas away, he leaned in and whispered. "I'll come for you, tonight. Be ready." That was his marriage proposal. I've often thought, had The Beast not ordered Thomas out, had we had a few days to plan, I might have lost my courage. I'd likely have convinced myself that my sins, my unholy body, and the curse upon my back made me unworthy of such a man. The rush, and Thomas's confidence, swept me up, and I had no time for doubt.

Once in America, when the letter arrived telling me of Sabine's death and of the infant daughter left under *Le Bête's* roof, I had to tell Thomas the whole truth. Crossing the Atlantic in a steel steamboat was arduous and dangerous, to say nothing of entering the villa. He had to know why I asked him to risk his life to steal an infant from her bed and take her out of France. I wasn't far into my confession, when he stopped me and held me, his rough chin against my cheek. "In a thousand ways," he said, "you've already told me."

Now, I watched Willow and Clay and how their relationship evolved from the afternoon he carried her into the house and up the wide stairs to Mémé's bed, her head dropped against his chest. Brushing hands moved into holding hands. A first kiss quickly became passionate kissing. At times, Willow felt Clay couldn't be real, that she'd awaken from her dream of him and find he was as imaginary as weeds growing out of flagstone. She was certain Papa would tell her to 'Slow down.' He'd be afraid for her, but she believed Clay was different. Still, there were times when she knew he kept parts of his past a secret.

Clay wasn't at Farthest House the bright afternoon Willow held Prairie's small hand as they moved at the child's toddler pace along a garden path and off between flower beds where roses bloomed in great bushels of perfumed red and farther still under shade trees. They walked to the edge of the yard where Willow loved to stand. There, under the great bowl of blue sky, she had the farthest view and the widest perspective. She breathed deeply, inviting the wind over her face and through her hair and almost believed her fear of Mary stalking was imaginary.

I'd stood there, too, watching the road with the same dull ache in my stomach, checking for signs of Thomas returning after days on another photography expedition. Afraid that he wouldn't come back, that he'd been caught in a massacre, or imprisoned in a damp dungeon an ocean away from me.

Willow marveled at the blooms on the slope leading down to the river and how they changed with the seasons, going from pink and white wild flowers in the spring to yellow and gold in the fall. Currently, it was wild mustard, sunflowers, black-eyed Susans, and Mad Apple with its white trumpet-shaped flowers. Some few minutes passed before Willow realized there was also a haze of bees working over the acres, thousands, maybe tens of thousands, low over the plants. She tugged on Prairie's hand, "Let's hurry and visit Jonah."

He stood in the shade of his tool shed with an overturned shovel, the scoop against his hip, as he cleaned it with a wooden scraper. Black dirt crumbled down one pant leg. His overalls looked empty and held up only by the hanger of his shoulders. A knot tightened in Willow's stomach. The two of them had yet to have a meaningful conversation, and their relationship felt like torn fabric. She missed what they'd lost, and she had no idea how much longer she'd be at Farthest House, though she wanted never to leave. And there was his age. The few long and slow good-byes that Death allowed were only a ruse: Death loved to surprise.

As she approached him, she realized that in the years she'd been away, Jonah had become the "outside man." When Mémé lived, he'd often been in the kitchen handing over his tomatoes, fixing something, or just sitting with Mémé over seed catalogues while Mable peeled potatoes or stirred cookie dough. Willow wondered, too, who neatly stitched squares of almost-matching fabric on the worn knees and elbows of his clothes, who purchased his coffee, his eggs, his underwear? Who cut his hair?

He lifted his head, the skin on his neck stretching as he sighted them from below his sagging lids.

Willow smiled. "How are you?"

Seconds passed, then a barely audible, "Yup."

So much for small talk. "I'm feeling better today," she said. There it was again, a childish confession, an obvious attempt to receive love.

He continued scraping his shovel, his age also evident in the tremor of his hands. She longed to put an arm around his stooped shoulders, to tell him she cursed time for its cruelty to him, but mentioning anything of the sort would only call attention to his palsy. She wanted him to believe she didn't notice.

"You're seeing that college fellow now," he said.

"Clay?" Had Mable told him? Or did he see more through his cloudy and closing eyes than she supposed? Had he seen Clay and her earlier through the library window? Clay leaning against the desk, his arms around her waist, while she leaned dangerously close into the vee of his open legs and they played at verbal badminton? Had Jonah seen the long kiss?

"Thought you'd go home by now," he said.

A webby rash of goose flesh fanned across Willow's back. Before she could answer, Prairie, with her dimpled knees and unsteady waddle of a run, started after a butterfly, heading across the grass. "Prairie stop. Come back here."

Prairie did stop, and Willow frowned at herself. Did she really suppose the one-year-old would bypass the manor and head down the driveway for Old Squaw Road where Mary waited with her passenger door open: *Come in, little girl.* Yes, exactly that.

Jonah tucked his wooden scraper into his back pocket and drew out a snakestone. His file hit the shovel in short, hard strokes, sunlight ricocheting off the burnished steel. His jowls, soft and round floated beneath his skin. "This ain't a place for young people."

"We're still not welcome?" Willow asked. "What part of Farthest House isn't good for us?"

Jonah didn't answer.

Two bees entered her space, and she took a quick step back, her stomach sinking. Were they attracted to worry and irritation? She had plenty of both. Jonah wasn't going to talk, the bees refused to move on despite her batting at them, and Prairie threatened to run off. Coming outside had been a bad idea.

She felt the tiny touch of a bee landing on her hand, she jerked, shook the insect off and swatted at the air as the bee lifted but threatened to land again. "Jonah! Why are they doing this?"

"Quit dancing."

A third and then a fourth orbited her.

"Are you siccing them on me?"

His yellowed eyes fixed in her direction, but they looked into the past. "They ain't acted this way since your mama."

A bee touched her neck, and she tried to swat it off, but she felt it roll once under her fingers and then the quick fire of a sting. The bee dropped, and she palmed the pain. "Dammit!" For Prairie's sake, she managed to keep back a far bloodier scream.

Jonah leaned the shovel against the shed and turned toward his cabin. "I'll fix that."

The other bees were still bothering. Jonah's cabin was nearer than Farthest House, and he'd actually extended something of an invitation. Hadn't he? She hurried after Prairie, grabbed her up, and returned so quickly on Jonah's slow heels, she almost ran into him. His stiff and laborious walk, full of age-shortened steps, added to her sense of a world grown hopeless. When he stepped through the narrow door of his cabin, a shadow into a shadow, she followed, Prairie on her hip, and pulled the door shut so hard and quick the thin cabin walls shook.

Absolute darkness. Odors close and strong: boiled onions, cabbage, turnips, raw honey, old work clothes, rotting wood. She feared Prairie would slap pudgy hands over her nose and say, "Ack."

Squares of diffused light, like blocks of faint auras, she counted four, made her squint into the darkness to try and understand.

A harsh bulb above the kitchen sink flashed on, and the long, frayed string Jonah had pulled swung in the air. She looked around, unable to stop herself. Jonah's place, like his body, looked pared down to a line drawing. If the whole of his wealth was there, she could count his possessions on her fingers: a small table with two unmatched chairs, one wood, one aluminum, a refrigerator, a slouching brown sofa with lighter areas where the fabric pile had been worn away. Through a doorway, a small, unmade bed, a nest really, with its mattress sunken in the middle and looking so lumpy it might have been filled with stones, and an old Bible on an end table. She could imagine the Bible splayed across his bony knees, his shaky hands slowly turning the stained and yellowed pages, his eyes reverent over the words and evoked images. Though the Bible held no fascination for her, she imagined Jonah entering the verses the way she entered her paintings, as if through wickets in hedges.

He opened the refrigerator with its door as round as a coffin top. With trembling hands, he brought out an egg, cracked it on the side of a cup, let the yolk and white fall in, and scratched at the lining of the empty shell, lifting out a piece of thin membrane the size of his thumbnail.

The small wooden table butted the wall, and Willow took one chair, keeping Prairie in her lap while Jonah shuffled to her, his chin raised so he could focus on her wound. With fingers she felt wobbling against her skin, he fumbled his egg-membrane remedy over the pain. Instant coolness. For a few seconds, he remained standing at her side, examining his work so closely Willow could have leaned and rested her cheek against his chest. "Thank you," she said.

He reached for a porcelain teakettle I'd given him as a Christmas present.

Over the decades, the porcelain had chipped so much the original color was nearly lost. He'd kept the pot, though, and I told myself his doing so proved he carried no animosity towards me for what happened later.

Only a pencil-thin stream of water leaked from the faucet, but he stood at the sink watching the kettle fill. Willow searched for the mysterious lights she'd seen: wisps of eerie moon-colored glow, vague as smoke rings, large, square smoke rings. Her stomach fell. His windows. Each had been covered in a thick tarp-like material and was held tight with a row of nails hammered up and across and down. The shrouding couldn't be seen through, although in the dark, traces of light seeped in around the edges. She remembered the black, construction-paper rings Sister Dominic Agnes draped around the classroom window, and she had to swallow back a moan of sadness. Who did Jonah fear might look in? Had he been as afraid when Mémé was alive? Did his hiding away have something to do with the long-ago murder Tory told Clay about? Or the graves across the yard?

The teapot scraped on the stove burner. "The bees don't mind me," Jonah said.

She watched the blue flame licking around the bottom of the kettle.

"They don't mind color," he continued.

Growing more accustomed to the dim light, Prairie pushed and squirmed to be put down. Willow let her stand on her own feet and then toddle out of reach, cold rushing the tips of Willow's now-empty fingers. "They mind me," she said. "What color am I?"

He stood so close to the stove she wondered that he didn't feel the heat and step back, but he only turned his body slowly in her direction, looking so stiff he might have been one calcified piece. "Yell-ow," he said.

Willow needed a moment. "Yellow?"

"We're the same color. Yup. A bad color."

Tears threatened her eyes, and she looked to Prairie who walked around slowly, still not touching anything. Jonah had become a cruel old man. Why did she remain sitting there in his worn-out chair, trying to have a conversation?

"I came here to get safe," he said. His heavy bottom lip, always partially turned out, glistened with moisture. "I didn't find safe. The past catches up."

Willow was confused. According to Tory, a mob threatened to hang him the same way one hung Willie Brown, but hadn't Farthest House kept him safe? Wasn't the garden where he spent his days an Eden?

"They stung your mama, too. I thought it might have to do with her being like she was."

He remained stooped and too close to the stove, his overalls hanging low off his drooping shoulders. Visions of Papa lying in his hospital bed, swathed in bandages, made Willow bite her lip to keep from warning him, treating him like a child. "You mean her being pregnant?"

He nodded over his teapot. "Ain't the bees' fault."

"Well, I'm not pregnant, and they still sting me." Exposed to the air and the warmth of her body, the thin egg membrane was already drying around the edges, pulling back ever so slightly and feeling like a small breath on her neck. "Why keep them? Wouldn't buying honey be easier?"

He might not have heard.

She couldn't stand watching his nearness to the flame. She stepped up beside him, ready to beat fire from his clothes. "That water is plenty hot for me."

He continued to ignore her, waiting until the water boiled hard and steam poured from the mouth of the pot. He turned the stove knob, letting the flame limp away. "My bees come home." His words slow and thick with emotion. "They come by my door all day long." His bottom lip went in, reappeared. "They don't have to hide until dark." He raised his chin and looked at her through the slits of his overcast eyes. "You never been alone. First your grandma and Papa, and now, a baby and that college man." He breathed, leaving the names listed in the air. "You ever stick your arm over a hive? Just so you feel something alive on your skin?"

She walked back to her chair, her emotions sinking further as she remembered Mary and Derrick waiting until dark to knock on her door. She thought, too, of the cockroach a school-aged Jonah wanted to protect and wondered if his staying single was connected to the murder in Omaha. None of which explained why he wanted them away. He'd become crotchety. What would he gain if they left?

He carried two cups from the rubber dish-drainer beside his sink, banging them down on the table so hard Willow jumped. When she did, he nodded at her, understanding in his otherwise unreadable eyes. "Yup."

She watched him move back to the stove for the kettle. He was right and wrong about her. She *had* ached for touch. After having sex with Derrick, she lay deathly still, needing him to turn and acknowledge her, to reach back across the column of cold space already separating them. She'd felt ugly and unloved, like the slit between her legs was the only acceptable part of her and at the same time the Catholic sin of her? She thought, too, of Mary's cruel touch, her claw-like finger tracing the protrusion of bone, carving ugly into Willow's heart. "There was a time, before 'fancy college man,' before Prairie, when I could have used bees. Nice bees, that is."

Spilling only a bit of the hot water, he filled her cup and then his own. On the table were generic tea bags in a paper box and honey in a mason jar. She thanked the bee that had gotten her to Jonah's table. "I know you don't give straight answers," she said, "but why don't you want Prairie and me here?"

He lowered his bone-thin body onto the chair opposite her. She doubted the chair even felt his weight. "Only old folks here, finishing up. Start a life somewhere else."

The water in Willow's cup rippled as she lifted and lowered the tea bag, the auburn stain drifting into the clear water, the fine swirls of color turning it a rich brown. Was she disappointing Jonah the way Tory disappointed Mémé? Marrying herself to a house? Was that what he feared, that she'd hole up, never risking again, forgetting about college or forward dreams? Or were his fears moored in his own past, a man regretting his own marriage to a place and sameness?

"Most days," she said, "Farthest House is the only branch keeping my head above water. If you're telling me to let go of my little hand-hold and reach for a boat, I'm telling you, right now there is no boat."

Prairie came to the table, sank against Willow's legs like touching a base, and then started off again, stepping onto one small rug and then off and onto a second, the rugs soiled and worn to the color of scrub water. From the rugs, she moved down the length of the sofa, her shoulders moving alongside the seat, a palm running over the tatty fabric, as if the texture tickled or spoke.

Willow sipped her tea. Jonah's cabin mirrored his body: small, dark, and its eyes closed on the world. No newspapers, no radio—she doubted the old 1940's box on top of his refrigerator still worked—and no television. What could touch him? After so long, did he still think someone might reopen the murder case? Was she really all that different—shuddering at every flash of a yellow or gold vehicle, certain Mary had come to get Prairie? Clay thought her fears as unreasonable as she thought Jonah's, but Mary had killed Friar and Papa, and Mary still had the picture she stole of Prairie. Prairie unborn, floating in a sea of blue.

37

That night brought little sleep for Willow who tossed with a headache aspirin didn't reach. Too early the next morning, Prairie jarred her awake, coming into the room and trying to pull herself up onto the bed, only to change her mind when Willow sat up, running for the door as though she could tease Willow into chasing her.

Willow flopped back down, closing her eyes. She could hear Mable in Prairie's room and knew the toddler was safe. Just one more blessed moment of rest, she thought, and she'd get up and finish dressing Prairie herself.

A gentle rain fell on the roof, the kind Mémé called cleansing. Willow moved her heavy feet over the edge of the bed, tested the floor for balance, walked to the window, and slid up the sash. The cool mist on her hot skin felt so delicious she knelt down and leaned in almost to the screen.

Outside, Tory's voice speared up from below: angry, several octaves higher than normal.

Willow tried to hear, leaning in until the wire screen's grating roughness pressed on her forehead, and she feared it would pop out if she pushed any harder. She could just see Tory and Jonah standing on the wet grass below. The top of Tory's head was matted, and her wet shoulders made her white blouse transparent over the straps of her bra.

Water dripped off Jonah's hat. "Send 'em home." Then, a "Yup." Not easy sounding, but guttural, demanding.

Willow didn't have to wonder who *them* was. His words were a wind that buffeted and stung when he said them to her face, but saying them behind her back, including another person in his disapproval, turned that wind into a gale.

Couldn't he see she never wanted to leave, never wanted to go back to the loud and busy streets of Omaha, never back to where the cemeteries held only strangers, to a city filled with so many bad memories and fears? She meant to get well and find a job in Greenburr. She'd rent one of the village's old Victorian homes where she'd have more than enough space for her easel, where the large rooms full of dark wood played the music of Prairie's footsteps, where Prairie would have more than enough room to grow, and they could remain close to Mable, Tory, and Clay. She would start at Briarwood.

Mable walked into the bedroom, Prairie tugging on the yards of her caftan, and Willow jerked back, knocking her head on the window sash as she pulled out. She eased the window down.

Mable laughed, coming up to the window. "Peeping are we? Fresh air ought to be good for a sick room. Why not keep it open."

"I'd better not."

She nodded at Willow's forehead. "Looks like you tried to squeeze through a garlic press."

"Very funny."

"What's out there?" Mable looked down and caught sight of Tory, just vanishing inside, and then longer at Jonah, heading for his cabin. She shook her head. "In the rain mind you. He'll catch his death."

"What's so important they had to talk outside? And why not at least under the portico?"

"Stubborn, the both of them. She never walks across the garden to him, and he avoids her when he can. He'll come in if she's gone," her voiced trailed, "that is, if I need him for something."

"Are you blushing?"

"No."

Willow picked up Prairie, shifting the toddler's weight from one hip to the other, but her attention stayed on Mable. *You are blushing,* she thought. "So, you, the two of you?"

"He's a good man."

"The two of you are in a relationship, aren't you?"

"Nonsense."

But Mable spoke too quickly and adamantly, actually confirming Willow's suspicions. "That's nice," Willow said. She sat Prairie on the bed and cuddled her. "Wow, I didn't realize."

"Stop it right there." Mable's face was still flushed. "Don't you start trouble over something you know nothing about."

"You think I'm going to become the town crier? And anyway, who cares?"

Mable stepped up to the bed, jerking at the top sheet. "This here's a small town. There isn't a place to hide."

"I'll make the bed," Willow said, "and I'll stay out of your business, but you answer a question for me. Why doesn't Jonah want us here?"

"He worries too much. Imagines trouble everywhere." She punched pillows and laid them back. "He can't be blamed."

"So, you guys do talk?" Willow was grinning. "I mean more than about tomato harvests."

"The world's full of cruel people, Willow."

"I'm not one of them."

"If you're not needing help with Prairie," she turned to go, "I've plenty to do in the kitchen."

"Did you know," Willow asked, "that Jonah came here because of trouble in Omaha?"

"The murder? He's innocent, of course."

"Tory thinks he did it, doesn't she?"

Mable walked back to the window and opened it. Fresh air blew her sleeves against her wide arms. She eyed the patch of lawn where Jonah stood a moment before. "I don't know. I've never asked her. I don't need to."

"In all the years you've worked here, you haven't asked? That's as strange as their talking in the rain."

"Like I said, I've never needed to ask. I know what sort of man Jonah is. There's a lot I don't ask."

The wooden comb Mémé had favored, its teeth as round as infant toes, lay on the dresser, and Willow took it up and sat down on the bed again with Prairie. "Like what?"

Mable's brows lifted. "Is it *you* writing a book now?"

"You were here the night I was born. Why wasn't my mother taken to a hospital?"

"Your dad blamed Dr. Mahoney." She shrugged. "It's been twenty years. No one remembers exactly, and who can say the same thing wouldn't have happened at a hospital."

"He never talked about it. He kept so many secrets."

Mable slid her hands up the opposite forearms, irritated, but she wasn't leaving the room. "This family runs on buttoned-up lips."

"Meaning?"

"Those two out there whispering in the rain. The way Tory keeps her bedroom door locked and all her clothing across the hall. She's had racks moved into that bedroom, and her twenty pairs of black shoes are all laid out." She let herself grin over her wit and went on. "I suppose, with a house this size, it makes sense to spread out. I do what she wants and stay clear of her room."

"Her door is always locked?"

"For as long as I've worked here."

"Aren't you curious about what she's hiding?"

"Hiding? It doesn't mean she's hiding a thing. Could just be she wants her space left alone, no pesky maid moving things around to dust or fuss over how she keeps it."

Prairie twisted away, putting her hands on top of her head to signal 'no more.' She stood up on the mattress and began trying to jump.

"At first, it bothered me," Mable said, "her being just eighteen when I started and locking her door. I thought she expected I'd steal." She realized she might be saying too much, but warred with herself. "Luessy always told me, 'Leave her be.' So, I did. After Luessy died, Tory was writing my paychecks. I was mighty happy to be kept on. I figure part of my job is leaving her to her privacy. Some people just need to feel a power over one thing."

"Tory would never fire you. Who else would work for decades and never snoop?"

Mable left the room, then stuck her head back in grinning. "There's been times when my vacuuming at the end of the hall was a bit more aggressive than need be, a bump here or there into the door. I've noticed odors, weedy-smelling things I'd like to clean out, but the door doesn't open. I remind myself she's never been inside my bedroom, either."

"Whoa," Willow said, "grass? You suppose she smokes pot?"

"I didn't say so. She's got her sherry for that. The old aunt used to collect every living bloom and weed and she'd paint pictures of them. Tory went on the hunts, too. They'd go into the trees, even down to the river. Wild flowers, weeds, she'd pick anything that caught her eye."

With Mable gone, Willow considered how Jonah was likely a big part of the reason Mable so valued her job. How else could she be near him without society freaking out? True, there were a few mixed-race couples now, but very few. And when Mable and Jonah were young, their relationship would have caused an upheaval. Jonah might have been run out of town, or worse, for being with a white woman, and Mable and her family right behind him. Was their relationship tied to Jonah's covered windows? There were shades for that.

38

"Que serà, serà." Whatever will be, will be."

Clay held Prairie, waltzing her to the music and making Willow wish for the umpteenth time that he was the father. How Prairie loved being in his arms, and how natural she looked there.

"Come join us," he coaxed.

Curled at one end of the sofa, Willow smiled but shook her head. Her stomach felt settled, so long as she didn't move, but her exhaustion was a lead blanket she couldn't push off.

Clay winked and went on swinging Prairie. He still spent his mornings in the library and afternoons helping Jonah with the heaviest work, pushing a mower or dragging heavy hoses. For the last week, however, Jonah's begrudging tolerance of him had waned to the point of outright resentfulness. The afternoon before, he told Clay he didn't need help. Then today, "Go finish up your own work."

Which Clay wasn't doing. He drove up the hill with every intention of writing, but again, he left the library after only a couple of hours. "Something's jinxed me," he told Willow. "The writing's not happening."

She gave him a weak smile, knowing he tried, but she thought the same of his attempts. Somehow, they weren't working. So much of what he wrote about Mémé wasn't new to Willow, and the new he did write seemed lifeless and too scholarly. To capture Mémé, his prose needed wings, not the boots of academia, and his aim needed to be spherical, not arrow-straight. She couldn't tell him. Maybe, her criticism was really of her own work, which she wasn't doing either, and all that she failed to capture of the Crones because she, too, failed to imagine enough.

She shook off both concerns. At the moment, they were minor. Derrick had called. When Mable announced he was on the phone, Willow's stomach dropped away, and her whole body gave an involuntary shudder. Shaking, she refused the call. "No, I won't talk to him. Tell him I'm sick, or I'm not home, anything."

The record ended, and Clay put on another before he came to sit beside her, letting Prairie squirm from his arms and hurry away to the stack of records on the floor. "You feel like talking?"

"To say that I think about Mary every day? That it kills me to think she's getting off scot free?"

"Criminals end up in jail. If she's guilty, she'll slip up and get caught. Criminals never act just once."

That's exactly my fear, Willow ached to say, *She's not done!* But what good would it do rehashing everything yet again. "What's your secret?" She looked into his eyes. "How come you're never afraid?"

He kept his voice low, not wanting to distract Prairie from her play. "*Never* is a bit extreme. Though, for one thing, I don't have a child to worry about." Prairie laughed, a baby's deep, abandoned belly laugh at how the records slid apart. Her laughter tickled him, and he knew he did have a child he worried about. If Willow had reason to fear letting Prairie go off with her ex, and some psycho named Mary, he'd do everything in his power to prevent it from happening.

"Things will get better. Everything passes eventually, and everyone feels horrible at some time in their lives." His eyes darkened. "I mean *slain,* really bad stuff."

"But not you."

The Adam's apple in his throat slid down, rose again. "If you believe that, I've done a great job of hiding the truth."

For a time, they sat in silence watching Prairie continue to stack two LPs, put both hands on top and push, which sent her sliding forward until her arms gave out, and she collapsed in giggles.

Clay spoke. "I've told you my brother Robbie had Down's, but there's a lot I haven't told you." He paused, "My brother, Robbie . . . ." Then, "My family . . . ." Finally, "You sure you're up for this?"

She nodded.

"You're not feigning interest, the way you do with my writing?"

"That's not . . . completely true. It's just that I'm not the right critique partner for you. I have my own memories, maybe myths, about Mémé, and I want to keep them."

"Myths? That's interesting. To know your conceptions of them are myth, and still you want to keep the fables. I've never thought of my family as the stuff of myths, maybe, as a Gothic theme park."

She frowned, trying not to laugh.

"Okay." His legs stretched out in front of him. "Where to begin? I think as soon as my folks knew about the Down's, Dad started concocting a way of covering it up. Not covering up Robbie." He took a deep breath, feeling his way in. "Dad needed to deny something more personal, as though he and Mom had failed on some profound level, and Robbie proved it to the world."

Tension ran down the arm he had around Willow.

"Robbie was only four months old when Mom got pregnant again. Nine months later, I arrived to prove my dad could sire a normal child."

She thought of Papa. His death was still an open wound, something that couldn't begin to heal until Red came with the news that Mary had been arrested. At the moment, she didn't want to hear about the pain it caused a man to sire a less-than-perfect child.

"Mom stayed home, and I mean *never* left the house. Dad carted me around to little league games, spelling bees, Boys Scout ceremonies, and school sports. Any place he could parade me and show the world he had this non-Robbie son."

"A trophy son? That explains the arrogance." He didn't laugh, and Willow could feel how remembering brought pain. He needed a moment, and she tried to give him that. "Papa thought my grades made up for our being hermits, for about anything he needed covered up, I guess. After Jeannie died—"

"Your mother? You refer to her by her given name?"

"Whew. Maybe we shouldn't dig up the past."

"There are things you need to know." Again, he took his time. "I loved my brother. Loved him. We learned to walk about the same time, played blocks together, shared baby bottles. It was like Robbie waited developmentally for me, so we could be twins for a small span of time. Then, I went forward, and he didn't. From crib to preteens, we slept in the same bed, usually holding hands. We'd fall asleep that way and wake that way. When we grew too large for one twin bed, we still shared a room."

He moved an inch, his shoulders, his arms, his legs, as if the whole of his body had felt the need to shudder. "The first day of kindergarten, I left him crying at the kitchen door, while I walked out holding Dad's hand. I felt like I'd socked him in the gut. I had. I could go and learn, but Robbie couldn't." He shook his head, "I know all this isn't rational."

She shrugged, unsure of what to say and afraid of where the story would end.

"Walking to the car that day, I realized, even if I couldn't have articulated it, Robbie was different, and I was breaking this huge promise to him. An unspoken promise, sure, but we'd said it in our hearts. The two of us, we were in it together, Chang and Eng. Starting school though, my job was suddenly to separate myself from everything Robbie was, to put the biggest damn gap between us that I could. To be the most *not-Robbie* possible. Is there a larger betrayal of a brother?"

"But this wasn't your fault."

"Darling, you haven't heard anything, yet."

He needed still more time, and she thought about the story of Mother Moses, and how with each telling she had to consider the starting place.

"We even celebrated our birthdays on the same day, my birthday. It went like this, on my fifth birthday, five candles. I blew them out. Dad re-lit one for Robbie. Sixth birthday, six candles for me, a re-light for Robbie so he could play at growing up, too. And the kicker? I could have been twelve before it hit me." He swallowed, "All along, I hadn't seen it. It was natural as hell that Robbie got his one candle on my birthday. And the best part?" He looked into Willow's eyes. "He loved his candle and never had any trouble blowing out that one candle, never thought there should be more. Of the four of us sitting around those birthday cakes covered in red globs of bleeding frosting that Robbie squished out of a corner of a sandwich bag—more like wounds than roses—he was the happiest."

"You don't have to dredge this all up."

"I do. If we're going to spend our lives together, there are things you need to know. Like how I never want a birthday cake. You present me with a cake, and my guilt over Robbie will probably force me out of the room. We'll celebrate Prairie's birthday, yours, but don't do that to me."

He does mean to stay. The thought rushed down from Willow's head to her lungs and into her heart. She snuggled closer, feeling the surety of his body. What couldn't she endure with him in her life? She wanted him: his health and vigor, his honesty, and his sex. She wanted to take his clothes off slowly, one item at a time, and discover him. "Prairie will grow up wondering why we never celebrate your birthday. She'll think me mean and vow to treat her husband differently."

"In the whole of English literature, is there a single example of a child growing up who wants to be just like Mom and Dad?"

The sound of the doorbell chiming in the foyer made Willow lean back from Clay. She meant to go to the door, but Mable, squat and square in her flowered caftan, and looking like an upholstered chair on the move, was already crossing the foyer and opening the door. "Willow," she called after a moment, "it's a registered letter for you. Can you sign?"

Panic burned Willow's face and seared her hands. A registered letter could mean only one thing, Derrick. This had to be the letter, or the subpoena, or the court order forcing her to give Derrick equal time with Prairie, which meant equal time with Mary.

"Let's calm down," Clay whispered at the way her face blanched. "It's probably nothing."

She rose from the sofa but went to Prairie, taking the child into her arms. "I don't want it! Refuse it."

Clay gave her a minute before continuing, "It could be anything. Nothing. Either way, eventually you're going to have to sign or be served papers. If it's important, you're going to find out." He walked with her to the door where her frightened signature on the postman's form had all the pitches of a tiny scream. Still, she refused to touch the letter, hurrying back to the sofa with Prairie.

Clay followed with the letter in his hand. "Do you want me to open it?"

"Yes," she said. "No. Yes."

"That's two yeses and one no." He began opening the envelope, taking as much care as if he were unwrapping a wound, giving her time to yell, *Stop!* Or decide to open it herself. She only closed her eyes and held Prairie tighter.

He read the letter silently and then sat down beside her. "It's not what you think."

She'd been holding her breath. She let the air ease out, but she was far from relaxed. Was Clay sure? Positive? If Derrick hadn't instigated the letter, it was good news, even if it informed her that she'd inherited some massive debt of Papa's.

He handed her the letter as Prairie flopped across both their laps. Still Willow hesitated, her gaze avoiding the body of the letter and lingering on two words in the letterhead, "Law Offices." When she could, she read the letter. Then again, more slowly, "Is this possible?"

"That's what it says. It looks official to me. Luessy left the place to you. It became yours on your twentieth birthday. You've owned Farthest House for a couple of months." Willow couldn't find words, and Clay continued, "You had no idea?"

Overcome by what the letter did not say, Willow struggled to keep her mind on what it did say. "I own Farthest House?"

Clay touched the letter. "This makes more sense than Luessy leaving the property to Greenburr. You've told me how close you were."

The letter trembled. She *owned* Farthest House? A gift equivalent to a second soul? A home for Prairie? This meant she had a better chance, should the next letter be from Derrick's attorney, of keeping Prairie. "Why didn't I know? Why did it have to be a big secret?"

He was grinning at the joy on her face.

"I'll tell Jonah to get rid of his bees." The words made her heart leap again. Was she so scared that she'd strike out at the first person she could? "I'd never do that."

"I know," Clay said.

Prairie wanted down. She paddle-ran out of the room into the foyer and headed for the kitchen and Mable. Her speed always frightened Willow, but this time there was the windfall bigger than anything else. She read the letter again, carefully refolded it on its original crease lines, and when she finished, she unfolded the sheet, as if for the first time. Her voice trembled. "When Mémé stood by my bed the night she died, she gave me Mother Moses and a rose. What better symbols for Farthest House? I think she was telling me this at my wedding, too. Telling me to 'hang on.'"

Footsteps sounded on the stairs, and Willow's eyes widened. "It's Tory. What do I say? Why did Mémé deceive her and make her think Farthest House was hers?"

The footsteps had yet to land on the foyer floor, but Clay lowered his voice to a whisper. "She'll be glad the place isn't going to Greenburr. They'd tear down walls and put walls up and turn it into city offices or a medical clinic."

Willow wasn't convinced. "It's still a dirty trick . . . she trusted . . . I know how it feels to be double-crossed. Though nothing has to change, it might not seem like her home, anymore."

Tory stood in the doorway, "Whose home?"

Willow swallowed, trying to hold the letter so still Tory wouldn't notice it. At her side, Clay said nothing, and she appreciated his silence, his waiting for her to call the first play. But Tory had heard the doorbell, she certainly heard part of their conversation, and there wasn't time to come up with a plan for breaking the news gently. Honesty seemed not just the best way out, but the only way out. She handed up the letter, and Tory reached for it.

39

Willow started awake, her eyes wide in the darkness, her heart thundering in her chest. Another nightmare, this time that Prairie screamed for help, and though Willow searched frantically and the crying was so near, she couldn't find her.

The screams came again, and the thumping in Willow's chest that for half a second had slowed, kicked back up. Not just a dream, Prairie needed her. She threw back the covers and sat up, her feet hitting the rug and slamming a wave of dizziness into her head. Prairie cried out again, and the sound sent Willow running, the rug beneath her feet rolling on waves. Prairie wasn't just whimpering from bad dreams of her own, but shrieking. Something was terribly wrong.

In the hall, long and dark and empty of support, Willow nearly lost her balance but caught herself, both arms swinging into the air. She slowed. She'd be no good if she fell and broke a hip or sprained an ankle. At Prairie's door, she smelled the vomit. Only that, she told herself, Prairie was sick. While Willow could identify with how bad puking felt—the pitching stomach, the loss of control as the stomach convulsed, the headache, and Prairie probably had a nose full of bitter, stinging bile—still these things passed. Mary wasn't in the room hovering over the crib, and Derrick wasn't standing crib-side, reaching in to snatch the baby away.

Finding the light switch would have taken only a second, but Willow hurried to the crib using moonlight. "Mommy's here, it's okay." Prairie sat with vomit on the legs of her pajamas and on the sheet between her legs, but she'd not rolled in it, didn't have the rank stuff in her hair, wouldn't need a full bath, which Willow felt too shaky to attempt. "It's okay, sweetie." She shushed and soothed and cradled the child, grabbing a fresh pair of pajamas and heading for the bathroom.

Even washed up and in clean clothes, Prairie continued to whimper. She rested her head on Willow's shoulder, her tiny thumb in her mouth, as Willow walked the floor, rocking and waltzing a few feet down the hall and then back, never getting too close to Tory's door for fear of waking her. She did wonder that Tory wasn't already up. Who could have slept through the screaming, or if awakened refused to come to the child's aid?

Maybe, she wasn't being fair. Tory was in her sixties, and she did have the farthest back bedroom. She also kept the door tightly closed, even locked, and then there was her sleeping potion—a tall tumbler of sherry. Possibly too, Prairie hadn't cried as long or as hard as Willow feared. *Wishful thinking.*

She moved back into Prairie's room, still kissing and cradling and eyeing the rocker. Changing the crib sheet would require more energy than she had, and she didn't want Prairie in the crib anyway. God forbid the baby would need help again, and this time, Willow wouldn't wake. The safe thing was for them to sleep together, but not yet. Prairie still needed soothing, and if she was going to be sick again, there was no sense in soiling another bed.

Before Willow could drop into the rocker, moonlight beckoned out Prairie's window. She swayed up to the glass. A pale hue frosted the yard, not golden or white, but more suffused, as if low light bled through a sheet of blue tissue paper. Jonah's white cabin, so serene looking, contrasted with what she knew to be the somber, secretive interior. The magnolias and river birch were night-still, even the weeping willow looked like a fountain of inky frozen water. The roses, scores of dark and clumped bushes, each with unmoving fists of charcoal shadow, took a backseat to the moonflowers on the far left of her view. They climbed up tall trellises, each flower the size of a tea cup, a delicate and thin bone china cup bobbing like a beacon to night moths.

The trellises stood furthermost in the garden, just yards from the beginning of the wood, the trees serving as a windbreak, helping to protect the thin wooden laths from storms. The outermost trees reflected the pale light, the moon glowing off their trunks and leaves. But the path into the acres of oaks, maples, and poplars loomed dark as the opening to a cave.

Just as Willow was turning back for the rocker, a shadow emerged out of the trees and made her jump. "Geez," she breathed aloud. Who was on the property this time of night and why? Half a second later, she recognized the silhouette. Tall and thin in a long, dark trench coat, with a reaching gait, Tory stepped onto the grass.

Keeping herself back from the window, Willow watched her aunt advance toward the house along the cobblestone walk. When the walkway split, one fork going to the kitchen door and the other to the portico, Tory took the latter. She stepped beneath the roof so that Willow lost sight of her, but moonlight kept the tip of Tory's shadow in place, a stilled thing. A minute or two more and Tory reappeared, stepping back onto the path to the kitchen door. Willow was ready to run for her bed when a glint caught her eye. She studied what at first looked like a silver straw slowly snaking out across the smooth stones. As it grew, she realized it was water being struck by moonlight and coming from where Tory had stood a moment before.

Sounds of the kitchen door opening and closing made her rush across the hall, whispering in Prairie's ear as they moved, "Shh, it's okay." Standing just inside Mémé's room, she could hear Tory cross the kitchen floor, and when she felt certain Tory was in the foyer, she eased the door closed and crawled into bed with Prairie.

The sound of footsteps was so slight and careful on the stairs, Willow couldn't be sure she heard anything. Her mind raced. Maybe, she hadn't seen liquid on the flagstones. After all, that was the spot where she'd also imagined weeds climbing her legs.

She held Prairie close and stroked her back. Soft footsteps, which strained for quiet, reached the upstairs hallway, and a shadow stopped outside her door. The shadow passed after a bit, but Willow's heart still banged. Why was she so scared, and why didn't she simply step into the hall and talk to Tory? Was it because there was only one possible explanation for the water? Tory, classy Tory, had stopped, spread her legs, and peed on the portico floor. Or was it that Tory had been out in the wood by herself at night? Had she gone to meet someone? A coven?

Prairie began to cry again, and then, she gagged.

"Oh, poor baby," Willow soothed. "I know just how you feel." Her stomach gripped. She did know exactly how Prairie felt. What was happening?

40

Two nights later, with Clay in a chair to her left, Willow lay in Luessy's bed watching the evening light shrink and sicken until darkness pushed, bullied, and blackened the turret windows. An hour earlier in Prairie's room, she stood on aching legs and watched Clay dress Prairie in pajamas and tuck the toddler under her blanket. Clay did the lifting, Willow the kissing and cooing, a strained smile of exhaustion stretching her lips.

Then Clay went to the library for manuscript pages, and while he was a floor below, Willow made her way, losing her robe and crawling into her own bed.

Now, Clay read, his voice clear and enunciating though his words slid in and out of Willow's attention. A week had passed since receiving the letter, and while the time ought to have given her a new sense of freedom and foundation, she spent the days more bound by illness than at any time over the summer. She was plagued with flash impressions and questions—some of which felt trustworthy—others ludicrous. At least Prairie was fine. All children were sick here and there, and yet, one question would not quit bobbing in and out of Willow's awareness: Had Prairie eaten something tainted that hadn't been meant for her? Willow wouldn't let herself believe it.

Her right hand circled the area of Mother Moses within reach, resting on a walnut-sized hole. "Just this one," she said. "The rest of the birds and flowers are all intact." She was certain that just days before there'd been several holes, or had she dreamed breakage and unraveling?

Clay stopped reading. "You all right?" She wasn't paying attention to his writing, and that seemed fair; he wasn't either. He knew the two of them needed to talk, but bringing up the subject plaguing him wasn't going to be easy.

Willow had been staring, and she brought her gaze back from a middle, unseeing distance and turned to face him. "I'm listening." She wanted the drone of his voice in the room, the background noise that required nothing of her while still promising she wasn't alone. "Keep reading."

He nodded at the manuscript. "I feel like I'm sitting on a fence. I'm not sure of my direction."

"Humpty-Dumpty died that way." His expression changed to quizzical, and she went on. "You know, sitting on a fence or wall."

"You're funny," he said. He scooted his chair forward until his knees touched the side of her bed. He leaned in, "We need to talk."

She bit her bottom lip. All week she'd spent more time asleep than awake, rowing through lucid dreams full of bright, colored illustrations. Waking to the dim, sepia-hued world around her was jarring, leaving her mind slippery, untethered to either place. Even now, Clay's voice wasn't the only one she heard, and it wasn't the most insistent. Mother Moses spoke through the cotton string, and stories whispered from the room's dark and paneled walls. Behind the tiny door she'd opened to the attic staircase, a cane tapped faintly.

She tried to concentrate on Clay and the intense set of his mouth. She not only wanted him to stay, she wanted him in her bed, naked and holding her steady, the long length of him warm against her, his body a ballast against her fears and what the room would tell her.

"You'll let yourself out?" Tory stood just inside the door, her body in shadow, and her glass of sherry in her hand.

The amount, too much nightcap for one skinny, elderly woman, always surprised Willow. Was part of the liquor saved for the middle of the night, sedating Tory again after her nocturnal stroll?

The blame was mine. *Sip, sip,* I told Tory so many years ago.

"Of course," Clay said. "Good night."

Willow waited, and when the sound of her aunt's door closing traveled back from the end of the hall, she whispered. "When you were reading Mémé's and the Sherlock Holmes mysteries, did you also read Daphne Du Maurier?"

"Some."

"*Rebecca?*"

He thought for a moment, "Yeah, I believe I saw the movie, too."

She rolled her eyes toward the door Tory had just exited.

He was quiet for a moment and then chuckled. "Mrs. Danvers? No. Tory's a sweetheart."

"I'm just saying. Sometimes . . . ."

"Did you know," he said, "that after the Salem witch trials, the town changed its name to Danvers?" He grinned back at her surprise, "I'm just saying." He motioned around the room. "And is this Manderley?"

"No. This is Farthest House."

They grew quiet, and Clay cleared his throat. "Something strange happened today."

"Let me guess, I'm not going to like it."

"It's not that big of a deal, maybe not even worth mentioning."

"Then don't."

He stretched, kissed her, and studied the strain in her eyes. "Is there something you want to tell me?"

"Derrick called again. I won't take his calls. Prairie seemed fine, didn't she? I told you she was sick?"

He thought about Mary's "Looky here," as the camera flashed, but this wasn't the time to bring it up. Willow was struggling with enough. "Yes, Prairie is fine. How about Tory? How's she taking the news?"

"I think we're both still in shock. Some days, she appears happy for me, even sort of celebratory over the news. Other days, she's withdrawn. I suppose she's hashing over what her mother did and what she should do now."

"She's not thinking of leaving?"

"I don't think so. I have a story for you. The other night . . . ." she stopped. Was she absolutely positive Tory had peed on the portico floor? It seemed so long ago. "She has to feel betrayed, and I don't blame her."

Clay squeezed Willow's hand. "You could give the house back."

"What have you been smoking? We did talk about my having a will drawn up. I'm putting her name on it." She was aware of how slowly she was talking, as if treading through her thoughts. "She thinks Papa, not Mémé, was behind the deception. She can't think why though, other than maybe Papa was afraid to tell her the truth."

"That sounds like anger to me."

"She hopes I don't blame him."

"Maybe, your dad did it to protect her, to give her peace of mind for another ten years. What good would it have done to dangle the truth over her head?"

Willow didn't need to close her eyes to see the raven on the kitchen ceiling, the black and winged stain hovering and descending on Papa. The anger that morning, the day the will was read, turned the kitchen air fetid. Papa wouldn't have done his sister any big favors, at least not that day.

"Or," Clay said, "maybe, he thought she wouldn't keep the place up if she knew the truth. Or she'd move out completely and the place would really fall into ruin. It's good she's been here."

"There's no such thing as a perfect family, is there?"

"Last I heard, they were still made up of humans."

She let her free hand creep again, the motion hopefully not enough to catch Clay's attention. When she found the open place in the crocheting, her palm rested, widening over the broken threads. The center of her hand, the most sensitive part, was circled now by the rough outline of knotted string. She imagined a touch or tug, imagined she could slide down through the hole and away. She knew that sort of travel, mental or psychic. The flying thoughts were anything but new. For days, especially since the letter, she'd felt extra loopy, as though she were already half wings and wind. Right now, she could slip away, so easily.

The fear of going, even for a moment, made her shiver despite the summer heat and her blankets. She would not risk leaving Prairie. Not all journeys had roads leading back.

She closed her eyes, pushing her hand off the entrance but leaving her fingers on the cusp, trembling. She whispered Luessy's words, "I'm up here. Out here."

"No, Willow, you're not," Clay said. He let go of her hand and cupped her face, forcing her to look at him. "You're right here. You're with me."

She wished again that he'd crawl into the bed beside her, stay the night, and keep her from being alone. She wished it for Prairie too, someone who'd wake at the first sound of crying and know where they were and what should be done. She didn't trust herself, or Tory, who walked out of the house at night and prowled under the moon and peed on the flagstones. Who stood in shadow or created shadow.

The darkness beyond the turret's windows had turned to crepe. "I need everything on paper. A will, ASAP."

"Everyone needs a will, but 'ASAP'?"

She didn't miss his frustration, or blame him, but he needed to understand. "I want Prairie to have this house, eventually, and should something happen to me, Tory is the logical person to keep it until Prairie is grown. Strange as Tory is, she opened her door to us. Without a will," her fingers opened, reached for the broken threads, "there might be a way, as Prairie's father, for Derrick to put Tory out. Even sell Farthest House. Just as bad, suppose he and Mary ended up living here. I'd return from the dead!"

"This is crazy."

"Houses do burn down, Clay. People do die."

"Nothing's going to happen to you."

"There are no bogeymen, right? No lawyers for hire who'd kick Tory out? And where would Jonah go, to some state-run dump for old folks?"

"Does this mean you're agreeing it's time to see another doctor?"

"I thought you believed Dr. Mahoney."

With a soft plop, the pages in his lap landed on the floor. Whole paragraphs of the manuscript were scratched through, and marginalia crawled up the sides. "I do believe him. The point is, you don't. He says the migraines are from stress and are as likely to quit as quickly as they started. Losing your dad, and the horrible way you did, it's no wonder. When I lost Robbie," he took a breath and exhaled, "I came completely unglued." He ran his fingers back through his hair. "Remembering what I went through, the drinking binges, I'm lucky to be here." He leaned forward again and put a hand on her forehead. "I do believe Dr. Mahoney. Think about it, serious illnesses get chronically worse. They don't come and go like what you're experiencing. Right now, you're tired, but you're feeling pretty good, aren't you?"

"What is it then?"

"If not migraines," he shrugged, "appendix? Measles?"

"Measles?"

"I don't know," he laughed. "I do literature. Another doctor agreeing with Dr. Mahoney though might help you relax. Which might help you break through this wall and get better."

She considered his comment. "Have you've been talking to Dr. Mahoney?"

"Willow, I love you, and this week has been a bad stretch for you. I needed assurances." She didn't answer, and he tried again. "Your depression is bulldozing you, but I get that. Just give yourself more time. This is where Dr. Mahoney is wrong; it's only been a couple of months. The mind doesn't heal as fast as the body."

She longed for a cave of her own where she could go and hide until she figured everything out and gained some peace. Even Jesus needed forty days to get his head together.

"What are you most afraid of?" Clay asked.

"That Mary won't ever go to jail for murdering Papa, and that she'll hurt you or Prairie."

Looky here, Mary had said. He looked to the papers on the floor, began picking them up, worked at straightening the edges.

"All these years," Willow said, "I've blamed Jeannie for dying and leaving me. Now, being sick, I think maybe I was wrong. That's hard for me to admit."

"No one *decides* to leave a newborn. Why would admitting that be hard for you?"

"If I can't blame her, I'm left with only myself to blame. Have I spent my life *choosing* to be a victim? Don't answer that," she smiled. "In fact, I don't want to talk about any of this." He did make her happy, even when she feared happiness was risky and a precursor to loss. "You talk to me, great keeper of secrets." And then, daring herself, "In this bed."

He rounded the footboard and dropped down beside her on the mattress before she scarcely heard her own words. Before she could turn to face him, he held her, her back pulled into his chest. She stiffened, but he pulled her closer, his longer body spooning hers, his arms snug beneath her breasts.

"That didn't take much coaxing," she said.

"You might have changed your mind." He kissed her cheek, her ear, her neck, and then grew quiet for a moment. "You might not have had your mother, but you had your father, and having even one moderately-functioning parent is a blessing. You're right up there with the luckiest."

Pulled into Clay's warmth and feeling the strength in his arms, she could almost relax. "I was lucky then. I was so close to Papa I often heard his thoughts. I mean *verbatim*."

"Whoa. Thanks for the warning."

"Finish telling the story of Robbie. Don't leave anything out. 'If you don't know your stories, you don't know who you are. Or who you can be.' Something like that."

Again, she felt tension twitch through his arms as he took his time beginning. "Robbie defined our lives. That's not an exaggeration. He was the mirror we all had to look into, and our reflections weren't always pretty." He swallowed, lifted his head to kiss her cheek again, giving himself a moment. "As often as I could, to relieve my guilt, I tried to let Robbie win at things. Only if Dad wasn't around, though. He couldn't stomach the deceit. Once, sitting at the kitchen table playing checkers with Robbie—I was probably twelve, he thirteen—I left pieces all over the board, trying to lose mine without taking any of his. That was the object, my personal challenge, find plays that cost me, like playing the game with the rules reversed.

"Dad came home early, walked in and stood over the board. I was grinning inside, so sure he'd think I was brilliant. A minute passed. 'Robbie, is it your turn?' he asked. Robbie shook his head no, and Dad reached down, his thick fingers picked up one of my pieces. He started jumping Robbie, cleaning up the board. With each jump, Robbie's face fell more. He'd been sure he was winning. I thought Dad just didn't understand my master plan. Then, he shoved the whole thing off the table, checkers flying and rolling across the linoleum, the board landing on the floor. He grabbed me, hauled me out of the chair, slammed my tennis shoes into my chest and told me to run.

"Did he believe I insulted Robbie by letting him win? I don't know what it was, except I was so upset I ran over ten miles that day. I started angry, intending to never go home, but something happened and a rhythm found me: Arms, legs, breath, soul, just me, and what I could find inside. It sounds crazy, but it was a religious experience. No Mom, no Dad, no Robbie. I came home changed: I could run. I could push myself to near euphoria. My track career was no longer about Dad. It was about a place in me."

Willow clutched the arms he'd wrapped around her.

"You okay?" he asked. She managed to nod, and he continued. "Who was I to love? Robbie? My dad? Who to hate? Robbie? My dad? Dad was my biggest fan. Always on the track sidelines, or in the bleachers. He even carried my gym bag. I'd come out of the locker room after a meet or a basketball game, and he'd be there waiting for me and reaching out for it, 'I'll take that son.' Every time, I'd grow an inch or two taller. There weren't any other fathers waiting in the hall. If they'd come to the game at all, they were already in their cars, engines running, looking at their watches, pissed at having to wait. But me? The team's filing out, and Dad's got my bag.

"But Robbie was never there. Robbie would have loved watching me play." He sighed, "God, I wish I'd known then." He paused for several seconds, "You suppose Prairie will let me carry her gym bag?"

"Even if it's pink?"

"Absolutely." He took a moment getting back into his story. "Every race I won, every ball that swished through the net was a way of making Robbie matter less. I'm still ashamed; I was such a dumb-ass kid, wanting to be the best on the team, never thinking it through."

"And your mom?"

"She had Robbie. Somewhere along the way, she quit leaving the house. I'm sure Dad never meant for that to happen, but every year she shut down more. Dad started doing the grocery shopping, and Mom ordered anything else she needed from catalogues. Those big fat Sears and Penney's catalogues. Those and Robbie's picture books were the only books I ever saw her read.

"Crazy as things were, we managed to hold it together, until I graduated from high school and planned to leave for college. I wanted to be the one to tell Robbie I wouldn't be home every night, and that he wouldn't see me for maybe a month at a time, and he'd have to sleep in our room alone. One day, he and I were in the backyard tossing a football."

Willow's heart clenched.

"I told him," Clay continued, "and Robbie started crying. It really broke him up, or maybe, it scared him. The ball started rolling down this slope, a wobbly roll, and Robbie pushed me out of the way and started for it, tears running down his flat face. He ran as though getting the ball meant everything. I can only guess why beating me mattered so much. Did he think he'd be getting even with me for leaving, or he'd be showing me he didn't need me, or that reaching the ball proved he could go with me? He was short, never got exercise, and I was the runner, three heads taller, practically running in place, knowing this win meant something big to him.

"I didn't know Dad had come home. Robbie reached the ball, and Dad swooped down. We had a tool shed in the back, and he shoved me in there where Robbie couldn't see. Or Mom, I suppose. He pinned me to the wall with one arm, grabbed the end of the garden hose with the other, and started swinging. That rage again. He swung until I sunk down, my hands over my head, blood on my face, my head, my arms. I just kept taking it, not fighting back."

He took a breath before continuing. "See where this is going? I was as guilty as he was. At eighteen, I could have given him one hell of a fight, or I could have just ran, my specialty. Two strides and I would have been out of his reach. He could never have caught me. I could have given him time to cool off, and he would have. But the event was too incredible to miss. I was getting off on my martyrdom, hoping the bastard hurt me so bad he spent the rest of his life in guilt. And behind bars.

"I knew too," he continued, "at least I think I knew, that the more I let him hit me, the more pain he'd have later. So he was hitting me, but strike for strike, I was hitting him harder.

"As he's swinging, he's yelling, demanding to know if I thought I was a better person than he was. Did I think I cared more about Robbie than he did? Every time that hose whacked me, I felt something being explained just a bit more.

"When he was winded, nineteen years of *whatever* spent, he staggered back, his knees buckling. He slumped against the lawnmower, did a slow motion to the floor, panting like a horse after a race, ending up on one knee. That knee of his suit pants in an oily circle. Crying. Big sobs, slumped over. It went on and on, and still I didn't have the decency to leave him alone. I stayed there with my bloody welts, blood running down my arms—waiting for him to see what he'd done to me. He wasn't thinking about me, though, and I realized slowly that he cried for Robbie. Finally, I got it. Finally, I knew what it did to him to see his son that way and there not being a damn thing he could do to fix it. Robbie wasn't being kept from the public eye because of Dad's pride; Dad didn't give a damn what people thought. It was Dad's helplessness, and how that tore him up, that made him need away from Robbie. My leaving, it was making Dad face things he hadn't yet had the courage to face.

"A couple of hours later, after Mom helped clean me up, and feeling too sore to run, I took the car and pulled out of the driveway. I saw Robbie panting out of the house after me. Did he think this was the time I'd told him about, that I wasn't coming back? Had he been listening outside the tool shed, blaming himself? I couldn't deal with it, couldn't go back to where he and Dad were. I hit the gas, and in the rearview mirror saw Robbie run into the street. It was the first day of kindergarten all over again, and I didn't stop this time, either. I watched him, his sorry running, twenty steps, and he was gasping for breath. Then boom. Out of nowhere, a car."

"Oh, god."

"Robbie slid up the hood and flew off. It was over before the ambulance got there."

"Oh god, I'm so sorry."

"All my life I'd been promising him something. 'You and me, Robbie.' Not in words, but in my always being there for him, how close we were. I'd been promising." He swallowed, exhaled. "I did go off to school a few weeks later. Mom was dead within months of Robbie's death. Dad stayed in the house, lived another five years, and then he up and died. No one even knew he was sick. I visited him every Christmas. Five Christmases. An asshole. Not him, me. You know why I couldn't see him more? Guilt over Robbie, yeah, but that felt more between Robbie and me. It still does. With Dad, I was ashamed for not having run from him that day in the garage. He was my father—maybe crazy—but trying his hardest to have this family. I should have cared more, should have taken that hose from him, the way he took my gym bag from me. I should have said, 'Let me get that, Dad.'"

Willow turned to faced Clay and ran a hand across his chest, felt the rise over one pectoral muscle, the dip and rise again, and she let her hand rest on his heart.

"So there you have it," he said, wiping tears from the corner of her eyes. "You think you've got some huge issue happening on your shoulder. We've all got some kind of mark. Ninety-nine percent of us would trade with you. If anyone says differently, he's a bold-faced liar. Robbie would still be alive if I'd gone back for him instead of hitting the gas—if I'd thought about him instead of myself. He was crying for Christ's sake. I've got to live with that. We could have driven around, gone for ice cream. Mom, Dad, they might still be here, too. Can you stand living with me, knowing that?"

"Of course." He was turning her again as though they were on a dance floor, she responding to his lead, the touch of his knees into the backs of hers, waltzing her body into the same lazy S-shape as his, spooning her. Where his body touched hers, his chest solid and warm on her back, his groin and thighs a seat she settled into, her skin became harp strings and hummed. He kissed the top of her bare shoulder and continued kissing, his lips moving down to her shoulder bone. When he spoke, he whispered, not breaking the trance but deepening it. "It's such an easy thing, Willow. A lily bulb, maybe a chrysalis."

She shut her eyes to try and stop time, to feel the whole measure of the gift he was giving her. A lily bulb. A chrysalis. Mémé had spoken of a chrysalis in describing her own back and said something about the chrysalis being a way of traveling. Willow knew now where his mind went when he looked at her. He wasn't just willing to over-look her shoulder, to weigh it against attributes, her back made him conjure images she loved.

He lifted his head and looked closer at her arm. "What's this? All these little scars?"

The first hard darkness on the turret windows had softened. She turned and faced him again, her gaze locking with his. "Make love to me."

A slow smile crept onto his face. "Why, Miss Willow." Then, after a moment, "You're sure?"

"You've never pushed. I'm beginning to think—"

"Because Derrick did."

"I told you that?"

"Everything you do and say tells me that." He held her tight, his expression both serious and flirting. "You're sure?"

"I want to forget everything tonight but us."

He slid his hand under the strap of her gown and slowly moved the thin strip of cotton down her arm and then the second strap, his touch electric. As he pushed the fabric over her breasts, his palm caressing, he stopped, rolling her over on top of him, her breasts hanging in round, tear-shaped lobes. "It's incredible that we're together," he said. "For the first time since Robbie's death, I know I've found something good. I don't want to hurt us, what we're building. It's been a tough summer for you, and no matter how much I want you right now, tell me to stop, tell me you need a bit more time, and I'll stop. I'll wait as long as you need."

She quieted him with a kiss, her hand sliding down his flat stomach, feeling a pulse there and going deeper.

He sighed, "Thank god."

I left them their passion, and the house seemed to do the same, quieting into the night. Only in Tory's room did the lights remain on. Tory sat at her desk turning dried plants, counting and cataloging her apothecary stock, her tight heels still on her long feet, her pencil skirt still pulled down over her locked knees. Looking around at her horde, her lips twitched with pleasure. At last, she picked up a circle of muslin, wheedled her needle in and out, red embroidery floss, a slightly tipped, sneering mouth on the doll's face. "Sip, sip," she hummed to herself, sewing and drinking her sherry.

41

The following morning, the sun crested red and bled across the undersides of clouds. Wind set the oaks up and down the drive stirring. In the garden, the blowing was low and hot. Petals dropped from flowers, the fronds on Willow's tree went right and left, as though tossing in troubled sleep, and the bees stayed close to their hives. Farthest House seemed to shudder on its foundation and every corner to hold its ghost.

Clay had left in the wee hours, Willow telling him to hurry, afraid of Tory realizing he stayed the night. Though she got up and dressed Prairie, by noon Willow was sick again and sitting on the bathroom floor over the toilet, her stomach heaving.

I pitied her, but with so much happening elsewhere, I was glad to see her there, safe, albeit suffering.

Tory's glee was a thicker psychic rope, and it pulled me to her. In her room, she strode back and forth, a celebratory pacing. Her ceiling hung with more plants than had covered the ceilings of the barn and the kitchen at The Beast's villa. Many of these hanging herbs and weeds were so old they were only brittle stems, the pods and petals and leaves long since having dropped onto the floor and onto her bed. Behind her, a fortress of cardboard file boxes reached nearly to the ceiling. I thought of Julian and how alike the siblings were. In times of stress, they both hoarded, as if to keep a hold on some physical thing.

Tory's face remained stoic, despite the pleasure her success gave her. Thus far, all was going according to plan. She felt alive, exhilarated. Each hunt was a rebirth. She trailed a thin finger through the grainy dust covering Luessy's mystery, *Mad Apple,* and turned to her window at the sound of a bee dropping.

It's been said nothing destroys a mother's love, and though Tory wasn't of my womb, she was of my heart, an organ just as physically and emotionally deep. When she was little, I'd taken such pride in everything she did, even in her dreams: She'd go to the university in Lincoln, and she'd become a veterinarian, a decision made at ten years of age when she found a rabbit clutch in the wood, and one by one the tiny creatures died in her arms.

Then it all changed. And it changed again, as irrevocable as the letter arriving, telling me Sabine was dead. There were long months and years following, when I lived in fear of being found out, and for us to survive, I needed to convince her that murder had a place, that no one had the right to hurt her. Did I let myself belief I was slaying The Beast? That with The Beast dead I could bring back Sabine?

For all the emotional clamor in Tory's room, energy roiled even harder and faster across the yard where an old, black man was removing his clothes. Jonah's heart raced as he stuck his hand into a rusted coffee can and drew out a glob of grease and bee's wax mixed with a concoction of his own. His senses were keen, and the world around him lucid: his kettle, the old chairs, his damp walls, even his hands as he smeared his mixture over himself. He knew what he had to do. If it meant he died, he was willing. If he did return, things would be different. He'd tear the tarps from his windows, and he'd ask Mable to marry him.

He smeared his poultice thickest over his face and around his eyes. Willow wasn't listening to him, but she'd listen to *college man*. If college man went, Willow and her baby would go, too. They'd be safe. He'd known since the afternoon she sat in his kitchen with the sting on her neck that something needed to be done. Leaning in close, he'd smelled death on her. Unmistakable. The same smell her mother carried—an odor asleep in him for twenty years.

He finished coating his skin, set the rusty can in the sink, and for a long minute stared at it. He didn't know exactly what Willow and Prairie would be safe from, maybe the house and all the land around it was cursed. The dead were buried everywhere. He also didn't know if what he was about to do made sense, maybe it didn't make a single lick of sense, and still he needed to do it. He'd spent his whole life in the body of a whale. No more.

Everything had been clear when he woke that morning, his mind full of images: spook college man by taking him where he ain't ever been. College man had no business writing his stories about Luessy; college man needed to take Willow and the baby and keep them away.

Jonah opened his door and stepped into the yard. Men like Clay, college men, they were the ones who stirred up others, got themselves elected, made the laws, slammed down the gavels, drank the hardest liquor, and took what they wanted.

He shook his head, trying to clear his thinking. Some mornings the world seemed to ruffle backwards like pages blowing in a book, and it was 1919 again, and the mob was alive, breaking into the courthouse, lynching Willie Brown, dragging him through the streets, burning his body. And Willie's crime? The same as every Negro's in the city: his color. Or it was 1932 in Jonah's mind, and the mob was screaming, "Lynch the bug!"

"College man," he mumbled the moniker. No other way to make Willow listen. Only thing to do was scare college man, scare him hard, something he couldn't pencil out.

With his crowbar and smoker, Jonah puffed a bit of smoke into the bottom of the first hive, momentarily quieting the guard bees at the entrance. He pried off the lid and lifted only a few of the frames, turning them over before spotting the queen, twice as fat and long as the bees around her. She was old now, old like himself. After three years, her fertility was waning, but he had one more favor to ask of her.

Bees began to rear up, spewing in a cloud around him. "It's Bug," he told them. And to the queen, "Yup, it's me." He took her up between thick fingers and closed her squirming in the palm of his hand. More bees flared in alarm. He wasn't aware of the number of stings he was receiving, if any. He needed one more queen, and through the thick furry cloth of angry buzzing bodies, he pried up the lid on the next hive.

He was speaking to everyone who'd put him down over the years: the teacher who locked him in the steaming outhouse; the mob who tortured Willie Brown while Jonah hid in a cellar, watching through broken slats; those who wanted him dead, not because he'd killed, but because killing him would be as satisfying as using the toe of a boot and grinding out a cockroach.

As Clay's car climbed the steep gravel and he could see Farthest House in the distance, he felt a growing uneasiness. He had believed Willow's fears about Mary were mostly grief over her father's death, and he'd understood. A decade had passed and Robbie's death still impaled him. But given Mary's campus visit—he should have told willow the story—he needed to re-think Willow's position. Still, to suppose Mary started Julian's house on fire, knowing he slept inside? Clay shook his head, it was a huge leap from driving onto an open campus with a Polaroid.

He made the turn from the gravel road onto the bottom of the drive before he saw the wall of darkness. His breath caught, and he slammed on the brake. The car slid to a stop. Not a dozen feet ahead, thousands of bees, a mass that looked to be an entire hive, maybe two or three, made a twisting, seething blockade in the shape of a squat tree. Angry branches frothed and hummed, wasp-like.

There are sixty to seventy thousand bees per hive, Willow had told him. He stared at the swarm. This had to be more than one hive, and they were not bees just drifting in a swarm to start a new colony. This was a wholly unnatural phenomenon. The bees held an angry core and intentionally blocked his way. He thought of Willow. Even calm bees stung her. If she stepped out now, not knowing the bees were loose and dangerously upset, and if she had little Prairie in her arms, both would be seriously harmed. Adrenaline pushed through his veins. He had to warn Willow.

It takes over a thousand stings to kill a healthy man, she'd also said. How many to kill her or Prairie? he wondered. He scanned the space leading up to the house. There wasn't room between the oaks to swerve off and up the grass in his car, and suppose the bees followed him? The same catastrophe was likely to happen if he tried to make a run for it on foot. The closer he got to the house, the closer he got to warning Willow, the more danger he'd be putting her in, bringing the bees up to her front door.

His blood pounded as he stared at the maelstrom, then he squinted and leaned farther over the steering wheel. He'd been so surprised by the swarm, his attention on the whole, he'd not seen Jonah just visible in the middle of the eddy. Jonah's shirt was off, and he wore dark trousers, or no trousers beneath the cloak of bees, using his body as the black core they coiled around.

Grabbing for the door handle, Clay yanked it open, mapping a frantic plan of action. He'd shake Jonah hard, dislodge the bees, throw his coat over both their heads, cover their faces as best he could, pull Jonah into the car and head for Dr. Mahoney's office. And he'd pray he reached a phone before Willow stepped out.

A wave of the angry horde swung right, the sound sending chills down his spine, and in the second before they swung back, he saw something more frightening than bees gone feral. Jonah stared at him. Defiance in his normally weak eyes. Not affected by stings, not writhing in pain, not flinging his arms trying to save himself. He stood upright, resolute, threatening.

With the sound of bees in the air and Jonah's stance, Clay slammed the car door shut again. He locked it and reached across and back, each lock clicking with an only mildly comforting sound. Jonah's message was loud and clear: "Leave and don't come back." There was more, too, something about turfs and the order of things. Jonah wasn't an extra on the scene, scuffling around on the periphery of Farthest House. He was a force.

Clay clutched the steering wheel, veins in his hands pulsing to the surface. The scene was something straight out of Alfred Hitchcock: bees usually benign suddenly haywire, controlled by some demigod or dark gremlin. He had no way of knowing if Jonah could see and read his eyes, but if the old man could, he'd see the performance wasn't working. Clay wasn't breaking off his relationship with Willow.

Nor was Jonah relenting, and Clay's alarm increased. Had it been three minutes, five minutes? The longer the standoff continued, the more bee stings Jonah might receive. It was time to get him help and call Willow to warn her to stay inside. So his head told him, but his heart held him there. He couldn't drive off until he knew more, until he was positive Willow would be safe until he reached help.

The swaying tree of bees continued to hum and whine, a sound loud enough to be heard inside the car. When a bee buzzed at his ear, he jumped and swatted the insect and half a second later heard it hit against the back window, alive and angry. He tried to ease the cold from his shoulder muscles and unclench his jaw. With this kind of control over his bees, was Jonah responsible for Willow's stings? All along she'd kept faith in him, sometimes spooked by Tory, always spooked by Mary, but her faith in Jonah unwavering.

Yet, here was the swarm obeying Jonah. Clay's mind searched for reasons. Was it possible Willow sent Jonah after receiving Mary's pictures?

The questions were for another time, and Clay shifted the car into reverse. Jonah was an old and mortal man—nothing super human, and he played with his life. Clay would go straight to the fire station, tell them they needed the ambulance and hazmat suits.

As the car began rolling backwards, Jonah took a step forward, his arms lifted, flung in the air, and the swarm careened in a net, raining over the windshield and side windows in a hail of clicks.

Clay felt encased in a glass hive. Angry buzzing filled his ears. He envisioned bees crawling over the undercarriage, filling the car's engine, seeking and finding vents to the interior.

42

---✤---

At the sound of sirens turning onto the drive, Willow forced herself out of bed and to the window. She felt like cloud, drifting, pushed by wind, but she managed her clothes, and clutching the stair rail, she hurried down. Prairie met her at the door of the kitchen, and with a cry of relief, Willow swept her up.

She felt faint, but with Prairie on her hip, she met Tory at the window. "Is it Jonah?" Men in hazmat suits stood talking in a loose group, their headgear in their hands. Two others steered a stretcher into the back of an ambulance. Mable in a red caftan huddled over the gurney. "It *is* Jonah!"

"Dr. Mahoney is there," Tory said. "I'm sure Jonah will be fine."

As she raced for the door leading to the garden, Willow fought panic. Too recently, she'd watched her father's body being rolled into an ambulance.

Tory shouted at her. "Where are you going? His bees attacked him, and they might still be riled up. There's absolutely nothing for you to do."

Stepping away from the door, Willow held Prairie tighter and reached for the support of a chair back.

"Jonah," Tory said with emphasis, "isn't interested in seeing you."

Tory was right. There was no point in going out and certainly not with Prairie in tow. Jonah didn't want to see her. He wanted Mable, only Mable.

"You haven't forgotten our appointment with my lawyer?" Tory asked. "The day after tomorrow?"

"No." The question was distracting and in light of Jonah's condition, irrelevant. Mable would sit by Jonah's bedside, a place near grace.

"It's shameful," Tory said.

"Shameful?"

"Mable! Look how she's fussing. Crawling into the ambulance after him. Doesn't she care how people will talk? Just where does she think she's going?"

"We could go out the front door and follow."

Tory didn't move. "You tax yourself worrying about the wrong things."

"You're not worried about him?"

"How long did Clay stay last night?" She paused, strain on her face. "I'm not running a brothel."

And I'm not running an old folk's home, Willow just managed to keep from saying.

"I'm going to my room. I'm not interested in going to the hospital." As she stepped away, she pointed to the table. "There's something for you."

The manila envelope had Willow's name written on the front in large black letters. No stamps or postal markings, which meant it had been hand-delivered to the mailbox at the end of the drive. She shifted Prairie's weight, opened the envelope, and drew out the pictures.

Close to midnight, Willow carried Prairie to her crib and stood in the unlit room looking down at her daughter. They'd lain together in Mémé's bed, turning picture-book pages until Prairie finally slept, and then for another two hours Willow counted and recounted the whorls of brass on the chandelier above the bed and stared out the turret windows at the dark sky and the stars, searching them for pathways to deeper space. Finally, she painted Prairie on an imaginary canvas: the small arms flung out, the smaller fingers in a slight upward curl, fingernails tiny as satin paint chips, the folds of her closed eyes, and the spheres of her cheeks. All in an attempt to distract herself from her fear that Jonah might die. She'd dreamed of one day having real time with him, and now, when he was in a hospital bed, he wanted nothing to do with her.

Mable, in her last phone call, said he was stable, but the word didn't put Willow at ease. Was stable good, or did it just mean, "not-yet-dead?" Stable for an old man, stable for the hour, or the night? If stable meant he'd live, would he be able to return to Farthest House? She felt shut out, but Tory was right, Jonah didn't want her there. Showing up uninvited might cause his heart to heave and sink at the sight of her. He was too weak for upset. Suppose seeing him in his bed, machines strapped to him as they had been strapped to Papa, made her run out of the room? Then there was Prairie. Willow couldn't leave her with all the upheaval in the house. Mary's pictures were a flag waving in the air, shouting, *I'm right here.*

She ran her hand from the top of Prairie's head and down the child's back, before stepping to the window. The garden was empty and quiet with no sign of Tory out on a late-night tramp. She left the room, went back to Mémé's, and sat on the bed. The small door leading to the narrow staircase beckoned. How long since she'd painted, really painted? Not since seeing Papa consumed in flame? The realization packed ash around her heart. It was no wonder she used illness as an excuse to avoid working. Who might she see next? Did that mean Doctor Mahoney was right, and she'd let herself sink to the level of a Sleeping Beauty: a dormant object, helpless, with all doors to the psychic closed?

She rose and entered the narrow staircase where she ran her hands over the walls, still zinc white and absorbing what moonlight they could from the tiny window at the turn. She thought of Victorian novels and their long winding lighthouse staircases and the staircases in mythology.

The attic smelled of wood rafters and dust. Moonlight gave just enough illumination. She imagined Mémé working at the desk, me painting at the easel, and herself as a child sleeping in the cottage bed surrounded by crayons and paint boxes.

Two of the cardboard boxes the movers brought from her apartment were pushed against the back wall. She folded open the flaps of one and considered how long she'd been at Farthest House to only now be unpacking her tools. She removed a pad and charcoal pencil, avoided the desk and easel, and stepped outside onto the widow's walk. There, with her back against the house she sat down and faced the night.

Crickets, frogs, and myriad nocturnal creatures chirped and scurried and hunted below her. At tree-top level, she heard leaves rustling, awake and companionable. Sounds Mémé, maybe even Jeannie, also heard standing on that porch.

"Pagan," Sister Dominic Agnes once said of Mémé, but if the attic, the moon, the stars alert as votives, and the whispering trees were more pagan than a black, construction-paper chain, Willow would revel in the paganism. She wished Clay were there to share the beauty with her. Detained that afternoon by a sheriff full of questions, he arrived after the ambulance left with Jonah.

She heard him running up the stairs, saw him burst through the door of her bedroom, and then slow down seeing her safe with Prairie on her lap. "Thank God," he said. He frowned at seeing the two pictures on the bed. They were 8x10's of his face, complete with half-goofy smiles and Mary leaning over his shoulder.

Willow had remained sitting in the rose chair. "Jonah is *stable.*"

"That's good."

"Is it?"

He studied her a moment and sat on the bed in front of her, turning over the pictures. Prairie smiled at him and stretched out her arms to crawl from Willow's lap to his. "Those pictures," he said, "don't mean a damn thing."

"They mean everything. She's still out there, Clay. Just waiting." She lowered her voice to a whisper for Prairie's sake. "They prove you aren't safe either."

A line scored between his brows. He wanted to say he wasn't running, not from her, not from Mary, and that he hadn't run earlier when he left Jonah standing in the drive. He wished he could face the scene again to try and make better sense of it. He was certain the bees all left Jonah when they landed and struck his car, but his vision had been blocked. And after he left? What happened then? "Any idea when Jonah might come home?"

"I haven't heard. Thank God, Mable called an ambulance in time."

"I called the ambulance." He sounded desperate, half glory-seeking, half rationalizing.

"How did you know he'd fallen?"

"He stood at the end of the drive, covered in his bees, not letting me pass. He didn't fall. I went for help."

"You left him?"

"There was nothing else I could do."

She wanted to fall into his arms, and she wanted to make him take his words back. "You drove away?" She wasn't cursing him, only the craziness, like some dark shadow, that kept closing over everyone's heads. "It's been a horrible day," she said. "I don't blame you for anything, but my head is throbbing, and I'm too afraid for Jonah to think straight. On top of it, Tory is angry you stayed so long last night. I think you'd better just go." She motioned to the overturned pictures, "Burn the damn things."

"Will you let me explain?"

"I don't care how she got them."

"Well, I do. Let me talk. I was in the cafeteria grading papers. First thing I know, this blonde is leaning over my shoulder, pointing, 'Looky there.' I look up and a camera flashes. I thought it was some joke, a mug shot I'd see in the student rag with some banal comment in a balloon over my head. Only after she left with her little friend—druggy, goth-looking—did it come to me: long hair, a turtleneck on a hot day, and her interest in me. I should have told you before. I'm sorry." He watched her. "They don't mean a thing. You know that."

"They mean everything," she repeated. "I know they don't mean you're having sex with her or something, but they could mean you are her next target."

q

Alone on the widow's walk, Willow watched the moon track its slow course across the sky. Using only moonlight, she doodled, her pencil marking erratic curves over first one sheet and then another and another, her mind swirling around the eddy of assigning shape to her vast emotions and her equally vast need for answers. At times, she gazed through the door and into Mémé's aerie at the crone paintings crouched in the dark.

By the time the first notes of a sparrow began waking other birds, she'd gone back inside, turned on lights, and placed a canvas on the easel. As the sun crested, tree shadows appeared on the lawn, one over the top of the next like thatch, all pointing west. Willow continued working.

Later in the morning, she brought Prairie to the attic, and while the toddler prattled about, she painted. She painted during Prairie's nap. Still later, Clay climbed the steps, and she smiled to feel the rub of his cheek against hers. "Keep working," he said. "I've got the kid."

He turned to leave, but she reached for him, leaning against his chest and relishing the feel of his arms around her. "You can bring Prairie up," she said. "You have your own work to do."

"I'm okay. Actually, I accomplished more today than I have all summer. I repacked Luessy's papers and pitched my writing."

"What?"

"I'm not going to write the biography. If you were counting on it, I'm sorry." She was surprised, but he went on before she could object. "We both know it wasn't happening. I realize now that the whole project was something of a cop-out. Maybe a warm-up, but I need to go on."

"I don't understand."

He held her close. "The project helped me settle into Briarwood and Greenburr, but I'm settled now. I'm even going to survive Robbie's death. When I think of Jonah, covered with bees, that took some courage. He put it all on the line, and you, here, all this," he motioned around the attic, "art from the gut. Writing Luessy's life story would be playing it safe, talking about someone else's life rather than exposing my own. I need to write what's in here." He touched a fist to his chest. "Even if it's hard."

They stood in an embrace. "Jonah did that on purpose?" Willow asked. "Why?"

"It's been driving me crazy. Was it just to show me that he has the courage, when he knows I don't? Or because he needed to say he's still a man, a force, despite his age and frailty? Maybe that act spoke to his past and settled a score on things he wished he'd done or hadn't done. He also wanted to scare the crap out of me. You keep telling me he wants you gone. He doesn't care about me, but was he trying to scare me so bad I'd take you away?"

"Do you think he *is* siccing his bees on me?"

"I don't know. They're his bees, and something has him upset enough to risk his life."

43

Putting aside her fears for Jonah, Willow felt triumphant as she looked over her work area. Several brushes held remnants of paint, and tubes of color looked dropped or tossed onto her worktable. She had painted and without any visions of flames or bees dancing over the body of someone she loved.

She stepped back to examine the work. The emerging picture still needed many more hours, even days, for saturations and shading there and there, but in her mind she saw the completed image: a huge, century-old turtle in a wash of gold light. Inside and beneath the great dome of its carapace, she sat cross-legged and wide-hipped. Her figure was a composite of a wrinkled old woman and an oak tree. The tree crowned, green-leafed from the top of her head while her wider hips formed the tree's base. In her lap lay a picture, not of a sister she inadvertently sacrificed, but a picture of herself now, as a young woman.

The painting had come from the space of her dreams, and the magnitude of its message unspooled slowly. She lifted her hands, touched them to her face, her eyes, her cheeks, her breasts. No loose and creped skin, her face and breasts still vital, not the empty purses of Mémé's last years. In the painting though, she'd reached arch age, an oak's age. A rush of surety rose up through the soles of her feet. She would live to be the ancient crone who looked down at a younger Willow with motherly love.

Willow's euphoria expanded. She didn't doubt or question, she closed her eyes, reached her arms out, and opened her hands. Reality was not the hard ball the world supposed. Reality was more a balloon—able to stretch on all sides to accommodate the miraculous.

When the surge settled, she headed for the stairs and the people two stories below. If she remained in the attic even to clean her brushes and recap her tubes: Madder blue, Prussian green, terre-verte, and cadmium, she might pick up a brush, dab it in color, and be swept away for another twelve hours. She needed to hold Prairie, to tell her that from now on everything was going to be all right.

Coming out of the staircase into Mémé's room, Willow hurried across the floor, tossing her robe onto the bed, and pulling on the jeans she wore the day before. She opened the drawer on Mémé's stacked sweaters and settled on a raspberry-peach of wool and angora.

Hurrying made her dizzy. She came down the main stairs slower, with one hand on the rail, and her mind buzzing with excitement. She would paint more portraits like the one in the attic. Not copies of faces but inspirational works, trying to imagine and capture the essence of a person's highest, not-yet-realized divinity. The world was saturated with lavish imagery of the saints, angels, and gods, which humans were trained to venerate. Didn't un-realized gods also deserve spiritual images? Weren't they still gods, the way a sapling was still a tree?

She had another task before she joined the others in the kitchen. She went into the den and took up the paper where Mable had written Derrick's number. Using the phone there, she dialed, counting five rings before she heard his voice, "Hello."

"You've been trying to reach me?"

"Willow?"

She wished she had a cigarette to light and thumb down into a groove on an ashtray. Just how quickly could she be done with him? "How's your mom?"

"She's fine. She's found a church."

"How's Mary?" She was fishing. The pictures of Clay proved Mary wasn't there with Derrick, but how much did he know? And before he could answer. "Did you hear about the fire? About Papa?"

The pause was long, and Willow began to think they'd lost their connection. When she heard a muffled, "See you later," she knew he'd put his hand over the receiver and waited for someone to leave. "Mary, actually, is pretty pissed," he said. "Totally pissed. I think she believed that with Mom coming down here I'd be sending her an invitation."

"I think you should."

"Ha. Not a chance in hell. Ever."

"You've told her that?"

"Yeah, I've told her. And to quit calling. I hope I never see her again." He paused, and she could hear him draw in a breath. "She's a psycho, but it's hard to believe she'd kill your old man."

"Well, believe what you want. Why did you call?"

"There's this girl. I think she's the one. And Mom's hooked up with this priest, okay. They both think I should get an annulment." He swallowed the word, and he repeated it with more force, "An annulment. I wanted to warn you about the papers coming. Will you sign them?"

The proposition sounded wonderful to Willow, the severing of another tie, but it also tracked old regret, even fear, through her stomach. She took her time. In the kitchen, Clay was with Tory and Prairie eating dinner. In the attic she'd touched something holy, and Derrick had yet to ask about Prairie. This wasn't a conversation about him wanting to share custody. She should be shouting, *Halleluiah.* She'd sign the papers the moment they arrived, but she'd also make him squirm, "And if I don't?"

"The annulment will still go through." He sounded apologetic. "I'm sure Steinhouse will throw in his two cents, but if you just sign the papers and answer the questionnaire, the church tribunal will push it right through."

It was hard to believe how calm she felt. "You sound like your mother. If I do, will you sign a form for me? I want to have Prairie's name legally changed to Starmore."

"Why?"

"Because Crat rhymes with brat and rat, and it's a horrible name."

"You mean give up my rights?"

"You have no rights. Sperm have no rights; only fathers do. I could probably put your ass in jail for lack of support."

"I never wanted a baby."

"I'll tell her. I wish it wasn't true, but at some point, she may want to meet her sperm donor."

"Like when she's thirteen or fourteen?"

"Yeah, when she's thirteen or fourteen." Willow felt like laughing. Derrick had twigs were there ought to be brains, and he couldn't hurt her. He wanted an annulment and had no interest in Prairie. As the wonderful news fitted itself over her, she thought of what he'd said about Mary being pissed. With Mrs. Crat gone, Mary had no sounding board, and now, she knew there was no hope of getting Derrick back. More desperate than ever, she had nothing to lose.

44

⚜

"Get up," Tory said, her voice taut as wire, the hour on her thin watch alarming her. "We have the appointment. I've been waiting for you, and I supposed you were getting dressed."

"I'm coming," Willow said, her response half groan. "How's Jonah?"

"He's expecting us."

"Jonah?"

"My lawyer." She wore a black skirt reaching to mid-calf, a white blouse, and a rope of pearls twisting around her neck. "I've never missed an appointment, or been late for one, in my life."

Willow had slept soundly, one of the deepest nights of sleep all summer. So soundly, she felt groggy and slightly disorientated. Dreams, like pieces of winter clothing, weighed on her mind and didn't want to be shrugged off. She pushed back the sheet and Mother Moses, stood, and gained her balance before heading into Luessy's adjoining bathroom. "Is Mable back? Are we taking Prairie, too?"

"Of course not. Mable will stay with her." She watched Willow take a faltering step and bang a hip on the doorjamb. "You shouldn't have painted so long yesterday."

"That's not it." She sank down in front of the toilet and gagged. Fragments of the dreams, or dream, tapped on her awareness. Had she been in Tory's room?

"I'm disappointed in you," Tory hadn't moved from beside the bed. She crossed her arms over her chest. "I thought we had an understanding."

"I can't go. I feel terrible. Call Dr. Mahoney."

"You've been to him half a dozen times. At my expense. That's over now."

Willow wretched over the toilet.

"My lawyer might not have another opening for days." Anger plied Tory's face. "I've had this appointment for months, and I'll be charged if we miss."

"Can't you go alone? Not postpone the whole thing? Today was just to draft the will. You can still have it drawn up. We agree on what it needs to say, and I'll sign it once it's typed." Was she being too adamant? She took a breath and gagged. "You're right. You will be charged, and it's my fault."

Tory continued to mull and fume. "I don't know how you were raised, but I was raised to keep my appointments." Willow was right though, and the two of them agreed on all the particulars. The will needed to say that in the event of Willow's death, Farthest House would remain under Tory's care until Prairie came of age. Maybe there was even a benefit in going alone. There were questions she wanted to ask in private.

Willow remained on the floor, as Tory scowled another long minute before leaving the room. Her loud steps on the stairs and through the foyer contrasted with her weightless climb in the middle of the night. Only then did Willow congratulate herself and sink back on her heels.

Just as I sank back on my emotional heels. This was my Tory, and I had a huge hand in her upbringing.

Before Willow could try and concentrate on the dream, she hurried across the hall to Prairie's crib. Empty, always a startling sight. She listened at the top of the stairs, then relaxed when she heard Mable's voice in a sing-song patter. Both she and Prairie were happy. Jonah was surely better.

Back in Meme's room, the dream hunted her again, and she picked up her robe, slid her arms into the sleeves, and went to the window. Tory's car, a two-toned green Chrysler passed under the canopy of late August trees, peeked in and out of the leaf cover, and through the rusted-open gates at the bottom of the drive. Now that Tory was gone, Willow wanted to go back to bed. She wanted another chance to wake with her breathing steady, her heart beating at a regular pace, and with the belief that her aunt cared about her.

The dream followed her down the stairs. Tory kept her bedroom key in her sewing basket but then left the basket unattended, which made no sense, unless she only pretended to lock her room. Cinching her robe again, tighter than necessary, Willow forced herself on. Bluebeard handed his wives the key to his room full of skeletons, telling them they were forbidden to enter, guaranteeing they would, not so different from dangling a red apple in front of Eve. Maybe Tory's room was also a method of entrapment.

Tiptoeing across the foyer, she heard Mable coaxing Prairie into eating. It wasn't Mable's job, and surely, Mable would much rather be with Jonah at the hospital, which meant Tory refused to give her the time off. Likely, Tory couldn't tolerate for one more day the idea of her white housekeeper sitting by a black man's bed.

"Choo, choo," Mable said, "here comes the train."

Fear gripped Willow. That's what she should be doing, caring for Prairie, and regaining her health and painting. She could stop right now, forget all the flashes of dreams, and soon enough the terrifying images would fade away. But, if dreams carried messages—especially dreams as lucid as the one she'd had—she needed to pay attention.

The sewing basket sat beside a stuffed chair and in front of the den window. To Willow, it looked *placed*. Tory was half witch, could appear whenever she wanted, and even sitting in a lawyer's office, she could keep one lurid eye on her possessions.

"I thought I saw you sneaking around."

Willow wheeled. "Mable! God! Don't scare me like that."

The housekeeper stood in the kitchen doorway, drying her hands on her apron. "Only thing shaking your knees is guilt." She stopped wiping her hands, but she kept hold of the apron, gripping it, looking at the basket in Willow's hands. "I don't have to ask what you're looking for, and I suppose it's not my business."

"You're right. It's not." Willow's hand fished down through billowy tufts of batting, short stiff tubes of arms and legs, and she flinched at a pin or needle prick. "I don't want to get into it with you."

"I owe her."

"I know. Just as I owe you for taking care of Prairie." The sound of a plastic bowl hitting the floor made Mable frown and glance back. "I'll clean that up," Willow said. "I just need one minute, and then I'll be back."

"You suspect Tory of something?"

The question and the tone were surprising. "Do you?"

Mable let out a small harrumph, and her apron settled down over her caftan. "If you ask me, you're all acting strange. Jonah has been in a stew all summer long, and look what's happened to him. Tory's not herself, and she just left here with her mouth in a pucker. She may fire me still for riding with Jonah to the hospital and missing a day of work. Now, you're sneaking around like a dang fool."

Willow held the skeleton key in the air. "Bingo."

From the kitchen came the sound of Prairie slapping her wet highchair tray, a sure sign she poured her cereal onto the tray before tossing the bowl over and now entertained herself by splattering the milk.

Willow's nerves urged her on. She'd ask about Jonah when she returned. She headed for the stairs. "It's my house."

"I want you to know something," Mable said, raising her voice over Prairie's banging, the bottom of her apron back in her hands, "Jonah wouldn't sic his bees on you."

"I believe you." Halfway up the stairs, she leaned her head over the banister to say more, but the span of open space made her rear back with vertigo.

"It's because of him that I don't see this happening," Mable said.

Willow peered over the banister again, slower, less far. Mable's face held pain, and her eyes were damp. "You talked about the bees with him. Why did he do it?"

"He does want you gone, but I couldn't say why. He's fond of you, no doubt about that, but there's a bee in his cap, if you'll pardon the pun." Prairie was banging now, and Marble turned toward the sound. "It wasn't all for you, either. He needed to prove something to himself."

"By practically killing himself?"

"Do you know a man that's not a dang fool?" She headed back to Prairie. "Don't you touch one thing, and hurry, I'm not watching out for you. I have enough to do running a nursery at my age."

"You're an angel."

"No, I'm not," she called over her shoulder, "I don't know this is happening."

"Five minutes, and I'll take Prairie, and you can go to the hospital."

At the door of Tory's room, Willow stopped and tried for a deep breath. Only a fool would invade Tory's privacy because of a dream. If it had been only a dream, not that she could talk herself into that, but if it had been only a dream, there was nothing to fear in having a look. Tory wouldn't even know.

The key slid into the lock. A soft click and Willow gave the door a tiny push.

Closed-up air rolled into the hall, wafting over her in soft, but ripe arboreal, woody odors. She thought of a hundred-year-old potpourri shop, something out of a Dickens novel. The curtains were drawn, and she could make out only indistinguishable shapes, including what looked like ragged swags hanging from the ceiling. One smell drifted above the others, and she wondered where she encountered its muskiness before.

She stepped only a little way in, letting her eyes adjust. Her uneasiness grew. Tory's bed *was* the old-fashioned sleigh bed from Willow's dream. A graying chenille spread had been kicked to the bottom, also as she'd dreamed. Her heart gripped. She *had*, somehow, been in the room the night before. She'd stood exactly where she was standing now, looking at Tory sleeping slack-mouthed, the hair she kept pinned tight in the day, still fastened.

Along one wall, a wide desk held a mortar and pestle. Not the small kitchen variety for grinding cloves or cinnamon, but a large wooden mortar in dark wood and with the capacity to hold as much as a cup or more. Against the opposite wall was a narrow, cafeteria-length table, one end piled with books and the other with doll parts. In the room's dim light the limp muslin arms and legs held the tincture of bruised corpses. Willow's own legs felt as boneless.

She reached for the switch, hoping the light would give her courage. What she saw had the opposite effect. Clusters of plants tied together in fist-sized sheaves hung from the ceiling. Mushrooms, too, were strung like rosary beads, in all sizes and shapes. Some had round caps, some conical and some with spotted or dark scales. Most of the overhead swags were so old the colors had faded to parchment and become furry with dust, lint, and cobwebs. On the desk were constellations of tiny jars of powders and dried seeds, old prescription bottles with yellowed labels looking like the dregs of medications and pills Tory had been prescribed through the decades. Plant leaves and stems were in rows, as if placed for drying and identifying. As many as forty or fifty cardboard filing boxes sat stacked in a thick, almost ceiling-high block. She peered into one through the opening on the side. Dolls were crammed inside until the box bulged, and the lid was kept on only by the weight of the box on top of it. Decade's worth of dolls and none of them passed on to children. The number of boxes stunned Willow. How could one person, even sewing every day, make that many dolls? Because they hadn't gone to needy children, they felt *kept* from needy children.

Fighting nausea, she continued exploring, wondering how Tory could sleep in the room with the grime hanging over her? But in the morning, even after nights under the riot of fiber-shedding plants and dust mites, she appeared pulled together. The room explained why she kept her clothing across the hall.

Papa once told Willow everything was about money. Looking around the room, she felt everything was about fear. But what did Tory fear?

She moved cautiously, as though even the floor might hold traps. Many of the plants on the desk still had pigment and less dust than those overhead. Did that explain Tory's nighttime walks? Willow recognized only one plant with its long, distinctive leaves, jagged teeth, and host of names: Loco weed, ditch weed, mad apple, and datura. She was positive; she'd copied my watercolor. She stretched out a finger, touching the prickly surface.

What Willow didn't know was how much time, starting in childhood, I spent collecting and painting plants. When freed of *Le Bête* and not clawing through a cave trying to cleanse myself, I collected, learning the secrets of plants by gathering them and their lore from the old scullery maid and cooks in the kitchen. Mme. Francoise taught me that something taken straight from the garden could cure and relieve pain. Once in America, whenever possible, I learned from the tribes Thomas and I spent our first summers photographing. When the women walked up our hill for help, they often brought me the gift of some herb. Now, here was Tory, meddling in the same practice, believing herself knowledgeable and capable of handling the drugs, as though an understanding of plants and pharmacology were something she inherited as she had my hair color. The blame was mine. After her tribulation, I began taking her on even more hunts, trying to make our woodland treks as healing as entering a cave. I wanted her to feel nature's wonder and beauty. She'd already used poison successfully, and I wanted to teach her to respect it.

"This is it," Willow said aloud. This was the moment in her dream when fear sent her flying back to her own bed, but she wasn't dreaming now. This was happening in real time, and she couldn't hope to wake up and find herself elsewhere. The plants, the mushrooms, and her summer-long illness—she let out an involuntary cry. Tory was poisoning her.

The realization echoed through her, doubled back, and had to be realized again. *Tory was poisoning her.* She was putting bane in the soups and teas and everything else she served up. Datura, yes, but mushrooms, other plants—roots, stems, seeds—maybe even shavings from morphine pills prescribed in the 1940's for toothaches. Tory likely didn't even keep a record of her ingredients, and the combinations could be nearly fatal. Maybe they were only accidentally non-fatal.

This explained the invitation to Farthest House. It explained why Tory sent Mable to the apartment to befriend Prairie. Most hurtful was the realization that Tory used even her brother's death to her advantage.

Staying in the room, given all she knew, was impossible, and Willow rushed back into the hall breathless. An all too-familiar pain of rejection burrowed through her. She needed to pack up Prairie and be gone by the time Tory returned. Leave Nebraska altogether. Flee the way Derrick had and find a new life.

She tried to breathe deep, to use her breath like a ballast. She couldn't run far enough to outrun this. Back to Omaha wouldn't do it, nor across the country, and she wouldn't try. Prairie deserved a beautiful home, not a string of run-down apartments. She also deserved having Clay in her life.

Shivering in the hall, she half expected Tory to appear on a broom and come flying down the long corridor, cackling. She needed to hurry, and though she didn't want to go back in, she had to see and face it all. The dark bundles hanging from the ceiling, the pharmacy on the desk, and even the hoarded dolls were evidence of more than just an old woman's bitterness. She had no proof Mary set Papa's house ablaze, but she had real proof now of a crime, and she needed to take her time, not botch the opportunity. Evidence had a way of disappearing, and she needed to find out all she could before she called the local sheriff. If Tory suspected anything, she'd start flushing poisons down the toilet before the law arrived—she knew which ones to destroy first.

The thought of contacting the police filled Willow with dread. She wouldn't be believed, and she'd be tagged crazy. Red hadn't believed her before about Mary. Another call to him now, this time to say Tory was poisoning her, would sound like another cry of *wolf*. He'd think she, not Tory, needed to be locked away. Greenburr's local sheriff wouldn't believe a far-fetched story from an outsider about one of his own, either. Dr. Mahoney wouldn't be of any help substantiating her claim of being poisoned. He already believed her illness was mental. Nothing in his records would even hint at her being poisoned, and he likely scratched *hypochondriac* in red ink next to every chart entry he'd bothered to make on her. And if someone did issue a search warrant, would they find only an eccentric old woman's bedroom? Collecting plants wasn't a crime, nor was keeping old medicines.

She wished Clay was there. He'd drop whatever he was doing and hurry to her, but calling him wasn't what she wanted of their relationship. She wanted a lover and a partner, not to put her fate in his hands, not to commit herself to spending her life on the small pallet of his palms. She had to finally stand on her own, or she'd forever be swept from one Mary or Tory to the next.

She started back in, slower this time, dust beneath her feet. Again the swamp odors and the one scent like a familiar but distant hum. She stopped, raised her forearm to her nose, letting the sleeve of her robe slide back. She sniffed her skin, pushed the robe higher, testing the scent on her upper arm, and then her underarm. Yes, the odor was transformed, altered by her body's chemistry, but some trace of the odd fragrance in the room was there. She'd noticed it on herself before, especially during her worst days and nights of sweaty, fitful sleep, which likely meant after one of Tory's sickly doses. She brought her arms in tight against her body. If she could detect the scent on her skin, could bees? Was that why they singled her out?

The bees belonged to Jonah. As mean and cold as he had been all summer long, she still couldn't believe he wanted to hurt her. He wanted her and Prairie to leave, but did that prove he knew or at least suspected something evil? He lay in the hospital and would likely be back in a day or two. Meanwhile, she couldn't run to the police until she knew how he would be affected. He already had suspicion attached to his name.

Willow was happy to see half a dozen sketchbooks I'd filled with watercolors stacked on the table. All roughly the same two-inch thickness, hand-sewn, and with the same cardboard covers, the pages had warped and crinkled from the moisture of my paints. Not trusting what Tory would do when the whole hideous truth came to light, Willow took up the books and cradled them to her chest. She'd hide them for safe keeping. On the table was an ancient text on mushrooms titled *The Good, The Bad*. She turned several pages of large and detailed pictures before her gaze fell on the book lying beside it. Mémé's mystery: *Mad Apple*.

She stared at the picture of a bright red apple with two white trumpet flowers on the stem: Datura. She decided against taking Tory's copy; she could read Clay's. With her arms full, she turned to give the room a final inspection. Another white file box sat beneath the garden-facing window. The window shade had been pulled nearly to the bottom but stopped where a piece of rubber pipe came over the sill and down to a hole in the lid of the box. She moved closer, unsure of what she was seeing. The window was raised a couple of inches to accommodate the tubing, and the open space on either side of the pipe was sealed with black tape. Again, Willow felt an urge to leave immediately: *Run, go now.*

She took the final steps forward and lifted the shade. A slim hummingbird feeder, containing a substance that looked like honey, hung behind the windowpane, between the glass and the screen. Beneath the feeder, sheets of aluminum foil were taped to the walls of the encasement and twisted to form a cone that funneled into the pipe.

She didn't understand. As she studied the whole jimmied affair, her body growing more chilled the longer she stared, a bee lit on the wire screen. The insect walked back and forth and finally tipped through an opening—a slit in the mesh that looked made with a knife. The stab and drag of a blade. Inside the screen, the bee landed on the feeder. Seconds passed as it fed. Moments later the insect tried to lift but struck the screen spinning and went silent, except for the tiny sound its body made dropping onto the foil. She watched as it slid down and disappeared into the mouth of the funnel.

Her toes were an inch from the box, and her stomach lurched. With trembling fingers, she lifted one corner of the lid. Thousands and thousands, perhaps hundreds of thousands of dead bees. She glanced back to the wall of boxes she'd thought were all dolls.

Her body was clumsy with horror, and she fought for balance as she backed away. Her heel caught on something behind her, and it moved as though alive.

On the floor, leaning against the table legs was a large but thin object, more oblong than square and covered with a yellowed bed sheet. The dimensions sent new cold lapping over her feet. 24"x36," her preferred canvas size.

Her mouth twisted in shock and grief. Her heart pounded, and the noise filled her ears. When she could, she pinched and gave the sheet a single quick tug. The cloth scraped along the top but it moved only inches. She had to touch the dusty cloth again and give it a second yank. The sheet fell away, slowly, seeming to slither off its prize.

A cerulean blue sea and an unborn child.

45

Pulling into Clay's drive, Willow was reminded of her own childhood home; though her house didn't have a driveway, an attached garage, or forest-green shutters. That home, where she lived with Friar and Papa and cubbied up in a small room with yellow-duckling wallpaper, was gone.

There wasn't time for remembering or self-pity. She lifted Prairie from her seat in the back. Clay's door lay open, and through the screen, she saw him across the room, sitting at a wide desk. The stories he'd told of his childhood, especially of Robbie's death, made her wonder briefly how best to paint his visionary portrait. Like the rest of the world's occupants, his past held layers of wounds. The superficial ones, the skin-deep red welts healed in a few days, but a deposit of unhealed bruises lay beneath. How best to capture that on canvas? What features needed to be fore-grounded and brought to life, and which ones could rest? She was stalling.

"Hey, Willow!" His feet came off the desk, his book hit the desktop, and he hurried across the room to draw her inside. "I've been worried about you. How's Jonah?"

Standing in the circle of his arms, as he held both her and Prairie, she breathed deeply of his scent and tried to absorb his surety into her own body. "Are you all right?" he asked. He lifted her chin, "Are we all right? Is Jonah all right?"

"Yes. Yes, and yes." Whatever would happen now, she was going to be all right, as was Prairie. Though thoughts of Tory pressed a weight on her heart, and she had no idea what would happen next, Farthest House was hers, she'd never take another dose of poison, and most importantly, Prairie was safe.

"Welcome to my abode," Clay said, swinging his arms wide.

She'd not imagined his place; he always seemed at home in Farthest House. She took a step away, and keeping Prairie on her hip, looked around. Bookcases covered the wall at one end of the room, shelves crammed with volumes, some piled vertically, some horizontally, filled every inch of disorderly space. More books and papers teetered in wobbly-looking stacks on the floor, a leather sofa sat opposite the desk, and a golf bag leaned in a corner with a Yankee's cap hanging from one of the clubs. Her eyes stopped there. "Robbie's hat?"

"Good guess."

Not a guess, she thought. And not a guess that the stains on the brim were Robbie's and the clasp in the back was still fitted to the size of Robbie's head.

"Can I get you something to drink?" He took Prairie from her, and they moved to the kitchen where more papers, books, a backpack, even a frying pan and an open loaf of Wonder Bread sat on the table. His coat hung over the back of a chair, and she wanted it to lift and float through the air to her. He pulled a second chair out. "You don't look so good. Have a seat. Prairie, you want a cracker?"

Willow tried to sound light. "She's a child, not a parrot." Then, before he could quip back, "Has Mary paid you any more visits?" This time, the flesh on her arms did not turn cold at the thought. Tory was a much larger concern.

He sat Prairie down, filled a glass with cold water and ice for Willow, and brought it to the table. "No, and I'm sure she won't. She got her pictures." He moved a book on the table, putting it in front of her.

"*Mad Apple,*" Willow said. "You're reading it?"

"Remember my saying that one of the mysteries was missing from Luessy's library? I wrote down the titles the other day and compared the list to my collection. This is it."

She nodded at the book. "It's in Tory's room." And then, "Papa once threw it across the room. He wasn't a book thrower."

"You read it then? You remember the poor bankers?" He filled another glass with ice. "They're all getting sick."

He wore navy dress slacks with slim pressed lines down the lengths of his long legs and a pale blue oxford shirt open at the collar. She rested her gaze there, on his throat, and tried to remember the texture against her lips. "I need you to watch Prairie for a couple of hours. Tory and I need to talk, and I'm afraid it won't be pretty."

He waited. "That's it? That's all you're going to tell me?"

"There's too much I don't understand. I'm just not sure yet what's going on."

Clay forgot his glass, slipping his hands into his pockets. "You're not explaining much," he said. "What's going on?"

"What if you had one family member and they . . . " She couldn't admit Tory was likely poisoning her. Knowing she was hated that much made her feel loathsome. "I know Tory has done a lot for you, but right now I don't want to talk about it. I just need a couple of hours."

"Maybe I should be there, too."

She shook her head. "I need you to watch Prairie."

"It's not my business, is that it? Even now?"

She knew she was hurting him, asking him to watch Prairie, not trusting him with the truth. "Please, don't take this personally."

He took a step back. "Personally? I thought it's been personal for a long time, Willow. You're upset with Tory? It's not Mary, now? How about Jonah? Is he part of this little war?"

"He has nothing to do with this. I'll explain everything when I know."

"Sure. Whatever you want."

She was close to tears. "I know Tory has done a lot for the library, but—"

"But what?"

"I know you want to help, and I appreciate that, but you can't help me with this."

"How about I also can't let you walk into something dangerous. After Jonah's little trick, anything could happen. Do we need to call the sheriff?"

"No. Not yet." The question had plagued her since leaving Tory's room, but Tory was Papa's sister, and if she called the sheriff, what would she say? 'Throwing up and migraines?' She owned Farthest House—that couldn't be disputed. It was best to just rid the house of Tory, not press charges, and not have the whole town talking. She didn't want a stigma attached to the house, and she didn't want newspaper articles and rumors that would plague Prairie's school years.

"Well then, you work it out."

Prairie fussed at the sound of Clay's raised voice, and Willow reached for her, but Clay reached first. He picked her up and his car keys on the counter. "We're going for ice cream."

She felt panic flash heat through her hands. "You promised you'd never leave me."

"Willow, I'm not *leaving*, but there are plenty of ways to send a man away."

"What does that mean?"

He turned around and looked her in the eye. "Nothing. It doesn't mean one goddamn thing, okay?" He started to leave, Prairie's head on his shoulder, but he turned back, "No, it means I'm worried about you, and I'm fighting for us. I'd like to think you're fighting for us, too."

In the kitchen at Farthest House, the teakettle simmered on the stove, and steam lifted from the spout. Tory sat at the cleared table and looked up as Willow entered. "What's so serious that you couldn't join us for dinner? Mable said you've been up all day and also avoided lunch."

Willow hadn't planned how to begin, and Tory's frankness made her hesitate and glance out the window to where the garden was slowly being shrouded in dusk. She approached the table, but she couldn't relax enough to sit. Her aunt's hands were empty, and the doll segments were nowhere in sight. Her long fingers looked restless and sinister.

"Everyone is gone," Tory prompted. "Clay, Prairie, even Mable. Off to the hospital again. What now?"

The backs of Willow's knees felt damp with tension. Was Tory really adding toxins to the soups and tea she made? If only Dr. Mahoney could be right and the migraines and nausea were from tension.

"We're alone, Willow."

The sinister bedroom with its pharmacy lay directly overhead, and the kitchen was where the raven descended on Papa. "Can we talk in the library?"

Tory's impassive gaze remained fixed, her chin a wedge throwing a shadow down and across her neck. She continued sitting, her thin form ridged and uncompromising. So different from her childhood, when she was all legs akimbo over the back of a stuffed chair or swinging them as she lay on her stomach on a rug, playing board games with friends or Julian.

"If you prefer," Tory said, each word severed from the next. "But Willow, ghosts do not exist." And then, "*My* mother is dead."

Willow cringed. *My* mother, as though going to the library tread on some reverent ground to which Willow had no claim. "I do prefer, Tory."

"All right. I'll just get my sewing."

Crossing the dim foyer with its dark paneling and the day's last gloaming light, Willow listened to the sharp sound of Tory's heels striking the floor behind her. The rapping veered off, and Willow continued on, her bare feet as silent as the library she entered.

Surrounded by Mémé's books, both those Mémé wrote and those she loved, Willow took her time moving down the aisle, past the rows, each packed with volumes she knew hadn't been touched since Mémé's death. They were hers now, and if she lived to an ancient age, she would read them all. She thought of the watercolor journals she took from Tory's room. Tory certainly knew by now that they were gone and she'd been found out. She knew Willow had seen it all: the dried plants hanging from the ceiling, the hoarded dolls, the vials of powders on the desk, the dead bees, the painting. She knew, too, that she had to leave.

Tory marched down the aisle and took a seat at the small table in front of the tall windows where Julian held Willow as an infant. Pulling a round piece of cotton from her basket, Tory set it over the bottom half of a small wooden embroidery hoop, placed the top wooden ring carefully, squeezed the two pieces all around and tightened the tiny gold screw. Her fingers were mesmerizing in their waltz and flight.

Willow took the chair opposite, watching her aunt's long fingers, the same ones that worked the wooden pestle, strung mushrooms and opened vials of expired prescriptions. All the while she gauged or guessed Willow's level of tolerance, deciding day to day when to back off a bit and when to give another dose of her bane, maneuvering Willow's body like a puppet to be animated or dropped at will.

The physical distance between them was small. Willow could have reached across and laid a hand on Tory's wrist. "Papa once made me a doll," she thought she'd choke on her own politeness. "Maybe you inspired him."

"Maybe."

She'd try and keep things civil, not because Tory deserved civility, but because Tory had answers—the only living person who did. "How did your meeting go with your lawyer?"

"We missed you." Tory kept her eyes on her embroidery, giving the fabric in her hoop a final round of sharp tugs. Her head lifted then, and her eyes held a stunning force. "In the few hours I was away, you made a miraculous recovery."

"Well, I'm obviously not going to sign the will you worked on today."

Tory leaned forward, her face dark. "But if something should happen to you?"

Cold touched Willow's arms. She looked away and out the window expecting to see the trees churning. How crazy was Tory? "I'm not planning on dying soon."

"You decided all this today? Weren't you just as sick this morning as you've ever been? I suppose Clay put you up to this. He's too old for you." Her smoldering gaze lowered and stalled on Willow's weaker right hand. "You're not at all the type of person he'll have for a wife."

The hot attention on her hand and the supposition that she was unworthy of Clay felt delivered with the slap of a wooden paddle. Keeping her hand on the table required will power. "This is about us. Not Clay."

"Well, thank God for that. Haven't I nursed you all summer? Clay isn't family. Mom would turn over in her grave. This is a family estate. It must stay in the family. Anything else would be criminal."

Criminal? Willow's eyes narrowed. Was it possible that Tory hadn't noticed the missing books, or was she playing the biggest bluffing game of her life?

"It's your illness," Tory said. "It's confusing you. You may not think so, but you're not yourself."

"You need to live elsewhere. I'm telling you to go."

"This is *my* house." A long and thin finger pointed to the floor. "Everyone knows this is my house."

Watching the pair, I felt sorry for Tory. The things she'd done were wrong, but I still remembered the little girl. She'd never lived anywhere else; all her ghosts were there.

"It isn't your house," Willow said. "You know it isn't."

"I won't be sent away. I won't have people knowing Mom left this to you."

Willow watched her, wanting to rip the stupid fabric from her hands. She'd watched the charade of Tory's sewing the summer long. "Is that it? Your pride?" As she asked the question, Willow realized it had been Tory's pride, too, that benefited from the phony will. Papa hadn't benefited. He must have gone along with it though, and the thought made Willow shift in her chair. "Tell people whatever lies you want, I don't care. Tell them the house is too drafty or you have bad knees and can't manage the stairs any longer. I don't care what lie you tell them."

"I'm not going anywhere. I've earned this house, and it's mine." She dropped her eyes to her work. An easy and cold confidence controlled her movements. There was a long silence before she raised her chin, her face composed. "I'm sorry," she smiled. "You surprised me is all. I never expected this of you. Maybe there's been a misunderstanding." She put her hoop back in her basket. "We're Starmores." A second smile. "We decide everything over tea, don't we? The kettle is already on. Do you mind? I'll fix a pot and be right back."

Willow's mind felt wind-swept as she watched her aunt leave with a straight back and her carriage proud. She had no intention of eating or drinking anything Tory touched, and Tory's assumption that she would was as naive as locking up a room and publicizing where you kept the key. Pitiful, actually. So pitiful that Tory obviously needed psychological help, and Willow wondered if Papa had known this about his sister. Who killed bees and spent their life making the same dolls over and over and hoarding them in boxes?

46

In the minutes Tory was away, Willow paced the library. Too soon, her aunt returned carrying the tray, the teapot, and the two floral cups. Each cup already held tea—exactly as Willow expected. Seeing the cups and certain that the pansy with its repaired handle contained more than innocent tea, Willow's emotions went from anger to sorrow.

Tory set the service down, positioning her rose cup in front of herself and the pansy cup in front of Willow. Even the purple cup, Willow realized, which she'd seen as a special recognition, had only been a way of marking the poison. Furious, she reached across the small table, resisting an urge to fling the whole service onto the floor, and picked up the rose and set the pansy in front of Tory. "Drink your tea."

There was hesitation as Tory looked from the cup to Willow. "You were in my bedroom."

"Rather brave, wasn't it?" She might have smiled. "Do you really consider that your bedroom? How about your chamber? Laboratory? Dungeon? Maybe dumpster?" She watched Tory lift the pansy cup, touch the china to her lips and swallow.

"You don't scare me," Tory said. "I knew you'd been in my room because I smelled the invasion."

"There's more than one kind of invasion," Willow said. "They all stink." She'd told herself she wouldn't drink, swore to herself she'd not touch her lips to the tea cup, but she'd thrown down a gauntlet of sorts in switching the cups, and Tory hadn't backed down. She lifted the rose and drank. The tea, with neither cream nor Jonah's honey, tasted more harsh than savory. She tried to match Tory's outward calm, as her mind churned with possible scenarios. If Tory tricked her, putting the evil in the rose cup, so be it. She'd been sick all summer, and she would survive another dose. Tory wasn't going to give her a lethal amount—if Tory knew what that was—before she had the notarized signature she wanted. If Tory became sick, wonderful; she deserved a night, hopefully a week, of puking. The only thing that mattered was getting her out of Farthest House. If necessary, a lawyer could be called and papers served. A bit of her tension eased away, "How did you get my painting?"

Tory waved a dismissive hand. "Shall we talk about what's important?"

"That's important."

With a small sigh of irritation, Tory sipped more tea. "While you were in the hospital with Prairie, I went to your apartment to see Derrick. I had a baby gift." The cup touched back onto its matching saucer. "Julian was there, and I must say, all in a huff. Seeing me only made him angrier. He was hardly a man celebrating the birth of his first grandchild. They left me standing in the hallway and went off to their important business. I walked in."

"What did you want with Derrick?"

"I told you, I had a baby gift."

"Were you trying to find out how we were? Plotting ways to get your name on the will?"

She shrugged. "The painting was on the easel. You underestimate me. You're too much like Julian. Weak. I'm not leaving here. You can have the place when I'm gone. Until then, since we can't share, Farthest House will remain in my possession."

"I can have you carried out."

"You won't. Not unless you mean to send Jonah to prison." Her words swelled in the air between them and seemed to sweep and fill the library. "Julian," Tory continued, "knew all along you would inherit Farthest House, but he agreed to keep quiet about the will." For years Tory kept the secrets, and now she relished the telling. "He couldn't bear the thought of harming Jonah or Mom's reputation. Maybe, he even considered you. Or was it just his own reputation he couldn't see destroyed?"

Under the table, Willow crossed her legs, uncrossed them, crossed them again, the foot off the floor tapping in the air. She remembered the night Papa and Red fought in the backyard, Red knocking Papa down, shouting at him to "fight," and Papa lying on the unmown grass doing nothing. From the grass, he moved to the kitchen table and sat there seven years drinking wine and hoarding newspapers. "He managed," Willow said, "to destroy his own reputation."

"I see you with Clay. Telling him, 'Don't write that.' You're even having Prairie's name changed, aren't you? Drunk on the family name, no matter the cost."

"What does this have to do with Mémé's will?"

"Watching you squirm is such great fun. I've waited so long for this day." A sly smile toyed with her lips. "Did your precious Papa ever mention Mr. Phillip Jatlick? Our father? Did he tell you about the afternoon he walked into my room and found me being raped? Did he tell you how Mr. Phillip Jatlick grabbed him by the collar, punched him a few times in the stomach, and threatened to kill him if he told?"

Willow felt punched, her stomach filling with a hard ache. When Papa found Derrick with Mary, had the scene from his childhood flooded back to him? She stared at the narrow block of Tory's face.

"My little brother, doubled over and crying, left me with that fiend."

There was a tremor in Willow's voice. "How old was he?"

Tory laughed, a quick, hard shot of sound. "Thirteen. Throughout history, boys no older and some much younger have been soldiers." She took her time; she'd had decades to formulate her thoughts. "But he was no soldier. Later that same night, I found him hiding in the trees, cowering like a runaway, and I made him promise to kill the bastard. He never kept that promise. I had to do it myself. Your father lied to me. He failed me, Willow."

Though Tory spelled out the facts, Willow struggled with them. "He failed you, because at thirteen he didn't commit murder for you? Do you expect me to be ashamed of him for not doing that dirty work at thirteen or even thirty or fifty? Besides, I think you're lying. Am I supposed to pick up Prairie and run away afraid of you?" She leaned back, tried to settle into her chair, to appear calmer than she felt. "I'm not going anywhere, Tory." In the attic, she'd painted a picture of herself as a crone with roots growing from wide hips.

"He didn't do what he promised," Tory said. She finished drinking the rest of the tea in the pansy cup and refilled it. "I finally found my own solution, and with Jonah's rake, I beat the body."

Willow couldn't speak. There had been a woman in Omaha, she remembered, a murder there.

"You know the story, how Jonah was nearly lynched for beating a woman to death with a rake. With so much of Mr. Philip Jatlick's blood all over his rake and my testimony, he wouldn't have gotten away the second time."

"But he didn't kill that woman. That was never proven."

"Then, why did he bury Phillip Jatlick's body? Would an innocent person have done that? He knew there would be a mob after him."

The disclosures rattled through Willow's brain. "You framed Jonah?"

"I didn't frame him. His own fear did that. And society. I was seventeen, a young and innocent white girl. It would have been my testimony against that of a black man with a prior incident." She lifted her brows. "Well. He'd have been strung up for both murders."

"You would have let him go to jail?"

"You're not listening. He'd have never gotten to jail, never had a trial. He certainly wouldn't have lived all the way to the electric chair. The bloody rake would have sent the vigilantes off and hunting. By the time anyone wondered what I'd seen, it would have been over. He wouldn't have lived for more than a few hours, depending on how much fun the mob wanted to have. You know your local history, don't you Willow? You've heard the story of Willie Brown? Dragged through the streets, hanged, his body burned? Jonah witnessed it. We all saw the corpse in the newspapers." Her gaze left Willow and made a slow, almost amused circle of the room. "I'm seldom in here. It's very lovely, don't you think?" She looked back. "I wonder who Mom would have fought for, Jonah or me?"

Willow's heart was knocking. Her mouth was dry. "You murdered your father and framed Jonah, and you're telling me Papa knew and let you get away with it?"

"If you call the police," nothing in her voice conveyed concern, "I'll tell them where the bones are buried. They won't find any evidence against me, not after this long and without a coffin, but they just might find puncture marks on the skull."

"And if you lead them to the body, you'll be incriminating yourself."

"Not if I convince them I was traumatized and so afraid for my own life that I suppressed the incident. But now, it seems," her eyes widened a bit, "why, my memories of that awful night are returning."

For Willow, the air in the library had turned sodden and taken on the color of gravestones. "When did Papa find this out?"

"I told him the morning of Mom's funeral. He was letting himself believe Mr. Phillip had either drowned in the river or been sucked into the bowels of some far-off city. I thought that amusing." She smiled, "Julian patrolled Omaha's streets looking for criminals but never thought to look in his own family. Even more amusing Willow, he knew the truth for ten years before he died. He never came for me. He broke the law by letting me go free, and he broke the code of honor he'd sworn to keep."

Willow stood, paced, and stopped before Luessy's row of mysteries. "The raven. This explains it. Why Papa quit police work. He couldn't go back to arresting others while letting you go. And he couldn't arrest you knowing what he did about your father. You're a monster."

"Because I wouldn't be a victim again?"

"Because, after so long, you told him. You knew it would ruin him."

"He deserved to suffer. He was getting over Jeannie's death, I could see that. Did you know that in the years you spent weekends here he started dating?"

"But that ended when he heard your news and quit working. You denied him happiness, which was the whole point, wasn't it?"

"And there was the will, of course, which needed to say I owned Farthest House. That was all. Not so much, considering."

"You ruined your brother's life so that for ten years people would believe you owned Farthest House?" That was too mean even for Tory. "There was more, wasn't there? That was just the first step. The plan all along was to get your name on a legal will."

"I didn't know why he quit the force. I hadn't thought his not being able to arrest me would mean he couldn't arrest others. How honorable."

Willow dropped back into her chair, bumping the table, and sloshing the tea in her cup. "He should have locked you up. You're crazy." She leaned forward. "Most people wouldn't take that as a compliment."

"I'm his sister, and we were very close. He's the one who walked out of the bedroom that afternoon. The shame didn't just stay with him; it must have grown. He knew Mr. Phillip deserved to die. How could he arrest his sister for having killed a monster thirty-three years earlier? Let's not forget Jonah. Julian tried for years to clear his name in connection with the murder in Omaha. He wasn't going to implicate him in a murder cover-up, where he'd be charged, at a minimum of abetting a criminal and obstruction of justice. Suppose the case got away from Julian and ended up with Jonah being convicted? It was all too messy, too risky, over the death of a man who deserved what he got. Nothing made sense but to let it lie."

Tory's skin looked waxy in the lamplight. "'Mr. Phillip Jatlick,'" she repeated to herself, "deserved to die. Julian knew that. Maybe, he was ashamed at not being the cracker-jack detective everyone thought he was."

Willow's stomach rolled, but not from the tea. Her thoughts were on Papa swathed in bandages, the horrible face that had not been his face, and her mother: Jeannie. Like Tory, referring to her father as Mr. Phillip Jatlick, she never used the term *mother*. She turned to face the nearest library window, hoping to see out into the garden. The glass, however, only reflected the emotional squalor of her pinched face, the backside of Tory's head with its tight bun, and the woman's thin, bitter shoulders.

"All this time," Willow started to say and stopped. On his deathbed, when it seemed impossible that Papa could still care about Derrick, he wished he'd killed someone. That *someone* was his father. Had Tory said something to her brother while standing over his hospital bed? But Papa kill? That desire, as much as wanting to protect Tory and Jonah, Willow realized, may also have made him give up police work. He knew he carried the resolve to murder, and if he'd been a bit older or the circumstances different, perhaps if there had been a gun in the house, he might have done it. How then, could he continue to arrest others?

"Simple isn't it," Tory said finishing the last of her tea. "Julian was too upset over the murder to care about the phony will."

"You ruined his life out of revenge and for this house, and the phony will. How did you figure that would work? Mable and Jonah were sure to tell a few loose-lipped people, and all of Greenburr would soon believe you inherited the place? How soon after that did you start scheming the second phase of your plan: getting your name on a legal deed?"

Tory rose, her body seeming to stretch into the air. "I think we understand each other now," she said. "In the morning, you can take your brat and move back to Omaha."

"Why would Jonah stay here all these years?"

"He felt safest with Mom. Julian was trying to clear his name. Then age and Mable." She shrugged, "I did threaten a time or two to unearth the body if he left." She started down the aisle. "Finish your tea, dear."

"Taking over the house against Mémé's wishes is a way of getting back at her, maybe for not protecting you. Taking it from me is a way of getting back at Papa for the same reason."

Tory continued out, her walk erect, practiced, while the hoofs of a hobgoblin danced on my chest.

"Once your name was on the will, Tory," Willow was shouting, her hands in fists, "what did you plan to do with me? Up the doses? Then what were you going to do with Prairie? Force her on Derrick?"

Tory disappeared, and Willow stared at the empty doorway. Now, she had the answers and she wished she didn't.

After a minute, she lifted first the rose cup and then the pansy to her nose. Did the pansy cup hold the scent she'd smelled on her own skin? In which case, Tory drank her own potion. Hopefully, she'd not only be sick for a couple of days; hopefully, she'd also be stung by a few dozen of the bees she lured into her trap.

For the next hour Willow sat. All around were the old books Luessy loved, and there was the desk where Luessy read, her mind in flights of fancy. Finally she stood. Tory would be in her room by now, her tumbler of sherry in hand, and Willow wanted to walk in the garden with its moonflowers and winding paths a final time before she left. She'd walk under the stars and rein her scattered thoughts into a semblance of order.

She pushed in the two chairs and looked around with sadness. She was saying good-bye to the room, but only for now. She'd be back, but that might not be for twenty years. Jonah would be gone by then. Should she go to him, tell him goodbye and that Tory trapped his bees? He couldn't fight the witch, and knowing the fate of so many bees would only upset him and make him give up his hives. He needed them and deserved to keep them. Knowing might even make him leave Farthest House. He wouldn't go to Mable's for fear of the ridicule she'd receive. He hadn't married her, after all. He'd walk away, not allowing himself to be loved, and too soon he'd end up dying alone under some cold bridge.

Confusion, rage, fear, disbelief—Willow couldn't name all the wars being fought in her body. Leaving the tray behind, she hurried out of the library, her gaze sweeping up the wide and empty staircase for Tory. She passed through the foyer, into the kitchen, and went outside.

Stars hung so low she wanted to scale them, use them like footholds to crawl away, deeper and deeper into the depths of space, but blood tumbled in her ears and cemented her to the Earth. All summer, she worried about Mary, while Tory worked her stunning evil, and Prairie ate Tory's food and learned to walk under Tory's hateful gaze.

She walked down the unlit cobblestone paths and past roses turned black by the night. Across the yard, Jonah's cabin looked faint and powdery in the moonlight. Fragile. She wanted to go to him at the hospital and assure him that she was on his side, but of course, he wouldn't want her knowing about the murder. Hopefully, he was sleeping, the sound of lovely bees in his ears. He'd been right: at Farthest House the old *were* still finishing up a past. He tried to make her leave, but she wasn't sorry for having spent the summer, ill as she'd been. The months renewed her love of the house, the beautiful, souled house, and she'd gotten to sit in his kitchen and feel his hands tending a bee sting on her neck.

At the edge of the hill, she looked down on Greenburr and knew Prairie was safe with Clay. She'd wait until the house came to her, Tory dead or finally carried out like a stunned bat and deposited in a nursing home. There would still be long years within the walls, with the books, and in the attic painting. She didn't want Mr. Phillip's murder made public, Farthest House robbed of its rich and incredible environment for raising Prairie, turning it into a place her friends would shun, as would their parents. And there was Jonah to consider. She would not have him hauled off and forced to endure a trial. The law was still more likely to believe Tory than him, and he was guilty of tampering with evidence. No house was worth destroying him. Was this the real reason he never married Mable, because he might, at any time, be hauled off to jail? He wouldn't put her through that, have her married to a man behind bars.

She cursed herself. She should have recorded their conversation! Papa taught her that. How she missed him, and now that she knew the truth, there was so much she wished she could say to him. He'd been a good man, not perfect, but life didn't give anyone the space for perfection. He'd been a good man, a good father to her.

She felt uneasy again. If there hadn't been the fire, what had Tory planned to do with him? The two of them, with Willow's twentieth birthday fast approaching, must both have been bracing for a fight. He would have nixed any plans that included taking Prairie to Farthest House, and his name would have been the first on any will. Was it possible that Tory started the fire? Likely, she'd even had a key. Papa would have given her and Mémé one when he first purchased the house, back when things were good between them, and never thought to change the locks. Or if Tory had gotten caught in Omaha the night of the ice storm, Papa would have opened his door to her. At the hospital, Red said there were bottles on the table—a detail that still bothered Willow. Were they sherry bottles? Did Tory bring them? Papa and Tory might have had a drink; he could have been talked into it, and when he went to bed, how easy it would have been for Tory to light a couple of cigarettes. Already in bed, Papa wouldn't have questioned hearing her in the bathroom or walking around the living room.

A tremor grew in Willow's hands. What about Jeannie? Jonah said she was sick before she died, and the bees stung her. Was it possible Tory gave her poison? Could that have made her too weak to survive childbirth? If Tory hated her brother enough to kill him, she'd kill the wife he loved.

The phone rang in the kitchen. It could only be Clay, and Willow walked numbly back through the darkness. If Tory murdered her own father, Papa, and Jeannie, that was three murders. Why not Mémé, who got so sick after arguing with Tory and died within the week? Four murders? There hadn't been such a mass murderer in Nebraska since Charles Starkweather.

The phone rang on, and when she reached it, Clay's worry was obvious. "Are you all right? Willow?"

The sound of her name on his breath made her shut her eyes with relief and longing. "I'll never send you away."

"Are you okay?"

"It's terrible."

"What's going on?"

"Can Prairie and I spend the night there with you?"

"Of course."

She ached to feel his arms around her, to already be at his house where books covered his kitchen table and a golf club held the baseball cap of the brother he loved, and where Prairie slept in real safety. She'd tell him everything, and together they'd go first to Red. Reaching Clay, though, meant walking the impossible distance back through the foyer, climbing the stairs for the car keys in her purse—where Tory drank her sherry and gloated—then back down and out to her car to drive down the hill to him. A trek when she was just managing to breathe and stay on her feet. Even the thought of hanging up the phone was equivalent to the thought of cutting an artery. She needed a moment to regroup and gather strength. "How's Prairie?"

"Sound asleep. Has been for a couple of hours. I've been reading your grandmother's mystery and waiting for your call. I guess I spooked myself."

"*Mad Apple*? Did you finish it?" Trite conversation, but anything to keep him talking, to have his voice continue to hold her steady.

"I didn't see the ending coming. The poisons didn't kill them all. Not directly, anyway. For some, alcohol finished them off. Sooner or later, they took a drink, or had medicine containing alcohol, and bam. The deaths looked like heart attacks."

A slow shaking crawled up from Willow's feet, bucked through her stomach, and put rain in her voice. "Her sherry."

"What? Tory? What's going on?"

The rain battered in her throat, not forming words, only grief noises.

"You're scaring me," Clay said. "Should I call the police?"

She nodded as though he could see the hard and mute shakes of her head. "Willow?"

"Tory, I think, I don't know." She missed the phone's cradle the first time. The air in the kitchen crackled hot in her ears, and behind her, she saw the back door wide open. Her body felt Jonah-old, shuffling to close the door, to do for the sake of the house what the house needed. Then shuffling, fighting weight as if in a dream, back to the foyer where a god's eye hung without light, climbing an empty staircase, pieces of herself sloughing off: a hat, mittens, hands, legs, and a blue coat with the collar of a dead rabbit.

47

The following afternoon, Willow sat in the shade of the portico with one of my first watercolor journals, and Prairie pulled a clattering contraption on a string no longer than her arm. All across the garden, bees crawled over blooms, their legs round and fat with pollen, but none bothered Willow. She stared at the rocks marking Thomas and my graves, and she longed to speak to her father.

She hadn't slept in thirty-six hours, but she was too restless to try, and she didn't want to close her eyes on Prairie. Tory's disclosures and her death were cruel and crushing, and Willow doubted she'd ever feel real safety again. Suppose she tried to sleep and woke, and Prairie was gone, too?

She'd suffered the police and ambulance sirens racing up the long hill, the invasion of their red and blue flashing lights panning over the windows, the sheriff's boots striking the wood floors through the foyer and up the wide staircase, the sight of Tory's body being carried down in a zippered body bag, looking longer and more substantial in death than it had in life. All of it brought back the panic she felt that icy night in March.

No mention was made of the state of Tory's room, though after finding the body, Willow swept everything from the desk into the wastebasket. Tears flowed and anger made her hands swipe in wild motions: the pills, pestle, mortar, and drying Datura. Still, those who took away the body saw plenty. By now, word of the mess had likely passed through town, along with the news that Tory died of a heart attack. Dr. Mahoney had asked Willow if she wanted an autopsy, and when she said, "No," he agreed. "No point in it," he said, "I know a heart attack when I see one."

Prairie ran to Willow, sinking against her legs, and Willow rubbed her back, kissed her cheek, and just as quickly Prairie was off again as if she'd been refueled. *I have her,* Willow thought, trying to refuel her own depressed spirits, *and Clay. And Jonah is back.* Though she doubted the two of them would ever be close again.

She drew her legs up, her heels on the edge of the chair seat, and hugged her knees to her chest. On her jeans, a tiny red spider crawled over the rise of one knee and only inches from her face. She wanted to press her thumb down onto its small hairy back, and she wanted to take it up and keep it safe in the palm of her hand.

Forgetting the spider, her gaze crept back over the garden and the bees to the grave rocks. It all started there, and now Tory, too, was dead. Less than twenty-four hours earlier, Tory sat in the library, her thin fingers lifted the pansy cup—that marked cup—her eyes steady and piercing over the rim as she drank. Now she was dead.

Though Willow lacked the will to paint, all art healed, and she forced herself to open my old journal. In a moment of silence, when Prairie dropped her string, she heard the paper and binding whisper awake. The page corners showed the most disintegration, crumbling as light as the flaky tops of too-dry piecrusts. She ran a finger over the dusty edges and then down over lines I'd drawn.

While Willow looked at the paintings, my own emotions rose and fell. Unlike her, Tory's death didn't cause me undo grief. I knew Tory was as alive now as she'd been sitting in the library, but Tory, like Sabine, had suffered in the physical, and I had a hand in that. I was both guilty and innocent in both cases. Until I fully understood that scale of justice and forgave myself, I could not move forward.

When I received the letter from France and saw it was from Mme. Francoise, and not Sabine, I knew it contained the gravest news. Sabine, I was told, had become pregnant, and my mother, when Sabine could no longer hide her condition, took to her bed. Mother refused food from that day forward, and within the month, she was dead. I could imagine her in her bed, gradually fading away, starved as a saint, the holy ascetic, her bones lifting out of her body, while she forbid her daughter entrance to the room. Dying before the birth of her grandchild, glad to have missed the shame. And Sabine was left to carry the burden of her mother's death, too.

Sabine conceived even as I, a married woman, failed to do. Throughout her pregnancy, she never named the father. The Beast would only have denied his paternity and had her church-condemned for pointing at him. He would have called her a witch and turned the village against her. Perhaps, he was the first to suggest she climb the precipice, an act of contrition for her triptych of sin. I, the only one who knew him, hadn't brought Sabine with me to America, hadn't thought this thing possible for my little sister. I believed, like most children of abuse, that I deserved it, and that Sabine's life would be full of ease and beauty.

She didn't take her life for his benefit. She felt hers was over, and still she waited for the baby. Then one dark night, soon after the birth, she stood at a cliff's edge and leapt toward the stars. But not before shearing her hair and passing through the kitchen into the scullery where amongst the shadows she stretched out her small, white hand on the scarred tabletop. While her infant slept in a warm cradle, a nurse snoring at her side, Sabine raised the small hatchet used to rid skinned rabbits of their limbs and brought it down. I heard the cry across the ocean, calling me back to the night she and I studied Thomas's photograph of a woman who in grievous mourning had done the same thing. That night, Sabine had been in disbelief that a woman could suffer so. Sabine, by raising the cleaver over her hand, leaving the blood and her flesh there for the maids and Mme. Francoise, was telling me she knew pain that deep.

At her funeral, The Beast had Sabine's body draped in black, shrouding her broken bones and face, but he left her ruined hand uncovered, resting on a raised pillow, a warning to all would-be sinners of the ravages of fornication. He announced to the parish, with Sabine's shrouded body not five feet away, that the infant girl would not be sent away to a foundling house. He, the good bishop, would raise the child under his own roof. His flock, if not the house staff, nodded their approval. He would give her tutelage. I wondered if she would reach as much as eight years of age before that began. Or would she be only three years or four? And the infant, without a single protector. That was the reason Sabine needed to send a message—an act of mutilation so outrageous—that it was certain to reach me thousands of miles away.

Willow's sudden alarm drew my attention back to her. At the bottom of the page she was on, I'd written: *I, the only one who knew him.* And then: *Death rides into a village holding the reins of three horses. I will not let the infant be the third.* The words, displaced across time, startled her.

Clay stepped up to her, bent, and kissed her cheek. She hadn't heard him open the door or cross to her, and she closed the book, the words forgotten. He'd gone home for a shower and fresh clothes, and now, he'd returned shaven and neat, though fatigue lingered in his eyes. He sat down beside her, and Prairie came running to stand between them.

He'd called for the ambulance the night before from his place, and after reaching Farthest House and carrying a sleeping Prairie to her crib, he held onto Willow through the commotion and through the night. After Tory's body and the emergency vehicles left, they talked of a hundred things. Toward morning, they finally dropped fully clothed onto her bed. She stared at the stubble on his cheeks and watched his face gradually relax into sleep. As he slept, she fought an urge to wake him. Had he seen everything? The rafters of dying plants? The pills in the waste basket, the painting? Had he seen the box of dead bees? How many others in the wall of boxes did he think held bees? She even fought an urge to shake him awake and warn him: *You better leave. People in my life die.*

She looked out as the door of Jonah's cabin opened and he stepped into the light, his back slightly straighter and his gait less stiff. She expected him to move to his bees or to his shed for a hoe or rake, ignoring her as he'd done all summer. Instead, he stepped onto the walk, and step after step, his advance still that of a gentle old man, he came on. When he reached the flagstones, Willow was shaking, and Clay reached out, laying a steady hand on her back.

Jonah lowered himself into the chair on her right. He nodded first at Clay, his heavy eyes smiling, and then to Willow, "Yup."

48

I was already old the night it happened, leaving all our lives changed forever. That evening, I strolled up Old Squaw Road toward Farthest House among talking birds and chirping insects. I'd had dinner with another widow lady, and afterwards, we sat on her porch and remembered our husbands. I cried a few, shaky tears thinking of Thomas, and we laughed at a couple of young women walking arm in arm toward the town's small theatre. They had no male escorts and wore neither hats nor gloves. *The Great Ziegfeld* was playing and had young people spending their money to see it not just once but a second and, sometimes, even a third time. My friend and I laughed until we each peed a few drops in our knickers, and then, we laughed again, this time about the number of knickers an old woman can soil in a day.

I continued my stroll up the hill. The setting sun threw all the colors of a French villa across the sky, and the cooling evening air on my arms made me long again for Thomas's touch.

Julian, who liked to comb the newspapers with his mother, keeping up on recent crimes, had turned fifteen. He was in Omaha with Luessy doing research, a trip she made three or four times a year. She divided her days there between the main library on Eighteenth and Harney and the police station, where she combed public records, talked with detectives about the latest police procedures, and listened to the stories of the uniformed men who walked a beat.

I rounded the hilltop corner, stepping from Old Squaw Road onto the long drive of Farthest House. The sight stopped me. A black Plymouth touring sedan lurked at the top. Phillip Jatlick. He was the villain who fathered Luessy's children, and now he'd returned after weeks away.

My legs trembled from the climb, but I had a new reason to hurry. With my breath prickling my lungs, I struggled up the drive, until I finally puffed through the front door of Farthest House—my home too, since the fire that destroyed Little Nest.

Sobbing. The sound caught me, raced my heart and pinned me to the doorway. Victoria—still the name she went by at the time—and Julian were in high school, and I hadn't heard that sort of sobbing and wailing since they'd outgrown falling off bicycles and bloodying knees. I rushed across the foyer and into the kitchen.

Victoria, standing in the satin ivory slippers I'd given her, worked with a mop. The slippers were soaked to deep red and sagged on her feet. She shot the rag head back and forth, smearing a burgundy stain the size of a washtub into the size of a table top. Blood. The back door lay open and the wide swath of a bloody smear, surely a dragged body, trailed across the threshold and into the night.

I found my voice. "What happened?"

She screamed and jerked, and her shoulders heaved in great wracking sobs. The front of her dress was a slick red apron that clung to her body.

I prayed the horror in front of me was a hallucination, that the trek up the hill had blown blood vessels in my aged brain, or sent clots to stopper them, and I was suffering an aneurysm or stroke. Dying, my brain might have been reliving scenes snatched from deep in the pages of one of Luessy's murder mysteries. I'd have accepted anything for myself, if only Victoria could be saved. But I'd seen the car lurking in the drive, and on the table next to a soup bowl was a whiskey bottle with only an inch of alcohol still shimmering in the bottom: Mr. Phillip Jatlick. In the weeks of his absence, I'd been promising myself he was dead, safely rotting underground, his liver having finally drowned, or some woman wearing a red petticoat had mercifully pressed her derringer to his fancy shirt front and pulled the trigger.

Seeing Victoria soaked in blood, hearing her sobs, each one striking me with double-fisted guilt, I looked to her bloody hands. Between that blood and my panic, my mind saw Sabine's hand—cleaved. I'd dreamed, so many times, of my little sister in the act of chopping off her fingers: the nighttime kitchen, the household staff off to their beds, Sabine standing in the moonlight, and even Mme. Francoise watching unseen from a dark corner.

Now, in the kitchen at Farthest House, there was another bloody scene. And again, I was responsible, as soaked in guilt as Victoria was in blood. I'd kept myself imprisoned in denial, that mental coffin, to keep from knowing she was being abused. That rancid, acrid-smelling denial was because I'd been afraid of family upheaval and of what the truth would do to Luessy. Greatest of all, though, was my fear of once again facing what I'd gone through and what I let happen to Sabine. Just as my mother had, I kept my mind angled wide of the truth. I submerged myself in mind-fillers: playing games with them, painting, walks in the wood. All the while promising myself I was fulfilling the role of good grandmother.

"Jonah!" Victoria screamed that night. The name came over and over, cries for help, her body quaking with the ravages of stark fear. "Jonah! Jonah! Jonah did it. He killed him with the rake. He beat him with the rake, just like that woman he killed."

My poor Victoria, clearly too out of her mind with terror to hear the absurdity of her claim. Too crazed to think rationally and see that if Jonah was guilty, a madman on the loose, she'd have run down the hill toward safety, would have called the police, would not be working feverishly to cover up the crime.

I opened my arms to her. Dropping the mop, she started for me, her legs still child-gangly, her knees bending deep, starting to buckle. I held her, "Where is the body?"

"Jonah took it."

Her trembling body trembled mine. Here again was the insidious atrocity of men abusing children, as if little bodies were tools manufactured to appease fetid lusts. Doors slamming on young unlived lives. This time, the child reached such a nadir of despair and self-loathing that she committed murder. She was innocent of any crime; wanting to live was god-given, not criminal. Anger shot red and hotheaded through my bones. Another man would not destroy another child in my family. Phillip Jatlick deserved what he got, and I was so distraught, I imagined raising the rake over him myself.

I held Victoria and promised her that we would find a way. We had to. She did not deserve to suffer through a trial, having a fancy-talking lawyer hired by the Jatlick family destroy her character and disgrace her in front of the community, ruining every chance she had of a normal life. God forbid, she'd be convicted and forced to spend her life in jail.

It hurt realizing that Victoria, in going for the rake, had already planted evidence against Jonah, but I had to let that go. She'd not killed her father with the rake, that was certain. A weak-armed teenage girl against a big man couldn't have done it. I didn't see evil in her going for the rake; I saw anguish. I saw a child's understandable panic. The real fault rested with Mr. Phillip Jatlick, but since Victoria had already dirtied up the body with a rake, and she meant to tell a false story, Jonah's life was also in danger. The only way to protect them both was to hide the body.

"Phillip Jatlick deserved to die," I told her. The terror in her eyes brought my heart up into my mouth. "Jonah has done a good thing," I said. Why did I pretend to believe Jonah was responsible? Because at that moment Victoria wasn't strong enough to bear the weight of my knowing the truth. "Leave that mop," I told her, "you're making things worse."

The sun had set, and the garden lay in a silent gray. Jonah crouched against the trunk of a magnolia tree, his arms braced across his thighs, his face empty. The body, pulled from the house by the feet, lay not ten feet away, the arms stretched above the head. I approached it. Phillip's face, his entire head, looked like a spilled cherry pie. I'd seen Thomas dress a deer with less mess.

Again, my blood coursed hot and wild. This Beast deserved exactly what he received. I wanted to kill him again for what he'd done and the trouble his death was causing and would cause. He could not be dead enough, didn't deserve the respite of death. I'd count coup on him, just as Thomas told stories of Indians counting coup on their dead enemies. The act was symbolic, but I needed to beat him, somehow, to be a participant. Only a few yards away, a sapling had recently been planted and still had a supporting stake. I pulled the stake from the ground and struck the body—dull thwacks—until the thin plank in my angry hands broke and was but a few worthless inches of stick. "I'll cut off his twisted-up root," I screamed, "he won't have it for any afterlife."

Jonah, shadow, unfolded in the dark. "No. No, Miss Amelie," he said. "You ain't doing that. You already beat him good."

I paced, my mind frantic for the best burying spot: the garden, the wood Thomas planted, the hillside leading down into Greenburr? I ruled them out. We couldn't dig a grave deep enough to be certain no wild dogs would unearth it, or that a too-wet spring wouldn't float the body up. And a patch of disturbed dirt, clay brought to the surface, always flagged a grave. I even considered burying the body with Thomas and replacing the stones. Thomas would forgive me, but he didn't deserve it. And when the day came and I was buried, the body would still be discovered.

Victoria came to the kitchen doorway, her body silhouetted by the light behind her. Her arms hugged her chest, and she swayed, soundlessly rocking herself.

Jonah looked up from the corpse to her, and time began moaning, a low wail that morphed hours, days, years, passing them through him. His face, his eyes especially, began to sag, the skin melting like a thick wax, drooping and aging. His body became more windsock than man, as fifty years of unspent life gusted through the husk and away. A sound, half sigh, half cry, crept from his throat, worked over his tongue, crawled out from between his lips, a resigned, bitter, dying sound.

My body felt glacial. Guilt traveled through me like time through Jonah. I bore the weight of Victoria's actions and all the damages those actions wrought. My hands lifted, touched my face, my hair, feeling whether or not I was still fleshed.

Jonah, his face ancient now and his eyes half-closed, turned to me. I couldn't bear to hear what he might say, and I cut him off before he could speak. "We have to keep the bastard dead. We'll stick him under the portico floor."

"How?" The word drifting and empty.

I had no idea, but I'd seen Sabine's hand superimposed over Victoria's, and Victoria, fragile as her future, rocked herself and sobbed, and Jonah's unspent life had washed forever through him. I had to find a way. "We'll take up part of the stones and bury him in cement. For a hundred years, we can walk on him and pee on him."

"How we going to do that." It wasn't a question, but a statement of disbelief.

"We will! We don't have to be finished before Luessy gets back, and we don't have to tear up that much, just have the body buried." I was pacing, pointing. "That floor has several cracks, I'll tell her I tripped on a broken place and fell. I'll tell her I got so angry, and I was so sore that I put you to relaying the stones. We just have to get him buried. Relaying the stones can take the week if need be."

His face was old, the years a silence in him.

"I'll do the lying," I said. "Leave Luessy to me."

Jonah nodded, but his eyes said he wasn't listening.

I couldn't bear seeing that old-man look, and my need to save him had me ragged with fear. "Luessy will be surprised," I said. "She'll even look hard at me, but I'll limp around some, moan a bit, tell her that at my age I couldn't risk another fall. I'll blame her." There it was; I knew it. "I'll accuse her of being so preoccupied she didn't know the state of her own patio. After this trip, her mind will be even more knotted with new story ideas. Her writing won't stop, and she won't pay any attention to what's happening out here as long as the work is quiet."

Still, Jonah made no sign of hurrying off for a pick or shovel, and I'd winded myself. He stared at the body, the blood over the corpse turning it black. "Why'd she do that?"

"Because she's got sense."

"And I'm goin' get lynched for all that sense."

At least he was talking. I tried to answer honestly. "I don't know what's going to happen, but I give you my word, if this body is found, I'll tell them I killed him. It shames me to say so, and you know it's true, but I can't promise anyone will listen." We both knew the truth had little chance. He was a young black male with a suspicion of one murder already. Vigilantes would decide the rake was all the evidence they needed.

Victoria's wailing increased, and I worried about her mind. If we were caught, would she testify against Jonah? "I swear, if that body is found," I said again, "I'll try and take the blame. I'm a damn good storyteller myself, but Victoria's mind can't be trusted."

"However it comes down, I'm gonna swing."

"No. I'll take his car to the river. I'll leave the lights off, everything looking fine, like he just stepped out and into the water. I'll leave his whiskey bottle on the seat, open, empty."

"You don't drive a car." He was stirring, agitated, but moving.

"Watch me! I need you here starting the heavy work, and if you were to get caught in that car . . . ." I shuddered to think. "If there's a fingerprint left behind, it needs to be mine."

He looked in the direction of the trees. "I still got dark."

"Where would you go? They'd find you. One week, two weeks. I can't do this without you." I nodded at the log of flesh on the ground. "If that thing is found, and you've run off—even if I claim responsibility—there will be 'Wanted' posters with your picture sprouting up on every tree and in every storefront across the fifty states. How you going to escape, if you can't even board a train?" I gave him a minute to consider what he'd have to face. "I can't keep you here. You're a free man, but I don't think running is your best chance."

I was walking up and down alongside the body, wringing my hands, something I'd been doing since dropping the stick. I hated begging, but considering what a mob would do if they caught him rammed a stake through my heart. Even if he was brought in alive to face a jury, highly unlikely they'd bother with the formality, Luessy was already considered half-crazy for saving his life the first time. She wouldn't be believed again; she'd spent all the good faith folks had in her, and trying to save him over her daughter? Oh, God in heaven, she'd try and fight for the truth, but no mother deserved having to condemn a child.

I didn't know what was right and couldn't reason through all the probabilities with a dead body already stinking of old blood, and time a crucible lowering over us, but I knew I wanted Jonah to stay close. We were his only family. I didn't want anything to happen to him that didn't happen right here, where I could run into the fray and knock off a couple of heads.

"I need you," I said, "and you need me. That beast got his just desserts, and we don't deserve the trouble his body could bring. He won't be missed. Folks down the hill know all about his chasing one new pot of gold after another or some young thing with bobbed hair and a cigarette. They don't care if he walked into the river or left his car to crawl into some floozy's."

"Except if a black man can be blamed. Then they care."

How could I answer? He knew better than I. "A few bored locals might pull on fishing waders and tramp around in the water for a bit, but they won't waste more than a morning. By the time their noon burgers and fries are set on the table, they'll be done with it."

"Sheriff comes to tell Miss Luessy about the car, sees the stones all tore up?"

Jonah would stay. I stood shaking, realizing it wasn't because I'd made a lick of sense, but because he simply wasn't running again. He wouldn't have his name tacked to this murder, which leaving would do, and he wouldn't be forced from his garden and his bees. On top of that horrible list, he'd become an old man. Running was for the young, those who could jump trains, climb trees, and scavenge.

"People aren't murdered in Greenburr," I was pleading my case. "Bodies aren't buried under patios here. That only happens in books. The sheriff gets reelected because he hasn't got the imagination of a garden toad and beds down with the sun. That way no one's teenage son is arrested for drinking or speeding. He wouldn't think murder, if one happened in *his* kitchen."

We'd already wasted precious time, and Jonah would need help. The cracks winding through the flagstones would give him a place to stick a crowbar or the tip of a shovel, but the work would be hard. Still, I needed to settle Victoria first. Again, I feared for her mind, and I had to clean up the massive amount of blood in the kitchen.

I'd read all of Luessy's books, and I knew many of the ways murderers fouled up, leaving clues, and getting caught. I had to find out how Victoria really killed Phillip, especially if I intended to take the blame. If there was some obvious evidence I was missing, I needed to get rid of it. I steered her back through the kitchen door, her body trembling against mine, her feet stumbling with fear. Her terror made me stop and call over my shoulder. "Jonah, you remember this: Victoria is innocent, too."

I sat her down with her first-ever glass of sherry. I used buckets of water from the kitchen sink, scrubbing, dipping, and wringing out my rag until the water turned so soiled I couldn't bear putting my hands in it again. I poured the soup into the toilet and refilled my bucket with fresh water, over and over again.

With the kitchen clean and scalding water poured over the threshold, I coaxed Victoria out of her clothes and into a warm bath. Two hours, maybe more, had passed since I first walked into the kitchen, and still she sobbed and trembled. If her mind skipped away and she couldn't be trusted to keep quiet, if she climbed to the roof-peak like the village idiot and sang, what then?

I poured her a second glass of the sherry, the only liquor Luessy kept in the house for when Bess Streeter Aldrich visited. "Keep drinking," I said. "Sleep, forget what happened. Sip. Sip. Sip."

The glass trembled against her teeth, the fortified wine running red over her chin and onto her chest and into the bath. "Why'd Jonah do that?" she asked.

Was it possible? Was the mind so malleable that enough trauma could twist it into a new shape? Was she really convinced Jonah had done the killing? Even though *her* body was covered in blood? Again, I thought of Sabine. Hadn't her mind just finally given out?

I helped Victoria hold the glass, tipped it to her lips, slowly, the way I helped her learn to drink milk as a toddler, coaxing her to finish the sherry, and finally helping her into bed. All I wanted was for her to sleep. I knew she'd have to be watched, possibly for months, even years, but I couldn't think of that then, only that I'd stay close, keep her under my wing, and give her whatever sherry she needed to sleep through the night.

In the darkness of her room, waiting for her to sleep, I strode back and forth at the foot of her bed. My heart pounded with all I still needed to do and wondering how Jonah was faring. Then, I began to see: the dresser mirror lay shrouded with a ghostly sheet, as if she never wanted to see herself; her hope chest was thrown open, and the tea towels and aprons and handkerchiefs we'd embroidered were strewn about the room and soiled—looking stomped on with dirty shoes. Even the movie posters of Loretta Young and pictures of Anita Page taken from movie magazines were pulled from the walls, crushed, and torn on the floor. Dried and emptied Datura pods, the poisonous, almond-shaped harvested seeds, lay on the dresser.

Luessy worked on a new novel: *Mad Apple,* and I'd given her the idea of doing away with several characters by using locally grown toxic substances. She and Tory had followed me down to the river and through Thomas's wood to pick Datura seedpods, and Luessy even visited a chemist at the university in Lincoln. They came up with a possible combination of mushrooms and plants so poisonous even dumb cows knew to avoid them. It was a mixture that could *conceivably,* when combined with alcohol, prove fatal. *Mad Apple* was still a work of fiction, and she had the recipe so vaguely written that she never supposed someone would try and copy it.

I stood in that dark room, Victoria tossing in her bed, while I wrestled with my dread. Had she figured out an exact formula, or was she just lucky? My stomach rolled, and I promised myself she had happened on to a lethal dose. Because if she hadn't, if Phillip had only passed out, she'd taken a rake to a live man. A rake she knew would cost Jonah his life, as well.

49

Tory's funeral ended and finally, the post-funeral luncheon hosted by Greenburr's Altar Society. Willow walked toward the parking lot and Clay's car, with one arm slung through his for support. Prairie, with her little-tyke gait, scuttled ahead of them.

Standing at Tory's gravesite, Willow had refused to mumble along with the prayers, and she looked across Tory's casket to the headstones of Jeannie, Papa, and Mémé, all possible victims of Tory.

Prairie continued her toddler running, getting as many as twenty steps ahead.

"Stop, don't go so far," Willow cried.

Clay slipped his arm from hers, hurried up on Prairie's heels, and swooped her into the air. "Where do you think you're going?"

"Don't let her down. Keep hold of her."

He turned to Willow, raising an eyebrow at the panic in her voice.

"I know," she said. "I may never be relaxed again. Deal with it."

"Give yourself time."

She still had Tory's room to clear, that stifling closed-up dungeon, where more dire findings might still be lurking, the filthy nests hanging from the ceiling, likely full of dead spiders, the boxes of dolls likely mixed with bees. She wouldn't leave it to Mable. Clay would help; she wouldn't be able to keep him away, and if there were more secrets, he'd help her destroy them. Maybe then, maybe with that task out of the way, she'd feel better.

She couldn't be sure when she had her last dose of poison, at least the three days since Tory's death, but with the prior crippling weeks, the discovery of Tory's room, the sheer horror of Tory's death, and her own role in that, she felt as exhausted as she had all summer long. She scolded herself for not feeling more relaxed. She needed a break from thinking about anything connected to Farthest House. "Could we drive out to Briarwood and see the library?"

Clay's face brightened, "You got it."

The afternoon was warm, and at the car he removed his coat, tossing it into the back where he strapped Prairie into her seat. Watching the two of them gave Willow hope. As crazy as the last few months had been, she still had things to be thankful for, and as Clay drove, she looked out over the serene lawns and family homes. This was her hometown, now, and she needed to fit herself into the rhythms of its people. She needed to build a life forward, an artist's life.

Clay reached over, the back of his hand running a warm line down her jawbone from her ear to her chin. "However it unfolded, Tory is the only one responsible."

She did her best to smile. Of course Tory's death was Tory's fault. But entirely? Tory hadn't been alone in the library, and Willow wished there was a way of going back to that moment before she traded cups. She wouldn't. She'd carry the tea back to the kitchen and dump it. Pride and anger made her challenge Tory. She knew Tory would never back down.

Greenburr continued to pass by her car window. So many times Papa had driven her down this road. Papa. Now that Tory was dead, she'd do exactly as he did, hide more truth than she told. Except this time, no one was going free, and no more people would be hurt.

Clay pulled onto the campus grounds, driving slowly over the narrow and winding streets and past old buildings. "*Loeffler Hall*, right there," he said. "My office, second floor."

She could see through the glass panes in the heavy wooden double doors to a broad wooden staircase. She sighed, remembering the delicious weight of new textbooks and the groan of such stairs in ancient collegiate buildings. "Who's Loeffler? Another rich alumni?"

"He was one of the music world's greatest and most famous composers. The music hall is in the basement."

"Sounds noisy."

"I don't hear anything unless I go downstairs, which I love doing. At the top of the stairs is a replica of a large, charcoal portrait of Loeffler, the work of John Singer Sargent."

"Really?"

He enjoyed her surprise. "You'll want to see it. Someday, we'll visit Boston and see the original, if you'd like."

From the backseat, Prairie began singing a sleepy-sounding song, her small hands clapping. Students moved between classes. Two squirrels ran one after the other across a green lawn. Everything *looks* peaceful, Willow thought, and yet, her stomach fisted and sent pain shooting toward her ribs.

"There it is," Clay said.

They parked at the curb. The library sat twenty yards away, across a wide sweep of grass. Groups of students sat in pairs or small clusters beneath stately burr oaks spared during the library's construction. At the building's entrance, balloons bobbed on strings, and carved above the door was the inscription, *Luessy Starmore Library.*

Studying its size and the new stone and glass, Willow couldn't help but wish Papa and Mémé were there to see it. "It's beautiful." The pride on Clay's face pleased her. "Mémé would love this." She lifted a shaky hand and ran a fingertip down his jaw, solid, yet soft. Flesh and spirit. "You really like being here, Greenburr and this school."

"It's become home. I am happy here. What would a bigger, over-crowded university offer me? Probably a much smaller office for one thing, so many students I'd never learn their names or anything about their lives, and have less time to write."

From the backseat, Prairie kicked in her seat, and Clay reached over and squeezed her toes through her soft shoes. "Okay, okay," he said. And to Willow, "She's ready to get out and move."

I ought to be ecstatic, Willow thought. *I have everything I wanted.*

"Hey, if this is too much too soon," Clay was studying her expression, "we can do it another day."

"I thought I was ready, but seeing the library . . . ," she stopped, thinking of all the time he spent on the project and how she had whined about one thing or another their entire relationship. "It's beautiful, it's amazing. You don't see any yellow cars, do you? Or Tory's ghost peering out from some shadow?"

He looked around, "No. Do you?"

She took a deep breath. "We're here. I'd love to see it."

"We won't stay long. Next time though, you'll have to suffer the campus-wide tour."

She stepped into the warm air while Clay unstrapped Prairie, and she told herself her uneasiness was just nerves. She'd spent so much time afraid, that now, fear nested in her hair.

They started up the walk, Prairie in Clay's arms when he stopped. "Hang on a second, I'm going to grab my coat." He set Prairie down and turned back for the car. "You never know who you'll see. Tory's funeral may have pulled donors from the woodwork."

Prairie started off in the direction of the balloons. Willow started after her but caught herself. *Today's the day. The day I start learning to relax.* Prairie wasn't running for the street, but away from it, and twenty pairs of eyes watched her.

Two male students passed, hardly catching Willow's attention until one stopped. "Hey," he said. "How you doing?" A smile cracked across his face.

She smiled back. She supposed she might not have caught his attention had she been in a pair of jeans, the every-campus uniform. But in her black skirt, quitting just above her knees, and her heels, she stood out.

Beside the car, Clay unrolled his sleeves before reaching for his coat. "Hey, Butler," he called, "the lady is with me."

Both students turned to him and grinned. "Dr. H., how you doing?"

Willow wanted to run back to the car and kiss Clay for announcing their relationship to his world, but she couldn't let Prairie get too far ahead. She mouthed the words, "I love you."

His voice rose over the top of the car, "Very well, I might add."

On the sidewalk, Prairie moved quickly, still with a toddler's forward tilt, as though her feet tried to keep up with the rest of her body. "Prairie," Willow called. Something unquiet had begun to tick in her ears, "Stop."

Half way up the walk, Prairie did stop and turn to watch Willow.

Safe. Still, breath by more rapid breath, Willow found she struggled to pull air into her lungs. Each gasp left her more desperate. She opened her mouth wider, wheezed harder for oxygen, and felt as if her lungs were quitting on her. Her peripheral vision began to darken, heavy curtains slowly closing on a stage. A classic panic attack? A heart attack? Would she actually drop, or worse, in front of Prairie? She waved her hand, tried to shoo her daughter on, keep her from seeing. "Balloons," she said. "Prairie, get the pretty balloons."

Clay caught her as her knees buckled. "Whoa, there, you okay?"

Slunk against his chest, the world spun, but she managed an apology. "I'm sorry," or hoped she did. Her voice sounded reedy in her ears.

He held her tight. "Come on, let's get you back to the house."

The world continued to circle. She didn't understand the ticking, only that it came from within the listening, talking place. It wasn't residual poison in her system, but the "listen up" hollow, where she saw images of crones, where warnings caught her, and she'd seen Papa dying.

"Prairie," Clay called, "come on back, now."

His voice in Willow's ear startled her. Pieces rattled down and clicked into place. *Mary was there.* The line from my journal slammed into her head. *I, the one who knew him.* She was the only one who truly knew Mary. Then a second line from my journal: *Death rides into a village holding the reins of three horses.* Papa and Tory, Willow counted, her heart hammering. "Prairie! Get Prairie!"

"She's okay," Clay said, "I'm watching her." Willow twisted in his arms, but he held her. "Hang on would you? Let's get you in the car first, Prairie's not going anywhere."

Trees spun faster. The ticking increased. Her dizziness put Prairie there and there and there. She struggled to force words that would not rise over the crest of her panic. She heard Mary's threat from nearly two years earlier: *Your baby is going to die, too.* "Get Prairie," she was sobbing.

"Okay, okay." He let her go, took a small step back, but kept his hands out as if he might have to catch her again. "Calm down. You're scaring the hell out of me. I'll get Prairie, and we're going straight to the hospital."

He had heard her words, but the way he hesitated told her he didn't understand the urgency. "Prairie!" she wailed.

A yellow car. Impossible. She didn't know from which direction the car approached, possibly it dropped from the sky or swelled up through the ground.

The TR6 jumped the curb behind a parked car, bounced onto the grass, settled on its shocks, and headed for Prairie.

Willow's reaction was instinctive. Before her mind could think of the best thing to do, her arms lifted into the air, and she stepped from Clay and onto the grass, waving, "Here I am." Leaving Clay baffled, keeping herself the center of Mary's attention. *Not this time, not again,* she told herself, *nothing and no one would take another from her.*

She'd keep herself the target while Prairie escaped. How simple it seemed now, she and Mary. That's how it started and should have remained. She wanted to yell but didn't dare for fear the sound would distract Prairie. "Come on," she only mumbled through clenched teeth. Mary couldn't kill her. Tory hadn't been able to. Papa's death hadn't. She waved her arms, both arms feeling strong, healthy, and fixed. *Come on.* She'd need only a second, half a second to jump behind the oak at her side.

"Hide!" Clay shouted. He pushed her behind the tree, upsetting her balance in the shove.

"No," Willow screamed, as Mary's attention turned to Clay and then to the child he raced toward. Time slowed, nearly stopped, as milliseconds curved in slothful loops. The yellow car changed trajectory, slow now, too. Mary could take both, double the loss, wait for just the right moment when together they entered her riflescope.

Students in the car's path screamed, cursed, and scattered. Hearing the fright made Prairie, who'd reached the steps, turn and look back with fear. She saw Clay and began running back into the open, back to him, her arms out, her tiny dress flouncing, her small soft shoes patting, her face stricken.

Willow lay paralyzed on the ground. Her body frozen, as frame by frame the unfolding images struck her. She couldn't outrun Clay, and she couldn't look away.

Clay, who raced both for Prairie and Robbie, who could save one by saving the other, who might lose both, had ten yards. His fear made Prairie stop, made her knees bend to nearly a squat, her arms lift higher for him, screaming now.

With each of his long strides, horror hammered deeper into Willow's chest. Her ears roared. She struggled to her knees, felt her whole body rocking, even with her hands flat on the grass. Mary was on them now, had hit the accelerator, her pearly hands clutched the steering wheel, and her white wolf eyes narrowed. Around her neck was the ruined black paper chain she'd pulled down.

With the car only seconds from impact, Clay grabbed Prairie around her waist. Slowing enough to pick her up caused an unwanted break in his stride, not the clean *plant, pivot, and jump.* Prairie was in the air and nearly slipped from his grip. Secured by his other hand, her head tucked under his arm, he led with his head and free arm. His hips and feet followed the momentum as he jumped, striving for perfect parabolic trajectory, his shoulder turning, his back hitting on the far corner of the hood, his body tucked as he rolled off.

Willow ran. Clay lay immobile on his back, Prairie still in his arms, close to his chest. Willow dropped to her knees at their side and saw Prairie lift her head, a stunned look on her face as she reached for Willow. Clay's squinted eyes proved bells rang in his head, but he was conscious. "Is she hurt?" he managed.

Only then did it register to Willow that she had heard a crash and students and faculty closed in, streaming like ants from across the grass, coming in all directions. Mary's car was slammed into an oak tree, the front end as crumpled as newspaper, the windshield shattered.

50

❧

They gathered in the kitchen over coffee and cookies, and Mable presided in her brightest gold caftan, smiling as if at her brood. Clay, bruised and with bandaged ribs, turned pages in a seed catalogue. Jonah sat on one side of him, and they talked about ordering and planting bulbs before the first frost. Jonah's eyes looked so clear that my heart soared. Willow sat on Clay's other side, enjoying coffee in a thick white mug, occasionally leaning into his shoulder, or dropping her hand onto his thigh. Prairie pulled pans from a low drawer. Several banged.

"I think she needs a puppy," Willow said.

Jonah set his cup down, kept his hands spooned around the warmth. "Always good having a dog around."

Willow watched him, her hands matching his in the way her palms hugged the substantial cup and its warmth. She'd never have tea again, would rid the place of the thin chinaware, and would make Farthest House hers. "We'll get two," she said. "Two, as much like Friar as possible. We've got more than enough space." The idea excited her, and she leaned forward, drawing one foot up under herself, and sitting back taller. "Puppies are just the new life we need around here. Two from the same litter, so they can play together, but one will be yours Jonah, if you want. He'll spend his nights with you. I owe you a dog."

Jonah tried to hide his emotion. "Yup," he said. "Your grandmother always had a dog."

Mable leaned over his shoulder, "More coffee, old man?" She topped off his cup and took a place beside him. "Did you know?" she said to Willow, "Luessy's aunt came from France? She had your back. She was a tall, striking woman."

Clay winked at Willow as if to say, "See what you are."

"What made you think of that?" Willow asked.

"I used to watch her," Mable continued, "she moved like a long ribbon. Even in her eighties, she carried herself that way. She turned heads. Your grandmother, was a little rounder. The night you were born, Luessy walked through the house saying, 'Amelie-Anais has returned.' Like she was telling the rooms. I think it helped her accept your mother's death. She was promising herself that we all come and go, and Amelie's return proved Jeannie was all right. She took a piece of your umbilical cord and buried it out by those graves. She believed this hilltop belonged to you. She meant to return it to the aunt who saved her life."

The information, though only some of it felt new, settled over Willow. "Mémé once said, 'I see my dreams are true.' That's what she meant, isn't it? She thought I was Amelie-Anais?"

Clay grinned, "Maybe you are."

"That's superstitious," Mable said. "Though who wouldn't be with a graveyard out your door and your drowned husband in the river at the bottom of the hill."

Willow dared not glance at Jonah who turned pages, a thick finger occasionally punctuating an interesting plant. She wanted him to believe his secret was safe.

"I hear he was a louse," Mable went on. "A drinking louse. Now," she enjoyed every bit of information she supposed she possessed, "he drowned a year before my time here, but everyone knew Luessy couldn't keep help because of him going after everything in skirts. They found his car there but never any sign of his body. By now, there wouldn't even be bones twisted up in the tree roots."

Jonah's eyes went from pink gladioli to the steam rising from his cup.

"Then, after he drowned," Willow asked, "Mémé had her name legally changed back to Starmore?"

"She'd always kept Starmore as her writing name."

"And Starmore for Papa and Tory?"

"The aunt insisted. Luessy might have done it, anyway. Of course, she would have, but the aunt wanted everyone to be Starmores, and it couldn't happen fast enough. She took to saying, 'Tory Starmore.' She changed both of Tory's names and called them out every chance she got like she was trying to give her a new identity. A she-wolf that one. When she died, didn't any of us believe it. We never supposed death could win out and take her."

The phone rang and Clay stood first. "Yes, sir," he said a couple of times into the receiver. "I understand."

They watched him. When he said good-bye and hung up, he returned to the table. "The University's official report is that Mary's death was an accident. She lost control of her car while speeding through the campus, where she was not a student and was unfamiliar with the grounds. She hit a tree because of reckless driving. There will be a toxicology report as well."

Willow stood, picked Prairie up, and walked to the window. Fall was in the air, but Damask roses bloomed in more proliferation than she'd seen all summer. "I wonder why she picked the day of Tory's funeral."

"The Omaha paper announced it," Jonah said. "Front page. A nice article about Luessy and how her last child died. Yup, Mary must a seen it, too."

"If she knew you'd be at the funeral," Clay said, "away from Farthest House and out with Prairie . . . " he let the sentence drop. "She was likely at the service and followed us out to Briarwood."

Willow turned back to the window. Behind her was her unlikely family, and she loved each one of them. Looking out to where the hill dropped away, leaving only the blue bowl of sky, she put her lips to Prairie's ear, "Angels are coming tonight."

Epilogue

───────────────❦───────────────

Watching the group and their fondness for one another, I felt light. I knew Willow would heal. It would take time, but she'd go on and realize her dreams. I hadn't come for her. I knew that, too. I'd come to see myself through the mirror of her life.

My lightness increased, a rolling sort of drifting, lifting up and out of gravity. Without a chance to think how I might say good-bye, I was simply losing my hold, and Farthest House was receding in a wash of warm colors. It wasn't Thomas I needed to see. In another world Tory waited for me, and there Sabine sang my name.